Also by Philip Caputo

A Rumor of War

Horn of Africa

Delcorso's Gallery

Indian Country

Means of Escape

Equation for Evil

Exiles

The Voyage

Ghosts of Tsavo

In the Shadows of the Morning

13 Seconds: A Look Back at the Kent State Shootings

Acts of Faith

Ten Thousand Days of Thunder

Crossers

The Longest Road

SOME RISE BY SIN

SOME RISE BY SIN

A NOVEL

PHILIP CAPUTO

HENRY HOLT AND COMPANY   NEW YORK

Henry Holt and Company
Publishers since 1866
175 Fifth Avenue
New York, New York 10010

www.henryholt.com

Henry Holt® and ☖® are registered trademarks of
Macmillan Publishing Group, LLC.

Copyright © 2017 by Philip Caputo
All rights reserved.
Distributed in Canada by Raincoast Book Distribution Limited

Library of Congress Cataloging-in-Publication Data

Names: Caputo, Philip, author.
Title: Some rise by sin : a novel / Philip Caputo.
Description: First edition. | New York : Henry Holt and Company, 2017.
Identifiers: LCCN 2016030634 | ISBN 9781627794749 (hardcover) |
    ISBN 9781627794756 (electronic book)
Subjects: LCSH: Clergy—Fiction. | Informers—Fiction. | Drug traffic—Fiction. |
    Cartels—Mexico—Fiction. | Mexican-American Border Region—Fiction. |
    GSAFD: Suspense fiction.
Classification: LCC PS3553.A625 S66 2017 | DDC 813/.54—dc23
LC record available at https://lccn.loc.gov/2016030634

Our books may be purchased in bulk for promotional, educational, or business
use. Please contact your local bookseller or the Macmillan Corporate and
Premium Sales Department at (800) 221-7945, extension 5442, or by e-mail
at MacmillanSpecialMarkets@macmillan.com.

First Edition 2017

Designed by Meryl Sussman Levavi

Printed in the United States of America

1   3   5   7   9   10   8   6   4   2

Well, heaven forgive him! and forgive us all!
Some rise by sin, and some by virtue fall;
Some run from breaks of ice, and answer none,
And some condemned for a fault alone.

—*Measure for Measure,* act 2, scene 1

SOME RISE BY SIN

hrouded in his brown Franciscan robe, Father Timothy Riordan stepped out into the sharp, dry cold of early morning to look at the stars. The sky, moonless and clear, gave no hint of dawn. He stood still in the rectory courtyard, eyes raised toward Polaris. Then, looking like a medieval monk performing some occult ceremony, he turned slowly left to right, taking in Orion as it fell toward the western horizon, the Dog Star blazing low in the south, Spica hovering over the Sierra Madre, where the sun would rise in two more hours. Completing the circle, he tracked the Dipper's pointers back to Polaris.

He'd read somewhere that six thousand stars were visible to the unaided eye; here in the Sonoran Desert, far from city lights, the air so transparent he could have imagined himself an astronaut on the moon, there seemed to be ten times that many: a profligate splatter of glittering worlds, each a window into the mansions of God. That was how he liked to think of them, even as the astronomy enthusiast in him knew that if they were windows into anything, it was the past: the light striking his eyes had begun its journey to Earth when the Roman Empire fell, when men were painting images of bison on cave walls, when dinosaurs wallowed in Jurassic swamps.

Did these contrary views of creation suggest a mind at war with itself? Riordan didn't think so. Observing the heavens produced an awe akin to a religious experience: behold the eternal, behold the shoreless ocean of space and time; and the constellations' procession along the ecliptic— stately, harmonious, predictable—had the same soothing effect on his soul as the drone of Latin chant.

The habit's cowl slipped to his shoulders, exposing his cheeks and ears to the chill as he turned again, this time from right to left. He ended with his gaze once more on Polaris, the north celestial pole. These rotations had become, in recent months, like the ritual of an obsessive-compulsive; he felt that if he failed to perform them, dreadful things would happen. That dreadful things continued to happen anyway hadn't convinced him that this practice was a superstition as futile as a rain dance. He entertained the possibility that it worked a kind of prophylactic magic, preventing still greater evils from afflicting his parish. Mexico had taught him many truths. One of them was: Things are never so bad that they can't get worse.

He returned to the rectory, made coffee, and, holding the steaming mug in both hands to warm them, went to his room. It met the standards for Franciscan austerity—narrow bed, desk, armoire, bookshelf, walls bare except for a crucifix and a shell painting of the host and chalice—though Riordan wasn't austere by nature. The knotted cord girding his waist was supposed to bind him to a life of self-denial, but physical pleasures—the smell and savor of *pollo mole Actopan*, the burn of a good *bacanora*, the wind chafing his face when he opened up his Harley on a paved straightaway—often made the spirit's struggle with the flesh an unequal one.

He switched on the space heater—the rectory's thick adobe walls seemed to produce cold rather than merely trap it—made his bed, then read his breviary, his cowboy boots clomping as he paced the clay-tile floor. He liked wearing cowboy boots; they made him the six-footer his driver's license falsely claimed him to be. Though he'd kept all his hair—uniformly gray except for a few reddish strands streaking both temples—he'd lost nearly an inch in height since his ordination, twenty-six years ago, and now stood exactly five ten and a half in his stocking feet. Everyone shrinks with age, Lisette Moreno had told him; the spinal disks compress under the prolonged pull of gravity. He'd joked with her: What would happen if people lived as long as turtles? Would gravity eventually crunch them down to the stature of six-year-olds? Would we live in a world populated by wizened dwarfs?

Finished with his breviary, he dragged the glowing heater over to the desk and fired up his laptop to read over the homily he'd composed last night. He was distracted briefly when his eye fell on the desk photograph of the Riordan clan, taken at his parents' fiftieth wedding anniversary. They were the very picture of Irish Catholic fecundity: the elderly couple surrounded by eight children and twenty-two grandchildren, a population recently increased by two. Riordan stood on the far left, the absence of a spouse and kids making him appear isolated. His mother and father had that hale and hearty look seen in billboards plugging retirement communities for "active adults" with images of shined-up gray-hairs swinging golf clubs or riding mountain bikes. They were in their mideighties now, his father recently diagnosed with Parkinson's, his mother with rheumatoid arthritis, both bound for some assisted-living facility lying beyond the golf courses and bicycle paths. "We're rounding third, and home base is a hole in the ground," his father had written in his last letter (not an e-mail, a letter, handwritten in a spidery script). The universe delights in change, Riordan thought, recalling something he'd read in Marcus Aurelius. Old age and death were nothing more than change, and therefore not to be feared. *Dad might find that a debatable proposition.*

The homily. He would deliver it at today's Requiem Mass, the *Missa Defunctorum*. He considered the Latin more appropriate; as far as their earthly existence went, the dead were defunct, all right.

Only two of those he'd buried recently had died of natural causes in the fullness of years. The others, like the two young men to be interred today, had been booted out of life well before their time, usually by a burst from a nine-millimeter or a *cuerno de chivo*—the AK-47. The lucky ones, that is. The luckless had been tortured to death or burned alive. Kyrie Eleison. Lord have mercy. The Lord better have, because it was in short supply around here.

He'd said so many requiems that his sermons had become variations on a theme, like the one he was reading now: messages of assurance, of comfort, of hope borrowed from Scripture or from Shea's *Spiritual Wisdom of the Gospels for Christian Preachers and Teachers.*

"We cry out, why did Ángel Reyes and Hector Díaz have to die so early in their lives? All we can say is that they were called to heaven for our Lord's own purposes, and all we can do is pray that He will forgive their sins that they shall be justified on the day when the Earth dissolves in ashes."

He didn't believe his own words. There must be something else he could say, closer to the truth.

Two days earlier, a detachment of paratroopers had attempted to quell a demonstration in the town plaza, a protest against the orders to disarm the pueblo's *autodefensa*, its citizens' militia. A gun went off—whose, no one knew for sure—and the soldiers opened fire. Whether they'd shot over the heads of the crowd or into it was another thing no one knew for sure. The former, Riordan figured, because Ángel and Hector had been watching the demonstration from up on the bandstand when the paratroopers' rifles cracked and the bullets found them.

He stared at the screen, as if expecting the laptop to write a revision automatically. What would it say if it could? If they'd been standing a few inches to one side or the other, they would have lived, that's what; therefore, the Lord had not summoned them for His own inscrutable purposes. Their deaths had resulted from the random convergence of the bullets' trajectories with their positions in the plaza. That was the truth, but to declare it would be to rob their families of all solace. It would be to tell them that they lived in an absurd universe. Or in a universe ruled by a God as careless of human suffering as the stars Riordan had gazed at this morning. No sparrow falls that the Father does not see it. But it falls regardless, so what difference does it make if its fate is observed by the eye of heaven?

A second after that heretical thought, his organs seemed to liquefy and spill out of him. Doubt was the antidote to complacent self-righteousness; lacking doubt, there could be no faith, as there could be no courage without fear. But this sudden emptying wasn't the physical manifestation of doubt. This was how it would feel to lose his faith entirely. How it would be to live in the absence of God. Mexico, drowning in a blood-dimmed tide deeper than any Yeats had imagined, the *sicarios* killing as much for kicks as for money (*And why not?* he thought. *Might as well enjoy your work*), was testing his faith. That struck him as . . . what? Strange? Peculiar? Ironic? The conversion of the Americas had begun in Mexico. He'd seen the fact proclaimed on the gilt-edged pulpit in its first church, La Señora de la Asunción: *la evangelización del nuevo mundo comienza aquí.* And hadn't the late Pope proclaimed Mexico to be *semper fidelis?* Yet this nation ever faithful was putting his faith to the test.

He silently recited the Lord's Prayer and a Hail Mary, begging forgiveness for thinking that God did not care for His creatures. He prayed for his faith to be strengthened. Then he printed his homily and read it a second time, hoping the words on the page would ring more true than they had on the screen. Of course they didn't, but they would have to do.

■ ■ ■

The church of San Patricio de las Colinas was large enough to merit a full-time cook and a house cleaner. Their services seemed extravagances to Riordan, not in keeping with a Franciscan's dedication to a life of humility and poverty, and for a while after taking over as pastor he'd considered letting them go. Father Hugo Beltrán, the parish vicar, opposed him, arguing that the two women, though humble and poor, had not taken vows to those conditions of life. Wasn't it more Christian to give them some pride and income by providing them with honest work? "Besides, you are not so humble and poor as you think," he'd said. "One who is humble and poor does not ride a motorcycle with so much chrome as yours." Riordan wasn't sure if it was the bike or merely its chrome that brought the vicar to this conclusion. He agreed to keep the women on, but only if he and Father Hugo cooked breakfast for themselves and for the Resident, the man everyone knew as the Old Priest.

This morning was Riordan's turn, as it was most mornings—Father Hugo had once tried to fry an egg and had incinerated the yolk. Riordan had learned to cook years ago, when he was studying in Rome, to spare his finicky palate from the dismal fare served at the North American College.

He grabbed an onion and a tomato from a wicker basket and placed them on a cutting board.

"Would you dice the tomato and onion?" he asked, turning to Father Hugo.

The vicar did make a decent prep chef; he wielded the knife skillfully. When he was done, Riordan scraped the vegetables into a cast-iron skillet, ignited a burner on the propane stove, and set a wind-up timer.

"Five minutes, no more, no less," he said, and sat down at the kitchen table, which was thought to be as old as the church, its heavy planks, fissured and time-darkened, bound with iron clamps. The Old Priest sat beside him, wrapped in a serape over a wool cardigan, his brown, blue-veined hands quivering, either from cold or age.

"We are going to have a full house today," Father Hugo said after a silence. He sounded like a rock impresario.

"For the wrong reasons," Riordan said.

"What reason can be wrong to fill a church?"

"A funeral for two boys shot to death."

"You would prefer everyone to stay home?"

"I would prefer—" Riordan began, but he was interrupted by the timer's ding.

He rose, allowed the onion and tomato to cool for a minute or two, then broke six eggs into a bowl, adding a little salt and pepper, half a cup of grated Parmesan, and a sprinkling of oregano. He whipped the mixture into a froth, dumped in the vegetables, poured the lot into the skillet, and placed it on simmer.

"And what kind of omelet are we to have today?" asked the vicar.

"You are untrainable," Riordan admonished, with gentle humor. "Observe the flame."

"Forgive me, maestro. A frittata. An omelet is cooked quickly over high heat, a frittata slowly over low. Also, it is not flipped and served as an oval. It is served round, like a pie."

"*Exactamente*! Perfectly round. And the top is cooked like so." Riordan removed the skillet from the burner and slid it into the oven, under the broiler. "For no more than one minute."

Sixty seconds later, he pulled the skillet out of the oven. After letting it cool for another half a minute, he sliced it into thirds, lifted each wedge out with a spatula, and filled three plates.

Father Hugo led them in the blessing. With mincing care, he cut his frittata into bite-sized squares. He was a small, bald man with lazy black eyes and a profile that could have come off a Mayan frieze: the sloping forehead, the prominent nose.

"What do you notice?" Riordan inquired, after he'd savored his creation.

"It is firm but not stiff and dry. An omelet would be creamy."

"You pass, Father Hugo. I'll train you yet."

"You were saying that there is something you would prefer. About filling the church."

I would prefer not to talk about it, Riordan thought, feeling his jovial mood dissolve. But he spoke anyway.

"I would prefer that our parishioners come for the love of God or from the fear of God or even to give themselves something to do for an hour than to bury a couple of eighteen-year-olds."

Father Hugo bowed his head between his upraised hands to concede the point.

"I'm sick of funeral masses," Riordan went on in a louder voice. "Sick of burying people I should be marrying."

"Yes, of course . . ."

"And I'm sick of saying the same thing in different words. That they were called to heaven, as if God had something to do with it."

"Ah, it's your lack of originality that troubles you?"

The vicar's dark eyes sparkled with pleasure at what he considered a clever remark. Riordan brushed it aside. "No God that we worship can possibly have anything to do with what's been happening here. What's been happening all over Mexico."

"Are we to have a seminary discussion? How do we reconcile the existence of evil with our loving God?"

"The Hebrews solved that one." It was the Old Priest, speaking for the first time that morning. No one knew exactly how old he was; people joked that he'd said the first Mass when the church's construction was completed, in 1785. He himself had never revealed his age, though with his dingy gray hair cut in a monkish bowl and his gray beard and a face as creased and dry as brown wrapping paper, he had the look of a biblical patriarch. "There was the kingdom of Yahweh, and the kingdom of Azazel, where the sins of the people were sent," he continued, his voice thin and fragile. He folded a tortilla into a triangle, then bit off a piece and pulped it between his yellowed teeth. "On the Day of Atonement, sacrifices were made to Yahweh, but also to Azazel. He received the sins of the people. All their sins for that year were laid upon the scapegoat, and the goat was led to a high place in the wilderness and flung to its death."

"Giving the devil his due," Riordan said.

"I think that maybe Mexico has become like Azazel's kingdom. She crawls in sin."

"No more than anywhere else," Father Hugo said.

"It has been said, hasn't it, that Mexico is cursed because she is too close to the United States and too far from God?"

Beltrán shut his eyes and tilted his head backward to signal strained forbearance. He thought the Old Priest was getting soft in the head. "That's been said, yes, and much too often. It means nothing."

"Maybe he has a point," Riordan said, recalling the sensation of a divine abandonment that had come over him earlier. "Think of these atrocities. Is it enough just to kill somebody? Oh, no. The body has to be dismembered, decapitated, eviscerated."

"The newspapers say that it is done to intimidate. That is how each cartel terrifies its enemies."

Riordan agreed. That was what the newspapers said. And the TV. And the radio, all attempting to explain the inexplicable. But what they were really doing was denying the unacceptable.

"What are you talking about?" asked Father Hugo.

"To maim and mutilate to intimidate your rivals is barbaric, but it makes a kind of sense," Riordan answered. "What's going on now . . . the bodies the state police found in the van last month, heads and arms chopped off. Those people weren't narcos—"

"Yes, I know. Migrants," said Father Hugo, with a dour look.

"Exactly. Migrants heading north. Kidnapped and executed when their ransoms weren't paid. That's more than barbarism. It's delight in barbarism. That's what Father was saying." He inclined his head toward the Old Priest. "And it's what the newspaper will not say, so they invent this nonsense about terrorizing one's enemies. It's inhuman, it's demonic."

"But the Beast has been defeated," Father Hugo said. Whether he was being sincere or uttering another ironic comment, Riordan couldn't tell.

"He seems to be holding his own in Mexico," Riordan said. "Sixty thousand murdered in six years! Tell me, if it's not the work of the devil, then how does a country that produces Octavio Paz and Carlos Fuentes produce people capable of such things?"

Father Hugo stood and rinsed his plate in the sink. "In the same way that the country that produced William Faulkner produces maniacs who massacre people in cinemas and schools."

"I knew you'd say something like that."

"What did you expect?" Dripping a little venom into the question. "A gringo has no standing to lecture about the evils of violence."

Riordan had been the pastor in San Patricio for four years. But, he thought, he would always be the gringo here, the stranger who usurped the pastoral seat from a worthy Mexican, like his vicar.

"I wasn't lecturing," he said. "Remember what happened to our police chief three years ago."

"Who can forget it?"

"It was thought through, it was planned."

"Your meaning is . . . ?"

"The *sicarios* who did that were not crazy. It was an insane act committed by sane men."

"*Cómo se dicé in inglés?* A distinction with no difference?"

"There is a difference. It's moral insanity. And it's spread all over this country. A spiritual epidemic."

"What happened the day before yesterday was very tragic, but it wasn't *sicarios* who did it. It wasn't an act of insanity. It wasn't deliberate. It was an accident. The soldiers fired over the heads of the crowd."

"It would seem not high enough," Riordan said.

■ ■ ■

Father Hugo's forecast had been accurate: In every pew people sat shoulder to shoulder. More stood in the back. Still more would have jammed the side aisles if those weren't blocked by scaffolding. Up until a few months ago, painters and artisans had been restoring the chipped and faded murals of saints and biblical scenes and the inevitable Virgin of

Guadalupe. The project had been suspended because the workers came from elsewhere, and the roads into San Patricio had grown too dangerous to travel, even in daylight. Halting the work was a bitter disappointment for Riordan. Beauty, the harmony of shapes and colors, fostered harmony in human beings. He believed that as deeply as he believed in the communion of saints, though he lacked even the flimsiest evidence to support either proposition. The statuary and artwork in this church was said to rival that in the church at Xavier del Bac, in Arizona. His friend and fellow Franciscan Kieran McCarty had overseen its restoration, an achievement Riordan hoped to emulate here. He clung to that hope as much for his parishioners' sake as for his own. They mustn't think he'd given up. That was why he'd ordered the scaffolding to remain in place; to take it down would signal surrender as surely as lowering a flag.

Two simple pinewood coffins, closed because the bullets had cleaved both boys' skulls, were laid end to end at the foot of the altar. The Díaz family occupied the front pew on the right side of the aisle, the Reyes family on the left. Hector's and Ángel's mothers, dressed in mourning, sat primly, hands folded in their laps, faces blank.

Riordan led them and the congregation in the act of penitence, and as sometimes happened when he recited the words "in what I have done and in what I have failed to do," the face of another dead young man flickered in his memory and he beat his breast in the thrice-repeated *mea culpa* with more sincerity than usual. I, too, crawl with sin, he thought. I am marinated in it.

César Díaz, wearing a dark suit jacket and a white shirt too small for his neck, went to the pulpit to deliver the scriptural readings. He had a bulldog's nose and a cratered face, but his voice, an orator's, diverted attention from his looks. He read the passages from Ezekiel and Romans as if he were addressing a crowd through a bullhorn. "O my people, I will open your graves and have you rise. . . . If we have died with Christ, we believe that we shall live with Him." César, owner of a walnut orchard, head of the agrarian union, and chief of San Patricio's *auto-defensa* (vigilantes, they were called in the press), was probably the reason the church had been filled. Parishioners wanted to show him respect. Then, too, his nephew had fallen to army bullets. If Hector and his friend had been killed by La Fraternidad—the Brotherhood—there probably would have been fewer mourners. You did not want the cartel to think you grieved for its victims, lest you become one. But the army was a different story. The soldiers, even though they could play rough, were under some restraints, so people were not as afraid of them.

In the choir loft, the organist played the notes to the "Alleluia," the congregation sang it, and Riordan, garbed in black vestments, took his place at the pulpit to read the gospel—from Luke, chapter 7, "In the midst of life we are in death; of whom may we seek for comfort, but of thee, O Lord"—followed by his homily, with its recycled sentiments. The Credo followed, then Communion, then the concluding rites. "May they rest in peace," he said, looking past the coffins at the congregation. Townspeople mostly, a few Indians from the foothill villages, faces dark and secretive. "May almighty God, the Father, Son, and Holy Spirit, bless you . . ." Thinking, *Will He?* Because he didn't doubt that a few Brotherhood spies had infiltrated the service, keeping tabs on things. Those young men whose gold rings flashed as they sketched the sign of the cross with hands that had blood on them. "Go, the Mass is ended."

César signaled the pallbearers, who shuffled out of the pews, hoisted the coffins, and led the recessional down the center aisle. Outside, they loaded the coffins into the bed of a Ford F-350 that would serve as a hearse. In the plaza, in crisp winter sunlight, helmeted soldiers wearing ski masks stood in pairs, rifles slung across the fronts of their armored vests. They'd been cheered as liberators when they'd rolled into San Patricio less than two weeks ago; now the churchgoers eyed them with mingled fear and hostility. Riordan stood at the front doors and watched his congregation atomize, scattering across the plaza and down the streets angling from it like a wheel's spokes.

Only Hector's and Ángel's families, sorting out who would ride with whom to the cemetery, remained on the church steps. César shook Riordan's hand and thanked him for his most excellent sermon, a great succor for his sister-in-law, Lupita. Riordan cringed inwardly at what he thought was an undeserved compliment. "Come with me, Padre Tim," César said, donning a straw cowboy hat. "There is a thing I need to ask."

A few minutes later, his vestments exchanged for what he called "clerical fatigues"—a black jacket over a black shirt with white Roman collar—Riordan rode in the Ford with César at the head of the cortege. They proceeded slowly down cobblestoned Avenida Obregón, past colonial houses with pastel façades and iron-barred windows, then the Hotel Alameda and Quiroga's bakery. César did not speak until they reached the tin-roofed *taquerías* and *llanteras* near the town limits.

"I raised Hector like my own son, since my brother's death," he said. "To lose him like this . . ." He made a sound, not quite a hiss, not quite a sigh, to indicate that he couldn't find the words. "I would like you to have a talk with that officer, that Captain Valencia."

"Me? What would you have me say?"

"That if he wants our collaboration, he should apologize. Not to me only. Not to the Reyes family only. To the entire town. There was no need for his men to open fire."

César's pickup labored up the steep grade to the cemetery, as if it were towing the cars and trucks behind it, and then followed the road in its circle around the headstones. Colorful flowers, some real, some plastic, adorned the graves of others Riordan had buried. Most were under twenty-five, except for the police chief and two constables, slain in a Brotherhood ambush, and for a narco who had managed two unusual feats: he'd lived past forty, and he'd died not from gunfire but in an auto accident. He'd had enough money to rate a small marble tomb. A banner fluttered over it—NAZARIO, YOU ARE WITH US ALWAYS—and a bottle of Jack Daniel's, placed there on the Day of the Dead, two weeks ago, stood upright at the entrance, in case his soul needed a drink.

César parked, his grille nearly kissing the rear of the last vehicle in the line, not a line now but a ring of metal forming, as it were, a protective barrier around the graves. Two fresh ones had been dug in the Díaz and Reyes family plots, each a miniature necropolis enclosed by low stone or cinder-block walls. The plots were side by side, which would allow Riordan to stand between them and conduct a single service for both boys.

"Why don't you speak to Valencia yourself?" he said to César.

"He'd arrest me before I could open my mouth."

"It would be a job for a mayor, if we still had one."

"But we don't. Besides, you are more respected than the mayor ever was."

"Not by Valencia, from what I've heard. It is said that he has no love for priests."

Outside, men were removing the coffins from the Ford's bed. As the mourners began to exit their vehicles, grackles burst into flight from the trees, like dark blossoms torn and flurried by a strong wind. César opened his door to climb out, then paused, a foot on the running board, his hat brim casting a shadow across the lunar landscape of his face.

"We don't want him to love you, only to listen," he said. "This Valencia has ambitions, I am told. He's overdue for promotion. If he can be convinced to work with us instead of against us . . ."

"I understand," Riordan said. "Let's talk about it later. It's time to bury your nephew."

■ ■ ■

Funeral masses and graveside rites, all the ceremonies of mourning, blunted the sting of irrecoverable loss; but once the last hymns and mumbled requiems had fallen silent, it struck like the pain of an amputation after the anesthetic has worn off. So it was that the sight of the coffins lowered by ropes into the raw graves and the thud and rattle of stony dirt striking the coffin lids tore from Hector's and Ángel's mothers primal cries of grief. There was no need now for the decorum they'd shown in church. They were in the deepest realms of sorrow, where sorrow, gorging the throat with its bile, can be tasted. Though they were only in their early forties, recovery would take more years than they had left to live.

Anna Reyes was embraced by her husband, who tried to look strong and stoic; César held Lupita Díaz as she let out a howl, there on the hilltop, under a sky cold, blue, and void. Riordan's familiarity with such lamentations did not make them any easier to bear. He heard clearly a hopelessness in the women's shrieks, and it made him question how deeply they believed in the consolations of his sermon. *I am Death, I have taken your sons from you forever* was the voice they heard now. For the second time that day, Luis sprang into his mind. He recalled how he'd felt, reading about Luis's death in a three-paragraph story deep inside the newspaper. Nothing even close to what these two women were suffering, but it allowed him to participate, however faintly, in their anguish. César, one arm around his sister-in-law's shoulders, led her toward his pickup. When she was inside and the door shut, he glanced at Riordan, who whispered, "I'll try to see Valencia. But surely you don't expect an army officer to apologize."

"I have learned not to have expectations," César said.

CHAPTER TWO

The next day, after bolting María's lunch of tortilla soup, Riordan donned Levi's and a black biker's jacket and went out to the rectory veranda, where his Harley was sheltered, locked to a stout oak post. With a chamois, he wiped dust off the fenders and buffed the chrome headlight and tailpipe, a tenderness in his movements, as if he were currying a beloved horse. The bike deserved his respect and care. It had served him well for almost a decade; it had carried him nearly a thousand miles from his last assignment, in Los Angeles, to the new one in San Patricio without a single mechanical hitch. His arrival on it had caused a stir—a Harley-riding priest was a novelty. After they'd gotten used to the sight, the townspeople gave the bike a name: *Negra Modelo*, after the dark Mexican beer.

He rubbed smudges off the gas tank, then put the chamois away. For no reason he could think of, the black metal's gleam and the mirror-bright chrome made him a little more confident about meeting Captain Alberto Valencia. Not that his doubts were entirely dispelled. His role as emissary did not seem fitting for a parish priest, yet he was flattered that César had asked him to play it, as well as pleased that his friend wanted to do the Christian thing: make peace with the military rather than seek vengeance. No, César did not expect to win an apology or convince Valencia to cooperate with the militia; but such an outcome was not impossible. His nephew's death had dealt him a strong hand. The plaza shootings reflected badly on the captain of paratroopers; he just might be willing to make amends.

Riordan had never met Valencia and had seen him only once, riding in a Humvee with his troops. In the two days that had passed since the funeral, he had been debating with himself how best to approach the man, what attitude to strike. Angry and demanding wouldn't do; neither would obsequious. In the end, he'd decided he would have to play it by ear and hope he hit the right notes.

Bending at the waist, he checked his appearance in the sideview mirror. His thick gray hair, he thought, should give him a certain gravitas, while his nose, dented at the bridge and slightly askew—it had been broken more than thirty years ago—lent a tough-guy look to his otherwise mild face. Riordan was not a tough guy but scholarly by nature, a former teacher of art history and something of a marshmallow, the kind of man who not only gives money to panhandlers but patiently and sympathetically listens to their stories. During his second (and final) year at Notre Dame, he'd joined the boxing club to put some steel in his spongy soul and emulate Sean, the eldest of his four older brothers and his boyhood hero—a Golden Gloves light heavyweight, a marine who'd won a Bronze Star for valor in Vietnam. To the amazement of everyone in his large family, including himself, Riordan qualified for the finals in Notre Dame's Bengal Bouts tournament in 1979. That was when his fine, slim nose met a straight right he never saw coming and his rear end greeted the canvas.

Riding slowly out of town, returning the waves of parishioners out on the street, he reflected on the things he'd learned in his four years as pastor. Things not taught in the seminary. Some were tutorials in economics—a kilo of uncut cocaine wholesaled in Mexico for around $12,000 and retailed in the United States for twice that—but most were vocabulary lessons. The slang for cocaine was *perico*, and for marijuana *mota*. The AK-47 was called a *cuerno de chivo*, or goat's horn, for its long, curved magazine. The AR-15, with its black barrel and black plastic stock, was a *chanate*, after a nickname for a grackle. A *sicario* was a hit man, the word deriving from Sicarii, the assassins hired by Roman emperors. To kill someone was to *darle el piso*, give him the floor. A drug boss was sometimes called *el jefe*—the boss—and sometimes *el mero-mero*, an untranslatable term that roughly meant "the main man." He'd also been taught, in a seminar given by César, about the plaza system, the arrangement by which a governor, a senator, a high-ranking cop, or all three licensed a drug boss to traffic in a certain territory in exchange for kickbacks, which were called *mordida*. The boss was then said to *tiene la plaza*—hold the plaza.

He hoped his familiarity with this glossary would be useful in his discussions with Captain Valencia. He didn't want to come off as a naïf with the street smarts of a five-year-old.

He dropped his helmet's visor and bumped across the Río Santa Teresa, dry as an Arabian wadi. Only one road tethered San Patricio to the greater world: a two-lane blacktop leading west to Hermosillo, the state capital, where it joined the broad federal highway, Mex 15. The road Riordan was on, called the Mesa Verde, went in the opposite direction, writhing through the foothills toward his destination, the *base militar*, headquarters for the company of paratroopers commanded by Valencia, as well as for a detachment of the Policía Federal, the famed— or infamous—*federales*. Beyond the base, it turned to dirt, eventually branching off into a web of jeep tracks that climbed into the Sierra Madre. Some years before Riordan had been assigned to San Patricio, this section had also been unpaved, so ribbed and rutted, he'd been told, that driving it could rattle the fillings out of your teeth. In the dry months, which meant most of the year, it coated cars in a fine, rust-red talcum; during the summer monsoons, it was almost impassable, the surface mud slick as ice. The town fathers had petitioned the state government to pave it. The government promised everything and of course delivered nothing, mostly because the project wasn't big enough to generate graft in amounts attractive to the politicians.

The appearance one morning of road graders and bulldozers and asphalt trucks, along with hard-hatted workmen carrying picks and shovels, was therefore regarded as miraculous. Some weeks later, several miles of the old road—from San Patricio to the edge of the Sierra—lay under a foot of bituminous black; a drive that had once taken an hour could now be done dust-free in less than half that time, and your fillings stayed put. It was later learned that the civic improvement had not been a supernatural occurrence: the entire project had been organized and paid for by Joaquín Carrasco, *mero-mero* of the Sonora Cartel. Your narcotics dollars at work. If anyone in San Patricio had known what Carrasco looked like (there was only one photograph of him, a mug shot taken years ago), a bronze statue would have been commissioned to stand alongside General Obregón's in the plaza, overlooking the bandstand.

A quarter mile beyond the town limits, where the Santa Teresa's east-west course bent sharply southward, three of César's militiamen, armed with sporting weapons, waved him through a checkpoint. The sand-bagged sentry post and the trench line zigzagging from both sides marked San Patricio's outer defenses and made it look like what it was: a town under siege. From there, the road coiled upward in ever-tightening switchbacks above the riverbed. Riordan's reactions being no longer what they'd been, he cruised along at a processional speed, thinking about what the Old Priest had said this morning. He supposed it was indicative of Mexico's distance from God that people were now nostalgic for the time when Carrasco had held the plaza in almost all of Sonora. He was known then as Don Joaquín, as if he were a character out of *The Godfather*, his underlings as *los valientes*—the brave ones—though there wasn't anything particularly valiant about smuggling dope. But Riordan had learned—more tutelage from César—that the plaza system kept organized crime in Sonora on a leash. So did Don Joaquín's temperament. He was first and foremost a businessman.

"He cut deals, you know, not throats," César had said. "He didn't make life harder for people—sometimes he made it easier, like when he paved the road. He preferred to talk than to fight, and if he had to execute someone, that's who he executed. He didn't massacre twenty people just to get the guy he was after."

César also gave history lessons. In 2006, the country's new president ordered the military out of its barracks to battle the cartels. He was the new sheriff in town; he was going to clean up the entire country. The unintended consequence was chaos. The campaign splintered the big cartels into smaller ones, and then splintered the splinters. Each little gang fought for its share of the traffic, resulting in something close to a Hobbesian state of nature: a war of all against all. The plaza system fell apart. Here in Sonora, Carrasco lost his protection, and he went into hiding—some said in Guatemala, some said in Spain, and some swore he'd been seen in Costa Rica.

Leaderless, the Sonora Cartel fragmented, like the others, into warring factions. From the entire state, the territory under its control had shrunk to a few municipalities in the far south, near the border with Sinaloa.

■ ■ ■

Its ruin spawned La Fraternidad, the Brotherhood. A new thing on the scene, a whole new wrinkle, as much a terrorist organization as it was a mafia. It diversified operations, expanding from drug smuggling into extortion and kidnapping. In the past, you were safe if you weren't mixed up in the trafficking of dope or migrants; now no one was safe, big or little, rich or poor. Quiroga's bakery had been squeezed a percentage for every tortilla sold; farmers were "taxed" at harvesttime; and when the Mexican supervisor of a Canadian copper mine nearby refused to fork over for each ton of ore produced, he was murdered, his body dumped in the plaza with the Brotherhood's calling card pinned to his blood-soaked shirt: the image of *La Santa Muerte*, Holy Death.

The gang's boss was Ernesto Salazar, about whom little was known beyond his name (which was seldom spoken, as if he were a wrathful deity who had forbidden its utterance). Salazar had, in fact, set himself up as a kind of religious figure, authoring his own "bible," upon which his followers swore allegiance in an induction ceremony rumored to involve the sacrifice of a chicken, goat, or cow.

Riordan had never seen, much less read, this bible. Father Hugo had, and said that it mixed Catholicism, evangelical Christianity, Caribbean Santería, and Aztec paganism into an incoherent mishmash. *Los fraternidarios* venerated the traditional saints along with a pantheon of narco "saints," of whom the highest was the sacred female, Holy Death, represented by a skeleton clad in the Virgin's robes, clutching a scythe in her fleshless fingers.

Riordan had been in the parish less than a year the first time he saw her. He'd been summoned to give Last Rites to San Patricio's police chief, gunned down—on the very road he was traveling now—with two of his officers. The bodies were cold by the time he reached the scene, and he knew the instant he saw it that he would never forget it. The bullet-sieved patrol car. Shards of glass sparkling in ponds of blood. The corpses, which the killers had pulled out of the vehicle, sprawled on the pavement, the chief's left leg bent under him, a constable with an arm twisted scarf-like around his throat—it was as if death had made them double-jointed. What burned the sight into Riordan's memory was that each man's right hand had been lopped off and placed upright on the car's hood. A playing card with the picture of *La Santa Muerte*, holding a Kalashnikov instead of a scythe, had been pressed between the thumbs and forefingers. A piece of cardboard was jammed into the crack between the hood and fender, with a quote from Saint Matthew scrawled on it: *Y si tu mano derecha te es ocasión de pecar, córtalo y échala de ti.* "And if your right hand causes you to offend, cut it off, and cast it from you."

Another lesson not in any curriculum he'd ever studied. See what people are capable of when all the guardrails come down.

The sight transfixed him, but somehow he managed to kneel, anoint each body, and murmur, "Through this holy unction may the Lord pardon you whatever sins and faults you have committed and lead you to eternal life." No one but God knew when the soul departed the flesh, and if theirs somehow remained in the cold corpses, perhaps the ritual would help speed them to heaven. It did not help Riordan. He felt tainted in his own soul just by being there; it was as if the atrocity had made a sacrilege of the sacrament he'd administered.

News of the massacre had spread quickly to the most remote parts of the municipality. Rumor had it that the victims had been on Don Joaquín's payroll and remained loyal to him. That seemed to be their offense.

A day passed before Riordan could speak of what he'd seen. He'd witnessed bloodshed as a young priest on his first foreign mission in Guatemala, he'd said to Father Hugo, but nothing to compare with this black marriage of murder, mutilation, and sacred Scripture.

"The *fraternidarios*, you know, are like the Islamists in the Middle East," the vicar had told him. "For them, Allah and holy war sanctions whatever they do. For these butchers, it is Holy Death. They pray to

La Santa Muerte for everything because she justifies everything. She is the deification of death, the baptizing of murder."

That didn't help, either.

■ ■ ■

Riordan rode on. The country between the militia checkpoint behind him and the military compound ahead was a kind of no-man's-land, but the road was firmly under army and police control and safe to travel. Even without that protection, he would not have to worry about his own security. So far, La Fraternidad had not targeted priests for extortion or kidnapping. The exemption probably had nothing to do with respect for the clergy; a priest, a Franciscan friar in particular, wouldn't fetch much of a ransom. As for extorting him, he couldn't cough up more than a few pesos from the collection box.

He came to the stretch where the road switchbacked between two rocky cliffs streaked with bright green lichen. One rose on the left side to a fissured pinnacle; the other, no more slope to it than the side of a build- ing, plunged three hundred feet into the boulder-cobbled bed of the Santa Teresa. He could see the chasm in his peripheral vision and throttled down to five miles an hour, his palms sweaty on the handles, his gut turn- ing somersaults. As he approached the switchback's apex, a line of highway cones shunted him to the left—a military roadblock. A beige army troop carrier—a SandCat—was parked on a turnout barely two yards from the precipice. Three soldiers sat atop it, behind a machine gun protruding from its roof like a lethal ornament. Another soldier was in the cab.

A fifth, standing sentry beside the cones, signaled Riordan to stop with a swing of his rifle. Riordan dismounted, raised his visor, and took off his helmet so the soldier would see his gray hair and pale gringo face and not think him a narco.

"Mexican citizen?" the sentry asked, his accent, like his mahogany complexion, identifying him as an Indian from the far south of the coun- try. He was squat and bowlegged, his chest half as wide as he was tall; his shoulders began right below his ears, and his forehead slanted above close-set eyes into a maroon paratrooper's beret, set off by a silver emblem of an open parachute pierced by a lightning bolt. Riordan explained that he was an American missionary priest, the pastor in San Patricio.

The soldier told him to wait and conferred with the comrade seated at the steering wheel. In the middle of the road, attempting to appear unconcerned, Riordan unzipped his jacket—the day had warmed twenty degrees since morning—dropped the kickstand, and leaned against the bike while looking back in the direction from which he'd come. The road appeared and disappeared, unraveling downhill to the Santa Teresa valley, fractured by the sandy riverbed and fringed with *alamo* trees. San Patricio sprawled along the west side, rusted tin and tile roofs crowded around the central plaza and the church, whose domed bell towers loomed over all. Farther off, under a haze, the copper mine's tailings rose like the wall of a giant meteor crater. Looking in the other direction presented junipers, oaks, and thorn-bush scrub speckling a wide *bajada* that sloped down from the pine-darkened Sierra Madre, the Brotherhood's stronghold. Beautiful country that might have been designed by a fiendish landscape architect, everything in it created to bite, scratch, sting, or claw: scorpions burrowed in the dirt; rattlesnakes coiled in the rocks; pumas and the occasional jaguar prowled the mountains; the fish-hook barbs of barrel cactus waited, with infinite patience, to draw blood.

"Ohe! Padre! Ven aca!"

Riordan turned toward the voice. It came from the soldier who'd been inside the SandCat and was now outside, beside his shorter comrade. A sergeant. Judging from his peremptory tone, he was in command. A quiver rippled through Riordan's knees. To obey the order, he would have to go to where the two men were standing, very near the cliff's edge.

"Hey, you! I said come here!"

He forced himself to move until he was a few feet from the sergeant, who looked skeptically at Riordan's ashen face, sparkling with sweat.

"What makes you so nervous?"

"Nothing . . . I . . . It's become warm, and . . ."

"My *soldado* says you say you are a priest. You don't look like no priest to me."

He hadn't thought that his unclerical mode of dress would cause suspicion. "Well, I am."

"Identification," the sergeant said, fluttering his fingers.

Riordan produced his Mexican driver's license and U.S. passport. Both showed him in a Roman collar. The sergeant gave the documents a cursory glance, and Riordan a longer, more appraising look.

"I've never seen a priest riding a motorcycle. Where are you going on that motorcycle?"

"To see your commanding officer."

"My commanding officer? For what purpose?"

"It's complicated . . ."

"This is simple."

The sergeant clutched his arm, spun him around, and shoved him against the front end of the troop carrier, ordering him to spread his legs and keep his hands flat on the grille at arm's length. He beat back an impulse to resist. While he was patted down, the other paratroopers hovered around Negra Modelo, muttering in admiration while they searched the bike's saddlebags. The short private reported that it was clean.

The sergeant climbed back into the SandCat and spoke into a radio in military gibberish. Another voice answered, but Riordan couldn't make out what it said. Swinging the door open, the sergeant ordered him to lie facedown on the ground, hands behind his head.

"What?"

"You heard me."

"This is outrageous."

"The *capitán*'s orders."

A poke from the squat soldier's rifle convinced him that further protest would be useless and possibly hazardous. The thought that he was going to be arrested, or worse, flitted into his brain; he evicted it as too absurd to permit tenancy for longer than a second. He knew how to behave. Comply. Submit. Keep your mouth shut. He'd been in this position before—the actual physical position—in Guatemala. He'd been a young hothead then, preaching liberationist theology, and after he'd made some incendiary public remarks about land reform and justice for his Indian flock, the police had decided to scare him, throwing him down, jabbing his spine and ribs with gun muzzles.

With his hands clasped over the back of his neck, he could not read his watch, so he didn't know how long he lay on the gravel. Long enough to feel each and every stone jabbing his thighs, his abdomen, his forehead, his elbows. When he rolled onto his side for relief, the private nudged him with a boot and grunted, "No moving."

He heard an automobile pull up, the engine shut down, and the sergeant's voice again:

"Get up." His tone was flat, bored, as if Riordan's easy submission made him unworthy even of contempt.

He stood, brushed himself off, and, struggling to suppress his anger, turned to face two men, both about the same height as he, one a *güero*—a blond, light-skinned Mexican—dressed in civilian clothes, the other in a desert-tan field uniform, the three bars on his collar tips declaring him to be a *capitán primero*.

"You are Capitán Valencia?" Riordan asked, extending a hand.

The officer, without accepting it, answered with a quick nod and said, "*Y tú?*," stressing the informal *tu* instead of the more respectful *usted*. He glanced down at Riordan's cowboy boots, up at his biker's jacket. "You are a priest?"

"I think of myself as a sinner in need of redemption."

Valencia chuckled mirthlessly. He had the slightly underfed look of a long-distance runner, a complexion almost as pale as the *güero*'s, a long, narrow nose, cheekbones that made sharp ledges under gray, intelligent eyes. Take off the beret and put a crested helmet on his head and you'd have the portrait of a sixteenth-century conquistador. "What do you want to see me about?"

"Do you mind if we talk on the other side?"

"The other side of what?"

"The road."

"There is something wrong with this side?"

"We're too close to . . ." Riordan pointed at the drop-off, a pace or two away. "I'm not . . . well, it's like this: I'm not comfortable here. I'm afraid of heights."

This drew more humorless laughter from Valencia. "There are so many things to fear in these mountains, heights should be the least of them."

They crossed the road, Riordan worrying that he'd already screwed things up, making himself ridiculous. The captain and the *güero* leaned against their car, a dark blue SUV with the words "POLICÍA FEDERAL" on its door. The *güero* wasn't a civilian: as he folded his arms, his wind-breaker parted, exposing a holstered pistol and a *federale* badge pinned to his belt.

"If you're now comfortable," Valencia said, not without sarcasm, "tell me what you want to see me about."

Riordan fought down the temptation to come out swinging with objections to his treatment. "I didn't mean to inconvenience you, Captain. I had every intention of speaking with you at the base."

"You are not inconveniencing me. I'm here because of *my* intentions. I don't want you or any other unauthorized person setting foot on the base."

"You have made yourself clear."

"Do the same for yourself."

Despite the request, Riordan sensed that an oblique approach would be more appropriate, and he attempted one with a speech about common interests: Valencia's paratroopers and San Patricio's *autodefensa* had the same mission: to liberate the municipality from La Fraternidad's terror. It made sense, did it not, for the two to act in concert rather than against each other? The militiamen were shocked and angered when the soldiers moved in to take their weapons from them. Such pitiful weapons, too. Antiquated shotguns, .22-caliber rifles. And so the citizens demonstrated, they resisted, and now two young men who'd had nothing to do with it were dead, and—

"Listen, priest," Valencia interrupted, scowling. "Nothing would have happened if these citizens of yours had turned in their guns when I told them to. My orders came from the very top. All these vigilante bands in the country are to be disarmed, and you know why."

Riordan knew what the government claimed: there had been enough bloodshed without mobs of untrained civilians getting into firefights with the far better armed cartels. The real reason, most people thought, was to take the pitchforks from the peasants, just in case they got it into their heads that drug gangs were only part of their problem and decided to storm the castles of corrupt political power instead. That is, prevent a revolution before it got started. The country was ripe for one. The richest man on earth, Carlos Slim, was a Mexican citizen; Riordan didn't doubt that so was the world's poorest man.

"Still, it was a peaceful demonstration," he said to Valencia. "My parishioners feel that there was no provocation for your men to open fire."

"Peaceful? There was nothing peaceful about it!" The army officer pushed himself forward and brought his face to within inches of Riordan's. His breath was stale with the smell of tobacco. "One of your parishioners fired a shot before my men opened fire."

"The way I heard it, a soldier accidentally discharged his rifle, and that panicked some others into shooting."

"Don't argue with me! Panic? My troops don't panic. They showed great discipline, shooting into the air!" Valencia's pale cheeks reddened, not out of anger but, rather, embarrassment. A man who treasured restraint, Riordan judged, ashamed whenever he lost it. The captain collected himself. "I'm still waiting for you to make yourself clear."

"The people in town want to collaborate with the army," Riordan said. "I've been asked to ask you to make an apology, if you want their cooperation."

He spoke rapidly, almost incomprehensibly, like a voice-over in a prescription drug commercial, rattling off the remedy's unpleasant side effects. One look into that spare, stern Castilian face told him that its owner would sooner commit an obscene act in public than apologize.

"All I need to do is to go before them crying, *Lo siento, lo siento*?" the captain said, scorn in every syllable. "And then what? The *autodefensistas* will peaceably turn in their weapons?"

"I think they would like to fight alongside you, like an auxiliary militia," he replied.

Valencia said nothing. Riordan took his silence as encouragement to go on. People in small towns like San Patricio had been forced to protect themselves because they could not rely on the authorities to protect them, he said. There was one exception—

Valencia interrupted. "You approve of vigilantes?"

Riordan took a moment before answering with a brief speech: He did not approve, but he understood why people had taken up arms in their own defense. And, he added, he regarded the rise of *autodefensas* as a good sign that ordinary Mexicans were undergoing a change of heart. For far too long, they had carried on a love affair with their outlaws, romanticizing them as insurgent heroes, singing about them in *corridos*. All that nonsense about *los valientes* dying with their rifles in their hands. Now they were beginning to see the brave ones for what they were: thugs and psychopaths.

"Their eyes have been opened? Only someone who believes in Virgin births could believe that," Valencia said.

"I don't respond to insults, Captain. I was going to say that there is one exception, and that is the army. People feel they can trust the army. The army is respected—"

"Don't try to flatter me."

"I wasn't. People will be more willing to give you information if they feel that the army isn't also their enemy."

"Who put you up to this?"

"No one."

"It's easy enough to guess who. César Díaz didn't have the balls to come to me himself, so he sends a priest to be his messenger boy. Or would you prefer to be called an ambassador?"

Riordan said nothing.

"I have no liking for priests."

"So I've heard."

"It's a tradition in my family. My grandfather's father was with *los quemasantos* in the twenties. Except he did not burn statues of saints. He burned priests. He put them in jail. He shot them. He hanged them." Valencia embraced Riordan with a smile as insincere as it was bright. "Don't worry. I'm not going to do any of that to you."

"I am very much relieved," Riordan said, offering an equally insincere bow of gratitude.

"This father of my grandfather wanted to free Mexico from black magic. He wanted to break the power of the church. He believed in the power of the state. So do I." Valencia's gray eyes grew shiny as new coins. He was relishing the opportunity to share his views on these matters, whether or not he'd been asked for them. "For example, a little while ago, on my orders, you were made to lie down in the dirt. Do you think that if your bishop commanded me to lie with my face in the dirt, I would have obeyed?"

"All right, I get it," Riordan said. "You don't genuflect to the church."

"Listen, priest. The government has deployed the army to fight these fucking narcos because only the army has the power to do it. With the assistance of the Federal Police, of course." He threw a little head twitch at his companion. "Why were we sent here? To smash the Brotherhood. To bring Ernesto Salazar out of these mountains in irons or in a body bag. Who but us can do that? You with your rosary beads? A mob of civilians armed with rusty rabbit guns?"

During this oration, Riordan had become aware that the police officer was studying him much as an artist would a model, only his gaze wasn't tracing the lineaments of his face. It was more like a probe of his interior, and it made him squirm.

"Please listen, Captain," he said. "With those rusty rabbit guns, the *autodefensa* kicked the Brotherhood out of town."

"Not entirely," Valencia scoffed. "Salazar still has operatives in the town, doesn't he? Spies?"

"Yes . . ."

"And as for the rest of the municipality, he controls it all. More than one hundred and fifty little villages. The mountains, the poppy fields, the *mota* farms, he controls them. And that copper mine, they pay him to stay in business. A copper mine!"

Riordan acknowledged that this, too, was true.

"*Con su perdón, Capitán*. That is my point. The militia secures the town, giving your men freedom to operate in the countryside—"

"Are you going to lecture me on military tactics?"

"No, of course not."

"In my opinion, your rabbit shooters did not force them out. Your pueblo is free of the Brotherhood because Salazar doesn't need it."

The *federale* then broke his silence: "What is it you want, Father Riordan? Besides an apology from Captain Valencia, that is."

Riordan was pleased to be addressed by his name and title rather than as "priest," as if he were an anonymous member of a separate species. He was also amazed to hear the question put to him in an English as American as his birthplace, Oak Park, Illinois.

"And you are . . . ?" he asked.

"A sinner beyond redemption," the *federale* replied, with a half smile. Gray stippled his blond hair. Riordan pegged him to be in his late forties.

He was handsome in an unremarkable way, with a pleasing face you would forget two minutes after seeing it—except for the piercing, pale blue eyes.

"No one is ever beyond redemption," Riordan said. "Although Hitler and Stalin may have been exceptions to the rule. You sound like you've spent a lot of time in the States."

"It doesn't matter where I've spent my time. No more than it matters who I am. You can call me Professor if you like. Most people do."

"Professor of what?"

"Arts."

"Something tells me not to ask what those are."

"Whatever voice that is, listen to it. What do you want besides an apology from Captain Valencia?" the cop repeated, continuing to subject Riordan to intense scrutiny. This was what he imagined: with the power of that stare, the Professor had thrust an invisible endoscope into his brain, and it was making images of his thoughts. "I'll give you a hint. *Libera nos a malo.*"

A Mexican federal agent who looked Dutch, spoke perfect American English, and knew church Latin? This produced a disagreeable sensation like the one Riordan had felt as a child when he was wading in the lake near his parents' summer cottage in Wisconsin and the sand had crumbled underfoot and suddenly he was in greenish depths with no bottom in sight. It was like that—a panicky foundering.

"You didn't come to us for an apology," the Professor went on. "You aren't anyone's messenger or ambassador. You came for your own reasons. You want to deliver your parish from the Brotherhood. Salazar is a cult leader as much as he's a gangster. He extorts money from the copper mine. What he means to extort from you are souls, and you, Padre Tim, can't allow that to happen."

For reasons he couldn't identify, Riordan found this observation unsettling. "Well, I . . . I never thought of . . ." he stammered. "I certainly wouldn't want him to . . ."

"What you want is what we want. We should be working together."

Recovering, Riordan pointed out that he'd said that very thing a minute ago.

"*Por supuesto!*" Valencia said. Apparently, he'd had no trouble following the English conversation, but now they were back to Spanish.

"However, you were speaking of cooperation between the army"—his arm swept wide to take in the soldiers on the SandCat—"and your idiot vigilantes. We"—the arm made a shorter swing between him and the Professor—"are talking about *you* cooperating with *us*."

"No matter your dislike of priests?"

"I am a professional soldier. I don't allow my prejudices to interfere with what needs to be done. There are people, many people, in your parish who work for the Brotherhood."

"Most because they were forced into it. It's the old question: *Plata o plomo?*"

"And for some, there was enough silver offered not to require the threat of lead, true?"

"I suppose, yes."

Then, from the Professor: "You hear things, don't you, Father Riordan?"

"I hear a great many things."

"Some true, some not."

"I couldn't tell you. People are afraid of their own neighbors these days. Is Pablo with the Brotherhood? Is Miguel? Who knows? There is no trust any longer. People make up stories. Most of the time, they don't say anything. The whole municipality has become one big *casa silencio*."

Valencia nodded solemnly. "But there is one place where they do say things, and the things they say are not made up." A glance passed between him and his companion. It looked to Riordan like a prompt. "The narcos are also in need of redemption. Even the worst of them hopes for a ticket into heaven. And you are the man in the ticket booth."

"*Ego te absolvo tuam peccatorum, in nomine Patris, et Filii, et Spiritus Sancti.*" The Professor, his expression a grimace or a grin or a fusion of both, drew the sign of the cross in the air.

The day had advanced to midafternoon, the sun rolling down a sky without clouds or even the possibility of clouds. The clarity of vacancy but a clarity for all that. The sobs of widows and mothers had been among the many things Riordan had heard; likewise, every now and then, the confessions of the men who'd murdered their husbands and sons.

"We need precise information," Valencia said. "Who did what when. Who has been ordered to do what by whom. We have our *dedos*, of course we do. But everybody knows that the best evidence is a confession."

Dedo. Finger, Riordan thought, recalling more underworld vocabulary. It was clear, from the way the two men were tag-teaming him, that this proposition wasn't an inspiration of the moment; they had discussed it before.

He said, "You know I could never do what you're asking."

"To know that a crime has been committed and say nothing makes one an accessory after the fact." The cop who called himself a professor sounded as if he were lecturing in a law school. "And to know that a crime will be committed and say nothing makes one an accomplice."

Dedo. Finger. Snitch. "The seal is inviolate," Riordan said.

"But there are circumstances when—"

"No circumstances, Captain. It is absolutely inviolate."

"Is it truly? What about altar boys' assholes? They should be inviolate, but you priests violate them all the time."

Riordan stood with his head bent and turned slightly aside, like someone hard of hearing. He felt a most un-Christian impulse to dig a left hook into the captain's liver.

The Professor gave Valencia a disapproving look. "My colleague shouldn't have made that remark," he said, reverting again to English.

"All the same, he did," Riordan replied. He lifted his glance to the hillside above the car. Swales of sharp, brown grass broken by ocotillo wands, each like a spiked whip, trembled in breezes eddying down from the heights. He turned to the captain. "I buried those boys two days ago. I consoled their mothers, but there is no consolation. No remedy for the pain of outliving your own child. What is being asked of you is very simple. A simple apology that will restore goodwill, and then, I think, you could hear all the secrets you need."

Valencia abruptly spun on his heels and reached into the SUV for his cigarettes. He shook one out of the pack and lit it, gazing sternly into Riordan's face. "What's being asked of you," he said, each word producing a puff of smoke, "is likewise very simple."

The Professor slouched against the driver's door. "That would be the quid for the quo."

Riordan no longer felt out of his depth; he'd kicked himself back into the shallows, and his feet touched bottom. "Your Latin is a little rusty. It's *ego te absolvo peccatis tuis*. I absolve you *from* your sins. Not *of*. Requires the ablative."

CHAPTER THREE

He rolled the Harley into the gated courtyard and locked the fork to the veranda post. The Old Priest was tending his herb garden: medicinal herbs mostly, ancient cures for arthritis, bellyaches, cuts and bruises and chafes. He was retired, no longer said Mass, the frequent genuflections too much for his creaky joints. All he did was pray, study rare texts in Greek, Latin, and Hebrew, and see to his garden, a life of monkish quietude that Riordan sometimes envied.

"There you have a sign of the times," Riordan said, sitting on a bench beside the bust of Father Eusebio Kino, motioning at the bike at the same time. "I have to lock it, even here, in a church rectory."

Clipping leaves from some plant or other, the Old Priest did not acknowledge him.

"I've been thinking about what you said, and my question is, Is Mexico far from God or God from her? Has He distanced himself because she has turned her back on Him to become the number one exporter of poison?"

The Old Priest faced him and pointed at an ear with his clippers to indicate that he wasn't wearing his hearing aid. *"Cómo? Qué dijiste?"*

"No importa," Riordan shouted.

"As you wish," said the Old Priest and, bending down in slow motion, returned to his task.

No longer said Mass. No longer heard confessions; even with the hearing aid, he could not make out the murmured transgressions well enough to grant absolution and assign the proper penances.

Ego te absolvo . . . Riordan reflected on Valencia's and the Professor's request, if it could be called that. Not the first time it had been made of him.

The plaintiffs' attorney was, as Riordan had been then, a redhead. She lacked the quick temper commonly associated with that hair color, simmering instead with a free-floating anger that had found an object in the person of Father Timothy Riordan, whom she was deposing in a class-action lawsuit: *John Doe et al., plaintiffs, v. Franciscan Friars of California*. Among the John Does was Luis Gonzalez.

After establishing that Riordan had taught at St. Michael's high school in Los Angeles with a defendant named Father James Brenner, she asked if Brenner had admitted to Riordan that he'd had sex with underage boys.

—I'm afraid I'm not at liberty to answer.

—Are you saying that Father Brenner confessed to having sex with minors but you are bound not to reveal what he said?

From the defense counsel: Objection. Leading.

—Sustained. Counsel will rephrase.

—All right.

Then she fired a surprise from her quiver of legal arrows. Did you ever hear a cleric, any cleric, confess to having sex with a minor?

—Objection.

—Did you ever hear a minor confess to sexual relations with a cleric?

—Objection!

—Your Honor, I'm not asking the witness to identify anyone; I'm not asking him to reveal the specific contents of any confession he's heard. I'm merely asking him to confirm or deny a fact.

—Objection! Plaintiffs' counsel is on a fishing expedition. What business does this or any court have in knowing this fact?

—Overruled. The witness may answer.

Riordan sat mute, his mind spinning. Did she know? But how? She could have learned only from Brenner himself, but it was very unlikely that he had told her. Still, he might have. Would a denial then bring a

charge of perjury? Would the truth open the door to a line of questioning that would lead him into violating his vows? Who and what did he
wish to protect? The Franciscan Friars from financial penalties? No.
Father Brenner? Absolutely no. The sanctity of the confessional? Yes, but
what was more, he wanted to protect one Luis Gonzalez, though Luis
didn't deserve it. The lawyer stood glaring at him.

—Please answer the question.

—No, he replied. I never heard any such confession.

No. Even now, nearly a decade later and in another country, he felt
the heat of shame rise in his face.

The Old Priest rose from his labors. It took him a few seconds to stand
up straight. He held what looked like beets in a freezer bag.

"Qué es eso?" Riordan asked, again shouting to make himself heard.

"Chicamilla. For the constipation. Señora Villarreal has the constipation."

His huaraches shuffling in the dust, the Old Priest went inside to boil
the root, carrying on in the tradition of the priest as physician, healer of
body and soul, a *curandero.* There was a quality of the eternal about
him; he served no purpose in the parish and yet seemed a permanent
part of it, like the antique iron rings on the church doors.

Riordan, left alone, studied Father Kino's bust, worn by time and
weather, the chips and black streaks on the great Jesuit's face a reproach.
The small monument had been on his restoration to-do list; he'd found
a sculptor in Tubac, on the Arizona side, who could make the repairs;
but the man had been frightened off by the State Department's travel
advisories, the signs at the border crossings: DANGER! ACTIVE DRUG
AND HUMAN SMUGGLING AREA. VISITORS MAY ENCOUNTER ARMED
CRIMINALS AND SMUGGLING VEHICLES TRAVELING AT HIGH SPEED.

Despite the skepticism in which he held Jesuits as a religious order—
too arrogant, too proud of their supposed braininess—he much
admired Kino. Kino the missionary who'd ridden the Pimería Alta's
river valleys on horseback, a Johnny Appleseed of the faith, planting
missions wherever he went, two dozen in twenty years. He'd established
this one, the southernmost in his realm, in 1697. La Misión de la Santa
Teresa de las Colinas it was called for a century and a half, till the name
was changed to San Patricio, honoring the Irish soldiers who deserted

the American army to fight for Mexico in 1848. (Leave it to the Irish to join the losing team, Riordan thought. We have a fatal attraction to hopeless causes.) He'd made a pilgrimage to Kino's tomb in Magdalena, peered down through the glass at his bones in the gray-brown dust. No question that a considerable brain had once filled that long-empty skull. Kino the astronomer who'd written an essay on his observations of a comet. Kino the cartographer who'd mapped the Pimería Alta when it lay beyond the rim of the then known world. And Kino the shepherd, protecting his Indian converts—Pima, Maricopa, Mayo, Tohono O'odham—from the hard Spaniards who enslaved them to wrest silver and gold from the Sierra Madre.

We live in a nation of sheep and wolves. That line jumped into his mind. He'd read it in a petition published in a newspaper a few months ago. "An Appeal to the People of Mexico," it was titled. The conquistadores had been the wolves of Kino's day. The wolves of the present were the narcos, the crooked cops, the corrupt politicians, and the sheep were everyone else. Right then, it came to him that the Professor's observation had been unsettling for its accuracy. How could a stranger have read him so perfectly when he had not been able to read himself? He did want to deliver his parish from the evil befalling it. More than a desire, it was a sacred obligation, for he was the shepherd, God his master, and the shepherd must answer to the master for the safety of his sheep.

But how? he asked himself. How?

■ ■ ■

He rode Negra Modelo through town only when necessary; the narrow streets amplified the sound of its 1,300cc engine to an ear-splitting roar.

The walk to César Díaz's house took him across the plaza and under an arcade covering the sidewalk that ran past *tiendas* and the town hall, its doors guarded by two *federales* in blue-black uniforms, its coral-pink walls papered with handwritten signs. *Afuera con la Fraternidad! Muerte a la Fraternidad!*

Only a few weeks ago, before the army's arrival, before Díaz's vigilantes reclaimed the streets from Brotherhood goons cruising in pickups with smoked windows, no one would have dared post such messages in public. Even with the improved security, these—"Out with the Brotherhood! Death to the Brotherhood!"—had been put up in the middle of the night; you never knew if La Fraternidad's operatives were watching.

The lights were on inside the town hall, functionaries busy making sure the water ran and the trash got picked up, the machinery of municipal routine clanking along even though San Patricio no longer had a government to speak of. Since the assassinations of the police chief and his two officers, the municipal cops did little more than issue parking tickets. The *autodefensa* had become its de facto police force, as the mayor's secretary had become the de facto mayor, the elected one and all four council members having fled. "They ran away with nobody chasing them," César had joked, adapting, Riordan supposed, the line from Proverbs: "The wicked flee when no man pursues." A fear of retribution, springing from guilty consciences, had convinced them to pack their bags. The mayor and the councilmen had been collecting "taxes"—that is, extortion payments for the Brotherhood—and sharing in the profits.

A shopkeeper greeted him, as did a woman sweeping dust from the sidewalk and the driver of a pickup transporting five-gallon water jugs. *Buenas tardes, Padre Tim! Dios los bendiga!* Riordan felt as much as heard the warmth in their voices. Yes, to Father Hugo (and the other priests in the diocese), he would always be an outsider; but his parishioners loved him, requiting his love for them. You are more respected than the mayor ever was, César had told him. That wasn't a great accomplishment—a stray dog would have earned more respect—yet he couldn't help but feel a flush of pride, a reaction, perhaps, to the humiliation he'd suffered at Captain Valencia's hands. Pissing in the corners to mark his territory. *I have the power, gringo priest, to make you grovel in the dirt.*

He emerged from the arcade and headed up Calle Insurgentes, climbing steeply between villas built by Spanish silver barons more than two centuries ago, now carved into apartments for grocers, mechanics, waiters from the pueblo's only hotel. One of the dwellings had been restored to its former elegance by an American expat who, heeding the State Department's warnings, hadn't occupied it for two years. Riordan began to feel the climb in his calves and lungs as he went by Lisette Moreno's house and clinic, shaded by an enormous mesquite said to be over three hundred years old. The past alive in the present, like the archaic light from distant stars.

Then came an antiquated sound: the clatter of shod hooves on cobblestones. A man with a face as fissured as a dried date sat astride a light-boned bay, his posture erect and proud. A would-be *caballero*, though he was in reality a guide who, in the days before the narco wars, had taken visitors touring the Mission Trail on pony treks through the countryside. Another encouraging sight. Not very long ago, he wouldn't have had the temerity to be out on the streets, exercising a horse.

But his ride, Riordan knew, would not take him beyond the militia's trenches and checkpoints. It would not take him to the outlying ranches, farms, and villages, or to the Indian settlements in the Sierra, or anywhere near the tenebrous canyons where the poppies and the cannabis grew and meth brewed in the Brotherhood's labs. Riordan, Father Hugo, and Dr. Moreno were among the few who could venture safely into those parts, the two priests protected by their poverty, Lisette by her profession. Narcos suffered headaches and fevers like anyone else, not to mention gunshot wounds.

He paused at the top of the hill to catch his breath, then walked on to César's compound. Behind it, his walnut trees marched in orderly ranks, many of them fire-blackened. A cracked adobe wall with an iron gate surrounded two flat-roofed, mud-brick casitas facing each other across a dirt courtyard. Three young men, César's security detail, slouched against the wall, pistols jammed in their waistbands. The only one Riordan knew, Moises Ortega, had a rifle slung crosswise over his back. No rusty rabbit gun, but a *cuerno de chivo*. Moises was smoking a joint, which he flipped into the street when he saw Riordan approaching.

"Yo! Padre Tim," he called, displaying a sheepish grin, followed by some elaborate acrobatics with his fingers—a gangbanger's salute.

"I could smell it, you know," Riordan said. "You three look like you couldn't guard a chicken coop."

"Hey, we're cool. Read-ee for anything."

Moises and his companions were San Patricio natives who had lived most of their young lives in Los Angeles, acquiring a command of English and a facility with firearms in barrio turf battles. They'd been deported back to their hometown, following convictions on drug and weapons charges, and promptly enlisted in the self-defense force. They liked to romanticize themselves as bad guys gone good, putting their criminal skills to righteous use, like the outlaws in *The Magnificent Seven*.

"So, Moises, *que tal*? What's happening?" Riordan asked, pointing at a van parked across the street, its panel lettered XHNOA-TV.

"César's being interviewed." Moises was now all restless energy, shifting his weight from one foot to the other, twitching his head, the silver crucifix draped from his neck swinging pendulum-like across his protective vest. "National TV, man. He'll be, like, a celebrity."

Riordan stood on tiptoe to peer over the wall into the courtyard. He was looking over the reporter's shoulder directly at César. Clad in the same too-tight shirt and suit jacket he'd worn at yesterday's funeral, sitting stiffly in a plastic chair, a small mike clipped to his collar, his eyes flitting in search of something to fix on, he didn't look like a celebrity. More like a suspect undergoing interrogation.

"Please! Look at me or at the camera," said the reporter, a woman with short black hair.

His wandering gaze settled on the camera, shouldered by a sallow-cheeked man in a satin baseball jacket. A technician squatted nearby, fiddling with audio equipment while a slab of meat and muscle stood off to the side, an assault rifle in his hand. Mexican reporters also needed bodyguards. In matters of news management, the narcos were as lacking in nuance as they were in their business methods. Any number of journalists had been murdered for writing or speaking the truth.

The reporter leafed through the notebook in her lap. "You have told us what happened at the demonstration," she said. "But let me ask one thing: The *autodefensa* still refuses to disarm?"

"Yes, that's right," César replied.

"Under what circumstances would you give up your weapons?"

"When the army brings us their heads."

Moises, squatting beside Riordan at the window, pumped his fist and whispered: "The boss is a badass."

"Excuse me, 'heads'?" the reporter asked, startled by the response. "Whose heads?"

"Ernesto Salazar and his lieutenants, Enrique Mora, the one they call *El Serpiente*, and Rubén Levya, who is known as *El Tigre Negro*. The

Snake and the Black Jaguar. Do you know the nickname for Salazar? *La Mariposa.*"

She tilted her head. "The Butterfly? Why?"

"Because he has never been married, never has no girlfriends."

"You said you want the authorities to bring you their *heads*? Do you mean—"

"No! Not to chop off their heads. But we want them dead. We want to see their bodies. And we want the DNA, for proof that they got the right guys. These *fraternidarios*, you know, they work miracles. They do miraculous things."

"Such as . . . ?"

"Resurrections. They rise from the dead." César put on a look of mock astonishment. "Levya is two times reported to be killed and both times he is later seen walking around. Is this because the Jaguar is a cat having nine lives? No, it is a miracle. The same with Salazar. I think he has been killed three times and all three risen from the dead. A very great miracle. Even Jesus rose only once. So we want the DNA for proof that they are truly dead. Then we will surrender our weapons."

Riordan, relieved that his friend wouldn't go on national TV calling for beheadings, was nonetheless alarmed. César's remarks were rash, to say the least.

The reporter's pen danced across her notebook; then she flipped its pages with a snappy flourish, like a card dealer finishing a shuffle. "One more question. These vigilante groups like yours—"

"We are not vigilantes!" César interrupted, voice rising in indignation. "We don't take the law into our own hands, because now, here, there is no longer any law to take! We are only defending ourselves. No one else will. The army, the Federal Police, they ride around in their Sand-Cats, they patrol the plaza, and we tell them, Salazar is not in the plaza, he is in the mountains. Go after him. And what do they do? They try to take our weapons away from us. They shoot us."

"But to my question. There are rumors that Carrasco is delighted by the appearance of the *autodefensas* in Sonora. They do his fighting for him, then he returns from exile to reclaim his narco kingdom. What do you say to that?"

César made a chopping movement with one hand. "I know nothing about what delights Señor Carrasco. Nobody does. Nobody knows where he is or even if he is still alive, so what I say to these rumors is that they are *mierda*."

■ ■ ■

César filled two shot glasses from the unlabeled bottle on the table as he and Riordan sat across from each other in his living room, its sky-blue stucco walls bare except for two images that delivered mixed messages: a poster showing a half-naked beauty caressing a bottle of Pacifico beer and a framed photograph, cut from a magazine, of a life-sized statue of the crucified Christ. *The Lord of Atil*, it was called, named after the Sonoran town where it stood.

The two men clinked glasses: *Salud, Salud*. César drained his with one quick gulp while Riordan sipped his. The clear, silvery liquid, at first cold on his tongue, slid down his throat like warm mercury.

"Eh! Padre Tim! That's no way to treat a *bacanora* like this one. My cousin Javier made it. *El néctar puro de agave puro*."

They were conversing in the hybridized lingo of the border, Spanglish. César, a citizen of the United States and Mexico, had worked many years for a produce shipper on the Arizona side of Nogales.

"Such purity should be savored," Riordan said.

"*Mierda*! It has authority. It must be drunk with authority."

"All right. *Con autoridad*." He downed the drink, and the warm mercury hit his gut, then shot into his brain. "*Que sabe bien, que Dios me perdóne*."

"You have said it many times. He pardons us all."

"Little children and Irish drunks especially."

"You are not a drunk."

"No. But my father was, and I have an older brother who is. How was it to be interviewed for TV?"

"My first time. How did I do, you think?"

"*No tan mal*. You seemed a little nervous."

"Not because it was my first time. Because I was angry and I was worried I would say the wrong thing." He lifted the bottle. "*Otro vez?*"

Riordan shook his head. "One is enough."

César poured another shot for himself and drank it off as he had the first, his cheeks flushing so that Riordan was reminded of a reddened moon.

"The nephew I raised like a son is in his grave, and over there"—motioning out a window at the casita across the way—"my wife comforts my sister. Thank God Lupita has two other children. I think she would kill herself if she didn't. I was worried I would say, you know, 'The *chingado* goddamned army and Federal Police should be fighting the *chingado* Brotherhood, and instead they kill my nephew and the Reyes boy, those *chingado cabrones*.' You will forgive my language, Padre Tim? I am still angry."

"I'm sure I've heard worse." Riordan hesitated, marshaling his thoughts. "But that's what you did say, in different words. Valencia won't be pleased. And when Salazar hears that you want him dead, that you want his DNA for God's sake, he'll double the contract that's out on you."

Doubt crossed César's face. Riordan sensed that he regretted his intemperate words. But it was only for a moment; self-doubt and regret were not part of his makeup.

"Let him triple it—I don't give a shit," he said, falling back into his natural machismo. He'd formed the *autodefensa* after La Fraternidad, desiring a share in the bounty from his walnut orchard, set it on fire when he refused to pay. Everyone told him to take his losses, consider himself fortunate, blessed of God, that the arsonists did not toast him along with his walnuts. César would have none if it. *They want war,* he had declared, *I'll give them what they want.*

"I've come to tell you what passed between me and Valencia," Riordan said.

"*Así. Dime.*"

Riordan censored his account, redacting Valencia's proposal, which he couldn't risk revealing even to a friend like César.

"Valencia made you lie in the dirt at the point of a gun?" César asked when he'd finished. "Like you were a criminal?"

"I told you he wasn't fond of priests."

César was silent for a moment. Then: "I am disappointed."

In the outcome or in me? Riordan asked himself. Or in both? Bending forward, he reached across the table to clasp César's knee.

"An apology from an army officer? You knew that would be expecting the impossible."

"*Tal vez sea así.* All the same, I must have expected something, because I have this disappointment. And I'm disappointed because something is expected of me. I am expected to do something about what happened to Hector and Ángel."

"Who has these expectations?"

"The Reyes family. My sister. Those boys out there guarding my house. Everyone. I expect it of myself." He sat back, hands on his knees. "I have an idea. I need your advice."

With a swipe of his hand, Riordan told him to go ahead.

"I know the human rights commissioner for Sonora. I am considering asking him to file a complaint, to demand an investigation. What do you think?"

Riordan coughed into his hand and pointed at the bottle. "*Permiso?*"

"Ah, so one wasn't enough. *Por favor.*"

But as Riordan raised the shot glass to his lips, his eyes lifted to the Lord of Atil. It was only a photo of a statue, the image of an image, and yet it shamed him, for this Jesus was not the film-star-handsome Jesus who swooned gracefully in sanitized crucifixions in American churches. This Jesus, his skin dirty ivory—the pallor of death—his mouth half open in the rictus of a stifled scream, blood from the crown of thorns and the nails and the spearpoint's gash skeining his face, his arms, and his ribs, inspired horror rather than sweet reverence, and so portrayed more honestly the profound agony the incarnate God had endured to redeem a fallen world.

He lowered the glass and with two fingers pushed it toward César. "You drink it."

"I've had two, and that's enough for me."

"All right, then . . ." Riordan poured the contents of the glass back into the bottle, taking care not to spill any. "I should be saying my afternoon prayers, not drinking."

César glanced at the photo, then back at Riordan, and twisted his thin lips into a knowing but indulgent smile. "I don't think he'll mind at all. Sometimes you are too hard on yourself."

True enough, Riordan thought. He suffered from false guilt—scruples, the church called it—an overactive conscience producing fears that certain thoughts, desires, or acts were sinful which in fact were not. He couldn't account for his malady. Like his terror of heights, it was woven into the tapestry of his being, though it seemed to prick him whenever he felt that he had fallen short, as he did now.

César recapped the bottle and said, "So what do you think? Is my idea a good one, a bad one?"

"These human rights commissioners are ornaments," Riordan replied evasively. He was afraid, now, that whatever advice he gave would be wrong. "The Mexican government decorates itself with them so it can pretend it's a real democracy."

"Come on, Padre Tim. People want me to do something. I'm the chief of the militia, and it was my nephew the soldiers killed. I'm asking what you think I should do."

"I'm the wrong one to ask. It's not a thing for a priest."

"And what is?"

"Perhaps I should visit Lupita."

César whipped his head side to side. "That is also not for a priest. Right now she is angry with God. She'll get over it, but she has been cursing God all afternoon. I cannot promise that she won't curse you."

"You said my sermon was a great succor to her."

"It was good manners to say that."

Riordan was silent. As a man who needed to be needed, hearing that he not only wasn't but might cause harm made him feel as useless as a doctor with no remedies in his bag.

"I think maybe you're right," César sighed. "None of this has been a thing for a priest. I should have gone to Valencia myself."

The self-recrimination in his words was belied by the expression that closed over his face: *I have been let down.*

CHAPTER FOUR

Riordan walked back to the plaza, under high cirrus colored molten orange by the sunset, and paused by the bandstand to admire the church. It was an architectural mongrel yet as eye-pleasing as a purebred, or, as an old guidebook put it, "a harmonious blend of Moorish, Byzantine, baroque, and Mexican Renaissance architecture." Looking at its balanced façade—the twin domed bell towers, the tall oak doors flanked by baroque columns—soothed him; and thinking about its history gave him heart. Priests from his order began building it in the 1780s, after the Spanish king expelled the Jesuits from Mexico. They accomplished the feat with Indian labor and no machinery, while protecting their converts from plundering Spaniards on the one side and wild Seris and Apaches on the other. Was he less than they? If they could triumph over all that, why couldn't he shield his flock from both the Brotherhood and Valencia's paratroopers? The good shepherd does not run from the wolves.

He crossed the plaza, passing near a young couple necking on a bench. Really going at it, so lost in their passion that they weren't aware of him. Pretending not to notice them, he quickened his pace; but he wasn't quick enough to avoid glimpsing the girl's jeans, as tight as leotards, and the delectable S traced by her back, hips, and legs as she leaned into the boy's arms. A needle of lust jabbed him and expelled the serenity he'd felt just seconds earlier.

Keeping celibate had always been a struggle for him, and he'd lost it once. Not long after his ordination, he'd tumbled into an affair with a translator from the U.S. embassy in Rome, when he was studying at the North American College. Marcella Allegretti. Long, light brown hair, a straight nose above half-smiling lips, large gray-green eyes, a distant look in them—she could have been a model for Botticelli's *Primavera*. Owing to her work and his somewhat cloistered life, they did not see each other very often; but the infrequency of the assignations heightened their intensity. He went to confession every Friday, vowed to sin no more, and within minutes of leaving, plotted how and when he could do exactly that. He almost left the priesthood over her. In the end, he chose his vocation, telling Marcella that he could not fully devote himself to her with a divided heart. "Then by all means give your heart to your church, see if embracing a stone statue is the same as embracing me," she had replied. After the breakup, feeling both devastated and relieved, he confessed yet again. By this time, his confessor recognized his voice. "Don't tell me you're still screwing her," he sighed before Riordan could finish saying, "Bless me, Father, for I have sinned." Such was his guilt that he was disappointed by the priest's mild penance and imposed a sterner one on himself. During the summer break, he made a pilgrimage to Spain, walking the Camino de Santiago from the Pyrenees to Saint James's tomb in Santiago de Compostela. Five weeks, five hundred miles, all on foot. The journey did not entirely purge Marcella from his system. For years afterward, just when he thought he had forgotten her, she would gate-crash his memory, as she was doing right now.

She sang to him as he entered his room to change out of his biker's outfit, back into his habit. *Vicino mare / facciamo amore / a core a core, pe ce spassá.* Seated at the piano in her flat near the Campo de' Fiori, dressed in nothing more than her bra and panties, Valentine red. The fantasy produced a bulge in his own underwear—drab cotton boxers. *For I acknowledge my transgressions; and my sin is ever before me.* And there it was, a Pinocchio's nose poking out from between his legs. This is ridiculous, he said to himself. A fifty-two-year-old priest getting a wanger over a woman he hasn't seen in a quarter of a century. The Angelus bells tolled in the twilight. He pulled the coarse brown robe over his head; it concealed his erection nicely. To eliminate it, he prayed the

Angelus in Latin while pinching the third knot, which signified chastity, in the five-knotted cord girding his waist.

It seemed that in the contest between will and desire, desire had the upper hand. Semitumescent, he walked down the corridor to the parish office to attend to the business he'd neglected all day.

The room was cozy and quaint. It held a kiva fireplace, a large, if rickety, wooden desk, a couple of ornately carved chairs with cracked leather seats, a tall bookcase crammed with theological and philosophical works, two volumes of canon law, several Bibles, and leather-bound commentaries by church fathers. His eighteenth-century predecessors would have felt at home here, though they would have been puzzled by the steel filing cabinet, the overhead fan with electric light fixture, and the desktop Mac (at five years old, an antique by computer-industry standards). He sat at the desk, upon which Domingo Quiroga, the parish secretary, bookkeeper, and office manager, had laid out the water, electric, and gas bills, with blank checks attached; a proof of next week's parish bulletin; and an engineer's report on needed repairs to the church and rectory buildings. Riordan signed the checks, made a few minor changes to the bulletin, typed a schedule of visits to shut-ins. The dull administrative tasks succeeded where will and prayer had failed. Better than an ice-cold shower, he thought, skimming the engineer's report. Some rusty pipes in the rectory had to be replaced, a crack in the masonry dome over the altar had to be patched. Sergio Ramírez, María the cook's husband, was an all-around handyman who did odd jobs for the church. He could repair the plumbing, but the roof would require a professional. Finding one willing to come to San Patricio for an affordable fee would be difficult. He wished that faulty plumbing and cracked roofs were the only serious problems he had to deal with.

Domingo had also left him two notes. "Mr. García telephoned, asking for you. He wishes to make an appointment," read the first. Domingo and his brother were partners in Quiroga's bakery; his position in the church was voluntary. Even so, was it too much to ask for a modicum of competence? Which Mr. García? There were four García families in the parish. And why had Domingo failed to get a phone number? The second note—"Someone slipped this under the door"—was paper-clipped to a sealed envelope, which Riordan slit with a letter opener. It contained another note, written in a loopy schoolgirl's hand: "Dear Padre Riordan: I cannot meet with you at three o'clock tomorrow. I can only meet with you at four o'clock. I am sorry for causing you inconvenience." It was unsigned, but he knew it was from Cristina Herrera, a seventeen-year-old high school girl. He also knew the reason for the meeting, though it had never been stated. She was coming in for counseling; a little more than a month ago, she had been raped.

■ ■ ■

Dinner was served promptly at seven-thirty in the rectory dining room, which wasn't much bigger than a good-sized pantry and was sparsely lit by low-wattage bulbs in a cast-iron, hoop chandelier that had once held candles. Exposed wires snaked up one wall, crawled along a beam, and slithered down the chandelier's chain, threatening to electrocute anyone changing a bulb should the insulation fray. María, a tree stump of a woman, rolled in from the kitchen, bearing a bowl of Spanish rice and a platter of flank steak in chipotle sauce. Another trip to the kitchen produced a basket of fat, warm tortillas. She went round the table, filling each plate. Riordan bowed over his, inhaled theatrically, and tugged the single gray braid hanging down María's back like a bell cord.

"María!" he said, with an exaggerated roll of the *r*: Mah-r-r-r-ree-ah. "No one makes a chipotle like you. If I were not a priest, I would marry you."

"I do not think so," she replied gravely. "I am already married. A problem, no?"

He slapped his forehead. "I forgot!"

"Be quiet and eat." She laughed an indulgent laugh, like the mother of a mildly naughty son. "You are a disgrace."

After she left the room, Father Hugo scowled to let Riordan know that he considered the flirtatious banter no laughing matter—it really was disgraceful.

"I'm only trying to cheer myself up," Riordan said. "Our roof is cracking, our plumbing leaks, and only a few hours ago I was lying in the dirt with a paratrooper standing over me with a gun."

They said grace. Father Hugo minced his steak, slicing it horizontally, then vertically into kibble-sized bites. "Your discussions with the military did not go well?"

Riordan had told the vicar he was going to see Captain Valencia.

"I have had more cordial conversations," he said.

"You must tell us everything," the vicar demanded, in the way of a house-wife eager for gossip.

Riordan abridged the account as he had with César. He wasn't sure why. His listeners, assuming the Old Priest was listening, could be trusted to keep a confidence. Scruples again? Somehow he felt too ashamed to speak of Valencia's and the Professor's proposition, as if merely listening to it had been an offense.

"So this captain's grandfather . . . ?" Father Hugo began.

"Great-grandfather."

"He was an iconoclast?"

"*Quemasanto* was the word he used. I think it means the same thing."

"It does. In the nineteen twenties, *Los quemasantos* broke into churches to destroy the statues of saints, to burn pictures of Our Lord and the Virgin Mother."

"He said his great-grandfather did more than that." Riordan popped a piece of tortilla into his mouth. "That he burned priests. Hanged them and shot them."

"Yes. The soldiers of President Calles's army would string priests up from telegraph poles along the railway lines to make examples of them. That was in the Cristero War. Terrible times."

"*Ojo*, Padre Tim!" the Old Priest said suddenly, pronouncing his name "Teem" and pointing at his own faded eyes with two forked fingers. Droplets of chipotle sparkled in his pewter-gray beard. Riordan wanted to motion to him to wipe his mouth, but then thought better of it.

"What should I watch out for?" he asked.

"For the things you are asked to do."

"It's dangerous for a priest to meddle in politics," Father Hugo elab-orated, as if the Old Priest were incapable of explaining himself. "A foreign priest especially. Article 33."

This was the article in the Mexican Constitution prohibiting foreigners, under pain of deportation, from taking part in the country's political affairs.

Riordan speared a chunk of steak, swirled it in the tangy sauce, and washed it down with the tempranillo Lisette had brought down from her last trip to Tucson.

"I prefer to see what I did as a humanitarian gesture, not political," he said.

"It makes no difference how you see it," said the vicar. "For excrement to roll downhill it must first roll uphill. The captain goes to his colonel and says, 'I have this priest, a *norteamericano*, interfering with my military duties.' The colonel brings the complaint to the general, who brings it to the governor, who brings it to a judge, who orders the North American priest to appear at a hearing, where he is charged with violating Article 33. Now the excrement rolls downhill. To be charged is to be guilty. In no time, the priest finds himself returned to his native country."

Riordan studied Father Hugo's face, from the high forehead down to the rounded cleft chin, and wondered if his vicar had not given a warning but expressed a hope. The gringo interloper sent packing.

"I spoke to Díaz this afternoon. We agreed it was a mistake for me to go. Let us talk about something else."

Father Hugo dipped his head and spread his hands. There was in these gestures the annoying impression of an authority figure granting a request.

CHAPTER FIVE

The trip south got off to a rough start, rough anyway for Pamela, whose nerves were more fragile than Lisette's or Nick's. Nick was driving Lisette's 4Runner. She'd asked him to take the wheel; like any nineteen-year-old male, he would have been mortified to be seen riding as a passenger with two middle-aged women, one of whom happened to be his mother. Not that anyone would know he was Lisette's son, or give a damn if they did; but among the privileges of people his age was the conviction that the world's eyes were upon them at all times. Pamela sat beside him. Lisette had insisted that she take the front because she would have resented sitting in back, as if she were a maiden aunt: a small gesture to assure her that she occupied a place in Lisette's heart equal to Nick's. Pamela, prone to doubts and jealousies produced by a vivid imagination operating in concert with her low self-esteem, required frequent reassurances. Lisette was not always able to offer them—one of the disadvantages of a long-distance relationship. It was also one of the advantages.

Nick was on Thanksgiving break. That morning, after collecting him at the Delt house, they took I-19 south from Tucson to the border crossing in Nogales. Just short of the gate, they pulled up behind an SUV with Sonora plates and two men inside. A U.S. Customs agent, uniformed in a style Lisette thought of as "Fascist black," was questioning them. Normally, customs stopped suspicious cars entering the States from Mexico, not the other way around. Another agent, in plain clothes and big enough to play defensive end for the Arizona Cardinals, joined the first. The interrogation went on for ten or fifteen seconds more, at which point the uniformed agent motioned for the driver and his passenger to get out. The SUV disgorged a pair of Mexicans not much older than Nick. Lisette leaned forward and watched through the windshield as the driver opened the rear cargo door and gestured, as if to say, "See, it's empty." Then the big agent stepped between him and the vehicle and reached into the cargo bed. When he stepped back, Lisette saw that he'd opened a kind of trap door in the floor, revealing a hidden compartment in which three long, metal cases lay side by side, tied together with a padlocked cable. Defensive End hauled them out as easily as if he were lifting shopping bags and dropped them on the pavement. The Mexican started to argue with the smaller agent, who, it appeared, had ordered him to open the cases. Encouraged by a shove from Defensive End, the Mexican squatted down, his back to Lisette's car as he fiddled with the padlock. With the four men blocking their view, she and her companions couldn't see what was inside the cases before they were closed again. The next thing, in movements that looked choreographed, Defensive End jerked the driver to his feet, yanked his hands behind his back, and slapped handcuffs around his wrists while the other agent dragged the cases toward the customs booth. One wasn't shut properly, and Lisette caught a glimpse of its contents. Pamela gasped "Omigosh" when the other Mexican attempted to run. He didn't get more than a few yards before the big agent took him down, jammed a knee into the small of his back, and cuffed him. All this happened in seconds. Nick was taking videos with his iPhone until the big agent, waving a hand the size of a catcher's mitt, signaled him to stop. Another wave told him to move on.

"For God's sake, do as he says!" Pamela cried, even though Nick was doing exactly that. He pocketed the phone and pulled around the SUV. On the Mexican side, he eased the car into the traffic on Avenida Sonora. A green sign overhead read: MEXICO 15. HERMOSILLO 277 KM.

"Wow! What the hell was that all about?" Nick asked.

"A bust, what do you think?" Lisette answered.

"A bust? Who ever heard of smuggling drugs into Mexico?"

"You didn't see what was in those cases?"

"Nope."

"Guns."

"Guns? Guns?" Pamela said, a tremor in her voice.

"Drugs flow into the U.S.," Lisette explained. "Guns and cash flow into Mexico. Think of it as the North American Free Trade Agreement in action."

"Awesome!" Nick said, thrilled. A tale to tell his frat brothers when he got back to campus. He'd witnessed the arrest of gunrunners at the border.

Awesome! The corruption of that word into a hyperbolic commentary on things not in the least inspiring of wonder or fearful reverence bugged Lisette. Someone, usually a young person, asks how you're feeling, you reply, "Pretty well, thanks," and he or she exclaims, "Awesome!" as if you've announced that your Stage 4 cancer has gone into spontaneous remission.

Pamela retreated into a gloomy silence. She had an unstable climate, her emotional barometric pressure subject to unpredictable rises and falls, which Lisette tolerated because they were not so sharp as to be pathological and because she was in love. Or thought she might be. This particular drop, unlike most of Pamela's ups and downs, had an easily identifiable cause: the incident confirmed her darkest imaginings about Mexico. Though she'd lived all over the world, studied art in London and Florence, and traveled throughout Europe, her experiences south of the border were confined to two or three fly-in, fly-out holidays in Cancún and Puerta Vallarta. Otherwise, the country was terra incognita. All she knew about it was what she'd read and heard, none of it good. Mexico was one vast bad neighborhood, East L.A. or the South Side of Chicago on steroids.

That would be an exaggeration if you were talking about the resort towns or Mexico City. But it was not an inaccurate metaphor for the Sierra Madre or any of the border cities, like Nogales and Juárez.

Mex 15, the federal route, led through Nogales's downtown, quieter now than it had been in anyone's memory, quieter as much in the right way as in the wrong way. The shops on Avenida Obregón that had catered to day-tripping tourists, hawking ceramics and glassware and copperware, Indian rugs, straw bags, belts, purses, and turquoise jewelry, were shuttered, victims of the recent war between the Sonora Cartel and the Brotherhood. There had been ambushes in the city parks, a couple of assassinations at the bus station, gun battles on the streets in broad daylight, and the rifle fire and grenade blasts had been heard on the Arizona side, behind the high steel fence dividing the city. So the tourists, their wallets already pinched by the Great Recession, no longer swarmed the Avenida Obregón. That was the wrong quiet. Everyone hoped the tourists would return and business revive, now that Nogales was safe once again (the right quiet), not because the authorities had restored peace but because one side had won, the Brotherhood.

Lisette mentioned none of this to Pamela. She did not want to alarm her any further. This trip, routine for Lisette, was to be a mild adventure for Pamela, a dip of her toes into the Mexico she hadn't seen in Cancún and Puerta Vallarta. What rotten luck, to arrive at the border crossing right in time to witness a gun bust. That took the mild out of the adventure. When they passed through Nogales's dreary fringes, Lisette tried to read Pamela's reactions to the plywood and mud-adobe shanties that covered the scrubby hillsides like invasive weeds or perched precariously on hilltops under low, thin reefs of smog.

"More of NAFTA in action," she said. "A lot of the people who live in those dumps work in the *maquiladoras*."

"The what?" Pamela asked. She sounded distracted.

"The border factories. Otherwise known as sweatshops. There's more than a hundred in Nogales alone. Foreign-owned, mostly. American, German, Japanese. No environmental regulations to worry about. Cheap labor, happy to work six days a week, ten hours a day, for ten bucks a day, and no overtime. Pay overtime to your workers and Walmart might have to charge an extra dollar or two for that hot new flat-screen TV."

"My mom, the socialist," Nick said, in a tone that communicated affectionate forbearance for her political tirades.

"I'm no mealymouthed socialist, I'm a communist," she replied, and Pamela laughed.

Lisette was glad to hear it, that light trill. Her partner (the term they used for each other, as if they were in a law practice) was over her fright and out of her funk. Lisette didn't expect Pamela to like her Mexico, poor, gritty, and perilous, but hoped she would not detest it and would agree to live with her in San Patricio through the coming spring and sum-mer. Pamela's schedule fit into the scheme; she taught art at the University of Arizona, but only in the fall semester. Half a year together, half apart—not a bad arrangement, Lisette thought. Better than their present setup, and they would not get bored with each other or on each other's nerves, knowing that they would catch a break when the fall term started. All Pamela all the time might be trying. She was high-maintenance. Not in the way Tony had been—sex every other night or he grew surly—but in her need to be assured that she was bright, talented, beautiful, desirable. She was forty-four and looked thirty to everyone except herself. There seemed to be a distorting lens in her head that wrinkled her skin, slabbed pounds onto her slender body, thinned her full, honey-blond hair, and dulled the luster in her hazel eyes. Witty, well-educated people intimidated her, though she'd graduated with honors from the Rhode Island School of Design. Galleries in New York, San Francisco, and Santa Fe showed her work, but a snippy review or, worse, no review—the ignominy of being ignored—could drop her into a whirlpool of self-doubt. "Sold three paintings," she'd e-mailed a while ago from an exhibition in Dallas. "*Art News* review attached. Maybe he's right—I'm like that guy in the Somerset Maugham story, only he had the decency to realize he was a mediocrity and quit." Lisette didn't know what story she was referring to, and the review (after she translated the art-speak argot into English) did not enlighten her because it made no mention of Somerset Maugham; nor did it say that Pamela was a mediocrity, only that her paintings, while very good, fell short of the brilliance her earlier work had promised.

What was wrong with being very good, if not quite a genius? Pamela's lack of confidence mystified Lisette. Pamela had been born into riches; Lisette had grown up in the North Carolina mountains, daughter of a part-Catawba waitress and a failed Christmas-tree farmer who died when she was seventeen. Pamela's talent was effortless, or seemed so; Lisette thought of herself as a grind, her sole gift the mulish perseverance, the slogging industriousness that had hauled her out of hillbilly country into the University of North Carolina on a scholarship, and had gotten her through med school at age forty-five. Pamela had a super-model's stature and beauty; at five feet three, Lisette was a bit undersized and plain besides, her best feature a head of curly, chocolate-brown hair that diverted attention from her workaday face, a mountain woman's face like her mother's, all hollows and sharp ridges.

During her undergraduate days at Chapel Hill, she had grown a grapefruit-sized chip on her shoulder. She was the upcountry hick surrounded by pretty, privileged sorority girls exempt from the need for scholarships or student loans, as well as from the need to study hard, either because their futures were guaranteed or because they were smart as well as loaded. She envied and despised them for their unearned self-assurance.

The chip had since shrunk to, oh, maybe a lemon, but it was still there. When she'd met Pamela in Tucson last fall, at a fund-raiser for Lisette's nonprofit, the Clínica Libre, her first impression had been stupidly knee-jerk. The host, Manny Cardenas, introduced Pamela as "Pam Childress, you know, the famous artist." Lisette looked up at the poised, statuesque woman in the dark blue cocktail dress, fully prepared to envy and despise her. "The most famous artist you never heard of," Pamela said, her smile revealing a mouthful of crooked teeth, her hand rising immediately to cover them. Lisette dismissed the remark as false humility. It was the imperfection and the quick, embarrassed gesture to hide it that moved her to hold off on the envying and despising.

"Lemme show you something," Manny said, gesturing with his chin toward his den. Carrying their margaritas, they followed him into the room, furnished with a few stylish pieces that were overwhelmed by nouveau-riche touches—hideous lamps, ceramic tchotchkes, a glass-fronted liquor cabinet displaying a single-malt scotch collection, a TV as big as a 1940s movie screen. (Manny was a San Patricio native who, with his parents, had scraped his back on a barbed-wire border fence when he was six. Now, fifty-odd years later, he was the luxury car king of Tucson, owning a chain of Lexus and BMW dealerships.) He pointed at a four-by-three-foot canvas hanging on the wall opposite the TV. It showed dramatic, jagged red shapes—rocks, Lisette assumed—thrust up from what appeared to be a canyon floor splashed with green and purple and yellow spots. Trees? Cacti? Desert flowers?

"Bought that way before I knew Pam. It's one of her best," he gushed.

"Five thou I paid for it, and an appraiser told me it's worth three times that today!"

Pamela cringed and said, "Manny, please . . ."

"Ah, you don't toot your own horn, so I'm tootin' it for you. It's a masterpiece, right?" Then, addressing Lisette: "But don't take my word for it. Lissen to this."

He lifted a corner of the painting and pulled a commentary from a plastic envelope stapled to the backing. "I don't understand half of what this guy is saying, but I get the idea—it's a masterpiece."

He held the sheet out at arm's length and began to recite, like a kid reading his sixth-grade essay in front of the class. Pamela cringed further. As Lisette would learn later, the applause and praises she craved discomposed her when she got them. "Manny, please, please stop it," she said, interrupting the oration.

"Okay. Whatever you say. But you're too polite, you know that?" His glance rested briefly on the cleavage peering ever so shyly from above the bodice of Pamela's dress. Briefly, but long enough to make it obvious that he had an eye for more than her work. "Lemme tell you what polite gets you in this country. The hole in the doughnut is what it gets you."

"I will be sure to keep that in mind. Thanks for pointing it out. I hope I'm not being too polite, thanking you," Pamela said, and Lisette liked the way she said it, in a husky voice, an unfiltered-Camel sort of voice, tinged by just the right touch of bitchiness.

After Manny left, the two women stayed in the den, talking on the sofa beneath the painting. Pamela was new to Tucson. She'd been teaching at the Art Institute in Chicago, but when a gig opened at the U. of A., she jumped on it. Couldn't face another Windy City winter. Wait till the summer, Lisette said. Hundred degrees in the shade, and don't listen to that crap about a dry heat. You'll be wishing for a blast of December air off Lake Michigan.

Lisette knew she should be circulating among the guests, chatting up potential donors instead of Pamela. That's what she was doing—chatting her up and feeling awkward about it. Always there was the awkwardness upon meeting a woman who charmed and intrigued her (though "always" was an overstatement; she'd had only two lesbian affairs). The awkwardness and looking for signs to answer the question, Is she or isn't she?

They kept the conversation on neutral ground. Pamela asked, Just what is the Clínica Libre? A private health clinic in a Mexican pueblo, San Patricio. About a six-hour drive from here. Six hours and somewhere between half a century and a century. We—that's a nurse and me—work with the public health clinics in the municipality. Five to serve more than a hundred and fifty communities. Lisette was aware that she sounded a little stilted, as though she were making a pitch for a contribution. Pamela edged closer, a knee lightly brushing hers, resting there. Unsure if the touch was intentional or accidental, Lisette resisted an impulse to return the pressure and swung her knees aside. But not too far, nor too abruptly, to avoid sending the wrong signal in case it had been intentional. Pamela said she was confused. A pueblo. A municipality. One hundred and fifty communities. What was all that? Ah, yes. A municipality in Mexico was like a county in the States, and it usually had the same name as its principal town, Lisette explained. So the pueblo of San Patricio was like the county seat for the municipality of San Patricio and all the villages in it. Indian villages, mostly. Mayos, Pimas, a few Tarahumaras, all so poor that they often paid her fees with chickens, tortillas, or something they'd grown. Tomatoes. Green chilies. Pamela laughed, the first time Lisette had heard her laughter, and it was clear and rippling and captivating.

"Manny would say you've got the hole in the doughnut. I mean, you could be earning zillions practicing here, couldn't you?"

"Not zillions," Lisette replied. "But for sure I wouldn't be depositing chickens and chili peppers in my bank account. That's why I'm hustling Manny's moneybag friends. Speaking of which, I'd better get back to it. A pleasure to meet the most famous artist I've never heard of."

She stood, smoothed her skirt, and extended a hand. Pamela rose and took it. Her eyes, cast down to meet Lisette's, wore a plaintive, almost childlike expression that made Lisette feel she was the taller of the two. Neither made a move toward the door.

"Are you in Tucson for long?"

"A couple, three days. Buy some stuff I need for the clinic, visit my son. He started U. of A. this fall."

"Oh! You're married?"

"Was. We split up a few years ago, after I decided to go back to med school. Tony's a doctor, and he felt that one MD in the family was enough. Or maybe it was because he's Cuban—y'know, he was Ricky Ricardo but I was miscast as Lucy. I kept his name. Moreno works better in Mexico than Bowden." She knew this was far more information than had been requested. She was under some compulsion to tell Pamela all about herself, or as much as she could in the next minute or two. "We met in Miami. He was interning there, and I'd just started med school. We met and got married and I quit when I got pregnant the first time."

"You've got two kids, then?"

"Nope. I miscarried. Nick came along three years later, and . . ." She put the brakes on her mouth. "Christ, listen to me. I'd best get back to the party."

"To be continued," Pamela said, a lift in her raspy voice turning the statement into a question, one that appealed for an affirmative answer.

"To be continued," Lisette said.

"When?"

The bottom seemed to drop out of her stomach as Pamela licked the salt from the rim of her margarita glass with the innocence of a school-girl licking an ice-cream cone. It was incredibly provocative because it didn't try to be. That's what kindled Lisette, damn near unhinged her, so that her voice trembled slightly when she answered, "Tomorrow. Lunch or dinner?"

"Dinner would be nice."

Lisette felt a squeeze in her belly. Lunch foreclosed on further developments; dinner promised them.

■ ■ ■

So they continued the next evening over tapas and glasses of malbec at Vicentes, in downtown Tucson. Lisette did not pick up where she'd left off, stifling another impulse to talk about herself. Self-revelation was not in her character. She'd inherited the reticence of her people. Those hickory-hard, work-worn Appalachians did not regard their lives and innermost thoughts and feelings as fascinating topics of conversation, as seemed to be the case with other Americans these days, encouraged by social media and something in the zeitgeist to blab incessantly about themselves. Another point in Pamela's favor: she possessed a becoming reserve, partly natural, partly indoctrinated by her upper-crust family, among whom, Lisette gathered, baring your soul was considered no less tacky than baring your ass at the country club, and wasn't half as much fun.

Pamela had grown up on Philadelphia's Main Line, in a suburb called Gladwyne. "Money so old it's senile," she said. Though it was intended as ridicule, the remark awakened the class warrior in Lisette. *Meaning what?* she wondered. *That it's so old and senile it's forgotten it's money?* She was tempted to come back with reverse snobbery, a recitation of the tough times in Watauga County, North Carolina, after her father died and the farm was lost to foreclosure and she had to waitress part-time alongside her mother at a diner in Boone to make ends meet. *I pulled myself up by the bra straps, pretty lady, and would've taken any money, regardless of its age or mental condition.* She stifled that, too, choosing instead to present a slightly amusing picture of herself as a tomboy, taking a chain saw to Fraser firs, baling and loading the trees onto trucks with her father and younger brother. Hunting and fishing with them on weekends and school holidays. "Ah kin shoot you a squirrel, gut hit, skin hit, and cook hit, too!" she joked, parodying the accent to draw a laugh from Pamela. How she adored that laugh, the tingling sensation it made, like fingertips running over her skin.

Pamela asked, "So how old were you when you went back to med school?"

"Thirty-nine, on final approach to forty."

"Holy moly! If I went back to high school right now, I'd flunk out."

Lisette couldn't remember the last time she'd heard someone exclaim "Holy moly." She said, "It took me almost five years instead of the standard four. The chem and biology courses were tough in Spanish. I'd studied Spanish in high school and I was married to a Cuban for fifteen years, but it was still tough."

"Spanish?"

"Right. I forgot to mention. I scored pretty well on my MCATs, but no med school in the States would admit a thirty-nine-year-old woman with a kid. Or without one, for that matter. I got accepted in Mexico, the Autonomous University of Guadalajara."

"And that's why you're down there?"

"Partly. If you're asking if I'm licensed to practice in the States, yeah, I am. I passed the exams."

"But . . . but . . . how do I say this? You go through all that, five years in your forties, with a kid, yet . . ."

"Nick—that's my son—Nick wasn't with me. His father took custody. I asked him to. I'll say that for him: he didn't object."

"All right. You go through all that and you end up in that little burg, getting paid with chickens and chilies. Why would you do that? It doesn't make sense. Oh, damn! That didn't come out the way I meant it to."

"That's okay. I get that all the time on this side of the line. Did I order my MD from Amazon? Am I on the run from a malpractice suit?"

Pamela's eyebrows arced. "Christ, no! I didn't mean that. I was just—"

"Here's the story, short version. The Mexican government requires each new doctor to work for a year in a public health clinic. The Mexicans are more civilized than we are when it comes to that. I was assigned to a clinic in Hermosillo, and that took me out to San Patricio and into the Sierra Madre, and, well . . . I thought I knew poverty, but that made me realize I couldn't even spell it. So when my year was up . . . not to sound all noble and altruistic . . . I saw a chance to make a difference, and I started my clinic."

Pamela met this speech with a transactional smile. The movement to cover her jumbled teeth was not as quick this time, and instead of her full hand, only two fingers went to her lips, as if she were brushing off a crumb. The flaw in her beauty—that was the key to her allure. It made her seem attainable.

"Nick thinks I'm fatally attracted to the marginalized," Lisette went on. "He thinks I get off on playing the great white medicine woman. He doesn't say so, but it's what he thinks."

"I don't think so at all," Pamela said in a peculiar, thrilling voice. "I think you're a remarkable woman."

A remarkable woman. Had anyone ever called her that before? Lisette didn't consider herself susceptible to flattery; but it wasn't flattery causing her to feel flustered and excited and embarrassed all at once.

"Don't make me blush," she said.

"How about the movies tomorrow night? There's a Turkish movie playing at that art house on Speedway. The Loft."

"I'm not wild about art films, but I'll give it a shot. I'll pick you up."

■ ■ ■

"You said last night, 'Don't make me blush.' Did I make you just now?"

Lisette flicked on the vanity lights alongside her rearview mirror.

"You decide," she said, her heart beating violently.

Pamela cupped her chin and turned her head to one side, then the other. "I don't think so. You're not the blushing type, I guess."

"Maybe it's shock. Nobody has ever kissed me like that."

"I'm normally not that way. So forward. I had to know. I was dying to know. You don't give off any signals . . ."

"You don't wave a lot of flags yourself," Lisette said.

"No? I thought I did. I couldn't tell about you and I had to know, and that was the only way I could think of to find out."

They were parked in the driveway of Pamela's small rented house in the Sam Hughes neighborhood, near the university. Lisette felt bold and wild and wonderfully irresponsible as she turned off the interior lights, then the ignition. "I think the old question *Your place or mine?* doesn't need an answer," she said.

CHAPTER SIX

From Nogales, Nick drove them on to Magdalena, where they stopped for an early lunch and a stroll afterward to walk off the *machaca* and *arroz con frijoles*. Pamela looked striking, the quintessential gringa, six feet tall in her cowgirl boots, radiant hair bouncing as she walked. Feeling like a tour guide, Lisette took her into a couple of shops in the plaza, showed her the church of Santa María de Magdalena, with its reclining statue of Saint Francis Xavier, believed to heal incurable diseases, and then Father Kino's tomb, his exposed bones stretched out beneath a painted dome depicting idealized scenes from early mission life.

"What a lovely town!" Pamela said, as if its attractiveness surprised her. It probably did, after the unpleasantness at the border and the Nogales slums and fifty miles of rubbish-strewn desert highway, scrawny goats feeding on the trash, barbed-wire fences beribboned with plastic bags.

"It's a magic town. See, it says so right there, to make sure you get the point," Nick remarked, mocking a street banner proclaiming the title the tourist board had conferred on Magdalena: PUEBLO MÁGICO. He didn't have any use for handicraft shops and miracle-working statues and the skeleton of a priest dead for three centuries. "But maybe we oughta get back on el magico roado?"

"All right," Lisette said agreeably. "It's another three hours."

Behind the wheel, fancying himself to be once again in control, in command, he swung back onto Mex 15. She forgave his sarcasms, the juvenile pig Spanish. He didn't have to be here with Mom and her "friend." He could have gone to Scottsdale to spend the holiday with his father and his vapid stepmother. A day quail hunting with Dad and his English pointers, another day riding one of Stepmom's Arabians, a Thanksgiving feast attended by their rich friends, the women decked out in Zuni jewelry no Zuni could afford in a million years. Some life the kid had, son of the Mayo Clinic's chief of neurology, a renowned lecturer invited to speak at symposiums all over the country, and now married into Scottsdale's horsey-set elite, the handsome doctor with the Ricky Ricardo hairstyle and his arm-candy wife photographed at black-tie benefits. Everything Lisette despised, and yet—she was jam-packed with contradictions—she was pleased that Nick had advantages she could not have imagined when she was nineteen. But it wasn't all Tony, Tony, Tony, was it? She'd had a hand in it. If she hadn't surrendered her ambitions to raise Nick and cook and take care of the house and smooth the way for Tony's advance, where would Nick be today? If she hadn't escaped Watauga County, if she had not studied and studied and gotten accepted to the University of Miami med school, she never would have met his father and Nick would not exist.

BIENVENIDOS! SANTA ANA. 1645, read the arch spanning the highway. Pamela marveled at the town's age. As old as a New England town. "You don't think of western towns being so old," she commented.

Darling, you are much too intelligent to have made such a banal and geographically inaccurate observation except for the sake of conversation, Lisette thought. To Pamela, she said, "Well, Dorothy, we're not in Kansas anymore."

Then Nick: "You haven't taken Mom's seminar on the Spanish settlement of North America?"

"Apparently not," Pamela answered, wounded by Lisette's wisecrack. Not seriously. A grazing wound.

"Coronado was in Kansas, way before it was Kansas," Nick said. "Fifteen forty or something like that. And Santa Fe was settled thirty years before Plymouth Colony. Like Anglos were parvenus."

He must have recently learned that word and was giving it a road test, Lisette thought.

"Newcomers. The English were newcomers, not parvenus," she corrected, taking an unmaternal pleasure in embarrassing him. Because he had his father's agile mind, he sometimes thought he knew more than in fact he did. "A parvenu is someone who suddenly comes into money, or into a position of power, but doesn't have the style, the dignity that goes with it."

"Christ! I thought I was on a break from classes. Did she forget her mellow-out pills this morning?" Nick asked Pamela.

"They don't work on her—her system rejects them."

Lisette liked them joking about her; it showed that they felt comfortable with each other.

Nick was still trying to reconcile himself to the fact that his mother was gay. He accepted it but had yet to absorb it completely. Lisette had noted the way he referred to Pamela as her friend, all but enclosing the word in air quotes. And she sensed that he felt a residual resentment, dating back to the divorce and her departure for med school in Mexico. Only eleven years old, he'd felt, justifiably, that his mother had abandoned him. There was a distance between them that had made her coming out more difficult than it might otherwise have been.

Not, however, as difficult as it had been with her family. It was shortly after the divorce, while she waited to hear if she'd been accepted to med school in Guadalajara. She was living in Phoenix with the first of her lovers, whom she had passed off as a roommate to her mother and brother. The charade became unbearable. She wrote two long letters, revising them several times. Her mother was a devout Baptist; Gene was religious, too, though churchgoing was for him as much a social occasion as it was an act of worship. She did not expect that her news would meet with a happy reception, and she was not disappointed. There was no response for a month; then Gene phoned her. She'd barely had a chance to say, "Hello, how are you?" before he took her on a guilt trip: What she did with her own life was her business, except when it affected the lives of others. The divorce had been hard enough on their mother, but *this*, this devastated her, it had turned her golden years into pure garbage. A blessing Dad didn't live to see this day. Mom is praying for you, Gene said. And so am I. Their minister likewise. They'd spoken to him, and he'd recommended a Christian camp where homosexuals could find freedom from their affliction through the love of Jesus Christ. My affliction? Lisette said, incensed. My affliction? Like I've got a disease? Like I'm crippled or something? Are you kidding? The conversation went downhill from there, and ended with Gene declaring that if she would not help herself, then neither he nor their mother had anything more to say to her. She hadn't heard from them since. Not a word. She was as good as dead.

Nick had been too young to be told anything then. After he'd started the U. of A. and she'd taken up with Pamela, she knew it was time. On one of her visits to Tucson, she invited him over for a home-cooked meal. Pamela thought it best to make herself scarce and went out with some friends from the Art Department.

Lisette saw little of herself in her son, only the high, acute cheekbones and aquiline nose passed down from her Catawba ancestors. Otherwise, he was all Tony. Tony's pale-sand complexion, his thick hair, shoe-polish black, his height and athleticism—Nick had played baseball in high school and was on U. of A.'s team, a first baseman. She waited till after dinner to reveal her secret. He reacted with a kind of hip indifference. Like no big deal, he said, though she could see by the way he blinked, as if staring into a bright light, that it was a bigger deal than he was willing to let on. Ask you a question? Sure. Did you ever love Dad? I suppose, sure, in my way. Well, he told me that when you guys split up, you told him that you never loved him, not for one minute.

"People say cruel, stupid things when a marriage breaks up. I didn't mean it," Lisette said. "I loved him in my way. Trouble was, my way didn't do him any good. Me neither."

She spared him further details: how the pretending to be what she was not and never could be, how the sham orgasms and faked emotions became impossible to sustain any longer, so that, toward the end, she could not feign simple affection, much less passion, her body rebelling against the masquerade, recoiling at Tony's touch, her mouth, seemingly with a will of its own, turning aside when he went to kiss her.

"Ask you another question?" Nick said. "Did you love me, or was that just in your way, too?"

That stunned her, brought her to tears. She rose from her chair and embraced him. "Of course I did, and I still love you. My God, Nick, yes."

■ ■ ■

After putting Santa Ana behind them, they crossed monotonous plains broken occasionally by vineyards and olive groves. Vultures specked the sky. Nick stopped for gas at a Pemex station outside Hermosillo. Lisette was pleased that Pamela did not complain about the condition of the ladies' room. A short distance south of the state capital, they turned off Mex 15 onto a secondary road that ran east through cactus-studded flatlands, descended into the Río Yaqui valley, crossed the river, and made a long, grinding climb into the foothills before topping out at a pass crowded with oak and juniper. On a mesa below, a mosaic of green woods and winter-browned meadows spread like a quilt under the Sierra Madre, tiering toward the sheer rock escarpment that limned the border with Chihuahua. Pamela, quite taken with the view, asked Nick to stop. She wanted to photograph the distant cliffs; their color in the afternoon light, a roseate gold, was fantastic.

Looking down, Lisette's attention was not on the scenery but on a police roadblock about a quarter of a mile away. A patrol car, roof lights flashing, barricaded one lane; a white pickup truck was parked on the shoulder opposite. A car approached in the left lane and stopped. Two uniformed figures gave it a quick inspection, then passed it through. She watched it struggle uphill toward her, an eighties-era station wagon, dusty, dented, its rear bumper almost scraping the pavement from the weight of its passengers, nine people at least. The scruffy driver, upon spotting her new, unblemished 4Runner, flashed his headlights in warning, and it was obvious that he wasn't warning about a hidden speed trap.

"I'll take it from here," she said to Nick when Pamela was done photographing.

"I'm not tired," he said.

"See those cops down there? Let me deal with them." She and Nick switched places. She said, "They might ask for ID from all of us, so make sure you've got your passports handy."

Nick saluted. "Yes, ma'am!"

She cruised downhill, not too fast, not too slow, a Goldilocks speed, and braked without fuss when the cops signaled her to stop. They wore ski masks and bulletproof vests. An insignia and the words POLICÍA ESTATAL marked the patrol car's door. State Police. Two other men, also in ski masks, occupied the pickup. They were wearing camouflage shirts, like hunting or military shirts, though a single glance told her that they were neither hunters nor soldiers. This was Mexico in the year A.D. 2012—it required you to size up a situation and make judgments at megahertz speed. In the next instant, she decided how to play this situation.

Both troopers came up to her side of the car. She lowered the window and said cheerily, in a pronounced American accent, *"Buenas tardes!* What is . . . I mean, *Que es problema?"*

"Estamos en busca de auto robado. Comprende?" said Trooper One, the heftier of the two.

"I think so. *Creo que si.* But this car belongs to me. *Esta auto es mia.* I have the registration papers . . . uh . . . *tengo los documentos para esta auto."*

"No es necesario," he said, then asked for everyone's identification. They handed him their passports, which he pretended to examine while Trooper Two sauntered around to the rear, presumably to check the license plate; then, without asking, he opened the cargo door and examined their ice chest and luggage.

"Qué son estos?" he demanded, rapping the ice chest with his knuckles.

Lisette turned around to look at him over the rear seat. "Food. A turkey and a cake. *Un pavo y una tarta."*

He slammed the door shut, hard enough to send a tremor through the car, moved to Pamela's side, and tapped the window. Lisette opened it with the control button on her armrest. He bent slightly and looked inside, quickly at Nick, longer at Pamela. All that could be seen of his face were his lips and his eyes, under whose insolent gaze Pamela hunched her shoulders and clasped her hands tightly on her lap.

Both cops walked away from the car to confer.

"Who the hell are these guys? They give me the creeps," she said, barely moving her lips, like a ventriloquist.

"State Police. Giving people the creeps comes naturally to them."

Trooper One returned with the passports. *"Son ustedes los turistas?"*

Lisette paused, as if she were translating the question. "Oh, yes. *Sí. Turistas.*"

Risky, this play-acting. If the cops found a pretext to search the car, they would discover her Mexican passport—she held dual citizenship— in the glove compartment. Things might get complicated then.

"Así, señora. Adónde vas? No hay muchos turistas vienen aquí. Comprende?"

She immediately grasped the reason for the question. Although her assessment of the situation had probably been correct, her response to it had definitely been wrong. Only now she had no choice but to continue her performance.

"No comprendo."

Trooper One tried his English: "Where do you go? *Turistas* not coming here."

"Ah! *Comprendo. Para San Patricio.* To visit a friend. *Un amigo in San Patricio. Un padre americano.* The turkey and the cake are for him."

He gave a dismissive jerk of his head, then backed off a step and, with a swat at the air, told her she could go.

Lisette said, *"Gracias, adiós,"* and drove on. She let out a sigh of relief, more audible than she wanted it to be.

"Okay, Mom. What was with the dumb-tourist bit?"

"Usually, the cops can't be bothered with dumb *turistas.* They just let you right on through, no questions asked. Didn't work quite so well this time."

"Because they're looking for a stolen car? I heard him right? That they're looking for a stolen car?"

"That's not what they're looking for. It's the standard line narcos use when they set up a roadblock. Next thing you know, if you're a Mexican who looks like money, your car ends up in a cartel motor pool and you end up held for ransom."

Seeing, in her peripheral vision, Pamela turn to look at her, Lisette regretted what she'd just said; but she couldn't think of a way to walk it back.

"So they weren't police, they were crooks?" Pamela asked.

What the hell, Lisette thought. *She's not a twelve-year-old. Might as well tell her the facts of life now so she'll know what I'm asking her to get into later.* She fell into her sachemic mode, which she relished: the tribal matriarch, wise in the ways and dangers of her world.

"They're cops working for the crooks. The crooks are the bozos in the pickup. They've got to be with a mafia called La Fraternidad—the Brotherhood in English. The Brotherhood controls everything around here. Kidnapping is one of their subsidiary industries."

"Whoa!" Nick leaned in, sticking his head between the front seats. "You mean that—"

"No, but the thought passed through their minds, I'll bet," Lisette said. "All the traffickers, and that includes the cops on their payrolls, obey the first commandment of the trade: Thou shalt not do what is bad for business. Kidnapping innocent Americans is very, very bad for business. That's where I screwed up, pretending we're gringo tourists. In a good year, this part of Mexico gets maybe a dozen more tourists than, let's say, Somalia."

"It made the cops' antennae twitch? It made them think that maybe we're not so innocent?" asked Pamela in the cautious but hopeful way of a quiz show contestant.

"Good for you," Lisette said. "They were asking themselves, 'What are these gringos doing in the dangerous Sierra Madre? Two women and a young man. Are they idiots? Or are they possibly freelancers trafficking without a license from the cartel?' That would have made us legitimate targets. They decided we're idiots."

"Whoa-ho! Like we had a close call!"

"No, Nick. It wasn't all that close. It wasn't awesome."

YouTube COMMUNIQUÉ #1

VIDEO: Full screen of a man in a ski mask and baseball cap, seated at a desk. On the wall behind him are: a photograph of Emiliano Zapata, a pencil sketch of Che Guevara, and a portrait of *La Santa Muerte.*

AUDIO: Good day, brothers and sisters, from the *comandancia* of the Brotherhood. This will be the first in a series of video communiqués we will issue from time to time. We have three purposes in making these announcements. First, to present accurate accounts of certain events in Sonora. You cannot trust the newspapers or the media because they are liars who serve the rich and the powerful. Second, to correct the misinformation, the deceptions, the filthy false-hoods our enemies spread about us. Third—and this is the most important—to enfold you in the beautiful butterfly wings of the truth, for whoever is without truth is without God, and who is without God is lost.

It is I, *La Mariposa,* the Butterfly, who addresses you today, all citizens of Sonora and in particular those who dwell in municipalities that have formed self-defense militias, so-called. Last week, the *comandante* of the *autode-fensa* in pueblo San Patricio challenged the army and the Federal Police to bring him human heads. He said this on television, speaking as the harlot Salome spoke to King Herod. She demanded only the head of John the Baptist. This man wants three heads: mine and two of my colleagues', members of the Broth-erhood's Executive Committee. Not only that—he called for the authorities to bring him our DNA. I'm not joking! He wants the very substance of our beings to be sucked from our bodies and brought to him! And yet we are called blood-thirsty barbarians.

This is an example of how our enemies spread dirty lies about us even as they do the very things—and worse—that they accuse us of doing. To this so-called *comandante, La Mariposa* says as Saint Paul said in Romans, chapter two, verse three: "Do you suppose, O man—you who judge those who practice such things and yet do them yourselves—that you will escape the judgment of God?"

This man who calls himself a *comandante* is a hypocrite in all things, a land-owner who grows walnuts but who pays his workers a few pesos and forces them to work long hours when his walnuts are harvested. Who would not pay just taxes levied so we of the Brotherhood could distribute money to the poor. Listen, *comandante,* to the words of Saint Matthew: "You hypocrite, first take the log out of your eye, and then you will see clearly to take the speck out of your brother's eye."

He also has no love for his family, no loyalty to them. You have all heard the story of how the soldiers and Federal Police occupying his pueblo wantonly killed his nephew and another young man. They were shot down for no reason. What action did this parasite take? Did he demand that the murderers be pun-ished? No! He begged the soldiers' commander to allow his militia to fight along-side them. What can you say about a man who bends his knee to make an alliance with the murderers of his own flesh and blood? Has he never heard the words of Emiliano Zapata? "It is better to die fighting on your feet than to live on your knees and be humiliated."

No member of the Brotherhood would behave in this way. We are all pledged to defend our families to the death, for the family is the rock upon which a just society is built.

A final word, brothers and sisters, about the soldiers and police who occupy our state instead of defending it as they should. They call us criminals, though they are themselves criminals. They who promise you justice bring only injustice. We of the Brotherhood also promise justice, and we keep our promises.

CHAPTER SEVEN

She knocked at the rectory door minutes after he'd finished meeting with the middle-aged ladies who were to decorate the church for Advent, coming in less than two weeks.

"Cristina?" he said, his voice rising to a question because he almost did not recognize her when he opened the door. At first, he thought it was the eye shadow and lipstick and the way she was dressed, as if for a fiesta in a bright red blouse, a striped, ankle length skirt, and wedge sandals that made her three inches taller. But those externals were not what had changed her appearance; it was the expression in her eyes. They reminded him of Sean's when he'd come home from Vietnam forty years ago: coated, as it were, in a hard finish that had cracked, like old lacquer, allowing an underlying sorrow to bleed through. Just as it had with his eldest brother, that look aged her, as though she'd leapt from seventeen to thirty in a matter of weeks.

"Please, come in," he said, and ushered her into the parish office, where, at his invitation, she took one of the two visitor's chairs. He sat in the other, opposite her, and composed a benign smile to put her at ease. The wooden chairs, with their high, straight backs, were unfortunately not conducive to making people feel comfortable, but they were all he had. She sat stiffly, her knees locked, her hands folded in her lap. She was a handsome rather than a pretty young woman, part Yaqui, with sharp cheekbones and a fall of charcoal-black hair.

"Well, Cristina, how are you feeling?" he inquired, maintaining his smile.

"How do you suppose I would feel?" she said, with a boldness that matched her mature look and threw him a little off balance.

"Do you mean you are nervous?"

"No. Should I be? I am angry, after what was done to me."

She sounded it, her voice, though subdued, whetted as a knife.

"You have every right to be," he said sympathetically. It seemed he was the nervous one, uncertain as to where this was going. Rape counseling was not what anyone would term his strong point. "Would you be willing to talk about that—what happened to you?"

"I want to ask you if I will be excommunicated and will burn in hell," she said, with a direct, challenging look in her wounded eyes. "I have heard my mother say that about another girl."

"That she was to be excommunicated because she'd been . . . ?"

"Violated," Cristina said.

Her mother, Paulina Herrera, went to Mass daily and made a great show of her devoutness, bowing more deeply than anyone else, genuflecting on both knees rather than one, spreading her uplifted hands a yard wide when the Lord's Prayer was recited. The Very Pious Señora Herrera was the title he'd privately conferred on her. But the view just expressed seemed too extreme even for her.

"You must not have heard correctly, Cristina. Your mother could not have said that."

"This girl was pregnant . . ." She hesitated and turned her glance away from him, toward the bookshelves. "She . . ." Her rigid posture slackened somewhat; there was a softening in her stern composure. "To say this to a man . . . a priest . . ." she stuttered; then came an unintentional play on words: *"Esto es embarazoso. Estoy embarazada."* This is embarrassing; I am pregnant.

He had thought as much. "You're certain?"

"I saw the doctor."

"Dr. Moreno?"

Her nod was so quick and shallow he almost didn't see it.

"Does your mother know?"

The negative movement of her head was likewise hurried.

"And you're sure . . . This is difficult to ask, but I have to—"

"Yes! No one else!" she interrupted with a flash of anger. Her shoulders convulsed and, her whole façade collapsing at once, she began to sob. Riordan's instinct was to envelop her in a consoling embrace, but such a gesture was out of the question, given the ongoing scandals in the church and the chance that it would be misinterpreted. Instead, leaning forward, he rested his palms lightly on her shoulders.

A man named Jesús Delgado, a Brotherhood mule, drove *mota* to remote points on the border, where other mules backpacked them into the United States for further distribution. (To college kids, Riordan thought, and to hard-core potheads and bourgeois baby boomers reliving their counterculture youths, none of whom knew, or cared, that they were sucking Mexican blood into their lungs.) This Delgado had abducted Cristina while she was walking home from school with her friends. Narcos could do things like that with impunity, confident that witnesses would plead sudden blindness if asked about the crime. Delgado took her to his village, Mesa Verde, and raped her for three days before she escaped, with a villager's help. When she recovered from the ordeal— physically, that is—she went to the San Patricio police to file charges against Delgado. Remembering what had happened to their chief and fellow officers, they told her to go home thanking God that all she'd lost was her virginity.

"I am terribly sorry," Riordan said to her. "But you must know that you're not going to be excommunicated or burn in hell because of what happened to you. If that is your mother's idea, I cannot imagine where she got it."

She wiped her eyes with the back of a hand. Reaching over to his desk, he handed her a tissue.

"She said . . . about this girl . . . she knew her when she was young. . . . This girl was excommunicated because she had an abortion and her soul would burn in hell . . ."

He braced against the back of the chair. "I see. So you were a little confused about your mother's words."

Cristina shrugged. "You must help me, Padre Tim."

"In whatever way I can," he said, and felt an unpleasant prickling up and down his arms.

She canted her head slightly backward and drew in a breath, marshaling her resolve, her nerve. His heart going out to her, he decided to make things as easy as he could for her. And for himself.

"Did you come here, Cristina, to ask about having an abortion? If it would be permissible?"

"I don't know . . . yes"—squeezing the damp tissue into a ball—"I . . . This child is . . ."

"You know I cannot tell you it is permissible."

"Why?"

"Because the church teaches that even a child conceived from rape is innocent, that to abort it is to meet violence with violence—"

"Innocent! Innocent!" she cried, her black eyes glittering. "This child is the devil's child. If you had had done to you what that man did to me, you would know that he is the devil," she went on in a furious rush. "It is his seed in me! Jesús Delgado. Jesús! What a name for a devil!"

"He's a bad man," Riordan said, in a level tone. "A criminal, but a man . . ."

It was a good thing that Delgado was not in this room with him, for he felt an urge to pummel him to within an inch of his life. At the same time, on another floor in his mind, he wished that a theologian, one of those whey-faced cardinals in the Roman Curia, were here, so he could pose the question: If this girl's pregnancy was intended by God, did that imply that God also intended the rape that caused it? Which wasn't possible, as the source of all goodness cannot intend evil, any more than He can square a circle.

"Why will I be excommunicated and burn in hell if I wash the devil's seed from my body?" Cristina asked, not so much speaking as vomiting the words. "That is why I have come. To find out why. Do you not preach that we should get rid of the devil in ourselves? Well, that is what I want to do. Why should I be sorry for that? Do you know what will happen to me if I don't? No man will ever want to marry me. I will be, you know, *mercaderías averiadas*. Damaged goods with a rapist's baby. That is what my—"

She stopped herself.

"That is what your mother told you?"

Her silence acknowledged that this was the case.

"So you weren't telling the truth? Your mother does know?"

"Yes," she weakly replied.

"And then she told you that you would be excommunicated and go to hell if you have an abortion?"

"Yes."

He decided not to ask if the Very Pious Señora Herrera had found out from her daughter or in some other way, while he pondered the contradictory counsel that had addled the poor girl's mind.

"Cristina, you should know that the church—"

She cut him off: "Yes, yes, yes, I know. I must have this child, I must learn to love it." Defiant now, impudent even—he was having trouble keeping up with the kaleidoscopic shifting of her moods. "How, Padre Tim? How can I learn to love the devil's child?"

"Cristina! Stop it! It is his child, but he is not the devil!" He paused to collect himself. "I was going to tell you before you interrupted me that the church makes allowances for girls your age. Girls under eighteen who have an abortion. There is no excommunication for a young girl who has been forced or frightened into it."

"So it is not a mortal sin?" Hopeful.

"I didn't say that. It is. A very grave mortal sin that would have to be confessed," he said, aware of how fine a moral line he was walking, all but giving her license. There was her mortal body to consider, as much as her immortal soul. "Please don't do anything without—"

Again, she cut him off: "It is legal in Mexico for someone like me. Who has had done to her what was done to me. It is legal. My friend told me that. I can go to a public health clinic and—"

"Did this friend tell you that you have to show a police report, and a doctor's report certifying that you were raped?" he said, interrupting her in turn.

"Eduardo. Eduardo López. He looked it up on the Internet. It is legal."

"Oh, then it must be true," Riordan said, abandoning any attempt to come off as kind and understanding. Pity without action is sentimentality, he thought. "I am counseling you not to have an abortion because the police did not report a crime. They should have, but they didn't. A doctor did not examine you. One should have, but he didn't."

She hesitated, her mouth opening a little as if she were about to speak. Whatever she'd meant to say, if anything, she thought better of it.

"Without documents from them, public health won't do anything for you," he said. "You will have to go somewhere else, and that could be dangerous. That is what I am trying to tell you."

She turned her gaze once more to the bookcase, crammed with the accumulated wisdom of two thousand years.

"You are not doing anything for me, either, Padre Tim. You are of no help to me. None."

Moments later, she was gone. He got to his feet and, looking out the office window, watched her cross the plaza. Slumping into his desk chair, he felt drained, and overcome by a sense of his own inadequacy. He had failed her, as he had César. She was going to go through with it, and his hope was that it would not be in some back-alley butcher shop in Hermosillo or Ciudad Obregón—or anywhere. His mind flying back to Luis Gonzalez, someone else he had failed, he prayed God not to withhold His mercy from a girl with a heart and spirit so battered.

CHAPTER EIGHT

She haunted him for the rest of the day and that night, and when he woke the following morning, he struck a bargain. *If You look out for her, I will fast for the next month.* To show the Deity good faith, he started straightaway, restricting himself to tea and toast at breakfast, clear broth and bread at lunch. As he was about to lie down for the afternoon siesta, Lisette phoned with an invitation to Thanksgiving dinner at her place. "You're the only other gringo in town," she said, which he would have taken as a mild insult if he hadn't known her better. He'd forgotten that today was Thanksgiving! He'd been in Mexico too long.

"Well, I'm on a fast," he said, but with a certain indefiniteness in his tone. "I can allow myself only one full meal a day, like we do at Lent."

"A little early for Lent, isn't it?" she replied. "But Thanksgiving dinner should qualify as your full meal."

Her son would be there, she went on, along with a friend, a painter who had done restorations for museums and who might be willing to tackle the work that needed doing in the church. "She'll be down here for the spring and summer, so she'll have the time."

He was dizzy with hunger when he rang Lisette's bell at five p.m. The heavy oak door swung open into the interior courtyard. She said, "So glad you're here right on the button."

She was all done up by the standards of San Patricio: a skirt and low-heeled pumps, silver bracelets on her wrists.

"So glad you invited me," he said. He caught the smells floating out of the kitchen. "I am famished."

"We'll take care of that if you can wait half an hour." She gave him a wet kiss that smeared lipstick on his cheek. "There's salsa and chips to take the edge off."

She motioned at the table, set with colorful plates beside a bubbling fountain and overlooked by an electric heater on a pedestal—a cold front had moved down from the north.

He denied himself the salsa and chips but accepted a glass of red wine from Lisette's friend, Pamela. The subject of Lisette's sexual orientation had seldom come up, not because Riordan objected but because she had an aversion to talking about herself. "Where I come from," she had said, "people don't wear their hearts on their sleeves." At any rate, he knew Pamela had to be more than a friend, and it was easy to see why. His father would have described her as "a looker": tall, blond, stylishly dressed in black slacks, a pale green silk blouse, a pearl necklace—and the pearls looked real. His first impression was of an aloof fashion model a little too aware that she was gorgeous; but after a minute or two of light conversation, he saw that her detached air was a disguised shyness. He tried to put her at ease with questions about her painting. Stupid questions, like "Are you into abstract or representational?" She responded civilly enough, while making it plain that she preferred to talk about something else. He checked his pantry of topics, could find nothing beyond the weather, and so turned to Nick, asking him stupid questions about college.

Cell-phone and wireless service in San Patricio being spotty at best, Nick could not flee into his smartphone, which lay idle on the table, and was forced to answer. When he and Riordan fell into male default mode—sports—Pamela picked up her wineglass and went into the kitchen, carrying herself as if she were on a runway. Nick said that he played first base on the University of Arizona baseball team, and Riordan admitted to being a lifelong Cubs fan. He gave an embarrassed smile, as if that were a character flaw.

"I feel sorry for you," Nick remarked. "That's gotta be tough."

"Oh, there's a certain masochistic pleasure in it," Riordan said. "My dad used to bring all us kids to Wrigley Field for the Crosstown Series against the White Sox. I was five or six the first time. Can't remember if the Cubs won or lost."

"I'd bet my car they lost," said Nick.

He was a big, enthusiastic kid, seemingly as uncomplicated as a single-celled organism. Uncomplicated, but not an idiot. After they had exhausted the topic of baseball, he mentioned that he was taking an introductory astronomy course and had been to the Kitt Peak observatory with his class. Through its thirty-six-inch telescope, they had seen the moons and bands of Jupiter, Saturn's rings, the Andromeda Galaxy. Riordan said he envied him the experience. His own observations of the cosmos had been limited to the naked eye or binoculars.

Nick was captivated by the phenomenon of archaic light. When he'd looked at Andromeda, 2.5 million light-years away, he'd seen it as it was 2.5 million years ago, right? Right, Riordan answered. A telescope was a time machine, in a manner of speaking. It took you out into space, backward in time. Nick speculated: "Let's say that last week, or last month, or even ten years ago, some really huge disaster wiped out the Andromeda Galaxy. So that would mean that it'll take two and a half million years for people on Earth to see the explosion and realize that the galaxy no longer exists, right?"

"Right, again," Riordan said. "Assuming there still are people on Earth by that time."

"But for two million years or so, they'd be seeing it like we do now," Nick said with an undertone of complaint. "So would it or wouldn't it? Exist, I'm asking."

Riordan felt like a parent who has been asked *Why is the sky blue, Daddy?* and can't find an answer.

"Well, objectively speaking, from God's point of view, so to speak, it would have ceased to exist," he said, taking a stab. "But from our point of view, it . . . it would be like . . . what? A fossil. Archaic light is called that sometimes, fossil light. The galaxy we now see would be like that preserved mastodon carcass they found in the Arctic ice some years back. Not a perfect analogy, but . . ."

Nick made a face. He thought it very imperfect. Lisette rescued

Riordan from further interrogations, emerging from the kitchen with Pamela and Anna Montoya, her nurse, a plump, pleasant woman who had been pressed into service as a sous-chef. She was carrying a tray covered in tinfoil.

"This will be a binational, bicultural Thanksgiving feed," Lisette announced and, with burlesqued élan, whipped the foil off five soup bowls. "First course: *posole sonorense*. Second will be turkey *norte-americano*."

Deferring to his companions' secularist sensibilities (Anna excepted), Riordan said a silent grace. Lisette poured tequila into small, blue glasses for everyone, and they toasted one another's health. In his half-starved state, Riordan gulped his soup with the table manners of Oliver Twist in the workhouse. He had to wait a few minutes before the others finished theirs. Then Lisette asked him to carve the turkey.

"I can do it myself—I'm trained in minor surgery," she said. "But it's traditional for the man to carve, and I am in a traditional mood."

The ceremony was performed in the kitchen. As he whetted the carving knives, he flashed on a nostalgic picture of childhood Thanksgivings among his populous family, Grandfather Riordan at the head of the table, scraping a blade over the sharpening stone. In his younger days, before he opened Riordan's Shamrock Lounge, a watering hole for varied species of Chicago wildlife—ward heelers, bookies, cops, newspapermen—Grandfather Riordan had been a meat cutter in the stockyards. He could disassemble a twenty-five-pound turkey before it got cold. Riordan's skills weren't up to those standards, but he figured he could do a passable job on Lisette's smaller bird.

"You do the breast this way, see . . ." He cut along the backbone, around the wings and thighs. "You take the breast out whole on both sides, then slice it crosswise." The smell, the steam curling out from the body cavity made him light-headed. Unable to resist, he snatched a small chunk of white meat and swallowed it whole. "You'll pardon me, Lisette? I've hardly eaten all day."

"So what's with this fast? Are you purging toxins?"

"No. It's . . . it's a personal thing." Anna came in with the soup bowls and spoons and stacked them next to the sink. Although she did not understand much English, he waited till she left. "It has to do with some-one who came to me for counseling . . ."

He checked himself, unable to think how to proceed without violat-ing a confidence.

"I think I know who." Lisette lay breast pieces around the edge of a platter. "She told me she was going to see you. What does she have to do with you fasting?"

"I'm not free to say." How far could he go, should he go? Had he gone too far already? "There were consequences. . . . I'm sure you know . . ."

"Let's us both be careful. We're on thin ice here. Patient-doctor priv-ilege," she said.

"I'm worried about her health," Riordan confided. "That there might be consequences to the consequences. I don't think she's as aware of them as she should be."

Lisette paused in her preparation and looked at him. Her irises were the color of old pennies.

"I think she needs to talk to someone besides me. A woman," he added.

Lisette piled drumsticks and stuffing between the ring of white meat and lifted the platter. "I'd say we're out of bounds, Father Tim."

"Yes, we are. We'll drop it."

"It's decent of you to be concerned, but she's not your responsibility. And not mine, either, unless she comes in and asks. I can't tell a girl I barely know to come in for a woman-to-woman chitchat."

"No, of course not. My meaning was . . . Oh, I don't know what the heck my meaning was."

"Get the gravy boat, please," she said, shouldering the kitchen door open into the courtyard.

They ate yellow rice and black beans, a Cuban specialty, with the turkey. That made it, Lisette said, a trinational Thanksgiving. She told Riordan about the experiences she, Nick, and Pamela had had on the drive from Tucson. Nick jumped in, declaring that he hadn't been scared, and the arrest of the gunrunners had been a rush. If this was bravado, it was the bravado of ignorance. A privileged American kid had not the haziest notion of what could happen in certain parts of Mexico if you were careless or just unlucky.

"Watch yourself while you're here, Nick," Riordan said, feeling obliged to offer counsel. "How you act, what you say."

"Hey, I'm cool."

"I'm sure you are. I'm also sure you've never been cut. My old boxing coach at Notre Dame taught us how to throw jabs and hooks and an axiom: 'If you've never been cut, you don't know shit.' I'm quoting."

He grinned to show that he meant no insult to Nick's intelligence. No offense intended, none taken. Nick merely laughed at hearing a Franciscan friar utter a four-letter word.

Lisette nudged the conversation to the church's refurbishment. She seemed eager to establish Pamela's credentials in art restoration, while Pamela was no less eager to play down her expertise. She had not worked for museums, as Lisette had claimed, but for a company that repaired murals in municipal buildings, and that had been years ago.

"A lot of the stuff we did was what you see in city halls and county court buildings—you know, big agricultural or industrial scenes, dreck, imitation Diego Rivera or Thomas Hart Benton."

It had grown twilit and chilly. Lisette lit candles in small jars and switched on the electric heater, which stood over them like a tall, mechanical servant awaiting orders.

"But surely the techniques, the materials are the same, no matter what," Riordan said.

"They are, but I'm way out of practice. I wouldn't feel confident taking on the paintings in your church."

"Nonsense!" Lisette cried. Then, to Riordan: "Pam is afflicted with acute self-effacement. It's her Waspy upbringing."

Pamela scowled, but not at the comment about her upbringing; she disliked being spoken of as if she weren't present. "How would you feel if you had to do an appendectomy when it had been years since your last one?"

"Actually, I've never done an appendectomy, except on cadavers," Lisette said. "But I wouldn't let that stop me if I had to do one."

Riordan, following his instinct to play peacemaker, stepped in to avert a quarrel. "Why don't you stop by the rectory tomorrow?" he said to

Pamela. "I'll show you the church. You can tell me what you think. No pressure. Around ten?"

"That would be all right," she answered as they took up forkfuls of pumpkin pie with far too much whipped cream for a man on a fast. Later, as Riordan left, Lisette planted another wet kiss on his cheek, and when he went to erase the lipstick, she grabbed his hand.

"Don't rub it off, Padre," she said flirtatiously. "Like Bonnie Raitt sang . . ." She belted out the lyric in a mock-bluesy voice, her abundant chestnut hair flying as she swung her head from one side to the other. "'Let's give 'em something to talk about!'"

There seemed to be something altogether excessive about this merry parting. "But not about that," he said. "We don't want them talking about that all over again."

She flicked her eyebrows comically at Nick and Pamela. "Once upon a time, there was gossip in town that me and the padre were gettin' it on."

"Oh, Mom," Nick groaned.

Riordan walked home, feeling bloated and more out of sorts than he should have after a fine meal in good company. Entering the rectory courtyard, beyond the plaza lights' glare, he looked up and saw Jupiter, as big and bright as a headlamp. On one of his morning vigils, he had spotted Callisto, the outermost of the four Galilean moons, with his naked eye. Poor Galileo, persecuted for daring to propose that Earth wasn't the center of the universe. Riordan had resolved, within himself, the mossy conflict between science and faith. The church wasn't as hidebound and intolerant as she had been four hundred years ago; she was capable of progress, though her pace was often glacial. The father of the big bang theory had been a Belgian priest named Georges LeMaître, and now astronomers from the Vatican observatory were charting the big bang's first children: galaxies so distant it had taken twelve billion years for their light to reach the observatory's scopes.

He went to his room, turned on the desk lamp, and began to read from his worn leather-bound breviary. He couldn't keep his mind on his evening prayers; it was fixated on that number, twelve billion light-years. A single light-year equaled more than six trillion miles, so the distance to those galaxies was twelve billion multiplied by six trillion. He could not grasp such a staggering figure. No human could, no more than a dog could grasp quadratic equations.

This thought led him to lay down his breviary and pull a volume of H. P. Lovecraft's writings from his bookshelf. He flipped through it to a passage he recalled underlining some time ago:

> Humanity with its pompous pretensions sinks to complete nothing-ness when viewed in relation to the unfathomed abysses of infinity and eternity which yawn about it. Man, so far from being the central and supreme object of Nature, is clearly demonstrated to be a mere inci-dent, perhaps an accident, of a natural scheme whose boundless reach relegates him to total insignificance. His presence or absence, his life or death, are obviously matters of utter indifference to the plan of Nature as a whole.

Riordan squinted at a note he'd scrawled in the margins: "The Holo-caust? 6 million Jews murdered? Not significant in the grand scheme of things?"

Quite a few people these days, some very bright people, shared Love-craft's view, and they reacted to it with a kind of insouciant despair that Riordan suspected was a pose; they went on living their lives as if they meant something. Lovecraft's response was more honest: his perception of a cold, limitless void, empty of love and purpose, terrified him. Rior-dan knew he could not live in such a universe; he doubted that many could. Absent the divine fire of God's love, which conferred value on human life, singly or in multitudes, it would be as toxic to the spirit and the heart as Pluto's atmosphere was to the body. Of course, that didn't prove God's existence, only the human need to believe in Him.

More of his notations, beginning at the top of the page, running down the right margin: "You might be vanishingly small, yet you are not nothing. What you do or fail to do does make a difference, even if the celestial bodies perform their usual motions with no regard to you or for you."

Those words snatched his mind out of the galactic, back to the tiny corner of the middling planet he inhabited and, finally, to the suffering microbe named Cristina Herrera. She was the source of the jangling discontent that continued to plague him, the sense of failure. Which brought him to the question he never could answer: Why do I think it's my responsibility to save people from the wrongs that are done to them?

CHAPTER NINE

Pamela knocked at the office door while he and Domingo Quiroga were searching the Web (when they could get online) and (when they couldn't) the Hermosillo phone directory for a roofer to repair the cracked dome.

He rose from his chair and let her in. She was dressed as if she meant to go to work that morning: a khaki shirt worn outside faded jeans, her hair pinned up under a bandanna. A straw tote bag swung from her shoulder.

"I didn't expect you so soon," Riordan said, smiling.

"You said ten."

"Around here that could mean any time between now and noon."

"Lisette calls me pathologically prompt—another condition from my Wasp upbringing."

Her hand made an awning over her mouth, apparently to hide the one blot on her beauty: teeth needing a good orthodontist. Odd, Riordan thought, that she hadn't had them fixed. He told Domingo to carry on with the search and led her outside, around the church, then into it through a side entrance, the front doors being locked.

"You've already started?" she asked, gesturing at the scaffolds.

"I had four people in here. They commuted from Hermosillo. They quit on me a few months back. Because of the narcos. They were afraid of being kidnapped."

"That's encouraging. Well, can I see?"

When he flipped the light switches, illuminating the twenty-four bulbs in the silver chandelier, she flinched.

"I know: it's a bit—well, more than a bit—busy," he said.

Her glance darted up, down, to each side. There was too much for the eye to settle on any one thing: trompe l'oeil tiles low on the nave walls; depictions of pomegranates, bells, Franciscan cords, vines, angels, and grotesques higher up; the ephod symbolizing Aaron, the first priest; murals portraying the four evangelists; the gilded, baroque *estipites* above the altar, looking like giant candles dripping golden wax.

"Busy? Busy?" she said, with a lift in her voice. "It's overwhelming."

"It is at first, and there's more in the transepts. But it's really quite harmonious. If you sit in here and meditate, you can feel the harmony seep into you."

"I'll have to take your word for it." She italicized the statement with a skeptical look.

"The harmony comes from mathematics. Mission churches in Mexico were built on mathematical principles. The idea is that mathematics leads you to God." He'd fallen into his donnish mode. "It comes from the Spanish, and they got it from the Muslims, from the Moors."

"The Mudejars," she said. "And they picked it up from the ancient Greeks. Pythagoras, Plotinus, that bunch of geniuses."

He'd never met anyone who wasn't a scholar of early Spanish architecture who knew this. "That's right! Right, right!" he gushed. "All numbers come from one, and the Creator is the One from whom all things come." He pointed at powder-blue cherubim flying across the white cupola toward its apex. "Under there are the trusses and beams that . . . what's the word I want? That *come forth* from the ridgepole. The trusses and the beams from the center of the circle are the radii. They represent the way God bestows being on his creation. The divine will is expressed in the radius. I'm boring you?"

She shook her head. "Confusing me maybe."

"I like people to know that all this in here isn't decoration, and the building itself isn't merely architecture. It expresses praise to God."

"Uh-huh. Can you show me what needs doing?"

"Everything. Which would take a team of skilled people three or four

years. I'm hoping you might be able to fix up the murals, those and those."
Waving his arms, he indicated Matthew and Mark, peering through the
scaffolds in the left side aisle toward Luke and John on the right. She
handed Riordan her tote bag, then scaled the rungs to the narrow platform fifteen feet above and sidled along it, examining flakes in the paint,
the blotches marring Saint Mark's face, like a skin disease. Riordan called
to her that he couldn't join her because he was afraid of heights. As she
climbed down, he found it impossible not to notice her shapely bottom,
not to feel an attraction. On home leave a few years ago, as he was driving with his father down Michigan Avenue, the old man—he was then
seventy-eight—ogled a woman young enough to be his granddaughter
and almost ran a red light. "Lord, Dad, does it ever stop?" Riordan asked.
"When you're dead," his father replied. "And if it stops before then, you
might as well be dead."

Crossing to the opposite side, Pamela went up again, nimble as a
gymnast, and studied the damage to Luke and John.

"He was the best writer of the four, Saint Luke was," Riordan said.
"Acts reads like an adventure novel. Shipwrecks. Imprisonments. Dangerous journeys in distant lands."

He turned aside as she came down to keep his eyes off the tight curve
of her rump.

"What Acts?"

"The Acts of the Apostles."

"You're talking to an arch-heathen. I haven't seen a Bible since my
parents forced me to go to Sunday school, and I don't remember a word
of it. Another reason I may not be the one you want for this job."

"Competence, not faith, is the requirement," he said, heartened by
the "may."

"Yeah. Like I said yesterday, I'm not too sure about that, either."

"To further disincentivize you, I couldn't pay you a penny or a peso.
We had a modest restoration fund, but most of it was used up. The rest
of it and then some is going to fix a crack in the roof."

"I wouldn't expect anything," she said airily. "If I come down here,
and if I decide to take it on, it would be for Lisette's sake. She seems to
think I'd go bonkers without some big project that would get me out of
the house. And maybe she's right."

"I hope you decide to help out. Someone with your eye, your talent, a painter of your caliber—"

"Could I hire you as my publicist?" she said, with a wink in her voice.

"I once taught art history in high school," he said. "Might have been a painter myself, but I've been told that to be a great artist, you need to have had an unhappy childhood. A cliché, I suppose."

"Sometimes clichés are clichés because they're true."

"I was the victim of a happy childhood," he said, aware that he was talking too much. "Oh, my dad drank too much before he quit. But he was a functional drunk. A fun-loving drunk. There were eight of us. He used to say that he and my mother practiced the rhythm method so all their kids would know how to dance. . . . Sorry," he added when she winced at the stale joke.

He brought her to the transepts to show her, on the west wall, the fresco of the Virgin of Guadalupe, her blue-mantled figure surrounded by an almond-shaped sunburst. Pamela squinted at it through the scaffold's lattice, the corners of her lips dropping to form pockets in her jaw, like dents in a walnut. Strange how he found even this sour look charming.

"The gold leaf in that halo—" she started to say.

"Mandorla, it's called."

"Restoring that would take a lot of work," she said, and sat down in the transept's front pew, placing a notebook from her tote bag on one knee.

Sitting next to her at a discreet distance, he felt an invisible yet tangible force flow through the space between them. It plucked at his sleeve, tugged at him to draw nearer. He resisted, his memory retrieving the scolding voice of Sister Josefina, his eighth-grade teacher. That time during first Friday Mass when she'd caught him passing a heart-shaped mint, inscribed with the question "How's Chances?" to a girl he was in love with . . . what was her name? Sandy. Sandy Cahill. "Here, in God's house? You're a bad boy, Timothy Riordan. Bad, bad, bad." A good thing Pamela was gay; it provided a restraint where his own will might fail, as it had once, though it wasn't raw lust pulling him toward her here in God's house: a yearning, rather, to touch and be touched by her, the hunger for human affection that, his confessor in Rome had told him, a priest could curb through a deeper intimacy with God. The implication being that his hadn't been deep enough.

Pamela began to make notes, then paused to gaze at the painting. An unusual depiction of the Madonna, she said. Nothing like the ones you saw in Europe—the dark complexion, the straight black hair.

"It's a mestiza girl," he explained. "This one's a copy of the original in the basilica in Mexico City."

He told Pamela about the legend: how in the early days of the Spanish conquest, a maiden appeared to an Aztec Indian named Juan Diego on a hill outside the city. The apparition identified herself as the Mother of God and asked for a church to be built there in her honor. Juan reported his vision to the archbishop, who instructed him to return to the hill and ask the maiden for a sign to prove she was who she claimed to be. Request granted: she miraculously cured Juan's uncle of a disease and caused flowers to grow on a hillside where none had grown before. Flowers not native to Mexico, Castilian roses. Juan gathered them up in his cloak and returned to the archbishop. When he opened his cloak, the blossoms fell to the floor, forming an image of the Virgin.

"That Indian and the archbishop must have been eating mushrooms that hadn't grown there before," Pamela quipped, then brought two fingers to her lips. "Oops! Sorry. Maybe you believe that story?"

"My parishioners do. Ninety-five percent of Mexicans do. The Virgin of Guadalupe is a kind of cult in this country. She's a national icon."

"So even if you don't believe it, you'd better pretend you do?"

This struck him as another "oops," but she did not apologize for it.

"How did you come to be a priest? Just curious. You don't seem like the type."

"I wasn't aware that there was a type."

"Maybe not."

"I'll tell you on the condition that you tell me why you became an artist."

"Fair enough."

"A long story," he said. "I'll abridge it. I dropped out of Notre Dame in the middle of my sophomore year. I was restless, and I hit the road. Three months later, I fetched up in Mexico, a town not far from where we're sitting, Yécora. Dead broke and half-starved. The local priest found me asleep in the church. He fed me, gave me a job washing dishes, sweeping floors, helping him out with one thing or another. He was a remarkable guy, Father Batista, a Franciscan. He was always fighting with the municipal government for his parishioners. Not a fist-pumping sort of fighter. He was the most serene man I've ever known. If there was work to be done, he'd pitch right in. Sometimes I'd work alongside him, and we'd be fixing a corral or nursing a sick burro and he'd be discussing Augustine's commentaries on Scripture or Aquinas's philosophy, like we were in a seminar room.

"The time I remember most clearly, because it made all the difference in my life, was when he got word that a crippled old man way off in the Sierra Madre wanted to take Communion. The only way into his village was on foot or on muleback. No mule to be had, so Father Batista walked. He was older than I am now. It was late winter, March, and a cold rain was falling. He left at daybreak, didn't get back till after sunset, drenched, shivering, beat to the bone. I asked him why he'd gone through all that just to give one old man Communion, and he said he'd done it for selfish reasons, meaning that it made him happy. 'Please explain,' I said, and he answered, 'The greatest happiness is to serve those whom no one else will serve.'

"I left a few days later, flipped a bus to the border with the money he paid me. I kept thinking about him and what he'd said, and sometime during that ride, I heard a voice inside my head telling me that I had to become like him. It was in my head but not my voice. And that was when I knew. Your turn."

She crossed her legs primly and, throwing an arm across the back of the pew, swiveled in her seat to face him directly. "Kind of the same thing."

"What is?"

"Art is a calling. I didn't hear voices or anything like that, but I didn't have a choice. I don't do what I do because I want to. I have to. Maybe I could have been a suburban hobbyist, you know, turning out passable stuff in a studio my investment-banker hubster built for me, showing at local galleries, drinking bad sauvignon blanc from plastic cups; maybe I would have done that if I hadn't been bi. But I was, I am . . ." She hesitated, then added, with a certain emphasis: "Bipolar, that is."

Riordan's cheeks warmed. Had it shown on his face, and had she noticed it? The little thrill of interest—no, of hope mixed with dread—that had flickered through him because, for an instant, he'd thought she'd meant bisexual?

"It set me apart," she continued. "Yeah, that's a cliché, too—that the artist has to be an outsider looking in, but she does."

Composing himself, he said, "I wouldn't have thought it. You seem so . . . is it reserved? Not that. Self-possessed."

"I'm not off-the-wall bipolar. The diagnosis was hypomanic. My ups don't reach the peaks, so my downs don't hit rock bottom, and lithium takes care of the rest. I know I started this, but let's stop before we get into too-much-information territory."

"I'll second that."

She resumed her note-taking. One list of the work that needed doing, she said, another of the necessary materials: ammonium caseinate, dehydrated mortar, retouching paints.

"Do I take it, then, that I can count on you?" he asked.

"No promises."

CHAPTER TEN

Returning to the parish office, an image of Pamela shimmering in his mind, he heard his conscience ventriloquize Sister Josefina: *You are a bad priest, Timothy Riordan. Bad, bad, bad.* Forget a deeper intimacy with God, he thought. Dad had it right: death alone is the way off the streetcar named desire.

Entering the office, he was startled to find the cop, the self-styled Professor, seated there. He had Riordan's Latin grammar open on a laptop covering his knees.

"*Buenos días*, Padre Tim," he said, his pale, piercing eyes beaming out from cavernous sockets. He was again in plain clothes, except for a windbreaker bearing the Federal Police logo, a seven-pointed star. And the gun, a black semiauto in a black ballistic-cloth holster. "I saw this on your shelf," he went on, in English, tapping the book. "Thought I'd brush up on my declensions and conjugations."

"This isn't a public library," Riordan said, flushed with indignation. "How did you get in here? What are you doing here? What do you want?"

"Are you curious or pissed off?"

"Both, and it's not fifty-fifty."

"I'll take your questions in order." The Professor noticed Riordan frowning at the pistol and zipped up the windbreaker to cover it. That was civil of him. "I got in here because your man let me in."

"Domingo?"

"He's one of the reasons I'm here. He and his brother have asked for police protection. It seems they're not confident that Señor Díaz's neighborhood watch is up to the job."

Riordan sat behind his desk. It gave him the illusion that he would be in control of whatever came next.

"It also seems that the Brotherhood isn't ready to write off San Patricio," the Professor continued. "We think they're going to try to regain control here. The Quirogas got a phone call the other night. They are supposed to start paying a *cuota* again," he elaborated. "Domingo's brother was the one who came to us."

"Adan," Riordan said. "An older brother."

"He was scared shitless, which I'd say is an appropriate response, but he wasn't ready to roll over. An installment was due early this morning, while the bakers were baking. You guys can bust the collectors when they show up, Adan told us. So we did. Two of them, young guys from right here in town. I wouldn't be surprised if you gave them Communion last Sunday." He said this jovially. "We're having conversations with them at the base. They're plankton, but they might lead us on up the food chain to the barracudas. Don't ask who they are. You've got your secrets, we've got ours."

A little gas bubble formed in Riordan's gut and bobbed into his throat. "Where is Domingo now?"

"Two of my men gave him a ride home."

"I was with him an hour ago. He never said a word about this."

"Why would he? Not the kind of thing you want to spread around. But I thought I'd let you know, since he's your employee."

"He's not an employee. He volunteers. Not that that makes any difference. You said police protection, Pro . . . Is there something I can call you besides 'Professor'?"

"Try Inspector. Inspector Grigorio Bonham. We'll have two officers watching Domingo's and Adan's houses twenty-four/seven, two more at the bakery, and we've beefed up security in the plaza to keep an eye on your church, since he works here part of the time."

"What did the caller say? Did he make threats?"

"A threat would have been superfluous," said Inspector Bonham. He clasped his hands behind his head and stretched out his legs, crossing his ankles, his trouser cuffs riding up to show costly, ostrich-skin cowboy boots with quilled toes. His relaxed pose and vigilant stare brought to mind a well-trained rottweiler at rest. Under different circumstances, he would have made Riordan nervous; but in a bad neighborhood, it was good to have an attack dog in your yard.

"I'm very fond of Domingo. If anything happened to him . . . Is there anything I can do to—"

"Nothing that we're not doing. You might want to encourage your parishioners to cooperate with us. If they know something, say something. Anonymity guaranteed."

"An apology from the captain might put them in a more cooperative mood."

"Forget that, but he might be in a better mood himself because he has to be," Bonham said. "The orders to disarm the *autodefensas* have been rescinded. The government figures disarming them would be more trouble than it's worth, so the neighborhood watchmen here and everywhere get to keep their flintlocks. And we—the army and the police—have been urged to cooperate with them. I doubt Valencia is going to be Díaz's best friend, but"—Bonham drew himself out of his slouch—"it's what you suggested, so congratulate yourself, Padre Tim. You were ahead of the curve."

Riordan noted the phrase: *ahead of the curve.* "How long did you say you lived in the States?"

"I didn't say."

"You can't blame me for being inquisitive. Your English, your last name."

"My father was a Brit, not American. A mining engineer. My mother was a third-rate Mexican actress, crazy enough to think she was a star. I got American citizenship for doing four years in the U.S. Army. The Eighty-second Airborne. We were in the Panama operation to nab Noriega in eighty-nine. My first drug bust."

"So you're a dual citizen?"

"Triple. I've got a British passport. Stifle your inquisitiveness. You're already well out of the need-to-know box."

"Are we done, then?"

"No."

Bonham got to his feet with a languorous movement, laid the laptop on the desk, then moved around it to stand behind Riordan. Leaning over his shoulder, he turned the computer on, tapped the keyboard. A still image filled a YouTube window. He clicked to full-screen display. Wearing a baseball cap, a man seated at a cluttered table was looking right into the video camera through the slits in the balaclava concealing his face. Centered on a wall behind him was La Fraternidad's emblem: the robed bones of Holy Death clutching an AK-47, her hooded skull grinning. Posters of Che Guevara and Emiliano Zapata flanked her, Guevara on her right, Zapata on her left.

Bonham clicked Play.

"Good day, brothers and sisters, from the *comandancia* of the Brotherhood," the masked figure began. "This will be the first in a series of video communiqués we will issue from time to time . . ." He went on for four minutes, thirty-seven seconds in a muffled voice as robotic as a recorded announcement in a train station. Then the screen faded to black.

Riordan stared at it, fascinated and appalled. "What . . . what is this?"

"Looks like the Brotherhood is opening a media campaign. Next thing they'll have a Facebook page. I thought you'd appreciate his religious sentiments. 'Who is without God is lost,'" said Bonham, positioning himself with his hands on the back of the chair, as if he meant to wheel Riordan across the room—or give him a shove.

"That was him? Salazar?"

"Yes. I recognize the voice."

"You would think a cartel boss would be embarrassed to call himself 'the Butterfly.'"

"He does because he was one thing that became another thing."

"I am mystified."

"Ernesto Salazar is an alias. Real name: Julián Menéndez. Julián was a pioneer in using new media in the trade. Back in oh-one, oh-two, he produced snuff videos for his mother. Mom's *sicarios* executing people, with snappy *narco-corridos* for background music. A bright guy. Has a business degree from the University of Texas."

"You seem to have gotten ahead of yourself," Riordan said. "And please sit down where I can see you."

Bonham spun around the desk and dropped back into his chair.

"Yvonne Menéndez was *la jefa* of the old Agua Prieta Cartel," he said. "Half Irish-American, half Mexican, and all bad, a mega-bitch. Next to her, Lady Macbeth looked like Little Bo Peep. Murdered her husband, with her son's help, so they could take over. Ten years ago, we raided her ranch to free three Americans she'd kidnapped. She killed one of them, and then I killed her. We smashed her operations, but Julián got away. Did I mention that Julián is also a dual citizen? Mom was an American. He changed his appearance—dyed his hair, some minor plastic surgery—and sneaked into the U.S. under a false name and with forged documents to prove that Julián Menéndez was now Ernesto Salazar."

Riordan raised a hand to signal for an intermission and said he was having trouble absorbing all this history.

"Are you? Well, there's more," the inspector said. "He got religion, became a born-again Christian, and joined a congregation in El Paso run by a nutball, James Showalter—Pastor Jim, they called him. Kind of a Christian jihadist. Preached a gun-totin' brand of Christianity. Torched abortion clinics, that sort of thing. Julián a.k.a. Ernesto became one of his apostles. Few years went by, he came back to Mexico. He'd learned a big lesson from his mentor: religion inspires loyalty and imposes discipline. And he used it to stitch the pieces of Mom's organization back together. Then he went to war with Joaquín Carrasco. You know that name, don't you?"

"He's a folk hero around here," Riordan said, nodding. "Or was."

"Joaquín was Mama Menéndez's nemesis. She was at war with him back in the day. Her devoted son wants to finish what she started, and he's almost there."

"You said you killed her . . . ?"

"When I was as close to her as I am to you," Bonham replied with a cordiality that didn't go with the statement.

"And there's a reason you've told me all this?"

"Partly for background purposes."

"And partly what else?"

Bonham steepled his hands under his chin. "You heard what he said at the end of the video: 'We of the Brotherhood also promise justice, and we keep our promises.'"

"Something is going to happen," Riordan said, another acidic bubble shooting into his craw. He wasn't thinking about Pamela now. He could scarcely remember what they'd said to each other, as if this conversation had recorded over that one.

"The question being what's going to happen," said Bonham. "What goes for your parishioners goes for you. If you know something, say something."

The steeple rocked forward, and with the dry sniper's squint behind them, Riordan imagined the joined fingers as a multibarreled gun aimed at him.

"I'm sure Salazar or whatever his name is won't be contacting me," he said.

"You get out into the boondocks. The Brotherhood's turf. All those villages in the Sierra Madre . . ."

"From time to time, yes."

"So does your doctor friend."

It would be foolish, he understood, to ask how the inspector knew that he and Lisette were friends.

"You might hear something. Or see something. Or she might mention something to you," Bonham continued. "I don't care if it's gossip, a rumor, second- or thirdhand, you let me know." He plucked a card from his wallet, wrote on it, and placed it on the desk. Hesitant to pick it up, as if that alone would commit him, Riordan merely glanced at it. A minimalist card if he ever saw one, offering only Bonham's name and the phone numbers he'd written below it.

"Call me on any one of those, with this," he said, producing a flip phone, which he set down next to the card.

"I have one," Riordan said. "An iPhone."

"Use this one. It's a burner, virtually untraceable."

"A what?"

"Burner. A prepaid phone with encryption."

"Aren't you being a tad melodramatic?"

"Careful is what I'm being. Call me. Any little scrap you might come across."

"Outside the confessional," Riordan said firmly as he thought, *This is preposterous*. "I want to make sure we're clear about that."

Inspector Bonham made a slight bow and said, "Right-ee-o," as if drawing on his British heritage. Then he stood, swept the laptop off the desk, and wedged it into its case.

"Your man told me you're looking for a contractor to repair a roof," he said, moving toward the door.

"You must have had quite a long conversation with Domingo."

Bonham shrugged.

"It's the dome," Riordan said. "It's two centuries old. A tricky job. But I don't see that our roof is any concern of yours."

"It could be. You never know. I might be able to find somebody. And if they're jumpy about coming out here, I could provide a police escort."

"Another one of your quid pro quos?"

"I won't need to rely on that, wouldn't you say, Padre Tim?"

The percipient look on Bonham's face made the question rhetorical.

CHAPTER ELEVEN

She loved the courtyard at any time of the day, but she loved it most in late afternoon, the mellow-yellow hour she called it, for the tone of the light. It fell not as sunlight does through a window but more like a mist, sifting down on the fountain, the plants, the floor's square paving stones. Her house dated to 1796; the year of its construction and the names of the Spaniards who'd built it were chiseled into the keystone arch above the front entrance: Don Francisco y Doña Isabella de Monteczuma, the surname marking Don Francisco as mixed race, a descendant of Aztec royalty.

The place had been a ruin, abandoned for decades, when she bought it for next to nothing. Restoring it to livable condition, converting the *sala* into a clinic and then equipping it, had cost considerably more than nothing. With her savings almost depleted, she'd been reduced to bartering for tradesmen's services: free treatment for new wiring; free examinations for new plumbing.

The courtyard being a luxury, its renovation came last. The fountain—a griffin standing on its hind legs in a basin shaped like a seashell—was sandblasted, the broken clay pipes replaced with copper. In the mellow-yellow hour, listening to the splash of water spit from the griffin's beak, Lisette would sit with a glass of wine and imagine Don Francisco and Doña Isabella joining her for cocktails. Sometimes, after one glass too many, the reins on her imagination slipped, and she conducted make-believe conversations with those ghosts, telling them about the commonplace events of her day, now and then relating a tragedy or comedy for contrast.

She was like a lonely child, inventing playmates to fill her solitude. Was that all Pamela was to her? In her ideal conception of love, Lisette thought, Pamela's happiness should be her first concern. This pulled her to another, more fundamental question she'd been trying to resolve: Was she in love? She'd approached it like a diagnosis, eliminating possibilities to arrive at the correct answer. She was drawn to Pamela's glamour and upscale style, but that wasn't love. Nor was the protectiveness aroused by Pamela's mania. Meds held it in check, though not always. During one of their weekend trysts in Tucson, she had stayed up all night rearranging her furniture, and woke Lisette at five a.m., crying, "Come look! Look what I've done to the place! Don't you love it! Tell me you love it!" That excitability, that neediness. Lisette wished she could throw herself, self-sacrificially, between Pamela and her neurochemical demons. If that was love, it was the maternal kind. She wondered, now, if probing the heart's motives was stupid. You knew intuitively when you were in love; if analysis was required, might that be a sign that you weren't?

"There. *There*," Pamela said now. They were in the courtyard, where she was applying finishing touches to a white cardboard poster, propped on a table against one of the pillars supporting the arcade. She stepped aside as if unveiling a portrait or an epic landscape. "Don't you think that's way better?"

Lisette agreed. The poster was a big improvement over the one she'd produced weeks earlier. On the left side, under the green-lettered word "*Sí!*," vegetables spilled from a cornucopia; on the right, under a red-lettered "*No!*," lay a trash pile of soda cans and junk-food wrappers. Pamela had drawn the images with photographic realism. Beneath them, neat columns listed the cornucopia's bounty—phytonutrients from blue corn, purple carrots, purple potatoes—and the evil fruits of Coke, Fritos, pizza—salt, sugar, trans fats. The poster was to be a visual aid in Lisette's nutrition classes, held monthly for San Patricio's housewives and schoolchildren.

"You done good, girl," she said. "You made the corn and carrots look appetizing and the crap repulsive."

"First representational stuff I've done in years," Pamela said with a laugh. She sat down, facing the poster, her back to Lisette, and picked up the cigarette in the plate dragooned into service as an ashtray. She was a social smoker, no more than two or three a day. Lisette considered it disgusting but didn't make an issue of it.

"Thanks for taking the trouble. I hope not to make a sign painter out of you."

"Hey! Anything for the cause. What is the cause, exactly?"

"Preventive medicine! Mexicans are the *número uno* consumers of junk food on the planet! Half the people I see have heart disease, diabetes, high blood pressure, immune systems fucked from the garbage they stuff into their mouths. If they can go back to eating the way they did a hundred years ago—"

Pamela turned and, looking at Lisette with gentle merriment, raised her hands. "Puh-leeze! I was only kidding."

"About what?"

"Asking what the cause is. You've told me."

Lisette chuckled at herself. "I can't help it. It's my grand passion."

"Not too grand, I hope. Not so grand it doesn't leave room."

She'd styled her hair in the way Lisette liked, pinned up with a butterfly clip. It emphasized her classic looks, exposed the full length of her pretty neck, which Lisette now kissed.

"Room aplenty. If the ladies and their kids weren't coming in half an hour . . ."

"Tonight," Pamela said, promise in her voice. She folded her arms across her breasts, tight, athletic, half again as big as baseballs. "Save it for tonight. It feels like it'll be a cold one."

"Snow predicted down to two thousand meters. We're at fifteen hundred. Ever think you'd see snow in Mexico?"

"Nope. But then I never thought I'd spend a morning in a church with a Catholic priest and find that I liked him."

"Tim's all right. Not the doctrinaire type."

"He knows you're gay, right?"

"Sure. A while back, when rumors started that I was the padre's secret squeeze, he got nervous about a scandal. No worries, I told him, I don't like boys. Never did."

"What did he say?"

"That it would stay between him and me. He warned me that his parishioners were pretty conservative when it came to that, the women especially. If they knew, or even suspected, I could lose them as patients. Their kids, too. *No problema*, I said. I'd grown up among hellfire evangelicals. I knew how to behave. So how did it go with Tim?"

"All right, I guess. He said there was enough work for a team, but I suppose I could get a start on it."

"You agreed, then? You'll come down and do it?" Striving not to sound too hopeful, too avid. Because this was so pleasant; it made her feel complete to sit in her own courtyard, conversing with a woman she cared for.

"I didn't agree. I didn't turn him down. I'll have to think about it."

"What is there to think about?" She wanted to take the words back as soon as she spoke them. Too sharp, too demanding.

"Are you kidding?" Pamela said, and held up a finger. "One: like I keep telling you and him, it's been years since I've done restorations." Another finger popped up. "Two: I wouldn't want it to interfere with my own work." And another. "Three: I don't speak Spanish. I can't even ask where the bathroom is."

Too much time in resorts where everybody speaks English, Lisette thought as she said, "*Dónde está el baño.* Give it a try."

Pamela bristled. "Come on, I know that much."

"Sorry. Look, I'm not asking you to throw your whole life over. Only to spend a few months down here. We can see how things work out."

"There's a couple of other things." She squinted at Lisette—a pained expression, as if to show how difficult it was to say what she was about to say. "It's weird down here, and dangerous besides, and I don't do danger very well. Those two guys who stopped us, the way the one looked at me, it made me feel like he was smearing slime all over me. And then there's what you said a minute ago. That you know how to behave. Back into the closet?"

"*Más o menos.* More or less."

"That's easy if you're alone. So what would I have to do? Make off that I'm just your friend or roommate or whatever? God forbid anybody catches us holding hands? I'm not sure I can go back to living that way, even for a little while. Are you saying you can?"

Ah, Lisette thought. *Here is the main objection.* She had had the same doubts herself, anticipating the strains that came from leading a double life. But they did not trouble her half as much as they seemed to trouble Pamela; for there had always been a hidden side to Lisette, an alter ego who liked being a sexual renegade. This part of her had taken a covert pleasure in shocking her family, and in their rejection of her. It was an anarchic streak that rebelled against any orthodoxy, finding the pieties of the gay rights movement a load of crap and the new tolerance of gays boring, the lukewarm bath of acceptance transforming social outlaws into bourgeois sanctioned to marry and adopt. Hot, once-prohibited kisses cooled into matrimonial pecks. *Your turn to drive the kids to soccer practice, dear, I've got to mow the lawn.* The romantic outrider in her believed that if eros was crushed by too much repression, it was shallowed by too little. Imagine Hester Prynne and Reverend Dimmesdale in a New England that winked at adultery. Yes, she and Pamela would have to sail their love boat under false colors in San Patricio. Fear of discovery would attend them daily; but deception's thrills would compensate for its anxieties. Not to mention the zip and zing of pent-up desires released in cloistered darkness.

But she wasn't about to reveal this secret self to Pamela, whose hands she now clasped. "I'm saying that it's a sacrifice I'm willing to make if that's what it takes to be with you," she said, with an earnestness not entirely genuine since it would not be entirely a sacrifice.

Pamela looked to her cigarette, three-quarters ash. She'd been put on the spot, unfairly, childishly. *If you're not willing, then you don't really care for me.*

"It's a lot to think about," she said.

The Quiroga brothers lived across the street from each other in new houses (new being defined in San Patricio as anything built within the last century), stucco over cinder blocks, Adan's sand-colored, Domingo's white. They took turns taking care of their mother, crippled by rheumatoid arthritis. This month was Domingo's turn, as today, Saturday, it was Riordan's turn to give Communion to the pueblo's shut-ins. Letitia Quiroga was his first call of the morning, a morning sharp with the penetrating cold of the high desert, a light snow flocking the junipers on the upper hillsides.

Domingo's wife, Delores, answered the door. She was tall for a Mexican woman, five-eight or so, with quick, alert eyes and a tough-cookie temperament. Looking past Riordan at the two *federales* parked in front of Adan's house in an unmarked car, the engine running for warmth, she expelled a dry, scornful spit at the floor.

"Half asleep, I'll bet. I myself could come up to them and shoot them both, *pah-pah,* before they could ask God's forgiveness."

He entered the house and blew on his hands and held them in front of a gas space heater before going into Letitia's bedroom with his kit. She was sitting in a wheelchair, her fingers frozen into talons. Her lips and tongue quivered spastically when she took the host and sipped the wine. *Cuerpo de Cristo, sangre de Cristo.* He spoke to her for a minute or two, then went into the kitchen, where Domingo was eating huevos rancheros.

"*Sentarse*, Padre, I'll make you something," Delores said.

He declined, but accepted her offer of coffee and sat down with her and Domingo to talk over what had happened. The *cuota* demanded had been ten percent of the bakery's weekly sales. Adan, who had taken the call, had not recognized the extortionist's voice. Nor had he or Domingo recognized the collectors who'd shown up early yesterday morning; they were masked. The *federales* arrested them without a struggle. Domingo did not agree with his brother about bringing the cops into it. He did not trust the cops. He did not trust anybody. He suspected that Roberto García, the young employee who worked the register and helped count receipts at the end of the day, had been in on the deal. Without someone on the inside to tell them, how would the extortionists know how much the bakery earned?

"They wouldn't need Roberto, a little clerk. They know everything," Delores said.

"Why didn't you say something to me yesterday?" Riordan asked. "I had no idea. You acted like nothing was wrong."

"One becomes good at acting," Domingo said. "We should all be in the cinema." He was a saturnine man by nature, lean and long-jawed, with concave cheeks, and today he looked and sounded more morose than usual. "We act like we do not see what we see or hear what we hear. We pretend not to know what we know. And so we live in—"

"*Una casa silencio,*" Riordan said.

"*Sí.* But not my brother."

Then a switch, slightly delayed, flipped in Riordan's memory. "Last week, you left me a note that a García wanted to make an appointment with me. You didn't say which García. It was this Roberto?"

"No, no," Domingo said. "A different one, an older man. Jamie."

"Did he say what he wanted?"

"No."

■ ■ ■

As he emerged from the base stockade, on whose floor the two *cuota* collectors lay semiconscious in dried puddles of their own urine, the

Professor blinked against the glare from the razor wire coiling along the top of the walls. The wire produced a sound heard only by him. The shape, those bright, sharp spirals, produced it: a low sibilance, like the singing of distant locusts except that it didn't vary in pitch. He crossed the drill field, half of which was taken up by the wall tents housing the Federal Police under his command, the other half a parking lot for the operation's vehicles. Clods of mud from melted snow flew out from under the boots of the paratroopers jogging around the perimeter to a martial chant, steam puffing from their nostrils and mouths. The words were different but the rhythm was identical to the one he'd sung when he was with the 82nd, and it created a shape only he could see: a reddish diamond flickering in time to the cadence. He had had synesthesia since childhood; it was as though the barrier between his ears and eyes did not exist, allowing him to hear forms and colors even as he saw sounds.

He scraped his shoes before entering the headquarters for 1st Compañía, 3rd Batallón, Brigada de Fusileros Paracaidistas, commanded by Capitán Primero Alberto Valencia.

He was standing before a wall map, large as a queen-sized bedsheet, with a sergeant and a sublieutenant. Two clerks were attending to paperwork, while a third soldier sat by a silent radio, almost asleep and no wonder: the propane heater made the room feel positively tropical.

"Inspector Bonham," Valencia said, turning. "It would have been a courtesy to ask permission before entering. We are in conference."

The Professor repressed an impulse to say that he'd stopped asking permission when he was a schoolboy. He was, after all, co-commander here, in practice if not on paper.

"My apologies. I didn't know."

Valencia gestured forgiveness. "No matter. We are just now finishing up."

After the captain dismissed the two underlings, the Professor moved to the map, its acetate cover decorated with arrows and runic military symbols drawn in grease pencil. Valencia pressed a finger on a square, in which widely spaced contour lines indicated gently sloping land and scattered black dots the village of Mesa Verde.

"We got a tip about this place. A poppy field somewhere nearby. Also a refinery for making *la negra*."

La negra—Mexican black tar heroin. The Brotherhood was responding to market changes. Heroin was on the comeback trail in gringo-land, the new junkies not street rats or jazz musicians but Mr. and Mrs. Everyday American, cut off from their OxyContin prescriptions.

"The tip—who from?"

"Anonymous. It could be bullshit, of course. I'm sending the sublieu-tenant and five men to check it out, as soon as I get authorization from the general."

Valencia made a face like he was in pain, because he had to take orders from a "straight-leg," that is, a non-paratrooper: Brigadier General Diego Carrillo, commanding the 2nd Military Region and Joint Operation Falcon, the combined army–Federal Police campaign to smash Salazar's cartel.

"I would think," said the Professor, "that you shouldn't have to ask permission from a general to send out a five-man patrol. Or are you just being courteous?"

"Your sarcasm is noted. And it's six, counting the *subteniente*."

"It would be better to make this reconnaissance by helicopter. But I suppose getting one would require authorization."

"*Por supuesto.*"

"I could get you one of ours, Alberto." The Professor addressed him by his first name to reestablish the fact that they were equals.

"*Gracias, pero eso no será necesario.*"

Valencia's pride was the reason it would not be necessary. His elite troops in a police helicopter? Never. Besides, it would be unauthorized. This was why, the Professor thought, deploying the army to fight the Brotherhood had been a mistake. It was a lumbering bison; its adversary, a wolf pack, light, nimble, and quick. All armies were hierarchical, naturally, but there was none quite so hierarchical, so hermetic and rigidly rule-bound as the Mexican. Christ, Valencia probably had to put in a requisition to take a piss. He was himself incorruptible, unlike some military officers the Professor had known; but his virtue harbored a flaw: it made him inflexible and self-righteous. The Professor was very flexible, a moral athlete who for years had hopped from one side of the law to the other; and he had never been accused of righteousness.

The captain asked, "What did you get out of them?," inclining his head to indicate the pair in the stockade. Suspected narcos, even those seized by the army, were to be interrogated and charged by the Federal Police. The protocol avoided sullying military hands with the measures necessary to persuade detainees that the benefits of squealing outweighed those of silence. In this case, no handoff had been required, as it was the Professor's men who'd arrested the pair.

"Not much," he answered.

"Not much? You've had them for almost two days."

"Let's go outside. It's like a greenhouse in here."

The fresh air felt good, still on the chilly side but warming quickly. Eastward, the Sierra's crests had already been stripped of snow. The two men sauntered along a crushed-gravel walkway, picketed by cypress trees, Valencia's hand popping up to his maroon beret to return salutes.

"You were in police intelligence. You have a reputation as an efficient interrogator," he said. "Please explain why you got nothing out of them."

Valencia's voice, high and sharp, caused a filmy, greenish curtain to shimmer before the Professor's eyes. Accustomed to these strange sensory experiences, he was not distracted by them.

"We got nothing because nothing is all they've got," he said. "In other words, they don't know shit."

"You mean they say they don't know shit."

"I mean they don't know. They don't know who told them to start collecting *cuota*. It's how La Fraternidad operates. In cells. Each cell knows only what it needs to know."

Right then, the burner phone in the Professor's left pocket vibrated, then stopped. He waited a beat. The phone vibrated and stopped again. On the third ring, he opened it. The message in the caller ID window flashed RESTRICTED before the caller hung up a third time. That was the signal—three times.

"An important call?" asked Valencia.

"It can wait."

He slipped the phone back into his pocket. They resumed walking and came to the main gate, an electronically operated barrier consisting of close-set vertical steel rails, with surveillance cameras mounted on concrete towers on each side. Combined with the walls and the radio towers rising behind the *comandancia*, the effect was of a colonial presidio with high-tech upgrades. The two soldiers manning the sentry booth snapped salutes, and Valencia's hand again went up in a casual movement, as if he were brushing away a fly.

"What did your priest have to say?" he asked. "Also not much?"

"He's not mine."

"And certainly not mine."

"But he is respected. The townspeople love him."

Valencia gave a rueful shake of his head. "My fellow Mexicans amaze me sometimes. How in this century they kiss the asses of these witch doctors. How they lay their hands on statues of saints thinking that will cure them of cancer. *Un milagro!* A miracle! How they will make pilgrimages, walk in sandals for two hundred kilometers, only to have a witch doctor bless them. One could forgive such idiocy, such superstition, a hundred years ago. But now? It's disgusting."

"So it's not amazing?"

"Amazing and disgusting. I am disgusted in my amazement."

"I think he's softening up," said the Professor. "He didn't object when I told him that if he knows something to say something, and to encourage his parishioners to do likewise. He did say that they would be more cooperative if you apologized."

"That again? Fuck that. I am already ordered to stop disarming the vigilantes. Now I must cooperate with those amateurs. Enough cooperation from me. Let us see some from them."

They started back the way they'd come. Pausing beside a SandCat, Valencia complained that he had felt humiliated last week, pleading with a witch doctor, a gringo witch doctor no less, to give him information. To be stuck out here in this wilderness among ignoramuses, pursuing lunatics who worshipped a skeleton, was not a fit occupation for a senior *capitán* in the elite Parachute Rifle Brigade.

"*Con perdón del capitán,*" the Professor said with sham formality, "but you did volunteer for this mission. To avenge your brother?"

Raúl Valencia, the Nogales correspondent for *Proceso* magazine, had been assassinated in his car a year ago for his commentaries on the narco wars. He was stopped at a traffic light when a *sicario* pumped five bullets through the door and into his heart. A card bearing the Brotherhood's logo was left under one windshield wiper, like a parking ticket.

"I was ordered here, Inspector," Valencia said stiffly. "My personal motives have nothing to do with it."

"You'll excuse me, Alberto? I have to return that call."

The Professor walked out the compound's rear entrance and hiked a burro track that wound uphill behind the base. Cell reception was better at the top, though his reason for making the climb had more to do with ensuring privacy. It wouldn't do for anyone to overhear, especially Valencia. Wouldn't do at all. He dialed Joaquín's burner, waited for a ring, and hung up. After doing this twice more, he let the call ring through.

"*Hola,*" Joaquín Carrasco said from the most secure of his ranches, high in the San Pedro Mártir mountains, on the Baja Peninsula. It was accessible only by air or by a long, unpaved, tortuous jeep track that would test the nerve of even an off-road Baja racer.

"*Hola.* How is your health?"

"For a man of sixty-two years, excellent. I could not be better. This mountain air, you know. The life of a vaquero, every day on horseback in the open air. My only problem is mental. I am going fucking crazy. So I have not heard from you for a while. *Qué está pasando?*"

The Professor apologized; he'd been very busy.

"Are you guys any closer to getting rid of that son of a whore?"

"We just got started not even a month ago, Joaquín. Julián is up in the Sierra, he moves around a lot. It's hard to get a fix on him. We've got some ideas where he might be—"

"A fact would be better than an idea."

"*Claro.*"

"I am anxious to get the fuck out of here. I'm going crazy, my wife is going crazy, and she is making me crazy. She's here twenty-four hours a day. I can't even bring girls in from Mexicali or Tijuana. I ride horses and look at cows. I think I understand now why vaqueros fuck cows."

"Sheepherders do that."

"Sheepherders fuck cows?"

"No, they fuck sheep."

The Professor pictured Joaquín, whom he hadn't seen for some time, lounging under the ramada where he liked to eat his breakfast, looking like Ernest Hemingway scaled down to five feet eight, his hair white as foam on a wave, his trim beard the same color. Was he still wearing a beard?

"Listen, do you know something? The people still talk about you. They still sing *corridos* about you," he said to make Joaquín feel better. "You are not forgotten."

"Very nice to hear. I am also remembered by the Americans. I would like them to forget me. Why don't you convince your friends there to convince whoever they need to convince to forget about me?"

"Which friends?"

"Are you kidding? In the U.S. Customs, in the DEA."

"We've been through this," the Professor said. "I have arrangements with them, but they aren't my friends. Even if they were, they are not high enough on the totem pole to do you any good."

"We have spoken too long, yes?"

They had, but the Professor remembered an item he'd almost let slip his mind. Carrasco had laundered millions via construction companies throughout Sonora. The Professor asked if he had any money in roofing companies.

"Sure. Two. What the fuck is this about?"

"Give me their names. It's for a good cause. Repairs to a church."

"What the hell," Joaquin said, snorting into the phone. "Maybe God will favor me. *Momentito.* I'll get them for you."

After he had the names written down, the Professor dropped the burner, stomped on it, and buried the remains under a rock.

He started back down the path, thinking about Mexican politics, a complicated and not-so-comic opera. Two years ago, when the PAN—the National Action Party—was still in power, Joaquín Carrasco had been indicted by a U.S. grand jury on multitudinous racketeering charges. The Americans were going to request extradition if he was arrested by Mexican authorities. It was understood that the government would grant the request, because virtually all of Joaquín's connections were in the opposition party, the PRI—the Institutional Revolutionary

Party—which had ruled the country for all but twelve of the last eighty-odd years. Word had come through back channels that the Americans were going to offer Joaquín a reduced sentence or confinement in a facility more pleasant than a maximum security prison, on the condition that he identify the PRI mayors, governors, senators, deputies, and cabinet ministers with whom he'd been in cahoots for three decades. The scandal would rock PAN's political opponents to the core, which would help PAN win the next general election.

Joaquín still had PRI friends in high places, but they were in the minority and lacked the clout to protect him. They urged him to flee the country. He went to sea on his two-hundred-foot yacht, the *Doña Isabella*, sailing as far as Australia on what became an extended fishing voyage. He loved deep-sea fishing. But his organization collapsed during his absence; it was no match for the Brotherhood. His prospects brightened after the elections returned the PRI to full power. The Chamber of Deputies, the Senate, the presidency. A message was flashed to him out on the blue waters: he could come home. Certain rules would apply to his repatriation. He was to keep out of sight, maintain a profile so low he could walk under a termite without mussing his hair.

The Professor had known little about all this high-level maneuvering until he was summoned to play a role. He had moonlighted for the Sonora Cartel for years; indeed, it was Joaquín who got him a position in the Federal Police; so Grigorio Bonham was the obvious choice to arrange for a civilian helicopter to pluck Joaquín off his yacht and ferry him to wherever he wanted to go. The Professor, however, was not to divulge the destination to anyone. The Americans were certain to discover that Joaquín had returned to Mexico, and to pressure Mexican law enforcement to find him and bust him. It would therefore be best if no one knew his whereabouts, for his PRI associates wished to avoid a dilemma: they could not agree to turn him over to the Americans, but refusing to extradite him would sour their relations with the United States. The simplest way out of that predicament would be to avoid arresting Joaquín, albeit with a plausible excuse. We're looking for him, but we can't find him!

And besides, the powerful, no less than the powerless, wanted him to run things again in Sonora. The Americans would get the drugs they craved; the politicians and cops would prosper on *mordida*; the common people would be able to come and go without fear; violence would be kept within bounds. No beheadings, no mutilated corpses littering city streets and rural roadsides. The publicly stated mission for Joint Operation Falcon was to rid Sonora of Salazar's gory chaos; the secret mission, known only to a handful of people (the Professor among them) was to restore Joaquín Carrasco and order. Eventually, it was hoped, the gringos would see that things were better off with him in charge, and the U.S. Department of Justice would lose its zeal to put him behind bars. The Professor had often said it: organized crime was far preferable to disorganized crime.

He had wiped the vessels with a cloth and packed them in his travel Mass case, each in its place. Chalice. Ciborium. Paten. He'd zipped his vestments into a hanger bag to keep the road dust off it, and with it and the Mass kit in hand, he met Lisette at her clinic. Organized and deliberate, Riordan was annoyed by her rushed, improvisational way of doing things. It tired him to watch her flinging equipment haphazardly into reusable grocery bags—portable ultrasound machine, nebulizer, digital thermometers, disposable syringes—then pulling pill bottles and antibiotic packets from cabinets as indiscriminately as a drug addict burglarizing someone's medicine chest.

They lugged the bags outside, dumped them into her Dodge pickup's rear seat, then dragged a portable plastic bathtub from the courtyard and wedged it into the truck bed between two jerricans (one for water, one for gasoline) and two spare tires, which he fervently hoped would not be needed; both were as bald as Hugo Beltrán's skull.

"Four stops before we leave," she said, climbing in behind the wheel.

"Couldn't you have gotten this done yesterday?" Riordan tried but failed not to sound disapproving.

"No time," she answered, a little out of breath. Drove Nick and Pamela to Tucson on Sunday, drove herself back Monday, and then had to see patients.

The twenty-year-old Dodge was her clinic's back-country vehicle, and it suffered from every off-road mile it had been driven. When she turned the key, a wheezing sound came from under the hood, prompting her to pump the gas pedal. On the third try, the engine caught. Lisette advised him, as she removed a thick silver bracelet from her wrist and turquoise rings from her fingers, to take off his watch.

"This old thing?" He raised a hand to display his forty-dollar Timex with its cracked leather band.

"It'll look like a Rolex up there."

"I've worn it up there before with no trouble."

She tilted her head, an ear halfway to her shoulder. "C'mon, Tim. Humor me, would you?"

He stashed the Timex in the glove compartment with her jewelry. She popped the clutch, and the Dodge Ram rattled down the cobble-stoned street to a *tienda de comestibles*, where she picked up beans and *nixtamal* and cans of fruit to pass out as gifts. From the grocery she went to a pharmacy for more antibiotics, from there to the Pemex to top off the tank, from the gas station to the bank for a quick withdrawal at the only ATM in San Patricio—the only one, for that matter, within a radius of about fifty miles.

Finally, she sped out of town, crossing the Santa Teresa, passing through mesquite and stands of columnar cacti resembling giant spiny pickles. They were stopped briefly at the roadblock, but this time Riordan did not meet with any unpleasantness. The road went past the army base before it turned to dirt and began its hairpinning—and, for Riordan, hair-raising—climb into the high Sierra. They were headed for the *aldeas* and *caserios*—the villages and hamlets—in the easternmost part of the municipality, near the Chihuahuan border. Wild country, puma and jaguar country, inhabited by Mayos, Guarijios, and isolated bands of Tarahumaras. Lawless country also, maybe the most danger-ous in North America. It had been so for decades—the last renegade Apaches had held out in the Sierra Madre well into the 1930s, and Pan-cho Villa had eluded General Pershing in its labyrinthine canyons.

The road twisted up and up, skirting shadowed barrancas. In one ascent, it slanted like a raised drawbridge and appeared to end in mid-air. Riordan shut his eyes, half-expecting the Dodge to fly into space.

Instead, it slid around a switchback and ran along a level stretch, the slope on the right side, steep as a chalet roof, plunging hundreds of feet. The oaks at the canyon bottom, speckled with the pink blossoms of the *amapa* trees, were reduced to the dimensions of yard plants. Lisette drove twice as fast as he would have dared on his Harley. She hit a pothole without braking, then another. Bang. Crash. Something was bound to fall off the truck at any moment.

"So who are you marrying?" she asked offhandedly, as if she were on an interstate.

He didn't answer. He felt nauseous, his breathing short, his palms damp.

"Did you hear me, Tim?"

"I did," he croaked. "I know you don't believe in heaven, but you drive like you do. Could you please slow down?"

"Oh, right. Your acrophobia."

She eased up on the gas pedal, but not as much as he wished.

"What was the question?"

"Who's getting married?"

"A couple in Mesa Verde. They've been living together, a kid to show for it now, so they sent word that they wanted to make it legal."

"Are you going to make them repent first for living in sin?" she wise-cracked.

"I make allowances for Indians." He let a second or two pass, then threw a barb: "For non-Indians, too."

"Ooooooh. Am I supposed to be grateful for your open-mindedness? I was only needling you, y'know."

He fluttered a hand in apology, pleading that the near-death experience she was putting him through made him edgy.

■ ■ ■

They topped out on the mesa from which Mesa Verde derived its name. It was as though they had traveled from Mexico to British Columbia in an hour. Patches of snow lay on pine-shaded hillsides. A vaquero rode by wrapped in a wool blanket, his burro blowing steam, and stove smoke like vaporous serpents rose from a *caserio* a short distance ahead. The mesa was off every kind of grid—no electricity, no phones, no running

water. If it weren't for a pickup truck parked off the road, Riordan and
Lisette might also have traveled from the twenty-first to the eighteenth
century.

The *caserio* was their first stop before Mesa Verde. There wasn't much
to it: half a dozen rock and adobe shacks, some with verandas sagging
on bent poles; a cistern perched on a mound; latrines covered by what
looked like discarded shower curtains; and non-eighteenth-century trash
everywhere—beer and soda cans, plastic bottles, food wrappers. Though
he'd never visited this particular settlement, he'd been to ones like it,
and the squalor always dismayed him. It bent his political correctness in
the opposite direction, inclining him to see the early missionaries' unflat-
tering descriptions of Sonoran Indians as largely true.

Lisette dove right in, laughing and hugging women and girls in long,
colorful skirts, her brown curls flouncing and bouncing. With the greetings out of the way, she and Riordan hauled the portable tub out of the
pickup and carried it to a hut that would have looked like a jumble of
rocks if it had not been roofed, the roof being a blue tarpaulin thrown
over interwoven branches. Inside, sunlight spearing through cracks in
the walls provided the only light. A mound of filthy sheets and blankets
lay in a corner, on a dirt floor smooth and hard as pavement. The room
would not have made a decent stable, though it smelled like one. When
Lisette poked the mound with a twig and cried, *"Yaretzi! Despertarse!
Soy yo, Dr. Lisette!"* he realized that someone was under it: the woman
Lisette had come to bathe, Yaretzi Olivares. She was believed to be one
hundred years old—no one could say for sure—and every day of those
years had scribed thin, deep lines into her coppery face. She sat up, iron-
gray hair tumbling down her back, grinned toothlessly, and immediately began to babble in some incomprehensible Indian patois. Lisette
responded in Spanish, telling her it was time to clean her up, Yaretzi
protesting that it was too cold. *Hace mucho frío. Mucho, mucho.* Riordan helped pull the old woman to her feet, then into a walker that
Lisette had brought along. Yaretzi had been lying for God knew how
long in her own feces and urine.

Lisette built a fire in the stone hearth, and Riordan hauled water from
the cistern, poured it into a galvanized basin, and placed the basin on
the hearth. While the bath water heated, Lisette put on surgical gloves

and pulled the foul blankets outside; then, fetching a twig broom, she brushed them off. Next, she filled a bucket, sloshed the floor, and began to sweep human waste out into the dusty yard. Two women and a teenage girl stood near the doorless doorway, watching. Yaretzi's great-granddaughters and great-great-granddaughter, Lisette said.

"You shouldn't be doing this—they should," he said, thinking at that moment about a commentary from one of those colonial missionaries, something to the effect that native Sonorans did not venerate parents and grandparents, showed no esteem whatever for their nearest kin. A racist observation? Or an accurate depiction of a reality that persisted to this day?

"The best way to teach is by example," Lisette said.

He grabbed the broom in frustration and said, "Let me handle this."

He hadn't taken two strokes before one of the women, the older of the two, yelped, "No, Padre. No!" and stepped in and snatched the broom from him. Apparently, the sight of a priest cleaning up shit had provided the teaching moment that the sight of a doctor doing the same thing had not. He looked to see Lisette's reaction, but she was preoccupied with the bathwater, dipping her fingers into it to test its warmth.

She declared it hot enough. He lifted the basin and poured the water into the tub, which Lisette had set outside, under a kind of porch roofed in the same manner as the hut. Yaretzi, her modesty undiminished by her years, asked him to leave while she undressed. He walked off a distance sufficient to preserve decency and sat down, leaning against the cistern, a huge fiberglass tank that had somehow been trucked to this forlorn hamlet. Across the road, brown, shriveled cornstalks rasped in fitful breezes. Underfed goats nibbled the grass at the roadside, and a Corriente steer, likewise underfed, grazed on the hillside above the cornfield. Yaretzi let out a shriek. Looking toward her dwelling, he saw her splashing in the tub like a child while Lisette, beaming and chatting like mad in Spanish and whatever native tongue was spoken here, shampooed her hair. He envied her joy. *La mayor felicidad es servir a los que nadie más va a servir* was how Father Batista had phrased it so long ago. The greatest happiness is to serve those whom no one else will serve.

"So it is true. You have come again to the mesa. Everyone has said you would be coming today."

The man was missing half his teeth, wrinkles spiraled on his cheeks, but his voice was strong, he stood straight, and dark hair peeked from under his frayed straw hat. It was hard to tell if he was a weatherworn forty or a well-preserved seventy.

Into Riordan's silence, the man asked, "You are Padre Tim, are you not?"

Riordan wasn't wearing his clerical collar or coat, only a barn jacket and Levi's.

"I am," he answered as he stood up. "And who are you?"

"*Mi nombre es Alonso Castillo.* You are going to perform a marriage in Mesa Verde today, and the lady doctor Moreno is going to make the sick better. Everyone has been saying this."

Riordan didn't doubt that everyone had. E-mail and phones were unnecessary in the Sierra. News of their visit, its spread probably accelerated by Brotherhood lookouts, had reached the mesa well before their arrival.

"I, too, am a healer," Alonso Castillo declared. "I am a *sonadoro.* I cure with my dreams. But, you know, lately, my dreams are not so clear. They have lost much of their power. I wish to ask you for a blessing."

Riordan brushed off the seat of his jeans. "To restore your powers, Alonso?"

"Not me. That, there." Motioning at the cornfield across the road. "Bless the field, please."

He'd blessed babies, children, houses, and, once, a new car. Never a field. This one, belonging to Castillo's brother, required supernatural assistance because of drought. The summer rains had been sparse, the autumn harvest poor, Castillo said. With Padre Tim's blessing, it would be more fruitful next season. Riordan, joking to himself, wondered what the shelf life of a blessing was. If he gave it now, would it expire before the spring planting? He fetched his Roman missal from Lisette's truck and flipped to the table of intercessory prayers. Thirty-eight altogether. One to say in Time of Earthquake, another to Avert Storms (no, he wanted to ask for them), still others for Times of Cattle Plague, Times of Famine. Ah, here it was: For Rain.

He stepped out into the road, Castillo alongside him, and just as he began, "O God, in whom we live, move and have our being, grant us reasonable rain—" a farm truck jounced around a curve and came to a sudden stop a few yards from them. It wasn't carrying produce. Seated in the bed against the wooden rails were half a dozen young men in dark clothing. Black jeans, black, purple, or navy-blue jackets, baseball caps and backpacks in the same colors. Gallon water jugs, spray-painted black, hung from their shoulders on rope straps. Two men were in the cab. The driver leaned out his window and yelled, "Get the fuck out of the way!" He had a broad, chubby face and wore a Mohawk haircut and a wispy mustache.

"Show some respect, Su!" Castillo called. "Show some manners! Don't you know who this is?"

"No, and I don't give a shit. Get the fuck out of the way. I'm in a hurry."

Drug mules riding in the back, and "Su" was short for Jesús. Riordan strode up to the truck, struggling to keep his temper in check, for self-preservation among other purposes. Delgado and his buddy were probably armed.

"*Hola, Su,*" he said. "I know who you are and what you did. Everyone in San Patricio knows. You got away with it for now but not forever, because God Himself knows."

From Delgado came a puzzled look that in seconds turned into a contemptuous glare, followed by a call for Riordan to commit a hermaphroditic act. He wrenched the floor shift and punched the gas, the rear wheels spewing clods of dirt.

"A dog, a piece of shit, that one," commented Castillo. "Those kids in the back are from up there somewhere." He swiped a hand at the mountains. "Tarahumara. Delgado is taking them to *la línea*, the border, to carry *mota* into the U.S. Fifty, sixty kilometers they might have to walk through the desert, each carrying twenty-five kilos!"

He went on: If the boys weren't arrested, they would then hike back into Mexico and hope that someone would be waiting to drive them home, where they would further hope that someone would pay them for their services. *El narco* preferred the Tarahumara above all others. They made such excellent *burreros*, famous throughout Mexico, throughout all the world as the greatest of runners.

"I am myself part Tarahumara, and I know we are truly Rarámuri—the light-footed people. *Oye*, Padre Tim, once when I was young I ran in a festival race more than one hundred kilometers. Yes, it's true. In my huaraches! Those kids—their fathers and their fathers' fathers ran in the races, they hunted deer on foot, and now they are mules for those people . . ."

Riordan stood silently in the road, indulging Castillo's soliloquy, part harangue, part lament. He seethed inside; it felt as if someone were thumping his breastbone with a mallet. The brazen look on Delgado's fleshy face, the way he'd spit those words, *Go fuck yourself.* He could not imagine how that poor girl had not lost her mind, assaulted by that animal for days. An animal but no devil. Delgado's evil was very much of this world.

He turned to Castillo. "I will finish the blessing now."

It was a short prayer, taking only fifteen or twenty seconds to read. Castillo thanked him and walked off toward the *caserio.* Riordan plopped down right there at the roadside, in the posture of a weary hitchhiker. His anger drained away, and a gloom dropped over him, like a hood over a man about to be hanged.

■ ■ ■

Riordan and Lisette set off for Mesa Verde a little before noon. It was only five miles away, but the road was in such awful shape it would take half an hour to get there, even with Lisette's driving. When she slammed over a hump, sending Riordan's head into the roof, he again snapped at her to for Christ's sake slow down.

"I don't want you to be late for the wedding."

"The wedding will be whenever I get there," he said savagely.

"Wow, what put you in such a sweet temper?"

He took a breath and, in a more moderate tone, told her about his encounter with Jesús Delgado. The Brotherhood was corrupting everybody, ruining everybody, she said. The Tarahumara had escaped the conquistadores in the distant past, they'd evaded land developers in the present, but the narcos had gotten to them.

"You were a teacher before you got sent here, weren't you?"

"At a high school in L.A.," he said.

"I'll bet that sometimes you wish you were back there."

"Hardly. And I hardly think St. Michael's or the Franciscan Friars would want me back. The school was involved in a big scandal . . ."

He was slightly too late in checking himself. He had never told her about what happened at St. Michael's.

"Was it one of *those* scandals?" she asked.

"Yeah, one of those."

"If this story is going where I think it is, maybe you don't want to tell it."

"I wasn't a defendant. I've done my share of wrong, but not that, for God's sake."

"Okay."

"When the whole sorry mess was off the front pages, I put it back on. I spoke out in a radio interview and another one with the L.A. *Times*. Creeps in Roman collars were making the church sick, is what I said. I wanted it to be healthy again, but the Franciscan Friars of California, I guess they figured I could do with an assignment to Mexico. That's how I came to be where I am."

They were silent while Lisette negotiated a sharp downhill slope with a deep, zigzag ditch in the middle. To avert a rollover, she positioned the wheels on the ridges astride the ditch and eased the truck down like a freight car on crooked rails.

"Well done," he said when they reached the bottom.

"You were saying . . ."

"There was a boy at the school I was mentoring. A bright, talented kid, a gifted artist, Luis Gonzalez. Horrible background. Mother had five kids by three men, and Luis was in a gang. The Chicano Kings, Chicano Lords, something like that. I got this idea to save him from the streets. He was my reclamation project."

"I'm guessing it failed."

"Sure did. I made a mistake about him. A common mistake, I suppose. I assumed that talent plus intelligence equals character."

"Of which he didn't have much?"

"He was a hustler. That was his real talent. Even at fourteen, fifteen, he could charm just about anybody into just about anything, and himself out of trouble, and he was in trouble a lot. A sociopath, that's what, but some way or another, I went on believing in him. He was suspended in his junior year, he was going to be expelled, and I went to bat for him and kept him in school."

They were bumping through an arroyo now, under an archway of pines and oaks. An Aztec dove flew out ahead, as if to lead them. Riordan pictured Luis: his mesmerizing smile, his earnest—and false— promises to do better.

"The scandal broke around then," he said. "A bunch of former students filed a class-action lawsuit against five Franciscans: three priests, two brothers. One of them, James Brenner, taught at St. Michael's. Luis jumped in at the last minute. I think he saw a chance to cash in. He gave a deposition that was a half-truth. Brenner had had sex with him—that part was true. Luis had initiated it—that part he left out."

"Uh-huh," Lisette said. "But it would still be statutory rape. It doesn't excuse that Brenner guy."

"I don't mean it did. What he did to those boys was vile, he betrayed their trust, but I can't help but feel that Luis betrayed my trust in him. He came on to Brenner, playing a sort of male Lolita. I'll never know why, but I do know that's what Luis did because—I can say this now— Brenner confessed to me. Later on, he admitted to everything he'd done in his own deposition."

"Sorry. I'm not tracking this."

"I was deposed too, but before Brenner came clean in his. The lawyer asked if I'd ever heard a confession from a cleric who'd sexually abused a minor, and I . . . It was an unfair question. But the judge allowed it."

"You lied under oath."

The road turned out of the arroyo and resumed its meandering across the mesa.

"I don't get that church of yours, Tim," she continued. "Here's this pervert, raping teenage boys. He tells you, but you can't tell anybody."

"For good reason. People would be reluctant to confess theirs sins otherwise. It's like attorney-client privilege. Or between—" He checked himself.

"Between a doctor and a patient," she finished for him. "Except that if a doctor knows a crime's been committed . . ."

"That isn't why I perjured myself, not completely." Riordan paused to line up his thoughts. "It was for Luis's sake. I didn't want it to get out that he'd done what he'd done. Maybe I was afraid of what his homeys would do to him. You're the first person I've told this to."

"A lot to carry around," she said. "So what happened to Brenner?"

"He was shipped off to a retreat house before the trial got under way. It was kind of a treatment center for pedophile priests." Up to this point, Riordan had told his tale without emotion, as if relating a story he'd read in a magazine; but now his throat began to swell with regret, with sorrow, with all the pain of bad endings. "He hanged himself there. Twisted his bedsheets into a rope, threw it over a beam in the basement, and hanged himself."

"Holy shit. What about Luis?"

"He was killed in a drive-by shooting three, four months later." Riordan's voice caught. "I read it in the L.A. *Times*. 'Gang Violence Claims Three Lives,' some headline like that. And you know, I felt like a father who'd lost a son. I felt that I'd failed him. It made me angry, but it hurt at the same time. It still does, now and then."

"I'm sorry, Tim." She paused. "I want to tell you that you shouldn't blame yourself, but I get the feeling you won't buy it."

"Haven't sold it to myself so far," he said.

CHAPTER FOURTEEN

The couple asked for a full nuptial Mass, and he gave them one, commandeering a table for an altar. The ceremony, which the villagers, starved for diversion, considered more an entertainment than a religious rite, was held outdoors. Afterward, the altar cloth was removed, the table reverting to its original function. Platters of fresh tortillas and dried beef seasoned with a hot sauce made by the bride's mother were laid on it, along with delicacies and drinks from Mesa Verde's dark little store: plastic tubs of Japanese instant noodles, potato chips, Coca-Cola, cans of Tecate. Riordan turned down the junk food (Lisette congratulated him for setting the example) but, abandoning his fast for this occasion, gorged on the tortillas and beef. He accepted a beer, which he drank with the fathers of the bride and groom under a madrone tree, its smooth, red-barked branches writhing like tentacles. Chimneys and cooking fires leaked smoke, dogs lay in the dust, chickens waddled by. The massive cliffs looming over the settlement took on the color of melted butter in the midafternoon light.

With his contentment restored, Riordan felt like taking a siesta, but Lisette pressed him into service, hauling her medical supplies and equipment from the truck. She started a generator for electric power, plugged in the ultrasound machine, and conducted a sort of health fair beneath a ramada roofed with sticks, showing a pregnant woman an image of her baby, passing out gift bags of beans and *machaca* and bananas, lecturing on their benefits and the evils of Coke and potato chips. She dispensed aspirin and swabbed ears and treated a small boy for a respiratory ailment, instructing his mother about how to administer the medication.

A vaquero arrived in a battered truck carrying a burro, a calf, and a goat. He walked up to the ramada with a rolling gait, watched the proceedings for a while, and then said that there were many sick children in a Tarahumara village farther up in the Sierra, where he'd been looking for loose cattle. The kids were coughing worse than this one, he added, gesturing at the boy. Some were gasping for breath.

"Probably what this kid has, syncytial virus," Lisette said. She turned to the vaquero. "Can you guide us to these Tarahumara?"

"Yes," he answered confidently. "A lot of narcos up there, but it will not be a problem. They know me."

"How far is it?"

"Not too far," he said. "We can drive most of the way, then we have to walk or ride a burro."

"Damn. I wanted to be out of these mountains by dark." Lisette traded looks with Riordan. "No way I could make it back before nightfall."

"'We,' you mean. You're not going by yourself," he said, thinking of what Father Batista would have done.

Lisette stowed her equipment in the pickup, stuffed water bottles and packets of Virazone into a backpack, and left with Riordan in the vaquero's truck, banging and slamming for perhaps twenty minutes until they came to a *ciénaga* beyond a village called San Tomás. The vaquero, whose name was Esteban, off-loaded his burro, saddled it, and gallantly offered it to *la señora*. Lisette slung her backpack over the saddle horn and mounted, and they sloshed across the *ciénaga*, spoiling an egret's careful stalk.

On the other side, they continued up a stock trail. Esteban trudged in front of the burro, Riordan behind, huffing in the thin air. Cool as it was, he worked up a sweat. Half an hour later, in a narrow, rock-sided defile, the burro raised its tail and dropped a load of green horse apples. Turning as he stepped aside, Riordan recoiled and almost yelped as his eyes met the motionless eyes of a human head set in a niche illuminated by guttering vigil candles. Coarse black hair matted the skull; a mustache bristled under a blunt nose. More than a head, it was a partial torso, the broad shoulders clad in white cloth. The cry that had started in his throat died there, with the realization that he was looking at a plaster bust of Jesús Malverde, the mythical bandit who had become a saint in the narcos' pantheon. Coins, small wooden rosaries, and other offerings had been laid around the idol. Recognizing that it was nothing more than a sculpture did not completely dissolve Riordan's terror; it lingered, like the terror of a nightmare after awakening. The object's placement, there in that dim, constricted passage, seemed like a macabre warning. He walked on feeling an uneasy alertness.

The trail led down into a mosaic of meadows and trees. Through bare stalks that sprouted in one of the meadows, he saw fifty-five-gallon drums ranked against a tin shed partly concealed in a pine thicket. Smoke curled out of a stovepipe in its roof, and a breeze from its direction carried with the resinous scent of pine an alien, industrial stink that heightened his apprehension, though he couldn't say why.

His ignorance was dispelled in a moment. Lisette reined in the burro and stood in the stirrups, looking toward the shed.

"Did you know that was here?" she said to Esteban, a hint of alarm in her voice.

"*Sí, señora.*"

"Lisette, is that what I think it is?" Riordan asked in English.

Turning to him, she nodded. "A poppy plantation, and that shed is a heroin refinery. That smell? Like ammonia? Poppy sap being boiled down into morphine." She said to Esteban, "Why didn't you tell us they were making heroin up here?"

"I did tell you. A lot of narcos. It is not a problem. They know me."

"But they don't know us."

"I am well known here, señora," Esteban repeated. "It is not a problem."

But it was, despite his fame. Nor, it seemed, had his notoriety spread to the two men who roared up from below on an ATV, pistols in their waistbands.

"Who the hell are you? What the hell are you doing here?" the driver asked, making it clear that there could be no right answer to the second question.

Esteban, giving his name, explained that he was guiding these people, a doctor and a priest, to the Tarahumara village, where there were many sick children.

The driver said nothing. His sidekick said nothing. They stared with the concentration of the predators they were, then swung off the ATV. Riordan thought that the Brotherhood had hired them for their menacing looks alone. The driver wore a walrus mustache, his eyebrows formed a single black line, as if someone had scrawled a Magic Marker across his forehead, and the onyx eyes below them were as hard and shiny as buttons. The other man's face was gaunt, a famished face, the skin stretched so thin that the outline of his skull was visible.

The driver braced Esteban against the ATV and patted him down. (Professionally, Riordan noticed; the guy had probably been a cop, and maybe still was, this being Mexico.) While Gaunt One kept an eye on Esteban, Mustache searched Lisette's backpack, pulling out the cardboard packets of the antiviral drug.

"What is this?"

She told him: medication for the sick children.

Taking two or three quick steps toward the ATV, he tossed the backpack inside.

"What are you doing?" Lisette cried.

He ignored her and said, looking first at her, then at Riordan, "*Oye,* a doctor and priest. So you must be the North Americans from San Patricio. Señora Moreno and the priest they call Padre Tim." He pronounced it "Teem."

"Seems like they know who we are after all," Riordan murmured to Lisette in English. He did not mention that he found this knowledge disturbing.

"What did you say to her?" Mustache demanded.

"We're surprised you know us," Riordan answered.

"Who gave you permission to come here?"

"No one," Lisette said.

"So you do not have permission."

"We were not aware that we needed permission," said Riordan.

"You do. Now you are aware."

"Who do we ask for this permission?"

"If you don't know, find out. This is as far as you go. Turn around."

Lisette protested: There were sick children in the village! Mustache replied that she was not to concern herself with the sick children; he would see to it that they got the medicine. She hopped off the burro and faced him.

"Are you a doctor? You don't know what to do!" She jabbed a finger at the backpack, on the floor of the ATV. "Give that to me!"

Her temerity astonished Riordan but amused Mustache. At any rate, he smiled, though there was something in the smile that said it was temporary. A nation of sheep and wolves, Riordan thought. Now, confronted by two members of the ravening pack, he did not feel much like the shepherd. More like one of the sheep.

"Easy, Lisette," he said, touching her shoulder, making sure he spoke in Spanish. "We'd better do what he says."

Mustache commended his wisdom, and warned that he better not see them again without their permission slip. Looking at a cowed Esteban, he added: "That goes for you, too, Señor Vaquero."

The trio headed back down the trail, Lisette leading the burro by the reins, muttering that she was fed up with these goddamned narcos with their guns and arrogance. Riordan didn't speak; it had occurred to him that he wasn't a helpless little lamb after all. He was an angry little lamb. He began counting silently each time his left foot hit the ground. One pace equaled about five feet. Six hundred paces equaled approximately one kilometer. He made note of the terrain and the trail's general direction; with some turns north or south, it ran eastward from the *ciénaga*, which, he determined when they reached it, was about four kilometers from the refinery. The odometer and speedometer on Esteban's truck were broken, but Riordan was able to estimate its average speed, and he timed the drive to Mesa Verde at precisely eighteen minutes. Call it twenty to make the math easier. Around seven kilometers, making eleven altogether.

These simple observations and calculations renewed his confidence. He felt rather good, in fact. *If you know something, say something.* Now he knew something.

CHAPTER FIFTEEN

In the early morning, as he performed his ritual, turning himself under the stars so that they seemed to be slowly wheeling above him rather than he beneath them, Riordan heard a rhythmic throbbing in the distance. The pounding of rotor blades grew louder, and it was close to deafening as the helicopters flew directly over San Patricio. He could see their navigation lights but not how many there were, or if they were military, though he assumed they were—they had come in from the west, probably taking off from the air force base near Hermosillo. He further assumed that their destination was the heroin refinery; two days ago, right after he and Lisette had returned from the Sierra Madre, he had called Inspector Bonham on the burner phone, reported what they'd seen, and relayed the results of his time and distance calculations.

His assumptions were correct, but he didn't know that until the next afternoon, when the Hermosillo newspapers were delivered. "ARMED FORCES DEAL THE BROTHERHOOD A BLOW," read a front-page headline. The raid was the lead story on TV, with video clips showing troops torching the poppy fields and the refinery, stacking morphine and heroin bricks (an estimated value, said the reporter, of more than $3 million) alongside a cache of captured weapons, and several handcuffed narcos, none of whom Riordan recognized as he watched in the rectory parlor with Father Hugo and the Old Priest. He hoped the two thugs on the ATV were among them.

Only Bonham and Valencia knew of his role in the raid. During the phone call, after he'd presented his information, Bonham ordered him not to tell anyone they had spoken. Not now, not ever.

"How about your girlfriend? Did you mention that you were going to call me?"

"She's not my girlfriend, and no, I didn't say a thing to her."

"And you're not going to," Bonham repeated, with a sternness that was a little frightening. "The fewer people who know, the better. It's for your own good. The narcos know you two were up there. After we hit them, they might do some simple arithmetic and finger you or her or both of you. And don't think for one second your Roman collar or your gringo passport will save you. I'll bet you didn't consider that, did you?"

Riordan was silent.

Bonham promised to "throw out some smoke" by telling the media that the crew of a military reconnaissance plane had located a heroin factory while on a routine patrol.

"You did a damn good job. Even Valencia was impressed," he said. "Don't worry—I take care of my assets."

The praise did not warm Riordan particularly; nor did the assurance. *Asset.* Is that what I am? An asset? he wondered. Then another question: What have I gotten myself into?

He answered it on the day following the raid, when he ran into Lisette and she remarked, "What a coincidence, right where we'd been last Tuesday. It *was* a coincidence, wasn't it Tim?" she asked. What troubled him more than his lie was the ease and sincerity with which he told it. He seemed to have a capacity for dissimulation he'd been unaware of. What if the Brotherhood didn't buy the cover story and did the simple arithmetic? He was ready—at least he thought he was—to suffer the consequences, but he couldn't live with himself if anything happened to her. That possibility chipped at his resolve to keep the truth from her. Someone had to strike back at the wolves. Why not him? Emotion without action is sentimentality, and words could be action. He'd known something, he'd said something. But in exiting one house of silence, he'd entered another—the one where informants dwelled. That's what he'd gotten himself into.

■ ■ ■

At the hour when last light drew the Sierra's ravines and ridges into sharp relief, he crossed the plaza and walked half a block down Avenida Juárez to the Hotel Alameda. Riordan dined there now and then to mingle socially with his parishioners—and to get away from the cloistered, hothouse atmosphere of the rectory. The Alameda dated back to the 1940s, when San Patricio began to be known as a destination for adventurous travelers on the Mission Trail. It would take a foolhardy tourist to visit San Patricio today. Not one of the hotel's ten rooms had been occupied for the past decade. But the bar and restaurant, grandly called the "Salón Alameda," were still in operation, catering to a local clientele. Riordan loved its Bogie-and-Bacall ambience: ceiling fans, white and black hexagonal floor tiles, a mahogany bar, faux-marble tables.

The place was depressingly empty this evening. The sole occupants, aside from a customer at the bar, were the bartender and a waiter wearing a starched white jacket. Riordan took a small table against a wall decorated with movie posters plugging Mexican and American films from a bygone time, the names of the actors and actresses no longer remembered, with the possible exceptions of a sultry Gina Lollobrigida swooning in Burt Lancaster's arms.

The waiter, rather ceremoniously, said that the hotel was pleased to see Padre Tim in its dining room once again. Riordan couldn't help it— the respect in the man's voice sent a tickle of pride through him.

"I know you like to read these when you eat," the waiter added, handing him copies of *El Diario de Juárez* and the Hermosillo paper, *El Imparcial*.

He ordered a Herradura on the rocks and, without looking at the menu, a bowl of menudo.

"Is that all? You look thinner than last time you were here."

"I am trying to fast."

"We have *cabrilla* tonight. Excellent *cabrilla*. Broiled."

"I promised God I would fast."

"This *cabrilla* is fresh, Padre Tim. It was shipped here today from Guaymas."

"You are the voice of the devil. Well, I suppose I can return to fasting tomorrow."

"Yes. Better to fast tomorrow, when the *cabrilla* will be stale and dry."

The news of the day required a stiff drink, and Riordan waited until the tequila arrived to read the papers. *El Diario* carried a front-page story about an attack on a drug rehabilitation clinic in Juárez, which had recently acquired an unenviable distinction: it was the deadliest city in the world, including Baghdad. Gunmen wearing "police-style" uniforms had stormed the clinic while the director was holding a prayer meeting, killing him and nine patients, some of whom were believed to belong to a drug gang called the Artist Assassins. No one was willing to say whether the killers were policemen or gang rivals disguised as policemen. A photograph showed a shrine to the Virgin of Guadalupe chipped by bullets, the wall behind it spattered with blood.

The waiter brought the menudo, steaming in a blue bowl. Tripe soup seemed fitting for his reading fare. EVITA CONTRERAS HABLAR SOBRE NARCOMENSAJES, read a headline in *El Imparcial*. "Contreras Avoids Speaking About Narco Messages." Octavio Contreras had been the losing candidate for mayor of Hermosillo in this year's elections. The messages about which he refused comment had been printed on bedsheets hung in several places throughout the city. They accused him of being an atheist, a front man for Carrasco's old Sonora Cartel, and a thief. They concluded ominously, if obscurely, *Ahora llega nuestro turno*, "Now comes our turn." And they were signed, "La Fraternidad."

No comment. No comment. Avoids speaking about . . . Riordan thought. The house of silence. The broiled fish arrived whole on a platter, its flame-whitened eyes staring through a crust of spices and bread crumbs. From out of nowhere, the melody to "The Sound of Silence" started to play in his memory. He separated the meat from the bones and began to eat. He could not get the tune out of his head—an earworm, burrowing a channel into his brain. He had finished only half his meal when he felt something moving through him, a kind of pressure as words flowed into the channel, a swift tide of words that burst the banks and flooded his mind. He asked the waiter for a pen and some paper place mats. The waiter frowned, quizzically.

"To write on," Riordan explained.

The requested items were brought. He turned a mat over to its plain side and began to write. He made no attempt to organize his thoughts, jotting them down as they came to him. He scribbled in a rush, compulsively, feeling like an overwrought coffeehouse poet. But he stayed within his theme: it was time for everyone in the parish to abandon their houses of silence. In fragmented sentences, he tried to express his contempt for the narcos and their savagery—and his disapproval of those in the parish who had shut their eyes, their ears, their minds and mouths to the scourge that was all around them. He had only a vague idea, at first, of his purpose in writing; but when he'd filled two mats with his near-illegible scrawl, it came to him that he was composing a rough draft, a very rough draft, of Sunday's homily. It would be like none he'd given before.

He wrote on, in a physical as well as a mental heat, breaking out in a sweat, until the waiter interrupted him.

"Pardon me, Padre. Jamie wishes to buy you a drink."

"What? Who?"

The waiter gestured at the customer at the bar, who swung around on the stool to face him. It was Jamie García, the man who had left the message with Domingo asking to speak with Riordan. How long ago was it now? Two weeks at least, maybe three.

"Another Herradura. On the rocks."

It was delivered shortly. He rolled the chilled glass across his forehead to cool the fever in his brain, then raised it in thanks to García.

"Padre Tim, can I join you for a moment?" the man called from across the room.

Riordan motioned to him, and he came over and sat down, looking as if he could crush the table with his bare hands. García was six feet tall, with an engine block of a torso and fingers as thick and brown as cigars.

"You don't mind? I see that you're busy."

"I don't mind at all. I should have called you days ago."

García wanted to have a word with Riordan about his middle son,

Danielo, who had been keeping odd hours, coming home at dawn, sleeping in till noon, driving off to who knew where in his brand-new truck. Danielo claimed to have a job at the copper mine, working a night shift, which may have accounted for those strange hours; but he was never dirty, and he could not possibly afford such a fine truck on a miner's wages. Jamie was worried that his son was using drugs or, worse, had become involved with "those people." (That was how nearly everyone referred to La Fraternidad, as if too fearful to utter its name.)

"Would you talk to him, Padre Tim? He's only twenty-one. He's young enough to straighten out if he's doing something he should not be doing."

"Have you spoken to him?"

"Sure. And not only once. But I can say nothing to him without making a big fight."

Riordan felt for the man. He knew that García had been a fairly prosperous apple grower whose small orchard in the Santa Teresa valley produced enough fruit for sale as far away as Mexico City, with some left over for export. NAFTA ruined him, along with a million other small farmers in Mexico. American apples, more aesthetic than the Mexican variety, tumbled into the country by the trainload, while those grown in the country fell into the grasp of agribusiness giants. García couldn't compete, sold out to one of the big firms for half of what his orchard was worth, and had been scraping by as a seasonal field hand ever since.

Yes, Riordan said, he would speak to Danielo, but only if Danny came to him.

"I thank you," García said, enveloping Riordan's hand in his.

■ ■ ■

He never expected to see Danielo, and so he was caught off balance when García's son showed up the next afternoon at the parish office, breaking Riordan's concentration—he was working on his sermon, revising, polishing, imposing order and clarity on the semicoherent sentences.

Danielo was built like Jamie, and an inch taller; his body communicated irresistible leverage. He was got up like a well-off young ranchero in a beaverskin Stetson, a suede jacket over a white shirt, starched Levi's with a crease that could slice butter, quilled boots polished to a high gloss.

"My father wants me to see you. I respect him, so here I am," he said, smirking, hooking his thumbs into his tooled leather belt.

"That isn't what I heard," Riordan said, annoyed by Danielo's cocksure manner.

"What did you hear? From who?"

"From him. That every time he tries to talk to you there's an argument."

"I promise not to argue with you," he said.

Surrendering all hope of resuming work, Riordan invited him to have a seat.

"Not here," Danielo said. "I don't want to talk here."

"Where would you find suitable?" asked Riordan, unable to keep a caustic note out of his voice.

"Would it be all right if we rode around in my truck?" Danielo said, now with more civility.

"Your truck . . . Where . . . ?"

"Just ride around."

Something to hide, Riordan thought.

"All right, but no more than half an hour."

It was a flame-red Chevy Silverado with a ton of chrome, and Danielo, like any twenty-one-year-old, was proud of it. They cruised through the pueblo for a while, Danny bragging about the Chevy: the big engine, the extended crew cab, the radio with Bose speakers, the GPS—

"I don't think your father expects me to talk cars with you," Riordan said to end the monologue.

"Okay. I guess you should start, Padre, because I'm not sure what he wants me and you to talk about."

"He's worried that you might be using drugs."

"Then this will be a short talk. I don't do drugs. Never use product—that's what I've been told."

Riordan recognized that phrase, the professional narco's rule of thumb.

"It's 'product' to you. So you're selling the stuff?"

"I don't sell drugs," Danielo answered, sounding rather pleased.

"Another thing on your father's mind is where you got the money for a truck like this. I'm not interrogating you, but do you mind telling me?"

"I don't sell drugs," he repeated, driving along slowly, casually resting the wrist of one hand on the wheel. "But maybe you're getting warm."

"What is that supposed to mean?"

Danielo shrugged.

"A truck like this must cost two hundred thousand pesos—"

"*Tres*," Danielo said smugly.

"*Trescientos mil!* On a miner's salary?"

"I'm not a miner, Padre Tim. I'll show you."

At a traffic circle, Danielo turned down a street that soon became the dirt road leading out of town toward the copper mine. After a mile or so, he stopped on a rise overlooking a huge wound in the earth from which pale dust rose in tendrils, like steam from a volcanic crater.

"What are we doing out here?" Riordan asked.

Danielo replied with his own question: "Do you know who owns that?"

"A Canadian company, Reliance Resources."

"They're part owners. I don't work for them. I don't work in the mine. I work for the partners."

"I see. And who are these partners and what do you do for them?"

"Anything you say to a priest is a secret, is that right?"

"Anything said in confession, yes."

Danielo switched the engine off and put the parking brake on and turned toward Riordan.

"Okay, then. I want to make a confession."

"Confessions are on Friday afternoons at four. If you came to church now and then, you would know that."

Too sharp, Riordan chided himself.

"Sure. But I'd like to confess now, here," said Danielo. "I'd like to go to Communion tomorrow. My father, you know, he goes every Sunday, and he wants all of us to go with him because it's almost Christmas. I think that's why he wanted me to talk to you."

His manner and tone had passed rather quickly—too quickly, it seemed—from cocky and flippant to earnest and reasonable.

"If you're not sincere about it, it won't be valid," Riordan said.

"Didn't I say I was?"

This would be another first for Riordan: hearing a confession in a pickup truck. He had an inkling that Danielo might be manipulating him, but there was no way to refuse him. He removed his purple stole from his pocket and draped it over his neck to make things look proper. They went through the ritual right there in the Chevy Silverado, Danielo admitting that he'd missed Mass for at least a year of Sundays, that he'd had premarital sex—he couldn't recall how many times, but a lot— that he'd fought with his father, dishonoring him, oh, it must have been on three or four occasions, but swearing, all the while looking into Riordan's eyes with a straightforward expression, that he'd never killed anyone, never touched a bale of *mota* or a brick of heroin.

"Danny, you don't have to confess to what you did not do," Riordan said, thinking that Danielo was angling to be excused from some as yet unconfessed trespasses. "Is there anything else?" he inquired.

"Like what?"

"Like what you do for these people you call 'the partners.'"

Shifting his gaze from Riordan's face, Danielo looked thoughtfully out the windshield.

"I . . . you know . . . I hurt a couple of people for them. Not real bad. I beat them up a little. They hired me because of my size and because I do some boxing."

"So did I when I was young—boxed, that is. Go on. Why did you beat them up?"

"The rule is this: If somebody screws up, like steals or something, they get a warning first. The second time, they get beat up. The third time . . . you know."

"I know, sure. But you swore to me that you've never killed anybody."

"I swear it a second time."

"You're forcing me to pull things out of you. Are you sorry for what you did? Do you still beat people up for these partners?"

"No!" Danielo replied. "I've been promoted. I'm like an executive who keeps the accounts settled. The mine owes the partners so much per ton of ore per week."

"Who are the partners? The Brotherhood?"

"The partners are the partners. All I do for them is check up on production and make sure the mine doesn't cheat. I don't see what's so wrong with that."

"Then let me help you see. It's called extortion," Riordan said, pouring judgment into the word. "Extortion would fall under the Seventh Commandment. Every week, you're stealing."

"That's what you call it," Danielo said, turning sullen.

"A mine foreman was murdered a while back for refusing to pay."

"I wasn't involved in that. How many times do I have to tell you that I never did anything like that?"

"Some other people have had to pay *cuota*. Do you collect from them, too?"

"The mine, that's all I do. It brings in a lot of money."

At a meeting last year of the diocesan priests, the assembled clerics had discussed what they should do, what they could do about the narcos. You must try to change their interior life, the bishop advised. You must try to change their values. Think of Christ entering the house of Zacchaeus. Appropriate in this case, Riordan thought. Zacchaeus had been a tax collector, and in a sense, so was Danielo. But the bishop's counsel seemed abstract and even silly now, as he sat in the shiny Silverado beside the young criminal. How was he to change Danielo García's values?

He said, "You know that to belong to a mafia is a sin. Anyone mixed up with those people cannot go to Communion."

"I do what I do because I have to," Danielo said, a plea in his voice expressing, if not contrition, then something like regret. "Come by our house. New furniture. I bought it. A new TV. I bought it. We don't have to eat beans and rice every day because we can afford chicken, pork, steak. I'm not going to be like my father, picking fruit for pesos."

I could hear the same argument from some punk dealer on the South Side of Chicago, Riordan thought.

"You must get out," he said. "If you care at all about your soul, you've got to find a way out."

Danielo's lips curled in scorn. "You don't quit those people—you know that."

"This truck, the TV, the steaks—maybe that's what you don't want to quit."

"I would if I could. I'm telling you the truth, Padre Tim."

"You had better be. God knows the truth of what's in your heart, and if sincere contrition isn't in your heart . . . The best way for you to show that it is is to change your life. I cannot absolve you if you aren't sorry for what you've done and you don't pledge to change your life."

Which Danielo did. Riordan did not believe one word of it, if for no other reason than Danielo was right: you did not quit "those people," because to quit them was to hand yourself a death sentence. He couldn't demand that a twenty-one-year-old kid sacrifice his life. There was in the end no choice but to take him at his word.

But when he returned to the rectory, he was troubled by the thought that he'd immersed himself in a charade, a simulacrum of a sacrament. He felt like taking a shower in the hottest water he could stand.

■ ■ ■

His sermon on that Sunday in Advent did not express the usual ano-dyne sentiments about the joy of the Christmas season—all Christians awaiting, anticipation in their hearts, the birth of their Savior. He mounted the pulpit and, for five or six seconds, said nothing as he swept his eyes over the congregation. This was long enough to provoke some uneasiness, people clearing their throats, squirming in the pews. Good. Discomfort was the effect he wanted to achieve. His dramatic silence was followed by a dramatic gesture: he unfurled the visual aid he'd cre-ated the previous night out of an old bedsheet and draped it over the front of the pulpit. Printed on it in red block letters were the names of the eleven men slain by narcos in the parish in the past year alone. And still he did not speak, allowing another few seconds to pass before he startled everyone by uttering a single word in a full-throated voice:

"SILENCE!"

After an interval during which the parishioners froze in their seats and lifted their gazes to his face, he began:

"Octavio Mirales . . . Roberto Sánchez . . . Miguel Patiño . . ." He read the rest of the names down to the last.

"What you have just heard are the sounds that silence makes," he said. "The names of our dead, young men torn from life by the criminals in our midst. This will be the topic of my sermon for today, silence and the sounds it makes." Looking over the pews, he saw that he had everyone's attention. No fidgeting or nodding off or wandering gazes—the typical responses to his homilies. "There are other sounds, the mourning of their mothers, their wives, their children . . . the grief that will shriek forever in the hearts of their fathers and brothers and sisters. What is silenced is the sound of gunfire, of a man's screams as he is tortured before he is murdered, and this, too—of young women brutally kidnapped and raped." He avoided making eye contact with Cristina Herrera, so as not to call attention to her. "It is the sound of our police officers telling the victim of a rape that she should consider herself fortunate not to have been killed." His glance fell on a municipal police sergeant, Rigoberto Ochoa. "And it is the sound of witnesses to all these abominations . . . SAYING NOTHING!"

Riordan paused and again scanned the congregation for several long seconds. "Most of you fear even to speak the name of the wolf pack that menaces us. I myself was reluctant to say it out loud—but no longer. . . . THE BROTHERHOOD! I will name them, too, the pack's leaders: Ernesto Salazar. Enrique Mora. Rubén Levya! They are the wolves who savage us with abductions, murder, extortions." Now he noticed movements in the pews, parishioners turning their heads right and left, as if expecting armed thugs to burst into the church at any moment, but he rolled on, praising the brave men who had volunteered for the citizens' militia, scathing those who thought the narcos were the true *valientes*, exhorting everyone to abandon the house of silence and speak out. "If you know something, then say it. Report it to the authorities. I know that because of what happened here last month, many of you think the army and the Federal Police are as much your enemy as the Brotherhood—but we must give them a vote of confidence that they will have the resolve and the intention to deliver us from this evil. They cannot carry out their duties if we do not carry out ours, if we do not STAND UP AND SPEAK OUT!"

Pausing once more, he looked from face to face and found Danielo García looking back at him with an obdurate tilt to his chin. "I want to remind you of another duty you have as Catholics," he said, in the rhythms of a hellfire tent revivalist. "Some of you have fallen into criminal activities, some of you have colluded with the narcos, and so you have contributed to this culture of violence and death. . . . You are in a state of sin if you belong to the Brotherhood. To any narco gang. You know who you are."

He gave his parishioners a final, measured look before stepping down to the altar. Many people were staring at him as if he'd taken leave of his senses; no priest had ever spoken to them as he had.

He felt light, relieved of a burden, as he led them through the Nicene Creed and the recitation of the Lord's Prayer—*Deliver us, O Lord, from every evil, for Thine is the kingdom and the power and the glory, now and forever*—and through the consecrating of the hosts and wine, arriving at the high point of the Mass, Communion.

Cuerpo de Cristo, he murmured. *Sangre de Cristo,* murmured the lay assistant beside him, proffering the chalice. Mouths opened at the Communion rail; the tips of tongues darted out. Like baby birds in a nest, he thought. Others took the host in cupped hands. *Cuerpo de Cristo*—Father Hugo was giving Communion at the rail on the right side of the center aisle. *Sangre de Cristo,* said Father Hugo's assistant, wiping the chalice's rim with a cloth before presenting it to the next communicant. Body of Christ. Blood of Christ. Intoned over and over. It seemed that everyone at Mass this Sunday had a spotless soul.

With the rail emptied, those waiting in line behind stepped up and knelt, hands folded. César and Marta Díaz, César's sister-in-law, Lupita. Was she still cursing God? Domingo and Delores Quiroga. He hesitated as he approached the next two: the Very Pious Señora Herrera and her daughter. Body of Christ, he whispered to the señora and side-stepped to Cristina, who, as her mother returned to their pew, bowed her head and crossed her arms over her chest. This gesture meant that she was in mortal sin but was asking for his blessing. Had she gone through with it? He blessed her, drawing the sign of the cross on her forehead with his thumb. The García family was at the end of the rail: Jaime and his wife, his three sons, Danielo the last. Riordan placed the host on his upturned palms. *Cuerpo de Cristo.*

Following the recessional, he took his customary place at the front door to greet his parishioners. Two or three mumbled congratulations for the sermon. César was more effusive, clapping him on the back. "You let us have it, Padre Tim, and good for you." But most people merely nodded to him or shook his hand and went on their way; and some steered clear of him, as if he carried a contagion.

As he went back into the church, he caught a movement in a corner of the vestibule. A figure stepped out of the shadows and stood still, hands crossed over his groin. It was Danielo.

Riordan's throat clutched. Danielo's face seemed to have undergone a transformation: it looked as hard, cold, and immobile as the marble face of some cruel Roman emperor, and the eyes meeting Riordan's were lifeless. It was probably the look Danielo put on when making his weekly collection, Riordan realized. But he couldn't permit himself to be intimidated by a twenty-one-year-old thug.

"What do you want, Danny?" he said brusquely.

Danielo stuck out his tongue. The white glob on it looked like a wad of gum. He spat the Communion host at Riordan's feet, turned, and walked outside, leaving Riordan so shocked that he could not move.

YouTube COMMUNIQUÉ #2

VIDEO: Women in bright pastel dresses that hang like scalloped draperies are lined up in front of a cave that's been converted into a house, the entrance modified and framed to form a door, the front faced with mortared river rocks. Some of the women carry dirt-smudged children in cloth sacks slúng from their backs, papoose-style; others hold toddlers by the hand. The children can be heard coughing and wheezing.

AUDIO (VOICE-OVER): Brothers and sisters! Good day once again from the *comandancia* of the Brotherhood in the Sierra Madre. It is I, the Butterfly, who spreads his beautiful wings and flies to you wherever you are to bring you news. In my last communiqué, I promised justice, and it is news of justice I bring you. Two kinds of justice.

Our Lord and Savior commands us to care for the poor and the sick. It is a command which we of the Brotherhood take seriously. This was the scene recently in the *aldea* of San Miguel, inhabited by the Tarahumara people . . .

VIDEO: Two men in sun-bleached denim jackets seated behind a table made of planks laid across sawhorses. Small boxes of medication are spread on the table.

CLOSE on a box. The label reads: Virazone. WIDE on the women as they step up one by one to the table, the two men handing tablets to each.

AUDIO (VOICE-OVER): These children were suffering from infections in their lungs, from bronchitis and even pneumonia. When we of the Brotherhood learned about this, we immediately dispatched a medical team to be of assistance. Our team obtained this medicine and dispensed it to the sick children of San Miguel. This is social justice, brothers and sisters. Perhaps our government could stop sending soldiers to terrorize the people and instead send medical teams to heal them when they are sick.

And now for another kind of justice, a stern but necessary justice. In my previous message, I told you about the murders of two innocent young men in the pueblo of San Patricio. They were murdered last month by soldiers while peaceably protesting against the military's oppression. Only last week, these same soldiers came to the *aldea* of Mesa Verde to spread more of their terror and oppression, but the Brotherhood was there to intercept them . . .

VIDEO: In a meadow, four soldiers wearing combat uniforms sit gagged, blindfolded, and bound by ropes to white plastic chairs. The gags and blindfolds appear to wrap around bare poles behind the chairs, as if to hold the soldiers' heads upright. A placard hangs from the neck of each, with his last name and the word *asesino* printed beneath it and, beneath that, the Brotherhood's logo. A burst of automatic weapons fire comes from offscreen. The soldiers twitch and jump from the bullets' impact, but they are trussed so tightly to the chairs that they don't fall. The camera lingers on them as the narration resumes.

AUDIO (VOICE-OVER): I, the Butterfly, send this video postcard to the families of the army's victims, so you will know that a just vengeance now is yours. As I said last time, we keep our promises.

FADE TO BLACK.

CHAPTER SIXTEEN

Brooding about Danielo's sacrilege, Riordan swung from self-criticism (he had failed to change that sinner's interior life) to an un-Christian thought (some people were beyond redemption) to an un-Christian emotion: rage. Alone in his room after Compline, when he should have been meditating, he would find himself wishing he were still a young middleweight so he could pound the fear of God into Danielo. And then he would swing back around to excoriating himself for harboring such an impious wish.

Preparations for *Las Posadas*, the procession of the Holy Family during the nine days before Christmas, saved him from further morbid reflections. There was a lot to do. Like a casting director, he auditioned couples who would play the innkeepers and listened to a young man and woman rehearsing for their roles as Mary and Joseph. He and Father Hugo met with the costume committee, the food committee, the decoration committee. He threw himself into these efforts, pitching in to string Christmas lights in the plaza. If he did not quite feel the joy he was supposed to feel in the season, he at least felt like a normal pastor in a normal parish in normal times. An illusion, but sometimes illusions were necessary merely to get through the day.

The pageant's first night fell, as was the custom, on December 16. The marchers, bundled up against the cold, assembled in the plaza, satisfactorily festive in the lights that garlanded the trees and twined around the bandstand's iron trellises like multicolored vines. Children lined up, carrying lanterns and wearing cast-off bed linens refashioned to simulate shepherds' garb. Draped in blue and white robes, the woman portraying Mary mounted a donkey; Joseph, with a costume-shop beard strung from his ears, stood beside her.

Riordan and Father Hugo led the procession twice around the plaza as the marchers sang "Feliz Navidad" and carols familiar to everyone in what used to be called Christendom. They trooped up Calle Juárez to the house of Domingo and Delores Quiroga, who would play the innkeepers tonight. César and Marta Díaz were to assume the role tomorrow night. A different house each night until the climax on Christmas Eve.

The marchers halted and gathered around the pilgrims. Their breath plumed in the brisk night air; lanterns formed a flickering semicircle.

Joseph stepped up to the door and began to sing:

> *In the name of heaven,*
> *Who will give lodging*
> *To these pilgrims, weary*
> *From walking the roads?*

From inside, Domingo sang his response, his terrible voice provoking giggles:

> *This is not an inn*
> *Get on with you,*
> *I cannot open the door,*
> *You could be a robber.*

The back-and-forth was supposed to go on, Joseph identifying himself as a carpenter from Nazareth, the innkeeper, increasingly belligerent, refusing to open his door, until Joseph proclaimed that his wife was Mary, Queen of Heaven, and soon-to-be mother to the Divine Word. The innkeeper was then to relent and bid the couple to enter his house. As they did, the procession would follow them, everyone singing,

Enter holy pilgrims,
Receive not this poor dwelling
But my heart.
Tonight is for rejoicing,
For tonight we will give lodging
To the Mother of God the Son.

But that was not what happened. The argument between Joseph and the innkeeper was interrupted halfway through by the frantic whoop of a siren, stroboscopic flashes, a spotlight's glare. A Federal Police SUV came up the street from the direction of the plaza and stopped a few yards short of the crowd. Behind it hulked a troop carrier crammed with soldiers, helmeted and bristling with weapons. A voice boomed from a bullhorn on the police car's roof: "Return to your homes immediately! A curfew is in effect! Until further notice, you will stay inside your homes from six at night till six in the morning! Anyone violating the curfew will be subject to arrest!"

The marchers milled around in confusion, shielding their eyes from the spotlight. Small children began to wail. Somewhere, a woman called out, "Padre Tim! Padre Beltrán! Talk to them!" Right then, the soldiers piled out of the troop carrier and blocked the street, holding their rifles and gas-grenade launchers at high port.

"If you people do not disperse immediately, you will be arrested. Return to your homes now! And stay there!"

Riordan stiffened and started toward the police car. *"Con calma, Padre Tim. Tranquilamente,"* cautioned Father Hugo, laying a hand on his arm. Riordan shook it off gently, composed himself, and approached the car, making an awning with his hand against the blinding spotlight. The *federale* in the passenger seat swung his door open. The bullhorn's microphone lay in his lap.

"Padre, you had better get these people off the street, or we will. You have three minutes."

"What is the meaning of this?" he demanded. "This is a Christmas pageant. It is not a demonstration."

"Did you hear me? As of tonight, there will be a curfew from six to six, until further notice."

"What for? We're not doing anything illegal."

"Now you've got two minutes," the *federale* said; then, tempering his tone somewhat: "Look, I don't want to arrest these people, but I will if I have to."

Riordan sensed a kind of static electricity in the air, a crackling of dread.

"One minute and thirty seconds."

"Let me have that," he said, indicating the microphone.

■ ■ ■

Riordan's illusions of normality underwent further demolition the following day. Squads of policemen and paratroopers ranged through town, barged into homes, and seized six or seven young men. No reasons were given for the arrests, no information as to where the prisoners had been taken. The next day, the acting mayor led a convoy of citizens toward the military base to protest; it was turned back at the roadblock, and the mayor himself arrested for his trouble. He was released within a few hours, but there was no word about the others.

Twenty-four hours later, a delegation of mothers and wives, swearing that their men were not narcos, fearing that they would join Mexico's *los desaparecidos*—the disappeared—appealed to Riordan to intervene. The authorities would not listen to them or the mayor, but if they had Christian bones in their bodies, they might listen to a priest.

Although he doubted that Inspector Bonham's bones had any religious affiliation, he made two tries to reach him on the burner phone, and got an answer on the third. What was going on? Curfews, arbitrary arrests that were nothing more than legalized kidnappings. Things were as bad as they had been at the height of the Brotherhood's reign of terror.

"Not in the Christmas spirit, I agree," Bonham said, and Riordan shot back that he didn't think this was an occasion for sarcasm. He then ticked off the roster of missing detainees: Álvarez, Durán, Rodríguez, and four more. Where were they, and what were the charges against them?

"Be at the base in an hour," Bonham answered, in a tone that left no room for discussion. "I'll notify the roadblock to let you through and make sure you have gate clearance."

Riordan quickly pulled off his Franciscan habit—the billowy garment could be hazardous on a motorcycle—and changed into his jeans and leather jacket. As he strode out to the Harley, recalling Father Hugo's and the Old Priest's warnings about foreigners who meddled in official state business, he wondered if he was being led into a trap. Maybe Captain Valencia, with Bonham's acquiescence, if not his connivance, intended to arrest him. That seemed a paranoid fantasy, but in Mexico the fantastic often turned out to be real.

■ ■ ■

In his rush, he had forgotten his helmet. The cold air that slapped his face and whipped through his hair when he opened the throttle exhilarated him. His skin burned from the ride as he dismounted and was escorted through the gate by a paratrooper.

"A good-looking motorcycle," the trooper said. "Leave it here. Nobody's going to steal it."

The base was larger than it appeared from the outside, about the size of a soccer field, and more intimidating, what with machine guns mounted on the armored vehicles and razor wire and dozens of soldiers and police officers in body armor. But he decided not to look cowed or apprehensive, and affected a swagger as his escort led him past a row of green wall tents to a low bungalow shaded by eucalyptus trees: Captain Valencia's private quarters.

He and Bonham were seated inside on identical easy chairs, the inspector in plain clothes, Valencia in his field uniform, the sleeves rolled up to the elbows with military precision. There was a laptop on a table between them, and on the wall behind them, a painting of some nineteenth-century battle. Valencia's greeting, while less than friendly, could not help but be more cordial than at their first meeting. He got up, shook hands, addressing his visitor as Padre Riordan instead of as "priest," and praised the accuracy of his intelligence. The poppy field and the heroin lab were almost exactly where he'd reported them to be.

"We had gotten a tip about it," he said in his lightly accented English. "You saved us a lot of trouble. It pleases me that you can do something more useful than spreading superstition."

That was more in character, Riordan thought.

Bonham motioned at a folding chair facing him and the captain.

Valencia, resuming his seat, expelled a breath and said, "So, you have some complaints." With a twirl of his hands, he invited Riordan to air them, which he did, feeling bold, more like the scrappy Irish kid he'd once been than a middle-aged friar. He pulled a list of names from his pants pocket and shoved it into Valencia's hands.

"What is this?"

"Those are the men you have arrested. What for? Where are they? What have they been charged with? What's the reason for the curfew? What gives you the idea that your men can break up a Christmas pageant and kick doors down and drag people off, like—"

"You're not making a complaint, you're conducting an interrogation," the captain interrupted, and what little warmth there had been in his expression vanished. "We do that, not you."

"About a week ago, I gave a sermon," Riordan said. "I told my parishioners to cooperate with the army and the police, that it's their duty not to be silent. I told them to have confidence in you, and now you do this. You behave like an army of occupation."

An angry edge had infiltrated his voice, but Valencia was unmoved.

"The suspects aren't here. We turned them over to the Federal Police." He handed the list to Bonham, who didn't bother to read it. "Perhaps the inspector can enlighten you as to their whereabouts."

A cute little game, Riordan thought as he said, "*Suspects*? What are they suspected of?"

"We'll get into that, but first you need to see one more entertaining video," said Bonham, opening the laptop on the table. "It was posted this morning. We want you to see it before it goes viral, if it hasn't already."

Riordan heard again the mechanical, monotonous voice of Julián Menéndez, a.k.a. Ernesto Salazar, a.k.a. the Butterfly. Three minutes, twenty-four seconds later, he sat staring at a black screen, much of the boldness and swagger draining out of him as he tried to process what he'd seen in the brief, final sequence.

"My men," said Valencia, his jaw tightening. "They went missing three days before your pageant. We found their bodies the next day, still in the chairs, with those cards hanging from their necks. We also found their SandCat, riddled with bullet holes, some distance from where we found them. Blood all over the seats. . . . You look perplexed, Padre."

Riordan said he was. He hadn't heard a whisper about this massacre.

"We have kept it secret. We did not want the press to get ahold of it. But now it's very public."

"But if they were killed in their SandCat . . . ?"

Bonham spoke: "This is the cartel's answer to the raid on the heroin refinery. But it's also a kind of two-part propaganda video. The Brotherhood winning hearts and minds in part one, meting out justice in part two."

"The medications they were passing out—"

"*Exactamente!*" said Bonham, making a stab with a finger. "The ones you told me were confiscated from Moreno. A windfall for the narcos, and they took advantage of it, showing what great guys they are, caring for the sick. And to prove what badasses they are, they staged the executions. Not one of those four troopers pulled the triggers that killed Díaz and Reyes. They weren't even in the plaza the day of the demonstration. The whole thing was faked. A fake medical team handing out medicine, a fake execution."

"You mean . . . ?"

"Oh, no. Those were real bullets and real dead men. But did you notice anything unusual?"

Riordan snorted. "It's unusual for me to watch a video of people being shot to death."

"That isn't what you saw. I'll replay the last few seconds—"

"No, thank you."

"All right. If I did, you would see that there isn't any blood. Any fresh blood. When the camera holds on the bodies after the gunfire . . . not a drop of blood. You would also notice that their heads are tied to stakes behind the chairs. For the sake of verisimilitude."

Riordan frowned in mute bewilderment.

"To make it look like they were alive. Those guys were already dead. Dead long enough to have bled out and for the blood to have dried and blended in with the camouflage pattern of their uniforms."

"It was a trap," Valencia spat out. Leaning back, he crossed his arms, the muscles in them like thin steel cables. "You see, we got another tip, also anonymous, that there was another poppy field up there. I sent the squad to check it out. They drove into an ambush on the Mesa Verde road, and then their bodies were taken somewhere else and tied up in the chairs and shot to make it look like they had been captured and executed."

"Salazar could have videoed the bodies after the ambush, but that wouldn't be half as dramatic as showing an execution," Bonham elaborated. "Their bodies were props."

Seated between the two men, Riordan swiveled his head from one to the other, like a spectator at a tennis match.

"But there is another possibility," Valencia said. He set his lips into a straight line. "Someone else ambushed my troops, maybe a rival gang. The Brotherhood discovered the bodies and saw an opportunity to make use of them."

"Another windfall," Bonham added. "But that theory is pretty far-fetched. The simplest explanation is usually the right one, and the simplest explanation for this bloodbath is that the Brotherhood did it."

"The question being, Who in the Brotherhood? Who pulled the triggers?" Valencia turned aside and, reaching across the table, plucked the list from Bonham's lap. "So you have these names . . ."

Riordan rediscovered his voice: "They couldn't have done it. I know those men. One of them—Durán—is a college student home on vacation. They're not narcos, and they're certainly not *sicarios*."

"Possibly you are right. But we think that they might know something—"

"And we're trying to convince them to say something," Bonham interjected.

"You have your list, I want mine, Padre Riordan," Valencia went on, with venomous calm. "I want to know, who was this informant who gave the false tip? I want the names of the men who butchered mine. If I have to arrest everybody in your parish to find out, I will."

"Do you want to know what that will accomplish, Captain? Zero."

"Then should I arrest and question you?" Valencia jeered. "Maybe you know who butchered my troops?"

"Of course not!" Riordan shot back. "I would be the first to tell you if I did."

Which, he realized in the brief silence that followed, had not been the best choice of words.

"How do I know you would? At our last conversation, you told me there are certain kinds of knowledge you must keep to yourself."

"I can tell you this much: no one has said anything about this to me."

"And if someone does?" The captain dropped his gaze and rubbed his temples, as if he had a migraine. "Without more precise information, what choice do I have except to arrest ten, arrest a hundred to find one?" He extended a pack of Marlboros. "Smoke?"

Riordan shook his head. The offer signaled that discussions would continue. But no one spoke. He understood that he was expected to.

"If I gave you a name," he said hesitantly, "would you agree to lift the curfew and release your so-called suspects before Christmas?"

Bonham let out a humorless laugh. "A quid pro quo! You're learning!"

"That's a lot to trade for one name," Valencia said. He lit his cigarette and squinted against the smoke curling into his eyes, giving himself a sleepy, hooded look. "It would have to be the name of a big fish. No plankton. No minnow."

"This man works for the Brotherhood. He's not a big fish, but he's more than plankton—or a minnow."

"What then? A snapper? A grouper?"

Ichthyological fine points were not Riordan's strength. He went with snapper, which Valencia rejected as a species too insignificant to warrant what was being asked of him. They negotiated for a while. Riordan felt as if he'd been taken over by an alien personality who was nonetheless himself, a heretofore hidden sharer in his existence, a doppelgänger. If in the seminary someone had predicted that he would one day be haggling over men's fates as if he were in a carpet bazaar, he would have thought it more likely that he'd be chosen as the first priest to fly into space.

Valencia relented a little: depending on the quality of Riordan's disclosure, he would consider lifting the curfew, but only until the day after Christmas. The holiday fell on a Tuesday, not quite a week from now. The suspects could be released by, say, Saturday.

They need time to clean them up, Riordan thought, and to hide or heal their bruises. He asked, "How can I be sure you'll hold up your end of the bargain?"

"You can't be—this is Mexico," Bonham answered, with another mirthless laugh, which Valencia echoed with one of his own. "Who is the snapper?"

"Jesús Delgado," Riordan answered. He wanted, in the deepest part of his being, to say "Danielo García," but Danielo was off-limits, protected by the seal of the confessional. Delgado, however, was fair game.

"Tell us about this Jesús," Bonham said.

"He's a famous rapist of teenage girls."

"We don't investigate rapists," Valencia said, disgust in his voice. "What does he do for the Brotherhood? What makes you think he'll do us any good?"

"He drives *mota* to the border, along with the mules to carry it over. He lives in Mesa Verde, and he's as familiar with the Mesa Verde road as anyone. He might know something about the ambush. It's possible he was in on it."

"I don't know, Padre Riordan. I don't know about this Delgado," Valencia said in a mocking singsong. "Sounds like not much of a fish to me. But you know what, priest? I'll take your offer, bad as it is."

Bonham was giving Riordan his invasive, mind-reading stare. "Don't worry, we'll keep our word," he said. "Like I told you, I take care of my assets."

Which, Riordan grasped, was the reason why they had agreed to the uneven exchange. They wanted to keep him on board.

■ ■ ■

"We don't want to get sidetracked," the Professor said after Riordan left.

Valencia lit another cigarette, letting the smoke drift slowly out of his mouth so that it veiled his bare-boned face. "From what?" he said as the veil lifted.

"The mission."

"How are we being sidetracked from the mission?"

"This idea you have to find the names of the *sicarios* who staged the ambush. You have almost no chance of that. Salazar would like nothing better than to have us off chasing a wild goose instead of a butterfly."

"Sixty thousand people have been murdered in this country in only six years. To put the best face on it, perhaps five percent of those crimes have been solved. You cops are experts on not finding out names. That's why you think there is almost no chance."

Valencia sprang from his chair, yanked a scrapbook from a desk drawer, and dropped it into the Professor's lap. Pasted into it were press clippings, with tabloid-gory photographs and headlines crying, JOURNALIST ASSASSINATED IN NOGALES or variations thereof. One article elaborated: "Raúl Valencia, 31 years of age, a reporter for the magazine *Proceso*, was shot to death on Tuesday morning . . ."

The captain waited for the headlines to sink in, then snatched the scrapbook back, as if the Professor's hands would contaminate it. He fell back into his chair and took another drag, again letting the dense blue cloud drift slowly from his lips; it looked like smoke rolling from under the door of a burning room.

"The police did a very thorough investigation," he said. "Yes, an excellent investigation. They collected the bullet casings—five nine-millimeters. They determined that the rounds were armor-piercing, because they passed through the door of my brother's automobile as if it were paper. They also determined that the *sicario* was a professional—the rounds entered in a tight group under the door handle."

The Professor nodded, having, early in his career with Joaquín Carrasco, eliminated a couple of snitches in exactly that fashion.

"The police interviewed eyewitnesses," Valencia continued. "Of course no one saw a thing, except one. He said the assassin was riding a motorcycle, a blue Kawasaki, and that he pulled up alongside my brother at a traffic light. My poor brother, he was not like most Mexicans: he believed a traffic light was a command, not a suggestion, and for his obedience his reward was death. The police concluded that the assassin knew about my brother's habit of stopping at traffic lights, that he knew the route Raúl followed when he picked up his daughter at the school. My niece, Andrea. And, oh yes, they even found the gun! The *sicario* had tossed it onto the street as he sped away—a Beretta—and they discovered that it had been purchased at a gun store in Arizona.

This is efficient police work, wouldn't you say? Please, give me your expert opinion."

The Professor had fallen into an impassive mood. "Come on, Alberto, I see what you're—"

"But then the police showed what they are best at, without parallel. They found no one! Not a single suspect. No names, Inspector Bonham. Not one! The case dissolved. Which is what happens to ninety-nine out of one hundred murders in this country. I think I can do better. I *will* do better. I will find the names. I will find the bastards they belong to."

The Professor listened patiently, and restrained himself from telling Valencia that his opinion of the army was as low as Valencia's of the police. "We're here to capture Salazar," he said in a tranquil tone. "This has nothing to do with your brother."

The captain raised his eyebrows. "But it has everything to do with him! We paratroopers are also a brotherhood. Those four men butchered for entertainment were my brothers. And I will lose the respect of their brothers, my troops, if I fail to do something about it."

CHAPTER SEVENTEEN

On Thursday afternoon, Federal Police officers in a sound truck cruised through town, announcing that the curfew would be lifted for the next five nights. Somehow the word got out that this had been Riordan's doing, and that he had also worked a greater miracle, securing the release of the detainees. Having said nothing himself, he speculated that Bonham had leaked this information to buff his asset's image among the populace.

If so, it worked. The pageant resumed that night, and the marchers thanked him, chorusing, *"Bendito seas, Padre Tim, bendito seas."* He accepted their gratitude with a show of humility. Inwardly, he was gorged with pride and a sense of power. He'd made something happen! Two kinds of wolves menaced his flock. He'd succeeded, temporarily at least, in driving off the ones dressed in police and military clothing. But would he be strong enough to take on the other, more dangerous pack?

By the next day, those who had not seen the Butterfly's video had heard about it. After Mass, instead of making the usual routine parish announcements, Riordan warned the congregation not to be taken in by narco propaganda. The Brotherhood had distributed stolen medicine to the Indians in San Miguel, and they had staged the soldiers' executions.

"They call it justice for the boys who were killed last month," he said. "But it wasn't justice, it was cold-blooded murder."

■ ■ ■

On the Saturday before Christmas, a police van delivered the detainees from Hermosillo, where they had been interrogated. It let them off in the plaza. Riordan met them there with their families. The mother of Miguel Durán, the college student, wept and kissed his cheek. The men had been in custody for less than a week, yet they had the wary, bewildered look of convicts paroled after long confinement; it was as if they didn't quite believe they were free. Their clothes, the same things they'd worn when they were taken, were rumpled, but their hair was combed, their faces scrubbed and shaved, and no marks were visible. Their interrogators knew how to make sure of that. The punch to the groin. The club to the backs of the knees. The electric prod to the buttocks. Mothers, wives, fathers, sisters, and brothers asked if they had been hurt. To a man, all said no. Perhaps not, though their furtive glances, their tense postures suggested otherwise. Probably, keeping their mouths shut had been a condition of their release. As Riordan shook their hands in welcome and they shook his in gratitude, he thought of Jesús Delgado. A fair exchange—him for them. Whatever these men had endured, Jesús was in all likelihood enduring worse, because of Riordan's denunciation. His conscience took a poke at him, but he slipped the punch, picturing Cristina pinned to the hard earth floor of some squalid shack.

■ ■ ■

The festival of *Las Posadas* climaxed in a grand fiesta on Christmas Eve, *Nochebuena*. Vendors' trucks and wagons, peddling ices and chorizo and *chicharrones*, made a bracelet around the plaza, above which piñatas swayed from poles. Bowls of rum punch were set on tables. Sausages and *machaca* sizzled on mesquite-fired grills. Riordan had made a renewed effort to fast for Cristina's sake and was light-headed from hunger. He thought he would faint from the savory smell of the smoke. He watched it rise into the black sky. His thoughts rose with it, drifting back to a Christmas Eve in the Piazza Navona, the scent of chestnuts roasting on braziers, the dirgelike drone of the Abruzzi shepherds' sheepskin bagpipes, when he and Marcella ate pasta carbonara and watched the water splash in Bernini's fountain while they anticipated the warmth of each other's bodies and the moment that stopped time.

"Golpearlo, golpearlo, golpearlo; no lo pierda. Si lo pierdes, pierdes el camino." Hit it, hit it, hit it; don't miss it. If you miss it, you'll lose the way.

The shouts tore him from his fantasy. Blindfolded people were swatting at the piñatas with sticks. The piñatas were shaped as seven-pointed stars, and they glittered starlike, covered in shiny wrapping paper that reflected the trembling candles in the lanterns, the streetlamps, the Christmas lights in the trees. The seven points represented the seven deadly sins. The people in blindfolds swung, trying to break the piñatas open and spill the sweets inside. The idea behind this custom was to ignore distractions, conquer sin through blind faith, and collect virtue's blessings.

César was one of the sinners. He was also drunk from the rum punch, twirling and staggering, like a top losing the momentum of its spin, after his friends finished turning him round and round. "Hit it!" He swung, missed, and almost fell. Laughter. "César! You're losing the way!" He swung and missed again, and dropped to his knees. Then things went wrong. He whipped the blindfold off, stood, and bashed the piñata as if it were a rabid dog. Hard candy and candy bars and peppermints tumbled out. Going down to his knees again, and with a kind of desperation, he began to scoop them up and shove them into his pockets. He looked like a penniless man falling upon found money. *"Que le pass a el?"* someone said. *"El jefe tenido demasiado. Muy borracho."* That came from Moises Ortega. Embarrassed for César, Riordan pulled him to his feet and walked him to a bench before the man lost more of his dignity. César flopped down, bending over as though he was about to throw up. Riordan knelt and spoke softly.

"Okay, César. What gives with you? *Qué sucede contigo?*"

"Go away. Shut up and go away," he groaned.

"I'll look after him." The voice came from behind the bench. Riordan turned. It was César's sister-in-law, Lupita. "Maybe he has been thinking about my son. About Hector. He drank too much to stop the thinking."

Riordan did not say anything. Over by the statue of General Obregón, someone else was taking a swat, the crowd chanting, *"Golpearlo, gol-pearlo, golpearlo; no lo pierda. Si lo pierdes, pierdes el camino."*

"Me, I could drink all the rum and tequila in Mexico and it would not stop me from thinking," Lupita said. She looked unbearably grave, there in the festive lights. "Go on, Padre Tim. Join the fiesta. I'll look after him."

Riordan stood. "Lupita, I know how hard this time must be for—"

"Shhhhhh," she hissed, placing a finger to her lips. "You have already said too much. You said too much after Mass. Forgive me, but you were wrong, Padre Tim. It wasn't murder, it was justice. *Feliz Navidad.*"

CHAPTER EIGHTEEN

He celebrated Midnight Mass, a High Mass attended by a platoon of altar servers and perfumed by incense. "Smells and bells" they had called such ceremonies in the seminary.

Father Hugo presided on Christmas Day, giving Riordan the morning off. Though he could have slept in, he woke at his usual hour—four-thirty—and after Matins, he went into the courtyard for a breath of air and his survey of the heavens. But a winter storm was blowing in from the west; a thick overcast extinguished the stars. Nor, when dawn broke, was the sun visible through the rolling, roiling, pewter-colored clouds.

In need of mild exercise, he paced around, feeling lean and fit; now, more than three weeks into his fast, and despite breaking it several times, he'd lost ten pounds and had found never-used notches in his belt. Gratifying as this was, he looked forward to the care package Lisette had promised to send from an Italian deli she knew in Tucson, where she'd gone to spend the holiday with her son and Pamela. Riordan had placed an order with her: aged provolone, soppressata, roasted red peppers, kalamata olives. He was already thinking of what he could make with them. An antipasto. Bruschetta. Sausage and peppers. Then, as if he'd willed its arrival, he saw through the iron pickets of the courtyard's gate a large box wrapped in brown paper lying on the ground. It must have been delivered last night. He opened the gate, picked it up—it was quite heavy—and lugged it into the courtyard. Ice cubes rattled inside. His name was scrawled on the top of the box. That was all—his name. No return address, no shipping label. Of course. A delivery service would not have brought the package on Christmas Eve, and if it had been sent all the way from Tucson the ice would have melted by now. It had to be a gift from someone local, although San Patricianos, adhering to a hallowed Mexican tradition, usually did not exchange presents until January 6, the Epiphany and the end of the Christmas cycle.

He removed the outer paper, then the candy-striped gift wrapping, its green ribbon tied in a squashed bow. Beneath it was a Styrofoam chest, with a greeting card taped to the top. His heart stopped when he opened the card and glimpsed a cartoonish version of *La Santa Muerte*, with a curved line connecting her rictal grin to a speech bubble that read, *"Feliz Navidad y próspero Año Nuevo."* Inside the chest, a Santa Claus hat topped by a white tassel stood upright on a bed of ice. He caught a faint but unpleasant odor as pulled out the hat with a quick movement, like a magician plucking a cloth to reveal an astonishing trick. As he did, the object beneath the hat rolled backward in the softening ice. There was a moment of incomprehension, a very brief interval—a couple of seconds at most—before his mind grasped what his eyes saw: the severed head of the parish secretary, Domingo Quiroga.

■ ■ ■

It was the Old Priest, shuffling into the courtyard to water his garden, who found him, some two hours later. Seated on the stone bench beside Father Kino's bust, he was staring at his discovery, its matted hair and shriveled flesh dripping moisture as they defrosted. Riordan had no idea how he had summoned the nerve to remove it and place it on the cooler's lid. He could not explain why he had not raised an immediate alarm and flown to Delores Quiroga's side, nor why he was sitting there, transfixed by her husband's severed head. He was in shock, of course, utterly numb and almost paralyzed; but there was more to his peculiar behavior. Something was stirring deep in his mind, vague as a mist, some insight or perception, some truth floating just beyond grasp.

It seemed that if he looked into Domingo's damp, dead face long enough, the bluish lips would part and he would speak, as it were, revealing the nature of the insight, the perception, the truth.

The Old Priest, unsure of what his weak eyes beheld—from his position in the courtyard, he could see only the back of the head—approached Riordan with the movements of a stalking hunter. When he stepped around the bench and recognized the object of his pastor's attention, he nearly fainted. Moving for the first time in a couple of hours, Riordan reached up and caught him before he fell and lowered the old man onto the bench beside him. The Old Priest made an unintelligible sound, an *"Ai, ai, ai"* before eking out two words: *"Dios mío!"*

"God has nothing to do with this," Riordan said.

The Old Priest's lips flapped silently. The horror exerted its magnetism on him as well—he could not take his eyes off it. "Do . . . do . . ." he tried to say.

"Sí, es Domingo," Riordan said. "I found him—it—here this morning."

He was amazed to hear himself speaking with such objectivity.

"Police . . . You must go . . ." the Old Priest said, recovering somewhat from his own shock.

"I will . . ." He waved a hand at the church. The choir was singing the "Gloria," their voices muted by the thick walls. "When Mass is over. I will go to the police then. We don't want to spoil everyone's Christmas."

The two men were silent for a few moments.

"Tell me again that story about Azazel," Riordan said, out of some hazy notion that the truth he sought to extract from his mind might be hidden within that ancient myth.

"Qué? Qué estas preguntando?"

"Azazel. Tell me again about him."

"A being . . . Some say a being . . . some say a place. . . . Both . . . some say both. The devil and the kingdom of the devil."

"Might that have been the ancient Hebrews' way of explaining evil? God does not have full dominion. He shares dominion with Satan."

Tearing his rheumy eyes away from the head, the Old Priest looked at Riordan as if he had gone mad. Riordan himself wondered if he had, the question was so wildly inappropriate.

"Padre, please . . . the police," said the old man. "You must go now."

"When the Mass has ended," Riordan said.

■ ■ ■

Domingo had been kidnapped shortly after he and his wife came home from Midnight Mass. The street was dark, which was why they hadn't noticed that both *federales* guarding their place had been shot to death in their car. Inspector Bonham speculated that they had been killed during the fiesta, possibly while Mass was in progress, to make sure there would be no witnesses. Their bodies, sprawled on the front seat, weren't discovered until midday on Christmas. Nor were there any outward signs of violence—no bullet holes in the doors, no shattered glass. The driver's-side window had been lowered, which led Bonham to conclude that the pair might have been talking to their killer. Both had been shot in the same way: two .40-calibers to the head.

He was interviewing Riordan in the municipal police station, just the two of them in an interrogation room furnished with a table and two metal chairs. Once, Rigoberto Ochoa—the municipal police sergeant—stuck his head in the door and asked if he could listen in. A sharp look from Bonham sent him away.

Dolores had spent all of Christmas, day and night, under sedation, but she was now able to speak more or less coherently, Bonham continued. She'd had the house keys in her purse and entered through the front door. Aside from the briefest glimpse of two men in ski masks and a crack to her skull, she remembered nothing. When she came to, hog-tied and gagged, Domingo was gone. Bonham examined the scene with an evidence technician and determined that the kidnappers had dragged Domingo out through the back door, where they'd broken in, and into a vehicle in the dirt alley. Tracks indicated a pickup with heavy-duty tires. Then they took him somewhere and decapitated him. "The rest of Domingo's body," Bonham related, "is missing—"

"Dear God, they didn't do that while he was still alive?" Riordan asked.

Bonham spread his hands and shrugged. If his kidnappers did kill him first, they must have shot him in the chest, because there were no wounds to his head. They'd wanted it intact.

Riordan knew he would see it the rest of his life, lying faceup, staring up at him through the ice, like the face of some ancient human discovered in a glacier.

"Your men were supposed to protect him, and they couldn't even protect themselves." Still dazed, he spoke in the voice of an automaton.

Ignoring the reproach, Bonham said, "This was a warning to Domingo's brother—better start paying your *cuota*—but it was meant for you, too. You more than the brother. I don't need to tell you what for."

"No."

"Do you have any reason, any reason at all, to think that Domingo was mixed up with the cartel?"

"No. I do not."

"Any idea who might have done this?" asked Bonham.

Riordan's eyes darted, seeking something, anything, to rest on. He would remember this moment, for he did not weigh pros and cons, pluses and minuses, and come to a decision. The decision had made itself. It had been sitting in his brain since the day before, waiting for him to find it.

"Talk to Danielo García," he said.

"You think this García murdered Quiroga?"

"I don't know. I'm not sure what to think."

"Then why should we talk to him?"

"He's not a little snapper. I'd put him in the barracuda category."

Bonham clasped his hands behind his neck and slowly flapped his elbows. "C'mon, Padre. Stop being coy."

"Danny thinks of himself as an executive, kind of an accounts manager in the Brotherhood's extortion division. He makes sure the bills are paid on time. I can't say if he was the one who put the squeeze on the Quirogas. His big—what should I call it? customer? client? victim?—is the copper mine. So much per week per metric ton. He didn't say how much."

Bonham squinted at Riordan. "He told you this?"

"Yes."

"When?"

"A couple of weeks ago."

"That would have been before our last conversation at the base."

"Yes."

"Why didn't you mention him then?"

Riordan answered by not answering. Bonham acknowledged with a low "Mmmmm-huh" and an almost imperceptible nod.

"It was privileged information?" he asked.

"Yes."

"So it took something like this for you to change your tune?"

"Don't trivialize it, Inspector, Professor, whatever you are. Domingo was a good man, a decent man. These monsters will stop at nothing, so I guess I'd better not let anything stop me."

The Inspector-Professor-Whatever-He-Was studied Riordan for a long moment. "You want to make things right, and this is the right way to do it."

"No, it's the wrong thing for the right reason."

Bonham let out a laugh that sounded like a bark. "I've been known to do the right thing for the wrong reasons." Standing, he leaned across the table and placed his hands on Riordan's shoulders. "I'll speak plain. Valencia wants those names. He's obsessed because we're in prehistoric times in the Sierra Madre. The name of the game is dominance, and at the moment the score is: the Brotherhood, four soldiers, two cops; soldiers and cops, zero. Valencia means it when he says he'll arrest every man, woman, and child in this town if that's what it takes to find out who killed his boys. If we catch whoever murdered Quiroga, you'll be the first to know. Which means that we had better be the first to know if some-day somebody walks into your dark little closet and tells you he pulled a trigger on those four troopers. And anything else we might find useful. Plain enough? You're in for a dime, in for a dollar."

"Quid pro quo."

"*Precisamente! Exactamente!*"

"The chances that anybody is going to confess to that are slim to nil," Riordan said.

"But there is a chance, and we want it covered."

"And the chances I could match a voice to a face, a face to a name . . ."

"We don't expect you to ID anybody. If you can, fine; if you can't, fine, too. All we want is to hear what you hear. You let us worry about the details." Bonham sat down again and rocked his chair backward, bracing it against the wall. "But it is too bad you don't have what I have."

"A badge and a gun?"

"Ha! Synesthesia. Look it up. Your voice makes me see green circles—like sunspots, only they're green. So let's say I didn't know who you were but that I'd seen you once or twice and heard you speak. Then let's say we were in your dark little closet, and you said something. I'd see the green circles and remember what you looked like. It's a gift, Padre Tim. Useful in my line of work."

CHAPTER NINETEEN

He had broken the seal, excommunicated himself. *Laete sententiae*, meaning that it was automatic, arising from the act itself, no trial or tribunal or public rite of expulsion necessary. If knowledge of what he'd done (in canon law, it was called "betraying the penitent") reached the bishop, he would be suspended from all clerical duties while his case rattled up through the hierarchy to the Vatican itself. Only the Pope could rule on such an ecclesiastical crime. And if the pontiff ruled against Riordan, he would be formally deposed from priestly office—that is, laicized; that is, defrocked.

But the only way the bishop could find out would be if Bonham or the captain told him, or if Riordan himself confessed. He wasn't going to, because he had every intention of carrying on as if nothing had changed. Otherwise, he would be an ineffective asset. The priesthood would be his cover. He had betrayed García, and if in the future others came to him seeking to be absolved of extortion or smuggling or murder, he would betray them, too. Again and again and again until the Brotherhood was smashed and Ernesto Salazar was, in Valencia's memorable phrase, carried "out of these mountains in irons or in a body bag."

The deception would be on his conscience alone. Ah, what had happened to his conscience, which in its scrupulosity had so often freighted him with remorse for doing or saying or thinking things that weren't wrong? Why did it not weigh on him in this instance? Maybe it had worn itself out through overuse.

■ ■ ■

Search parties failed to find Domingo's body. His head was placed in a wooden box—that would have to do for a coffin—and carried out to the cemetery overlooking San Patricio. Another requiem, another widow, another recitation of empty words. Dozens attended the funeral, but they were not as stunned and outraged as Riordan wished them to be. They were inured to abominations, and he later heard murmurings that maybe, maybe Domingo had been tied up with the narcos. The thought that a perfectly innocent man would be murdered and butchered, his head delivered to a church on Christmas Day purely for the shock effect, was too awful to contemplate; therefore, he could not have been innocent. That was the logic throughout Mexico: only the guilty were killed, and the proof of their guilt was the fact that they had been killed.

During the first week of the new year, *federales* disguised as miners arrested Danielo García when he walked into the mine offices with his black bag. He was taken to Federal Police headquarters in Hermosillo, where, Bonham reported, he admitted to a number of crimes but not to involvement in Quiroga's murder. The confession being sufficient, the formality of a judicial hearing was dispensed with, and he was shipped off to the Altiplano maximum security prison.

It was a farmer trucking produce into San Patricio for market day who found Jesús Delgado hanging from a tree alongside the Mesa Verde road. A piece of cardboard bearing the Brotherhood's symbol and the word *soplón*—stool pigeon—had been driven into his chest with an ice pick. Within hours, almost everyone in the municipality knew about Jesús's fate, and almost everyone agreed that it was justice—not for the crime he'd committed but justice all the same. When Riordan heard, his breath left him, as if he'd leapt into an icy lake. He picked up the burner phone and contacted Bonham, who informed him in the most offhanded way that Delgado had proved to be less than a rich vein of information. He'd supplied no details about the ambush or the fabricated execution, disclosing only the identities of a few low-level narcos—plankton, Valencia would say—and the locations of a meth lab or two. The plankton were arrested and the labs destroyed, after which the captain turned Delgado loose, ordering paratroopers to drive him to Mesa Verde and to make sure that everyone there saw them shaking his hand in thanks.

"Valencia should have told me he was going to do that," Bonham added. "I would have talked him out of it. A stupid damn thing. Now anybody who might have something for us is going to be scared shitless to give us the time of day."

Riordan ended the call and went into the church, intending to pray for Delgado's soul; but as he knelt in the nave under the fresco of the Virgin of Guadalupe, he thought that he should pray for himself as well. He had played an unwitting role in Delgado's death, yet he felt no remorse. All he felt was guilty about not feeling guilty. It seemed that his emotional temperature had plummeted to below freezing, carrying his moral temperature with it. He wondered if he was becoming like his enemy, the shepherd shape-shifted into a wolf.

Not long after the Epiphany, he had an epiphany all his own. He had gone out, late in the day, with Delores Quiroga to refresh the flowers on her husband's grave. A furious light filled her eyes in place of tears.

"The animals who did this to my poor Domingo must be found and killed like the rabid dogs they are," she cried.

It would have done no good to counsel her that bloodshed brought only more bloodshed, so Riordan kept quiet. But her words played and replayed in his mind that night, and would not let him sleep. The thought did come to him that doing whatever he could to find the "animals" would be the only way he could help her. Yet it was unacceptable for a priest to make himself an accomplice of vengeance. Agitated, he got out of bed, dressed in his warmest clothes, and went outside to seek calm in a survey of the stars.

Sirius, brightest of all, blazed in the southwest. As he looked at its blue-white glow, he saw that the shock he had suffered on Christmas morning had been more metaphysical than psychological. The daily cares of ministering had left him little time or energy for the Big Questions, such as: How can an all-just, all-loving God permit evil in the world? In the seminary, he'd been taught that the existence of evil was the price man paid for his free will. Without the capacity to choose between right and wrong, a human being had no more volition than a puppet. And if that explanation did not suffice, his teachers had argued, then one had to resign oneself to the inscrutability of the divine mind, whose intentions could not be fathomed by the limited human mind. Those rationales had served Riordan for twenty-six years, but what he had seen two weeks ago belonged to a higher order of evil. The demented humor in the gift wrapping and the Santa Claus hat and the card's holiday greeting, along with the fact that the atrocity had been perpetrated on one of Christianity's two holiest days, had struck at the foundations of his vocation, his faith, his entire life. On the day commemorating the birth of His incarnate Son, God had done nothing to prevent the horror. How to explain His failure except to argue that either He did not care or He did not exist.

This might have been the insight he had struggled to lay hold of as he sat transfixed by Domingo's bodiless head. For more than two weeks, it had skulked at the peripheries of his consciousness, like a jewel thief casing a mansion. Now he invited it forward: C'mon in, have a seat, have a drink, let's see if we can come to terms, me the excommunicated priest and you the Big Question: Is God a myth no more real than the Easter Bunny or is He a Supreme Being supremely apathetic toward His own creation? Whichever, we are in H. P. Lovecraft's cosmos, which turns on and on, as indifferent to man's fate and entreaties as the gears of a clock to a condemned prisoner's cries at the hour of his execution.

Then, an inspiration of the moment, a third alternative: Consider that the multiverse posited by cosmologists is a fact, he thought. There isn't one universe but millions, coming into and passing out of existence every minute, each in its own dimensions. God does reign with love and justice in one of those universes, the one I used to inhabit. But the instant I opened that chest and saw what lay therein, I was thrust into an alternate moral universe from which He is absent—a realm of the blackest wonders, where anything is possible and the worst monstrosities are permitted. In such a cosmos, my vow to uphold the sanctity of the confessional is an absurd abstraction, a parlor game, like estimating how many angels can fit on the head of a pin. Here, neither angels nor God are real. Delores Quiroga, lying bound and gagged while her husband is dragged off to be slaughtered, is real; the spattered blood and brains of the slain policemen are real; Domingo's head is real.

If he really believed what was going through his head, he understood, he would have no choice but to leave the priesthood and the church. The laicization procedure could be long and complicated—he'd looked into it years ago, when he was in love with Marcella. *Laicizing*—turning a priest into a layman—sounded like some transformative chemical or biological process. Homogenizing. Vulcanizing. He would plead that he was no longer able to live up to the standards expected of a priest. Then what? Go back to the States. Teaching was probably the only way he could make a living. Art history, as before, or philosophy. Not useful subjects as Americans understood learning to be useful. He would prefer astronomy, except that he had a sketchy background in math and no training, no experience beyond his amateur stargazing. Well, he could go back to school. The University of Arizona had a fine astronomy department. A teaching job or returning to college—either one was a reasonable possibility. But in the next whirl of thought, he knew he would never take such a momentous step. He had been a priest for half his life; he could not imagine himself as anything else. And he would feel like a deserter, abandoning his parishioners in a time of peril.

CHAPTER TWENTY

A roofing contractor from Hermosillo showed up one morning with a truck and crew and began to repair the dome. He said not to worry about the charges; those had been taken care of by a benefactor who wished to remain anonymous. The roofer must have come at Bonham's behest, but Riordan did not press him for any further information. Later, another contractor arrived, also from Hermosillo, and inspected the church's plumbing and electrical systems. Both needed work, he reported. Riordan had known about the plumbing problems, but the wiring, too? Yes, answered the contractor. It was very old and frayed, and if it wasn't fixed, there could be short circuits and a fire. He, too, said not to worry about the bill. As he had done with the roofer, Riordan showed his gratitude by not asking who had arranged and paid for his services. He found himself curiously incurious.

For the next couple of weeks, tradesmen crawled over the roof, scuttled through the interior of the church and the rectory, making a racket with their power tools.

■ ■ ■

Toward the end of January, every pastor in the Archdiocese of Hermosillo received a letter from the bishop, Arturo Peralta. It called their attention to a forthcoming visit by one Father Calixto Banderas, a prominent exorcist from Mexico City. Violence in Sonora—indeed, throughout the country—had become so perverse, so extreme, so hideous, wrote His Excellency, that he now questioned the political and sociological explanations for it. The ghastly crime recently committed in San Patricio, with which "you are all by now familiar," was the most recent example. Such violations of all human norms, and the utter failure of state institutions—the government, the military, the police, the courts—to contain them, much less to stop them, strongly suggested a diabolical influence. After conferring at length with his fellow prelates, the bishop had concluded that the country was suffering from an infestation of demons. These evil spirits might be punishment for the proliferation of pagan cults like the cult of *La Santa Muerte*; they might be a demonstration of what happens when people abandon their faith. Whatever the reason for the plague, Bishop Peralta had called for exorcisms in the parishes under his jurisdiction.

Riordan lay the letter on his desk and watched dust motes swirl in the winter sunlight piercing the rectory office window. Disbelief, fascination, and curiosity spilled into his mental blender, which pureed them so that he experienced them all at once. More than a dozen years into the twenty-first century, he thought, and things have come to the point that we are turning to a rite wreathed in the obscurant mists of the Middle Ages. In all his years in the priesthood, he'd never witnessed an exorcism except in a movie theater, watching Linda Blair vomit pea soup. Many priests his age regarded the ritual as an embarrassment; yet he had to admit that he was eager to see one performed. The bishop's word choice had caught his eye: an "infestation." He pictured the circuit-riding Father Banderas as a kind of spiritual Orkin man, traveling from parish to parish to exterminate demonic termites.

That evening, after dinner, he showed the letter to Father Hugo and the Old Priest. The dimly lit room, with its heavy antique table and sideboard, lent an atmosphere appropriate to the subject.

"Have either of you been to an exorcism?"

Father Hugo shook his head; the Old Priest nodded.

"Once, many years ago," he said. "It was very frightening. A young man was possessed. I remember him screaming obscenities when the exorcist commanded the wicked spirit to leave him. He had superhuman strength. It took three of us to hold him down. He raved like one gone mad, but the demon was driven from him. It howled when it left." The Old Priest squinted at Riordan through his thick reading glasses. "Do I observe skepticism on your face?"

Riordan answered with a noncommittal shrug. In his new role as a snitch, he thought, he might be more effective at ejecting demons than thousand-year-old incantations. But so far, he'd heard nothing worth reporting, only dreary recitations of quotidian sins. *I missed Mass twice without a serious reason . . . I masturbated five times since my last confession . . . I was unfaithful to my wife, Father . . . I took the Lord's name in vain many times.* Sometimes he felt terrible, deceiving his parishioners into believing they were confessing to a true priest; sometimes he trembled, knowing that every time he said Mass he was compounding his sin. But whenever his resolve began to falter, all he had to do was call on Delores Quiroga to offer what little comfort he could; all he had to do was walk into the parish office and look at the desk where Domingo used to sit, and feel the aching presence of his absence.

Father Hugo bowed his head over the letter. "It says this is to be an *Exorcismo Magno*—"

"I looked that up. It's rarely done," Riordan said. "It means a 'Great Exorcism'—"

"I know what the words mean," Father Hugo said peevishly. "But what is it?"

"An exorcism of a place or an area, not of a person," Riordan replied as he thought, *I do not believe that we are seriously talking about this.*

"I see. Maybe when this Father Calixto is finished here, he can go north of the border. Plenty of demons there, Padre Tim. A treasury of demons."

"What are you getting at, Padre Hugo?"

"The savages who did what they did to our poor Domingo, how did they get to be so powerful? Selling their poison north of the border." Father Hugo's voice swelled as he went on: "There is something wrong with a country where everybody cannot get through a week or a day without sticking needles in their arms or smoking their crack pipes."

"If you're looking for an argument, you'll get none from me on that point," Riordan said. "Except that it's not everybody."

"Flan! I have flan left over," announced Maria, barreling in from the kitchen. "Who wants flan for dessert?"

"Why is it always flan? Flan, flan, flan every night?" Father Hugo, apparently frustrated by Riordan's dodge, needed someone to fight with. "Can you make nothing but flan?"

Maria assumed an injured look. "Pardon me, Padre. I beg your pardon for asking your wishes."

"Oh, very well. Since there is only flan, I will have flan."

"Flan all around, María," said Riordan.

She bustled out and back in and slapped the custard on the table and bustled out again.

"You never answered my question," the Old Priest said.

"What question?"

"Was that skepticism on your face?"

"All right. Yes."

The Old Priest paused to dip his spoon into the flan. "I know what I saw and heard that day."

"I'm not doubting you, but—"

"I heard you say—I think it was in this very room—I heard you say yourself that what is happening now in Mexico is the work of the devil."

"It was a figure of speech. *Una metáfora.*"

"*Ah! Ah! Típico! Usted es un típico norteamericano,* a slave to rationalism. Satan is not a metaphor. He is real, and he has sent his lieutenants here to infest us. Because Mexico has been faithful, he has singled her out to destroy her faith. Where there is no faith, there is only darkness."

"I am skeptical," Riordan said, "that an exorcism is going to spare us from the next massacre."

CHAPTER TWENTY-ONE

Riordan expected Father Calixto Banderas to look gaunt, grave, and gray, projecting the austere demeanor of one who wrestled with evil spirits on a regular basis. But the man he met, a week after the delivery of the bishop's letter, was on the bright side of forty, with a cherubic face and a salesman's affability. He arrived in a dinged-up SUV, accompanied by a still younger priest, an exorcist trainee, whom Riordan dubbed (but only to himself) "the sorcerer's apprentice." His name was Father Franco Sandoval, and he carried the tools of his mentor's trade: a Bible, a book of exorcist prayers, a gold-plated crucifix, bottles of holy water and anointing oils, and a solid brass staff, its function a mystery.

The guests were shown to their room—the rectory always kept one open for visitors—and then came to dinner. Riordan enjoyed having someone other than Hugo Beltrán and the Old Priest to talk to. Banderas's hearty appetite was encouraging. The exorcist dove into María's *pollo mole*. He volunteered that he'd been trained in his occult art at the Athenaeum Pontificium Regina Apostolorum, in Rome, and told tales about his encounters with tormented souls and the demons who possessed them. So many demons! The need for exorcists was growing all over the world, and there were few places where that need was greater than in Mexico. San Patricio was the first call on his tour of the archdiocese because of the indescribable thing that had happened here. It had been an attack, he opined, on the church herself, on faith itself, and he was certain the heinous act had been committed by men conscripted into Satan's legions.

Domingo, Riordan thought, would have argued that the attack had been on him. The youthful Father Sandoval—he could not have been past twenty-seven or eight—drew booklets from a briefcase and passed them out to the three parish priests. They contained the prayers and litanies of the Great Exorcism, along with directions as to its performance. Banderas explained that he would recite the invocations; Father Sandoval, joined by Riordan, Father Hugo, and the Old Priest, would deliver the responses.

"I suggest we hold a rehearsal early tomorrow morning," Banderas said. He mopped up the *mole* sauce with a tortilla.

Suppressing his proprietary feelings—he didn't like turning his church over to a priest he considered wet behind the ears—Riordan looked over the service and the stage directions. He noticed that at each of the cardinal points on the compass, a prayer was to be said in a ceremony called the "Conjuración." The word jumped out at him. In Spanish, it denoted "warding off," but his mind automatically ran to the English, "conjuring," which, well, conjured visions of primitive rites, magic spells, the type of superstitious mumbo jumbo Captain Valencia scorned.

"Uh, Father Banderas, can you tell us what is supposed to happen?" he inquired, ironing all incredulousness out of his voice. "What can we expect this Great Exorcism to accomplish?"

"I am happy you asked that," the exorcist replied, eyeing an extra chicken thigh in the serving dish. "You will notice nothing, most likely. Nothing will be changed."

Riordan looked surprised. "Would you mind explaining, then, why we're going through it?" he asked.

Banderas's lips turned up so that, with his chubby, spherical face, he looked like a happy emoticon.

"Not at all! Few exorcisms work immediately. Some take weeks, months. Once, in San Luis Potosí, I exorcised a man five times before he was free. And the Great Exorcism? We may have to have three, four, five, six of them before we see any effect."

"The devil's minions are numerous," added Father Sandoval.

The Old Priest bobbed his head in agreement. "They roam the world, seeking the ruin of souls."

■ ■ ■

Riordan suspected that most of the parishioners who jammed the church the next day had been drawn in by the novelty. But those whose lives had been ravaged by the violence—Delores Quiroga, the Reyeses, the Díazes, others—came out of desperation, hoping for anything that promised deliverance. As for Riordan himself, he'd reflected on Giotto's painting of Saint Francis expelling demons from Arezzo the previous night, before he'd gone to bed. It was a purely mythological event; nevertheless, the picture of the Franciscan Order's founder conducting a mass exorcism swung him from skeptical to indifferent about the ritual. It could not do any harm, even if it did no good.

It began at noon. Booklets had been placed in the pews during the morning rehearsal. Clad in brocade vestments, Fathers Banderas and Sandoval stood front and center on the altar; Riordan, Father Hugo, and the Old Priest, wearing simple surplices, stood off to one side. Banderas bestowed a benign look on the congregation, bundled up against the midwinter chill, and told them to turn to the Litany of the Saints in the booklets. This they did. Then he chanted in a high, melodious voice:

Señor, ten piedad. Lord, have mercy.

Señor, ten piedad, the parishioners answered, raggedly, hesitantly.

Cristo, ten piedad. Christ, have mercy.

Cristo, ten piedad.

San Miguel, Arcángel, ten piedad. Saint Michael, Archangel, have mercy.

Ruega por nosotros. Pray for us.

The assembled voices grew stronger, more certain. On and on it went, through the archangels Gabriel and Raphael, through the prophets and patriarchs, the apostles, evangelists, martyrs, monks, Levites, and female saints, forty-five names altogether: Saint Peter, pray for us. . . . Saint Anthony, pray for us. . . . Saint Mary Magdalene, pray for us. The repetition of invocation and response was at once monotonous and entrancing, and not without an ascetic beauty.

From all sin, Banderas sang,

> *Deliver us, O Lord,*
> *From all evil.*

Two hundred voices appealed in unison:

> *Deliver us, O Lord.*

Now it was time for the procession around the church—the Rite of Encirclement. Banderas turned to face north, his back to the congregation, and intoned the first of the "Conjuración" prayers: "Lord, you are our defense and refuge. We ask you to free our Holy Church from the snares of demons. Surround it with the shield of thy strength, and show mercy. Through Christ our Lord."

"Amen," Riordan answered with Father Hugo and the Old Priest, their voices merging with the congregation's. He considered whether he was a slave to rationalism. Maybe this mystical drama was the needed weapon, for evil itself was irrational and could not be overcome with reason.

Banderas picked up the brass staff, and he and the other priests proceeded to the west nave, where more prayers were chanted, then to the east, before they wheeled, precise as a drill team, marched to the center aisle, and faced south. "Listen, Holy Father, do not let your children be deceived by the father of lies," Banderas intoned, his head bowed, one hand raised. Despite the chill, his forehead glistened. "Retire, Satan, by the sign of the Holy Cross, of our Lord Jesus Christ, who lives and reigns forever and ever . . .

"Amen."

Led by the exorcist, the priests filed at a solemn pace toward the front doors, there to send the infernal militias back into hell. The parishioners turned to follow them with their eyes, as they might the recession of a bridal party. Riordan's glance sidled quickly to the people standing nearest the aisle. He tried to read their expressions. Did they believe that the command "Retire, Satan" would liberate them from violence and ruthless terror? Hope it would? Did he? How many graves would he pray over, how many families console between now and when this rite had its desired effect, if it ever did?

"Lord, King of Heaven and Earth," prayed Banderas, loud enough to create an echo, "strike the powers of hell!" He hammered the floor three times with the staff. "Almighty God, through the intercession of Mary Most Holy and Immaculate, strike and crush the Ancient Serpent!" Again he pounded the staff three times. Riordan's pragmatic side cried out silently, *Not so hard! You'll crack the tiles!* "Creator of all things, strike, crush, and shatter all the hierarchies of the Abyss!" *Bang-bang-bang.* Ring of brass on stone. "I command thee, Ancient Serpent, depart from the Holy Church of God! Depart from this town! Depart from this diocese!" The members of the congregation were into it now, mesmerized, some swaying to the rhythm of the incantation. "God the Father so commands! God the Son so commands! God the Holy Spirit so commands! Through Christ our Lord . . .

"Amen!"

A shrill howl rose from a pew in the rear, then broke into a series of rapid, shallow gasps. Goose bumps scurried up the back of Riordan's neck. He spun and saw a woman on her hands and knees in the aisle— a young woman with thick, frizzy hair that looked like an Afro losing its shape. She attempted to crawl, then fell flat and rolled onto her back, her body jerking once before it went stiff, as if from an electrical shock. He rushed toward her just as another woman, somewhat older, pushed out of the pew and knelt beside her. He did not recognize either of them, but he couldn't shake the feeling that he'd seen them before, here in the pueblo. The one on the floor was staring blankly at the ceiling; her hands shook spastically while her jaw muscles flexed and her mouth worked back and forth, as if she were grinding something between her teeth.

Father Banderas, recovering from the shock of the woman's screech, hovered over her for a second. He went down to one knee and laid his crucifix between her breasts and called, "What is your name? Tell me your name!"

Riordan suddenly felt like a character in films of the occult, the one who doesn't believe in the paranormal until it confronts him.

"In the name of God the Father, the Son, and the Holy Spirit, tell me your name!" Father Banderas commanded.

"What are you doing?" the older woman said. A tough-cookie type, fair-haired and sinewy, with eyes the color of a thundercloud.

"What is your name?"

The prostrate woman came to, propping herself up on her elbows. Her lips moved soundlessly at first; then she croaked, "Miranda."

"Miranda, I command thee to depart. Depart, accursed one, from this child of God!"

Riordan looked away. People had spilled into the aisle, gawking as if at an auto accident. Some had raised their arms, palms outward, certain they were witnessing a struggle with an evil spirit.

"Depart, Miranda! Why do you still linger here, seducer? I adjure you, specter from hell, to cease your assault on this child of God!"

"Stop it!" said the woman's companion. "She is having a seizure. She has seizures. Miranda is *her* name."

But the exorcist was having none of it. Bowing low, face-to-face with the woman called Miranda, he summoned the spirit to be gone to its abode, a nest of serpents. Miranda stared at him, mouth agape. She was sweating now.

"Crawl with them, those snakes! You might delude man, but God you cannot."

Riordan saw that he needed to reassert himself. This was his church, after all, these people his parishioners. Another minute of Banderas's ranting might bring on mass hysteria.

"It is He who casts you out, Miranda," Banderas intoned. "It is He who—"

"Father, please. That's enough," he said, gripping the exorcist under one arm, as if to jerk him upright. "She's right. It's a seizure."

er laptop had announced the e-mail's arrival with a sound like an open bottle shoved underwater. *Glug.*

Hi, Lisette,

I am definitely coming down after the semester's over, but I'm indefinite about for how long. I mean that I'll be there longer than we planned. Can't say how long. At loose ends right now, really loose, stressed out, because I've been asked—Ha! Asked? Told, ordered, commanded—not to come back for the fall term. Been fired, in other words. The U. is cutting back. Budget problems. And my student evals weren't up to the mark. Did you know that? Teachers, even adjuncts, get evaluated by their students. Guess mine weren't happy with me. Shit shit shit. Don't need this right now. I guess I'm not good enough. Haven't sold a painting in MONTHS!! I'm not tenured, just an adjunct, so they showed me the door.

I've been busting my butt to sublease my apt. and put my stuff in storage that needs to be there and figure out what I need to bring to Mexico. You can tell the priest, Tim, that I can start on restorations. I've got the materials. So much to do, so little time, so I went off the meds, because they slow me down. Need rocket fuel to get through it

all. But I'm OK. Really. I'll go back on. Promise. You can look out for
me, you're the doctor.
    XOXOXO
    Pam

Lisette was troubled by the e-mail's stream-of-consciousness flow, its hyper tone, and by her own complicated reaction to it. She should have been happy to hear that they would soon be together, living as a real couple, and she was. But it was a happiness tainted by anxiety; their arrangement, originally intended to be temporary, a testing of the waters, an experiment with a built-in exit should things not work out, was now to be extended indefinitely. What if things did not work out? And then there was that business about going off the lithium. Lisette wanted to be Pamela's lover, not her doctor. Certainly not her shrink. But it would be irresponsible not to make sure she took her medications. Lithium or no lithium, Pamela was going to have a tough time coping with life in an isolated Mexican town where the dreadful had become commonplace.

Lisette had learned about the murder of Tim's parish secretary after she'd returned from the holidays in Tucson. It stretched her conception of what was possible in the way of human depravity. And then—an exorcism! Sweet Jesus! It was as if the whole town had fallen into a wormhole and come out in the tenth century. Lisette was tempted to attend the spectacle out of curiosity but decided to stay home. Tim Riordan came into the clinic after the ritual with two young women. The one with dark, tightly curled hair appeared dazed. She had had an attack at the exorcism, Tim said. A fit. *"No no no."* The woman's head whip-sawed. *"No ataque, no convulsión. Era algo más."* The other woman told her to shut up. She was tall and had the hard good looks of a film noir actress: long, straight, dull-blond hair, a knife-thin nose, gray eyes that were somehow bright and opaque at the same time, like the glass eyes in a stuffed animal. She made Lisette uneasy; waves of malevolence seemed to ripple from her. "Listen," Film Noir said, her tone icy, "my friend gets these convulsions, you know. So you give her something."

Lisette answered that she'd have to have a look at her first, which she did in the examination room. The young woman also had a certain tough-chick attractiveness, her cute ass shown to full effect by her sprayed-on blue jeans. A leather jacket and a denim shirt, unbuttoned to reveal a little cleavage, completed the picture of a biker's mama. She kept insisting that she hadn't had *una convulsión*, she knew what that was like, and this had been different. A demon had been inside her.

Lisette made no comment and diagnosed a petit mal seizure. "All right," said Film Noir, "whatever you have for that, give it to her." Lisette replied that she didn't stock medications for epilepsy. Even if she did, she wouldn't know which to prescribe. There were twenty different kinds, and some had bad side effects. "You should see a specialist," she said. Film Noir snickered. "Some great fucking doctor you are."

Lisette did not tell Pamela about the murder or the exorcism when she picked her up at the Hermosillo airport. A shrewd decision. Pamela had lost weight since Christmas. She looked almost scrawny and seemed brittle, radiating an unsettling mixture of tension and excitability. She talked incessantly on the drive to San Patricio, all stirred up about a new period in her work, experiments with light and shapes inspired by the Southwest—"Watch out, Georgia O'Keeffe! Here comes Paaa-mah-la!"— and about losing her teaching job—"Imagine, giving me the heave-ho because a few soggypants kids gave me a shitty eval"—and about the response from a New York gallery that had seen one of her new pieces—"I feel like I'm sitting on a rocket ship that's about to take off, whoosh, you watch, and let's see what the faculty has to say when they read about me in the Arts section in the *New York Times*. Their loss, if you ask me." And about the new luggage she'd bought, Louis Vuitton, and the new clothes to go with her new painting style, her whole new life. *New new new.*

"Are you back on the meds?" Lisette asked when she found space to get a word in.

"Sure. Why?"

"You seem a little . . . wound up?"

"Of course I am! I'm starting over! With you!" She wasn't in complete control of her voice; it hit shrill, grating notes. "What do you want? For me to feel like shit because I got the heave-ho? Well, I don't. I feel good, really good."

She whirled and twirled when they got home, unpacking the Louis Vuitton suitcases and the old-fashioned steamer trunk containing her art supplies. Lisette was dismayed by the new wardrobe: cocktail dresses that would be appropriate at an embassy function in Mexico City, flashy, fringed cowgirl blouses, and silver-buttoned *charro* outfits, as if she planned to costume herself for a folkloric gala.

"How much did this stuff set you back?"

"Oh, tons. Scads. So what?"

"So nobody around here dresses like this."

"What do I care?" Then came a laugh nothing like the laugh Lisette delighted in. It was sharp, artificial. "Maybe they'll start when they see me—maybe I'll start a trend. How do you say—excuse me: *Cómo se dice en español*, trendsetter?"

Lisette had seen glimmers of Pamela's need for attention before, but they had been only glimmers. This out-there flamboyance was new and, like her fast, pressured talking, more than a little disturbing.

Her sex drive was likewise in high gear. That night, she stripped down to a scarlet thong—a thong!—and, dangling a sex toy from her fingers, put on a lascivious expression as false to her face as the thong was to her middle-aged body. "C'mon, babe. C'mon and do me."

Do me? She sounded as if she'd been watching too much Internet porn. Her blatant sexuality was a bit ludicrous, and—this startled Lisette—arousing.

In the morning, while Pamela slept, Lisette phoned a psychiatrist she knew in Mexico City, asking his advice. He counseled patience; it could be anywhere from several days to two weeks before the lithium took effect, depending on how much time had passed since the last dose. "If you have any Xanax or Ativan on hand, give her some," he said. "It will help calm her." He couldn't say anything more without seeing the patient.

She had a supply of Xanax and presented Pamela with a capsule on her breakfast plate.

"What do I need this for?" Pamela said. "I feel terrific."

"Take the damn thing, please. You asked me to look after you, so I'm looking after you."

Pamela replied with a sulky, girlish "All right, if it makes *you* feel better."

The tranquilizer didn't do much good. They got onto the subject of their families, which Lisette knew, from previous episodes, could wind Pamela's spring to the breaking point.

"Iago, that's her, that's my mother," Pam said.

"Iago?"

"A whisperer whispering."

"Whispering what?"

And she was off, leaving most of her breakfast on the plate. "In Dad's ear. Oh, he was a wonderful man . . . not Othello. . . . A wonderful man, really kindhearted at heart . . . Whispering . . . Hsssss . . . She whispered suspicions about me, knew I was gay before I did and she was upset because she's very rigid, you know. We had to have dinner at exactly the same time every night. Six-thirty. The cook was under orders. We had a cook. Mommy dearest couldn't fry the proverbial egg and wouldn't have even if she knew how. I never came out. . . . Knew I was gay. . . . Why do you think my teeth are this fucking mess? We had enough money to buy ten orthodontist practices. . . . She wouldn't get them fixed because she thought I wouldn't need them to attract a man. . . . Iago whispered in Dad's ear, 'Pammy's a lesbian. Don't expect any grandchildren from her unless she goes to a sperm bank to make a withdrawal.' He didn't care, loved me anyway. Oh, he was a wonderful man. . . . She doesn't know about you, about us, no way I'll ever tell her, that awful woman. . . . Seventy-seven and still . . ."

Pamela's voice cracked and Lisette stroked her arm, not so much to reassure her as to cue her to dam the torrent of words. Lisette had learned that Pamela's favorite theme, when mania seized her, was to cast the people in her life as Shakespearean characters. She wondered what part she might be given. Cordelia? Glendower? When Pamela's serotonin levels dropped, the snakes in her pretty head hatched out. She wasn't insane in the sense that she heard voices or saw things that weren't there. She wasn't insane at all, medically speaking. Her type of bipolar disorder, bipolar II, acted on her like too much alcohol or cocaine, liberating the Pamela that Pamela otherwise kept chained in the attic: the hypertalkative, hyperactive, hypersexual, vulgar, self-aggrandizing Pamela B, filled with inflated notions of her talents ("Watch out, Georgia O'Keeffe!") and dark, furious memories of her bitch mother and kindhearted father. Lisette had fallen for the reserved, reticent, self-effacing Pamela A, and wanted her back.

She thought Álamos would be good for Pamela, hasten B's departure and A's return. But the getaway would also be good for Lisette. She had friends in Álamos, and she needed an escape from Pamela's exclusive company. Straight-line distance, the town was only a hundred and fifty miles south of San Patricio, but it was a thousand miles away in other respects: considerably larger, cleaner, and richer, a *pueblo mágico* crowded with American expats who had spent huge sums restoring colonial mansions or refurbishing them into B&Bs. Blood did not stain its ancient cobblestones; its citizens did not fear being kidnapped; extortionists did not prey on its merchants. It was neutral ground in the narco wars, a kind of mini-Switzerland, and every winter it staged a music festival, drawing opera companies and chamber music ensembles and music lovers from the world over.

The festival was on when Lisette and Pamela arrived. They checked into a casita at El Pedregal. Lisette knew the owners, an American couple who gave her a discount. Pamela had come down from her high—the lithium taking effect? A swing to the depressive cycle? She claimed never to suffer from deep depression, and Lisette had yet to see her in a black mood. Dark gray, maybe, when she got down on herself.

While Pamela sat on the patio, captivated by the white, disk-shaped blossoms falling like tiny parachutes from a *palo santo* tree, Lisette phoned her friends, the Hartigans—obscenely rich expats who lived in a hacienda with the square footage of a ballpark, the sort of people she normally disdained. But they were, like Manny Cardenas in Tucson, among the philanthropic donors who kept her clinic in business.

Louise Hartigan answered. "Lisette! You're here? Why didn't you let me know you were coming?"

"It was kind of a spur-of-the-moment thing."

"Well, you must stay with us. There isn't a room to be had this weekend."

"We found one. At the Pedregal. Lucked out. A last-minute cancellation."

"Lucked out, sure enough. Who makes the 'we'?"

"Pamela. Pamela Childress."

A pause, then: "The painter?"

"You've heard of her?"

"Heard of her? We caught one of her shows, in . . . in . . . Houston, I think it was. Last year. Right. Houston. We almost bought one of her oils. Or maybe it was an acrylic. It didn't quite go with our place. The colors were a bit off."

Lisette groaned inwardly. "She'll be thrilled that you know her work."

"We'd love to meet her. George is off in the reserve, checking on his trip cameras. He got a picture of a margay last week, hoping for a jaguar next. How about meeting me at the rehearsal for the opera this afternoon? *The Marriage of Figaro*. In the plaza at four, okay?"

"Sure. Thanks, Lou."

At lunch at La Terrasita, owned by another expatriate couple, Lisette told Pamela about the Hartigans. She was indeed thrilled that they admired her work. Maybe too thrilled, crackling with excitement.

"I should have brought my portfolio. I would have if I'd known."

"Save that for some other time," Lisette said.

"Save what?"

"Pitching yourself."

"I've got some on my phone. Or I could do a new one of the *palo santo* tree. Just the blossoms, falling, falling. Like teeny parachutes. They might like that. What do you think?"

"I think, honey, this isn't the time to go angling for a commission."

"When is the right time?" Her tone changed suddenly; there was an aggressiveness in the question. "I'm sure you'll tell me when the right time is to angle and pitch."

The waiter arrived with the tab.

"Sorry for the bitchiness," Pamela said, her voice softening as quickly as it had hardened. "I'll get lunch."

"So how do you like Álamos so far?"

"*Bello! Bello!* How do you say that in *español*? Beautiful?"

"*Hermoso.* Or *lindo.*"

"I like *lindo. Pueblo lindo mágico.*"

■ ■ ■

Louise Hartigan was an anomaly: an overweight vegan. Her height—she was almost as tall as Pamela—combined with her bulk made her an intimidating presence. Breasts like pontoons preceded her as she strode

across the Plaza de Armas with the momentum of a great ship. Her big
arms enveloped Lisette, and she gave Pamela an equally crushing
embrace, her deep voice booming greetings and praise for Pamela's art.
But Louise lacked a filter. Right after the encomiums, she said that she
and George had not bought the painting they'd seen at the Houston show
because it clashed with their decor.

"How do you mean, it clashed?" Pamela asked, her face clouding over.

"It didn't go with the wall where we wanted to hang it. The wall is
terra-cotta, and there was too much red and orange in the painting. It
would have been lost. We needed something with contrast, more blues
maybe."

"Why not repaint the wall?"

"Because we like the terra-cotta," Louise said.

"I am not an interior decorator," said Pamela, sounding at once
haughty and offended.

Louise finally realized her gaffe. She squeezed Pamela's arm. "Aw,
I've got a big mouth and the foot to go with it. It would have been a
shame to lose such a fine piece of work on that wall."

Mollified for the time being, Pamela whipped out her phone and
began swiping through photos of her recent work.

"Have a look at these," she said, passing the phone to Louise. "If you
see something you like, something that goes with your terra-cotta decor,
let me know."

Lisette was embarrassed for her. She sounded like a shopgirl, peddling sweaters. Louise returned the phone.

"Hard to see them in this bright light," she said.

"The first three in the stream, the thirty-six-by-twenty-fours—those
go for . . . how does fifty thousand sound?"

Louise drew back, giving Pamela a curious look. "Expensive is how
it sounds."

Lisette poked a thumb into Pamela's ribs, provoking a burst of high-
pitched, affected laughter. Louise smiled uncertainly and threw a look
at Lisette that asked, "What's with this woman?"

The soprano and the baritone stepped out of the old Governor's
Palace, now a theater, and began rehearsing on the front steps. A small
crowd had assembled to listen in.

"They're from a Spanish opera company," Louise said in an undertone. "He's playing Count Almaviva, and she's, I think, Susanna. No, Rosina, the countess."

The man was tall, thin, and too boyish to play the lecherous count, Lisette thought. The woman was ravishing, her pale complexion contrasting with her long, raven-black hair. The rehearsal got off to a bad start. The singers weren't half a minute into a duet when they were interrupted by the appearance of an odd conveyance: a four-seat golf cart decked out to resemble a carriage and drawn by a team of white fiberglass horses attached to the front. It circled the plaza, the carnival-ride horses pumping up and down on steel poles to a tinny calliope tune. A sign hanging from the fringed roof advertised guided tours of Álamos. The driver pulled to a curb nearby as the male half of an American couple called, "How much, señor? *Cuánto?*" The driver gave him the price, and the couple climbed in while the baritone scowled at the intrusion.

He and the female singer carried on. Pamela applauded, crying out, "Bravo! Bravissimo!" in a harsh falsetto, her *r*s rolling like barrels. She seemed unaware that she was cheering in Italian. Also that the duet wasn't quite finished.

Just moments later, to Lisette's alarm, Pamela ran over to the carriage and hopped onto one of the horses, sitting it sidesaddle.

"Avanti, signore!" She raised an arm, holding the pole with the other. *"Avanti presto!"*

The driver didn't appear to mind; he was laughing. So were his passengers and most of the people in the audience, all of them gawking at the long-legged blonde on the plastic horse. That was the point, of course. Pamela had stolen the show.

"Is your friend on something?" Louise asked with a bemused frown.

"She's acting like this because she was off what she's on."

"I understand." Louise made a gesture of sympathy. "I've got a relative with a problem like that."

Pamela tested Louise's understanding, and Lisette's patience, that night when they were invited to join the Hartigans and some of their friends at the *callejoneada*, the nightly street procession led by music students. Determined to make an impression, she had put on greenish eye shadow, dark red lipstick, and a *charro* suit consisting of a frilly blouse, a green jacket over a long skirt embroidered in gold, and high-heeled flamenco shoes. The costume, which would have looked ostentatious, if not ridiculous, on anyone else, made her more alluring than ever.

She flirted shamelessly with George as the procession flowed down streets ablaze with lights and jammed with festival-goers. She touched his arms and shoulders, lavishly complimented his tastes in art—he and Pamela shared a passion for Rothko—and feigned interest in his trip-camera photos of spotted cats. George was a good deal older than Louise, in his early seventies, a man whose once-handsome looks now had the charm of a ruin: hair gone white and thin, like strips of paper, face webbed with wrinkles, broad shoulders stooped. He pretended to ignore Pamela's flirting, but it was obvious that the attentions of a beautiful woman pleased him as much as it displeased his wife. At first, Lisette thought that Pamela was trying to woo him into buying a painting; then she thought that Pamela, for reasons known only to herself, wanted to make Lisette jealous; at last she realized that this seductress was but one more side to the many-sided Pamela B.

The music students, garbed in Renaissance costumes of maroon jackets and white knee socks, strummed guitars and sang old Spanish ballads. The throng following them joined in. Pamela skipped ahead and began to dance alongside the troubadours, marching behind an old man who led a donkey carrying cowhide botas slung from its packsaddle and two wine casks, one on each side. Pamela grabbed a bota and, raising it overhead, squirted wine down her throat. Lisette, feeling as though she were swimming through a river of human flesh, caught up and grabbed her by the arm, like a bouncer ejecting a rowdy. Wine dribbled down Pamela's chin, staining her white blouse. A couple of drunk young men nearby cheered her on. *"Bravo, señora! Hurra!"* Right then, a look of malicious merriment flared in Pamela's eyes. She broke Lisette's grip, hopped up to an elevated sidewalk and, using it as a mounting block, swung herself onto the donkey's back. The packsaddle slipped, dumping her onto the cobblestones. One of the casks broke loose, but it remained attached by a rope. The startled donkey bolted, knocking a bystander down, dragging the saddle and the cask. The old man ran stiffly in pursuit, shouting, "Gaspar! Gaspar!" George went to help Pamela up, but the young drunks got to her first. Giving her another *Hurra!*, they pulled Pamela to her feet. "Gracias! Grassy-ass, my amigos!" she screeched, laughing.

For days, Lisette been counseling herself to be forbearing, to remember that her lover's condition was not a character flaw but a disease no different than diabetes or cancer. Yet everything Pamela had done today seemed somehow willful and deliberate. Lisette faced her and told her to for Christ's sake get ahold of herself. Pamela laughed again—that harsh laugh with a hint of cruelty in it—and Lisette slapped her cheek, hard enough to feel her palm strike bone.

CHAPTER TWENTY-THREE

The Friday before Ash Wednesday. Riordan sat behind the confessional's privacy screen and looked at his watch. Fifteen minutes to go. Having listened, yet again, to tedious recitations of stale sins, he was feeling, in equal measure, relieved and disappointed that he'd heard nothing that merited reporting to Valencia and Inspector Bonham. He was also oppressed by the dismal banality of man's fall from grace. That an event as momentous as banishment from the Garden of Eden should produce some teenager joylessly pulling his pud while gawking at dirty pictures or some shop clerk filching a few pesos from the cash register showed a gross disproportion between cause and effect—the elephant laboring to bring forth a mouse. The whole of *The Divine Comedy* ought to have been confined to Purgatory, he thought; most people no more deserved the exquisite pains of hell than they did the rewards of heaven.

The door opened and clicked shut. A face, in silhouette, filled the screen. A female voice whispered, "Bless me, Father, I have sinned," so softly he could barely hear it. "My last confession was a long time ago. I don't remember when it was."

"Months? Years?" he asked. "And could you please speak up a little?"

"How is this?"

"Better," he said.

"Years," she said. "Three years, maybe four."

"May I ask, what has brought you here after so long a time?"

"I have seen God. God brings me here. I saw God when the demon was expelled from me in this church."

The young woman with frizzy hair, the epileptic. He hadn't seen her, in church or in town, since her collapse. What was her name? It began with an *M*. María? Melinda? That sounded right. Melinda.

"Please, begin."

"I am with them, Padre. The narcos. The Brotherhood," she said, falling again into near inaudibility.

A thrumming started in Riordan's chest. In as controlled a voice as he could manage, he asked what sins she had committed.

"I've done a lot of things. I think that I have murdered for them."

After an interval of silence, he said, "You *think* you've committed murder?"

"No! No! I have killed nobody. My partner, she has done the killing. She is what we call a *chica Kaláshnikov*, a *sicaria*. I have assisted her, but I have seen God and I know this is a mortal sin."

Sicaria. A female assassin! The only one he'd ever heard of. No banality now. The thrumming grew more rapid and irregular, like atrial fibrillation. "Yes, it is. And you want to confess to this assistance? How many times?"

"One time. I have helped her kill two people. Two *chotas*. Here, in San Patricio."

Chota—narco slang for "cop." Riordan had a sensation that he'd never before experienced: that he could hear with his pores. This hypersensitivity amplified her whisper so that she seemed, to him, to be speaking in a conversational tone.

"Do you mean the federal policemen murdered on Christmas Eve?"

"Yes."

"And how did you assist?"

She drew in a breath. A rivulet of sweat trickled down his ribs; his palms were damp.

"She told me that we both are to dress up like, you know, like *putas*, and we are to distract these cops. She doesn't say nothing about shooting them, I swear it, Father. We are to dress up, sexy, and flirt with them and make them think we want to, you know, party with them."

"Did she say why you were to do this?"

"No." The woman paused. "So we are dressed in short skirts and high heels, and we walk up to the police car and we flirt, we ask the *chotas*, 'Hey, you guys want a Christmas party you won't forget?' The one at the steering wheel, he lets the window down, and the next thing I know, my partner pulls the pistol from her purse and *pop-pop-pop-pop*. Four shots. Very quick. One-half of one-half of a second." Another pause. "I am as surprised as the cops, but they're dead and not surprised anymore. My partner, she has a heart of stone, you know. She says to me then, 'Okay, now we walk away, no running, we walk away,' and I am so scared my knees are shaking. I don't let it show, and she says that I did good, that this was a test for me, and maybe now I will be promoted to *sicaria* myself."

Riordan sat on his side of the screen, breathless. Then he said, "And you swear before God that you had no idea that she was going to shoot them?"

"I swear it, and I am sorry for what happened and I am here for your forgiveness."

"Please understand that it is God who forgives you, not me. God forgives you through me. You have committed an extremely grave sin."

"Oh, I know, Padre. I know. I know. I felt the demon inside me, and when I heard about the exorcism, I went to it . . . to get rid of the bad spirit. Then I saw the face of God and He told me to confess."

"I believe you." Riordan licked his dry lips, wondering what role, if any, Melinda and her partner had played in Domingo's murder, beyond killing the *federales* guarding his house. How far should he push this? At what point would he pass from confessor to interrogator, and risk arousing her suspicions?

"Did you assist in any other crimes that night?" he asked.

"No. We drove back to Hermosillo after it was over."

"Was your partner the woman who was with you at the exorcism? The blond woman?"

"Must I tell you to have you forgive me?"

"No," Riordan said, backing off. "That won't be necessary."

"All right. Yes," the young woman answered, apparently to further unburden herself. "That was her."

Miranda, he remembered now. It was Miranda, not Melinda. He massaged his temples as an idea came to him: he could avoid betraying Miranda without reneging on his agreement with Valencia and Bonham. The chance of success was vanishingly small; yet he had to try.

"I am obliged to urge you to surrender yourself to the authorities," he said with starchy formality. "To tell them what you have told me."

She said nothing.

"I know what you're thinking," he said.

"What am I thinking, Father?"

"That you would be crazy to do that."

"I am thinking you are crazy to ask me to. Pardon me if I insult you."

Gathering his resolve, he took one more step: "Would you give me permission to speak with the authorities?"

He could hear her breathing. The silence lasted for what felt like an unbearably long time before she spoke.

"That would be crazy, too. Do you know what cops would do to an assassin of police?"

"But you were not the assassin. If I were with you, if I were at your side, I could help you. . . . I think you could make a bargain with the police. Tell them who your partner is, who the *jefe* is."

Now I sound like a sleazy lawyer, he thought, urging his client to plea-bargain.

"Rat on them? Me? A *soplón*?" Miranda said with a sudden change of tone, a contemptuousness.

"You have made your point," he said, then tried another approach. "You said you may be promoted to *sicaria*. What happens now if you are ordered to . . . ?"

"I don't have a heart of stone. I don't know if I could do it."

"Then don't."

"But I do know what they would do to me if I refuse."

"You must have a firm resolve to amend your life, you must stop working for those people. Do you understand that?"

She did not respond.

"Do you understand that for God's forgiveness you must make a sincere act of contrition and do all you can to change your life?"

"*Sí, Padre.*"

"As for your penance, you are to say a rosary and make restitution to the families of the policemen. That will wash the blood from the money you were paid."

"How? Should I write them a check?" she said, with another abrupt flip in tone. "I don't know who they are . . . were . . ."

"I will leave the how of it to you," he said, and then he absolved her, though he was certain that, however sincere her contrition might be, her determination to change her life was not. Her first victim awaited her bullet. She might not pull the trigger for the money, but she'd do it if the boss told her to. As Danny García had said, you do not quit those people.

■ ■ ■

He opened the door to see if anyone else was waiting. No one. Miranda knelt in a pew below the mural of Saint Luke, face in her hands—the very picture of the penitent sinner.

Walking quietly past her and out a side door, he went to his room, unlocked a small compartment in his drop-leaf desk, and removed the burner phone. He hesitated, restrained by the image of Miranda praying. To inform on her would be altogether a different matter than informing on García. What could have driven her into such a life, what could have so corrupted her? Contrition was in her heart; she genuinely sought redemption. He sensed that, even though he couldn't prove it. Life still had value for her, and death had meaning, as they had no value or meaning for her partner, the woman with the petrified heart.

He put the phone back in the compartment, changed into street clothes, and told María not to expect him for dinner. She threw a fit—*Everything is ready, I only have to heat it!*—but he couldn't bear the thought of dining with Hugo and the Old Priest. Not tonight.

The plaza was deserted, except for three or four paratroopers in battle attire and a Federal Police van, antennae sprouting from its roof. Walking slowly toward the Hotel Alameda in the twilight, Riordan recalled an explication of canon law he'd read once: *A priest cannot break the seal of the confessional to save his own life, to protect his good name, to refute a false accusation, to save the life of another, to aid the course of justice, or to avert a public calamity.* He pondered a course of action.

He would go to the bishop, admit to what he'd done, and take whatever he had coming to him. The consequences might not be as terrible as he feared. An argument could be made—a weak one, true—that Danielo's confession had been a charade, a cynical ploy; therefore, betraying him had been a misdemeanor rather than a felony. He might be quietly placed on the "awaiting assignment" roster or transferred to another parish, preferably far away from Bonham and the relentless Valencia. He would be leaving his parishioners behind, yet he savored this appealing picture, allowing himself to imagine that it was a prophetic vision instead of an illusory hope.

César Díaz's bodyguards—Moises Ortega and two others—were seated near the front of the hotel restaurant. Their hands fell to their waistbands as Riordan came through the door; then, seeing it was him, they relaxed. The bartender and waiter had likewise tensed up, shooting nervous glances toward the front. Everybody in town was on edge, and had been since Domingo's murder.

Riordan went to the table in back, where César was dining with his wife, Marta.

"Buenas noche!" the animated woman said with aggressive zest. "So good to see you, Padre Tim! Please, join us! We are celebrating!"

César threw her a sharp look.

"What's the occasion?"

"I'll tell you sometime, in private," César said. He did not appear in the least celebratory—pensive, rather, and wary. "I'll buy you a drink, okay?"

The offer was intended to nullify Marta's, which Riordan had intended to turn down anyway.

"Gracias," he said. *"Nos vemos."*

Riordan took a table on the far side of the room. The waiter, as usual, brought him the newspapers and a Herradura on the rocks, saying that the drink was on Señor Díaz.

El Imparcial reported more mayhem. Armed men had stormed a migrant safe house, seizing ten people, whom they were holding for ransom.

So it appeared that the *Exorcismo Magno* had yet to evict Satan from the diocese. If I inform on Miranda, Riordan asked himself, what will happen to her, assuming she's caught? She'll probably be safer in jail than if she stays with the life she's leading now. She will kill someone, and then someone else, and someone after that, until she herself is killed and her soul numbered with the damned. So to betray her would be to save her soul, and it might save the lives of others. He should have called Bonham right away, while Miranda prayed. By now, she would be well on the way back to Hermosillo, where she would vanish into the city's crowded warrens. Really peculiar that she would drive more than a hundred miles to the scene of her crime to confess to it. Because she had seen God in the church, or believed she had? No point in speculating. On the other hand, maybe it was a good thing that he hadn't called immediately. Good for him, that is. If she were arrested so soon after confessing, she would have to be an idiot not to conclude that he had ratted on her. Word would somehow leak out, and then . . .

He had let sentiment get in his way. The image of her in a repentant pose, head bowed, face in her hands, had blurred the memory of Domingo's still, slitted eyes staring up at him through the ice. He was allowing it to get in his way now, because as he leisurely sipped his tequila, he made no move to return to his room and pick up the cell phone. He couldn't do it. That was peculiar, too: he could not be any more excommunicated than he already was.

César's bodyguards rose from their table and went outside. A minute or two later, they came back in and signaled that it was safe to leave. An observer who didn't know that César was chief of the *autodefensa* might think he was a cartel don, protected by *pistoleros*. He and Marta got up, but instead of following his wife and the phalanx of guards straight out the door, César veered to Riordan's table and leaned over it, his rough, rutted face inches away, the smell of beer on his breath.

"I can trust you with a secret?" he said in a low voice.

Suppressing a bitter, inward laugh, Riordan nodded.

César lowered his head and his voice still further: "My brother in the States, Ignacio?"

"Yes . . ."

"He's got a job running a warehouse in Nogales. A produce shipper. He told me they're going to need to replace a guy who's retiring. Twenty an hour to start."

"You're going to take it? I hope not."

"Well, I am. Mexico is fucked. We're leaving right after Easter. That's why we're celebrating. But only we know it. And now you."

He squeezed Riordan's shoulder and left, with no further word. Riordan wanted to cry out, *But the town needs you! I need you!* He drank off the tequila and looked around the room, now empty except for him, the waiter, and the bartender, whose profile was reflected in the mirrored back bar.

■ ■ ■

On a Monday morning, Bonham called Riordan and asked him to come to the military base. He said it was an invitation to lunch, but his peremptory tone was unmistakable: it was another summons.

What do they want now? Riordan wondered as he rode through a mid-winter sprinkle. The Sierra Madre mountains were a soft purple in the distance, the highest peaks wearing bonnets of cloud.

■ ■ ■

Seated around a folding card table, Riordan, Bonham, and Valencia ate in the captain's quarters rather than in the officers' mess—"for privacy's sake," Valencia said. Not complete privacy. They were joined by Subteniente Almazán, a quiet young man with the stretched build of a tennis pro.

"The troops massacred in the ambush belonged to his platoon," Valencia said.

The lieutenant nodded solemnly, as if the statement required his confirmation.

"With all our resources, we are no closer to finding out who was behind it," Valencia went on matter-of-factly. "Nothing, nothing, and more nothing. Which makes us wonder if the Brotherhood was not responsible. We are taking another look at the possibility."

Riordan gave a quick jerk of his head. "But you said that that was far-fetched."

Valencia did not respond as lunch arrived, delivered from the mess hall by the short, thickset soldier who had stopped Riordan at the roadblock a few months ago. Army food that purported to be roast chicken, the meat so stringy and tough it must have come from a fighting cock.

"Inspector Bonham was the one who thought it was far-fetched," Valencia said, picking up the thread of conversation. "Lieutenant Almazán has called my attention to the possibility that the fetching might not be far."

With another nod, Almazán elaborated: "The Sierra Madre is lawless. Like your Wild West. Anyone is free to do whatever comes into his head. It could have been some gang muscling in on the Brotherhood's territory. It could have been someone else. Anyone."

Riordan pointed out that this made no sense—the video proved it had been the Brotherhood.

"No sense whatever," Valencia said, tearing at a shred of the *pollo arrosto.* "We have looked at the video twenty times. It was shot in a meadow somewhere. But there isn't a meadow anywhere near where the troops were ambushed. So the bodies were taken to the meadow. Why go through all that trouble?"

Bonham spoke: "In other words, if it was the Brotherhood, why not stage the execution right there, at the ambush site?"

Riordan's ear was attuned to nuances in vocal inflections, and he detected an impatience in Bonham's, as though this ambush business was a subject to be gotten out of the way.

"I don't understand why you're putting these questions to me," he said.

"We'll get to that after lunch," Bonham said.

They finished the meal quickly and in silence. Valencia dismissed the lieutenant, who threw the captain a cursory salute and, after adjusting his beret, strode out.

"Well?" Riordan said to his hosts. "Did you call me here to listen to these theories of yours?"

Valencia shook his head slowly, as if in disappointment with a slow pupil. "In case you hear something about the ambush," he said. "A reminder that we are to hear what you hear. We want you to listen to something." He motioned at an easy chair. "Please."

Riordan moved to it, feeling disoriented and, suddenly, apprehensive. On the table beside the chair was Bonham's laptop, with a flash drive plugged into its USB port. A list of dates ran down the computer screen, and across the top, a time counter, paused at 27 minutes, 14 seconds.

"The sound quality isn't good. We thought you could fill in the gaps," Bonham said, tapping the laptop's trackpad.

Riordan heard noises he couldn't identify, followed by a low voice, fading in and out of audibility: "Bless me, Father. . . . Don't remember when . . ." and then his own voice: "Months? Years? And could you please speak up a little?"

Riordan's eyes widened, his jaw twitched; otherwise, he sat as still as a model posing for a portrait. He remembered the police van parked in the plaza, the one with the antennae. Now that he thought of it, he'd seen it there on previous Friday afternoons, but he'd failed to connect its appearance with confession times. With all the repair work going on in the church, a technician disguised as a laborer must have snuck in to plant the listening device.

"I am with them, Padre. The narcos. [Inaudible.] I've done a lot of . . ."

"Turn that off," he said, half-rising from his chair, his cheeks prickling. "Do you hear me? Turn it off! It wasn't enough that I'd agreed to . . . that I'd done what I'd done? You had to do this?"

Bonham paused the recording, gently pushed him back into his seat, and looked at him with a stare keen, calm, lusterless.

"We had to take precautions, in case you had second thoughts about what you agreed to," he said in his level voice. "And it looks like you've had them. We're disappointed, Padre Tim. Extremely disappointed."

Valencia flopped into a chair kitty-corner from Riordan's, rested his left ankle on the opposite knee, and flicked dirt off the toe of his boot.

"We also had to consider that you and that other priest trade off, so for two Fridays a month we would not be covered. It's been boring, listening to so many trivial sins. Then, *this*." He bared his teeth in what looked like a dog's angry snarl. "We have been waiting to hear from you, but you let us down. A finger who doesn't finger, what use is he?"

A confessional bugged like some low-rent motel room where drug deals go down, Riordan thought. It was a sacrilege.

"You're so clever, what do you need me for?" he said.

"Didn't we cover that? I thought we had covered that," Valencia retorted. "To place voices with names when you can. With this one, to tell us what this woman said. It is difficult to make out what she's saying, except that she works for the narcos, that she had something to do with assassinating the police officers."

"We can send the recording to Mexico City to enhance the sound," Bonham said, standing over the laptop, his long white fingers drumming on the table. "We have people who can do that."

"Where did you get the . . . to . . . This has to . . ." Riordan sputtered. "You will remove that damned thing. I'll do it myself, if I have to."

"The microphone is a miracle of miniaturization," said Bonham. "Smaller than this." His forefinger touched the flash drive. "You would have to tear your dark little closet to pieces, and even then I doubt you'd find it."

"I will not stand for this."

"Yes, you will. You're going to stand for it, all right," Bonham said with icy certitude.

"Unless you're willing to stand for what would happen if it becomes known that you have revealed what is said in your little closet," Valencia added. "You would be removed from the priesthood, correct?"

Riordan was silent.

"Is that correct, priest? I've done some research. There is a term for what would happen to you—"

"Laicized," Riordan said.

"Yes! That's it! You would be no more a priest. You would have to find a job, I suppose. Ha! I like that picture—"

Riordan started to speak, but Valencia stopped him with an upraised hand.

"I know what you're going to say. How can we prove anything. We don't need to. All we need is to start a rumor, plant some suspicions. But in case proof is required . . . you remember the conversation you had with Inspector Bonham? In the interrogation room in the municipal police station?"

"You're going to tell me it was recorded," Riordan said, feeling a little sick. Sick and stupid.

"Audio and video," said Valencia. "It was for our eyes and ears only, no one else, but consider what Señor García would think if he learned that you had fingered his son. Consider the opinion of your parishioners. If you can stand for the shame, the disgrace, the scandal, then you will not have to stand for this."

"What good would I be to you then?" Riordan said, dredging up some defiance.

"Why, no good at all. Really, you haven't been that much good as it is."

He went mute again. He understood now that as an asset he was more a convenience than a necessity. And this understanding bred another: his recruitment had not been entirely a means to gather intelligence; it was also to demonstrate who held power over whom, as Valencia had done when he'd forced him to lie in the dirt at the roadside.

Riordan glanced at three photographs on the captain's desk: one, an antique, showed a man wearing crossed bandoliers, a rifle in his hands; in another Valencia, flanked by a young man and a middle-aged couple—his parents, Riordan surmised—stood in the costume-drama uniform of a cadet; in the third, he was in civilian garb, beside a handsome woman in a blue dress, three children in front, two boys and a girl. That picture captured Riordan's interest, because it had never occurred to him that the captain had a life outside the army.

"That's my great-grandfather during the revolution, the saint burner," Valencia said, motioning at the sepia-toned photo. "And do you see the boy next to me when I graduated from the military academy? My younger brother. Three years younger. Tell me, priest, do you have a younger brother?"

"No. Four older brothers."

"Ah! Four. Did they look out for you when you were in school?"

"They were much older. I had to look out for myself."

"I looked after mine. He wasn't very good at looking out for himself. But, you know, there were so many things I could not protect him from." The martinet with the hard, conquistador's face looked at Riordan intently, loathing in his gray eyes. "He sang in the boys' choir. I'm not kidding you, he was a choirboy. The choirmaster was a priest. My brother wasn't like me—he trusted people. He trusted that priest . . ."

The captain trailed off. His gaze unwavering, he folded his hands and pressed his joined thumbs to his lips, as if to stop himself from speaking further. Riordan cleared his throat, suddenly remembering a comment

Valencia had made when they first met, at the roadblock. Altar boys, he'd said then, not choirboys, but the difference didn't amount to anything. So the poisoned well from which he drew his venom for the clergy wasn't admiration for his priest-hanging, revolutionary ancestor; it was far more direct and personal. The army officer had gained moral leverage. Riordan slumped in his chair, feeling that he should say something, but, really, there was nothing to say.

"My brother never got over it completely," Valencia went on. "But he did better than some others. He got married, had a daughter. He became a journalist—an odd profession for a trusting soul. The narcos murdered him. Have I told you that?"

"No."

"I couldn't protect him from them, either. Which reminds me of another thing you should consider. If the Brotherhood were to learn that you've snitched . . ."

Valencia trailed off again, leaving the consequences to the imagination.

"You're enjoying this, aren't you?" Riordan said.

"To be candid, yes. Immensely."

Bonham made a brushing motion with his hand. "That's enough chatter. Are you ready to continue, Padre Tim?"

Riordan did not respond immediately, trying to find an advantage.

"On the condition that you remove that thing from the confessional. And I want to be there when you do."

Valencia could no longer restrain his natural ferocity. He lunged off his chair, took one long stride toward Riordan, and leaned over him.

"Conditions?" he spat. "You think you can set conditions?"

"Alberto, not now," Bonham said, playing the good cop. Then, as Valencia fell back into his chair, he returned to Riordan. "You ought to be thinking about what they did to Quiroga—"

"I think about him ten times a day every damn day," Riordan interrupted.

"Well, if that doesn't open your mouth, then think about this: you're in the Brotherhood's crosshairs right now. They did what they did to Quiroga to show that they can get to you. All we have to do is leak that you've been working with us and it will be your head in an ice chest. I can't make things any clearer than that." He bestowed a thoughtful look on Riordan. "We'll remove the device, and you can be there when we do, once you prove that we can trust you."

"Yes, show us that we can trust you—priest," Valencia added superfluously.

"Blackmail," Riordan murmured. "What happens to her, the woman who confessed to me?"

"We'll go easy on her if we find her," Bonham said. "Now, are you ready to continue?"

The last tendons of his resistance snapped. He wasn't going to risk disgrace and the loss of his parishioners' love; he certainly wasn't going to risk his life.

"Go ahead," he said.

And they did, Bonham pausing the recording at key moments to question him. Did he know this woman's name? Her given name only: Miranda. Was she from San Patricio? No, Hermosillo. Bonham, not surprisingly, was particularly interested in Miranda's account of how she and her partner lured the officers into lowering their guard. It was the most difficult part to understand, her hushed tone reducing all but a few words into an unintelligible hiss. It was as if she'd been more embarrassed to admit to playing a whore than to being an accomplice to a double homicide.

As requested, Riordan filled in the blank spots.

Pressing a thumb and forefinger between his eyebrows, Valencia bowed his head, as if meditating upon some deep question. "So . . . so, a woman with the gang who murdered and butchered your secretary confesses her crime to you." He raised his head to look directly into Riordan's face. "You have an opportunity to see justice done, and what do you do? What do you say? Nothing, until this minute. What if this bitch told you she planned to blow up your church with dynamite during Sunday Mass? Would you keep your mouth shut even then?"

"Canon law would require it," Riordan said. "But—"

With a flick of his hand, Bonham gestured impatiently. They could discuss canon law some other time. He wanted to know about Miranda's partner. Apparently, Riordan had seen her at . . . what was it? An exorcism? Got a name on her? A description? No name . . . a tall, lean blonde, early to mid-thirties, good-looking in a hard-boiled way. Riordan said she reminded him a little of Barbara Stanwyck in *Double Indemnity*.

"*Double Indemnity*?" Bonham said with a wry smirk. "Are you an old movie buff?"

"Who the fuck is Barbara Stanwyck?" the captain growled.

"An American movie star, now very dead," Bonham responded. To Riordan, he said, "How tall, how blond? A *güera*?" meaning was she naturally fair-haired. "Did you notice a birthmark on her neck? About this big?" He curled thumb and forefinger into a circle smaller than a dime. "On the right side?"

He fired the questions quickly, with an intensity Riordan had not heard before. Normally, whether in Spanish or English, he spoke languidly, sounding almost bored.

"Do you know this woman?" Riordan asked.

"Never mind that. Answer the goddamn questions."

"Five-nine or ten," Riordan replied, hating Bonham, hating Valencia, hating himself, all the while silently begging forgiveness for his hatred. "I can't say if she was a natural blonde or not. And how would you expect me to notice a birthmark that small?"

"Try to be more observant," Bonham advised.

"I'll keep that in mind. Now, what happens to Miranda?"

"We'll track her down, and we'll question her. If she cooperates, I'll consider her an asset, and I—"

"Take care of your assets," Riordan finished.

■ ■ ■

Almost every seminarian knew the saga of Saint John Nepomucene, the fourteenth-century vicar to the archbishop of Prague and confessor to the queen of Bohemia, wife of King Wenceslaus IV. This was not the good King Wenceslaus memorialized in Christmas carols but bad King Wenceslaus, a philandering, paranoid tyrant convinced that even as he was cheating on the queen, she was cheating on him. He commanded John to reveal her confessions, under pain of death. John refused, for which he was imprisoned, tortured, and finally trussed hand and foot and thrown into the river and drowned—the Moldau in some versions of the legend, the Vitava in others.

Riordan's brother Sean had said this about Vietnam: *It was the place where you found out that you weren't who you thought you were.* Father Timothy Riordan's recognition that he was no John Nepomucene was in a way liberating. He saw, not in a sudden burst but, rather, in a gradual dawning, that who he'd thought he was had been a lie, a false self fabricated out of pride: pride in his parishioners' affections, pride in his self-assigned mission as the shepherd who would deliver them from the wolves. It had seduced him into one betrayal, which had led to another. To pride, add raw fear. The thought that he might be captured, murdered, and decapitated by the Brotherhood, were he exposed, made him physically sick. So now the sun was up, shining a merciless light on the truth of his character: he was a physical and moral coward.

He went about his pastoral duties as before, but it was all outward show, a simulation to maintain his clerical cover. Inwardly, he felt unmoored and adrift as, with Father Hugo, he smudged foreheads on Ash Wednesday; as he said daily and Sunday Masses; as he met with the parish council, signed off on the utility bills, checked in with Pamela Childress, to see how her restoration work was progressing; as he ate María's meatless meals on Lenten Fridays, and fasted and prayed and did penance for his own sins, which were now considerable. And as he heard confessions—every other Friday in town, and whenever he managed to get out to the Mayo and Pima and Tarahumara villages in the Sierra. No electronic bugs out there; he was the listening device.

Lent always brought an increase in the repentant population and in the severity of the misdeeds; no run-of-the-mill, off-the-rack transgressions now, as people seldom seen in church unburdened themselves of their gravest trespasses to fulfill their Easter Duty, which was to receive Communion at least once during the Easter season. A woman owned up to frequently stealing from her infirm parents to buy drugs, a man to violating his teenage niece, another to committing adultery more times than he could recall, and yet another to beating his wife in a drunken fury.

Two weeks into Lent, a man came in and admitted to being a Brotherhood *sicario.* Since his last confession, quite a long time ago, he figured he'd killed at least a dozen people. But he'd undergone a kind of foxhole conversion—he now feared for his own life (he didn't say why), and wished to scour the bloodstains from his soul should those fears be realized.

"Who did you kill and why?" Riordan inquired, hoping to hear that the *sicario* had been in on the ambush of Valencia's troops or Domingo's execution. The man's motives were simple: he killed to supplement his meager income. As for who, he could not say for sure. Most times he did not know even their names. He would be told to be at a cartel safe house at a certain time, some guy would be there, tied up in a chair or on his knees, and the *jefe* would say something like "Okay, do it and then get rid of him."

He was an unusually forthcoming penitent, and Riordan wanted to keep him talking because he thought he recognized his voice.

"You mean hide the body?" he asked.

"I have done terrible things, Padre. I cannot speak of them."

"You must, if God is to pardon you."

"We made *posole* of them," he said.

"*Posole*? I don't understand."

It meant dissolving the bodies in a barrel of acid so powerful that it liquefied everything but their teeth, the man explained dispassionately. The soup was then poured out into the ground, and the teeth buried.

So that was one way the disappeared disappeared. It might have been the way Domingo's body vanished, every last cell and bone annihilated. Riordan was silent for a few seconds, scarcely able to believe what he'd heard. In Azazel's kingdom, the power was upon men—and yes, women, too—to speak the unspeakable and do the unthinkable.

"There are no words to describe what you have done," he said, trembling inwardly. "I will absolve you only if you vow, here, this minute, and before God, to tell the police what you have told me."

"But, Padre, I have great remorse for what I have done. You must absolve me."

"No, I don't have to. Swear it. Swear you will, and remember that God knows if you mean it."

"But, Padre . . ." He faltered. "I *am* the police."

Riordan's instincts had been right. He very nearly laughed.

"There are federal policemen all around here. You can surrender yourself to them."

"Very well, I swear it."

The man's attempt to sound sincere failed, but Riordan had backed himself into a corner. He had no alternative now but to pronounce the old words: "I absolve you from your sins . . ." He assigned a penance that wasn't even a slap on the wrist: kneel and pray a rosary every day for the remaining thirty days of Lent, beginning immediately.

After dismissing the penitent, Riordan stepped out of the confessional and told the people in line he would be back in a moment. He needed to confirm that his suspicion was correct. And as he went up the aisle toward the sacristy, he saw that it was. Rigoberto Ochoa, the municipal police sergeant, was kneeling on the stone floor beneath the Virgin of Guadalupe, a rosary in his hands. A cop who moonlighted as an assassin and dissolved his victims' corpses in acid, on his knees before Our Lady. This image had the opposite effect from the one of the repentant Miranda. It was obscene, unnatural, grotesque, like a poster he had seen in front of a Tijuana bar when he was a kid hitchhiking through Mexico; it showed a naked woman fornicating with a man costumed as a gorilla.

Three days days later, Bonham's *federales* raided police headquarters and dragged Ochoa out in handcuffs and leg irons. Betraying him did not greatly trouble Riordan's conscience; he had helped rid San Patricio of a monster.

YouTube COMMUNIQUÉ #3

VIDEO: Full screen of the cover of a self-published book with no graphics, only the title, in bold green letters: MY REFLECTIONS.

Pull back to the same masked man who appeared in the previous videos, seated at a table, with the photo of Emiliano Zapata, the pencil sketch of Che Guevara, and the portrait of *La Santa Muerte* on the wall behind him.

AUDIO: Here we are once again, brothers and sisters, speaking to you from the *comandancia* of La Fraternidad.

The Butterfly flies to you today with exciting news: the Brotherhood will soon be moving into a new phase of its operations, and we hope all citizens of Sonora and, eventually, all of Mexico will join us in our crusade. I cannot present you with the details at this time, not until we are fully prepared to make the announcement.

But first, I wish to read some precepts from my book, *My Reflections*.

VIDEO: Tight on the Butterfly opening his book.

AUDIO: Precept One: The Brotherhood dedicates itself to the goals of love, fidelity, equality, and justice for all the people of Sonora.

Precept Two: The Brotherhood dedicates itself to bring strength where there is weakness, to give voice to the mute, and to the poor, generosity.

VIDEO: The Butterfly turns several pages.

AUDIO: Precept Sixteen: It is wrong to kill for pleasure. When the Brotherhood takes a life, it is only in the cause of divine justice.

Precept Twenty-one: We ask God for strength that He will present us with challenges to make us strong. We ask for wisdom that He will give us problems to solve. We ask for adversity that He will give us a brain and muscles to work.

Precept Thirty: Intelligence without love makes you perverse. Wealth without love makes you greedy. Power without love makes you a tyrant.

VIDEO: The camera pulls back as the Butterfly lays down the book and looks directly at the viewer.

AUDIO: These precepts, brother and sisters, are the inspiration for our new phase, our new endeavor, our new crusade. Think about the last one: Power without love makes you a tyrant. Is that not our situation today in Mexico? Has it not been our situation throughout our history? Our enemies call us criminals, but who is our enemy? It is your enemy. If we are criminals, then is not our government, which has power but lacks love, guilty of greater crimes because it permits extreme wealth to fall into the hands of the few while it allows the many to live in extreme poverty?

These are the questions I would like you to reflect upon as you await our next communiqué.

CHAPTER TWENTY-FOUR

A week after he'd finished interrogating Miranda Galindo-Flores and Rigoberto Ochoa, the Professor, along with Silvio Pérez, the commandant for the Northwest Regional District, rode in the back of an armor-plated Lincoln Navigator as they studied copies of a dossier that had been sent from the Intelligence Division in Mexico City. Pérez's driver piloted the Lincoln slowly through Hermosillo's empty, late-night streets, now and then exchanging a word with the Federal Police sergeant beside him.

There were few female assassins in narcoland. As for tall, blond assassins, the Professor had known of only one: Elvira Friesen, a Mennonite farm girl gone seriously rogue. He'd seen Elvira's photograph several months ago, when he was reviewing the files on the Brotherhood. Looking at it again now, under the glow of the reading light, he disagreed with Padre Tim's description: she was attractive but not as attractive as Barbara Stanwyck, her cheekbones too broad, too square; and the mole on her neck was larger than he'd remembered. The way it sprouted hairs, it resembled a brownish-red spider.

The dossier contained a few facts: Age: 34; height: 177 centimeters; weight: 58 kilograms. Hair, eyes, identifying marks, etc. Joined the army 1995; discharged 1998. Arrested on minor drug charges, 2001. Arrested for possession of an illegal firearm, an AK-47, in 2009. Served six months of a five-year sentence in the Tepepan women's penitentiary. It also contained much raw information gleaned from sources of varying reliability.

Elvira's ancestors had been among the Mennonite immigrants who had fled Russia for Mexico more than a hundred years ago. She'd grown up amid the tidy groves and orchards outside Nuevo Casas Grande in Chihuahua. The Professor guessed that she'd volunteered for the army at seventeen because some mutinous streak in her nature made her gag on the tidiness, on having to wear those nineteenth-century dresses and go to church every Sunday in a horse-drawn buggy. The army had been her ejection seat. She'd learned how to handle firearms and to use language never heard in the trim apple orchards, and she must have grown the emotional carapace that would later allow her to kill people without remorse.

How and when she'd been recruited by the Brotherhood wasn't known. The Professor had first heard of her when the war between La Fraternidad and the Sonora Cartel was at its height. She had played a kind of Mata Hari who slept her way into the higher echelons of Carrasco's organization. She'd vowed undying love to an Agua Prieta city cop who peddled *mota* for Joaquín, then turned him over to a Brotherhood *sicario*. She'd endured weeks of rough sex with a Carrasco underboss before luring him into a Brotherhood safe house, where he was decapitated with a chain saw.

She advanced to *sicaria* when a snitch was caught in a Nogales slum and dragged into a truck occupied by Rubén Levya, *El Tigre Negro* (then a death squad captain and now the Brotherhood's chief enforcer), two other hit men, and Elvira. In the tale told by an informant, Levya made her an offer: if she killed the snitch, she would no longer have to play Mata Hari. "No problem," she replied. The choice of weapons was hers: a nine-millimeter or a hammer. Elvira picked the hammer, with which she cracked the snitch's skull open like a coconut. Quite the young lady, Elvira was.

According to a parenthetical note in her file, the Professor told his colleague, she'd done only six months of her five-year sentence because the warden, in exchange for sexual favors, allowed her to escape. She was smuggled out of Tepepan in a laundry cart—

"Fucked her way back into fresh air?" asked Pérez, incredulous. He was a ponderous man who bore a resemblance to a turtle: goggle eyes, a receding chin, a nose that turned down into his mouth so sharply that the two features appeared as one.

That was shoddy information, the Professor replied. Another note was on the mark: she got out because her conviction had been overturned by a judge, a recipient of monetary favors granted by Rubén Levya, Elvira's boss. He was also her lover, a snippet the Professor had extracted from Ochoa, the San Patricio cop, and had confirmed by the epileptic, hysterical Miranda Galindo-Flores. That discovery excited him, in the way rumors of a gold strike excite a prospector. If they were able to flip Elvira, she might take them into the heart of the Brotherhood's ruling triumvirate, leading them to Levya, he to the number two, Enrique Mora, and then the prize of prizes, Ernesto Salazar, formerly Julián Menéndez. That was the reason the Professor had gone right to the top, to Pérez. This task was too important to be left to the second string.

"You're telling me you got all this from a priest?" the *comandante* said. He spoke with a wet, rough voice, sounding as if he were gargling.

"No. He put us on the right track with Ochoa and Galindo-Flores. I'm as surprised as you are. I never believed he'd come through with anything worth more than spit."

"A gringo priest, shit," Pérez said with a shake of his head. He leaned forward and told the driver, "We're through. Head for the address."

Circling the Plaza Zaragoza, they cruised down a broad avenue toward La Jolla, the upscale neighborhood overlooking Hermosillo and the Cerro de la Compana, picketed with TV and cell-phone towers, their aircraft warning lights flashing. It was good to be in a city again, away from the Sierra Madre and that hillbilly town and the base and Capitán Alberto Valencia, who was getting on the Professor's nerves with his monomaniacal pursuit of his troopers' killers. A couple of days ago, acting on some hazy rumor, Valencia had sent thirty men to a squalid little foothill village and interrogated and terrorized everyone in it. If there was such a disorder as a Captain Ahab complex, this man suffered from it.

Elvira lived well in a new, two-story bungalow in a gated community whose security guard, a tubby pensioner, didn't look capable of deterring a gang of determined six-year-olds. A show of Federal Police badges got them through the gate without delay. Elvira did not answer the loud knock, accompanied by the announcement "Federal Police! Open up!" The sergeant, door-sized himself, kicked hers in. The Professor came close to laughing when they nabbed her in the bedroom. The scene was straight out of a 1950s pulp magazine: four cops confronting a leggy blond femme fatale clad in a satin nightgown, *La Santa Muerte* tattoos decorating her arms, a gun in her hand. She'd probably pulled it from a drawer when the door came down. The driver and the sergeant, pointing MP5 submachine guns at her, restrained her from committing suicide by police. She laid the pistol on her nightstand. The Professor doubted it was the murder weapon, but he gloved his hand with a handkerchief and dropped the Beretta nine into an evidence bag. Pérez, in his liquid rumble, informed her that she was under arrest for the murder of two federal officers on December 24 of last year. Her face was immobile. The Professor gave her credit. She didn't utter any of the usual denials, the lame, shopworn things cornered suspects usually trotted out. All she said was "Well, are you going to let me get dressed?"

"No. Come along, and no funny stuff," Pérez answered.

"I'm not going to jail in this," she protested, pressing her hands to the nightgown's straps.

"You're not going to jail unless you want to," the Professor said.

"What . . . what do you mean?"

"Let's go, Elvira."

They led her to the Lincoln, sandwiching her between Pérez and the Professor, and drove off. For ten minutes, they rode around the neighborhood, then out to the bypass highway. They didn't speak to her, their silence, like the aimless driving, deliberate.

"Where are we going?" she asked, her stony indifference cracking.

"We're not going anywhere," Pérez answered.

"All right, all right, what the fuck do you want?"

"Ernesto Salazar, but we'll start with Rubén Levya."

"Who? I don't know who you're talking about."

Now the Professor was disappointed, and told her so. "Let's not waste time with children's games," he said. "You kill people for him. You've been screwing him for years. I imagine he visits you pretty often in that nice house of yours. Or maybe you shack up somewhere pleasant, a beachfront condo. We want you to keep us, oh, call it current, on what he's up to . . ."

She turned toward him, their faces half an arm's length apart. "Snitch? You want me to *snitch*?"

Her neck muscles strained and twitched as she spoke. He could see the spider-mole twitching with them, up and down her carotid artery. "A little more than that," he said. "We want you to do what you did during your apprenticeship. You screw him, you promise him eternal love, and then you deliver him—in this case, to us."

"You want this Levya delivered, call a delivery service."

"But we have one, right here in this automobile."

"Someone must have shit in your mother's womb for her to give birth to a turd like you."

The malice in the vulgarism was not in its expression; it sounded like a line she'd memorized and rehearsed. Pérez let out a sigh, a loud sigh, a fatigued, I've-heard-it-all-I-can-hear-nothing-new sort of sigh. "We know what a badass you are, Elvira," he said wearily. "You don't need to prove it with trash talk." He tapped the driver on the shoulder. "The station. It is very late, and we need to call it a night."

The driver turned off the bypass and headed toward the Centro, passing the bus depot, the children's park, the plaza. On the Avenida Jesús García Morales, he pulled into the parking lot behind the regional headquarters for the Federal Police, bright as noon under the sodium lights. The Professor reached under his jacket for his handcuffs and manacled Elvira's wrists in front of her, not without a little struggle, a little writhing and twisting that, under different circumstances, might have been a turn-on.

"What the fuck is this?" she squalled.

"You did not hear me?" Pérez said, in the same bored, tired tone as before. "The murder of two police officers, *federal* officers—"

"That makes them special? Federal?"

"Claro que lo hace."

"Nobody's special. Know what a life is worth? The money you spend for the bullets that end it, and I can get them for ten pesos apiece."

She was trying to buy time with cheap philosophizing; they indulged her, because once they brought her inside, the machinery would get rolling—the booking, the fingerprinting, the mug shots—and she would be lost to them.

"So you're confessing?" Pérez asked. "You shot them?'

"I'm not confessing nothing. I think I know who you were talking to—a little bitch who froths at the mouth." Elvira swung her wrists side to side, whacking Pérez in the shoulder. "Take these fucking things off!"

"I forgot to tell you that we are also charging you as an accessory to a third murder," Pérez added, ignoring her remark as well as the thump. "Of a baker. A simple baker, for Christ's sake. A man guilty of nothing."

"If he's dead, he's guilty. Better tears in his house than in mine, that's what I say."

"Do you?" asked the Professor, finally growing impatient. "Then listen to what I say. It is one forty-five in the morning. Today is the first day of the rest of your life! It's up to you where you spend it. Did you enjoy your stay in Tepepan? Maybe you'll go back there, but I think a maximum security place like Santa Marta Acatitla. It's overcrowded. You'll have to sleep on the floor, and you'll be sixty-five, maybe seventy when you get out."

"I don't think she will be in that long," Pérez said. "I don't think the rest of her life will be that long. There are some other girls in there like her, *chicas Kalashnikovs* employed by enemies of the Brotherhood. Besides, the word is bound to get out that she spent this time with us, that she snitched . . ."

He drew in a breath, exhaled another gargantuan sigh, this one sounding regret. Elvira said nothing. The Professor opened the door and clasped her by the arm, but not too firmly.

"Let's get started then," he said.

She wrenched free and raised her cuffed wrists. "Take these fucking things off!"

"Why?"

"Because I have something to tell you, and I'm not going to with them on."

CHAPTER TWENTY-FIVE

"If it's too good to be true, it probably isn't" was an axiom the Professor had found useful in dealing with informants. To determine if it applied to Elvira's intelligence a face-to-face interview with Rubén Levya would be necessary. Convincing him that it would be in his interest to sit down with a Federal Police inspector proved, unsurprisingly, complicated and difficult, requiring days of indirect, long-distance negotiations. But he eventually agreed. It might have helped that his girlfriend was under house arrest, guarded by police twenty-four/seven and electronically manacled to an ankle monitor should she effect an escape.

To allay Levya's concerns that he was being decoyed into a trap, he was allowed to choose the venue for the meeting, and to set conditions. He chose his ranch, where he raised competition cutting horses when he wasn't planning and ordering hits. The ranch was some thirty kilometers down an unpaved road west of Magdalena. The Professor was to come there alone and unarmed; and to make sure that Levya's bodyguards and ranch hands didn't know that their boss was talking to a cop, he was to pose as an American horse buyer. That suited the Professor, who had always enjoyed undercover work. He was good, very good, at pretending to be someone he was not. If the roulette wheel of his life had spun differently, he might well have become an actor, like his mother—only a better one than she.

On a cloudless morning in mid-March, driving a Ford F-250 and costumed in a suede jacket and a black Stetson, he was buzzed through a
barred steel gate with security cameras mounted on the posts. A short
drive through scabrous mesquite flats brought him to another gate, an
ornamental wooden one guarded on the outside by more security cameras and on the inside by men with assault rifles, two of whom hopped
into the Ford and directed him to proceed. The road led uphill to a small,
grassy mesa. After showing him where to park, the *pistoleros* escorted
him on foot to the ranch house, white as a hospital, tucked into a spring-
fed grove of oaks and cottonwoods and enclosed by a wall draped with
bougainvillea. There, eating his breakfast on the patio, sat Rubén Levya.
It was the first time the Professor had seen him in the flesh.

"Ah, Señor Carrington," Levya said, rising to shake hands. "Welcome
to Rancho Santo Niño."

The two gunmen left. The Professor assumed there would be several more nearby, keeping him under observation and themselves out
of sight.

"Please, have a seat," Levya said. "Have you had breakfast?"

"I usually skip it."

"Some coffee?"

"No, thanks."

They had agreed to speak in English, in which Levya was fluent, to
maintain the Professor's cover.

"You will pardon me for eating in front of you?" Levya asked.

The Professor nodded. Nice manners.

Levya dug into a platter of sliced mango and banana and quartered
oranges. His cholesterol was through the roof, he said, and a doctor had
advised him to lay off chorizo and eggs and eat more fruit.

He was dressed narco-garishly—a gold chain vanishing into a bright
blue shirt with dark blue stripes, yellow rings spiraling down their length;
a beaded belt holding up dove-gray pants; green western boots, their toes
as sharp as spear points. His underworld nickname, *El Tigre Negro,* had
been conferred for his skills as a killer and for his dark walnut complexion. His hair, of a shade almost identical to his charcoal irises, made a
straight line low across his forehead, giving him something of an Early
Man appearance. He was anything but a primitive, however. According

to his file in the Intelligence Division, he had a university degree and had taught high school French and English for a few years. The file did not explain how or why he'd gone from academia into his present line of work. There was the money, of course. On a teacher's salary he could not have afforded one square meter of a ranch like this; but, the Professor guessed, there must have been more—the unexpected, and captivating, discovery of a secret self, a killer whose existence had been hidden until some event revealed it. That was what had happened to the Professor. Almost twenty years ago, when he was a young DEA agent, he had jumped the reservation to track down and eliminate three men who had tortured and murdered his partner. He was successful, and his economy and marksmanship had thrilled him: three men, three bullets.

"Let's have a look at the horses I'm selling," Levya said when he finished eating. His Mexican accent was barely noticeable.

They proceeded down a paved walkway bordered by flowers—the man had an aesthetic sense as developed as his ruthlessness—passed an exercise ring, in which a trainer was working a bay, and entered a cut-rock stable housing some twenty horses. The Professor drank in the good smells of horseflesh, manure, and hay, and had a fleeting thought about retiring to a life like this. He owned a couple of Arabians himself.

"Here they are," Levya said, stopping at two stalls side by side at the far end, a sorrel in one, a roan in the other, their coats shiny as rubbed leather in the light slicing through the barred windows. A stable boy, mucking out a stall across from the two, greeted his boss—*"Buen día, Don Rubén"*—who told him to find something else to do.

"All right. Business," said Levya after the boy was gone. He leaned a shoulder into a stall gate, crossed his ankles, and dug the sharp toe of a boot into the dirt.

"These are some fine-looking horses. What are you asking?"

"I'm asking what my dear Elvira told you."

"That you're getting . . . disenchanted with Salazar."

"She said that? 'Disenchanted'?"

"That's my word."

"What is the cause of this disenchantment?"

"First, Salazar gave you a warning because you'd moved some *merca*—heroin—on your own, without his okay. It pissed you off, getting scolded like a schoolboy. Second, and this is the big thing, you think he's going off the deep end, and you don't want to go with him."

Levya said nothing, his dark face expressionless.

The Professor pressed on. Salazar had begun to think of himself as a messiah, divinely ordained to liberate Mexico from tyranny. According to Elvira, he was talking about transforming La Fraternidad into an insurgent army, financed by its drug profits. He wanted to start a revolution, in the name of the weird, gun-toting Christianity to which a Texas preacher named Showalter had converted him. Car bombs in front of government buildings, takeovers of TV and radio stations, kidnapping senators to exchange for Brotherhood prisoners . . .

Levya half-turned and stroked the sorrel's cheeks. "She told you all that?"

"Except for the part about the Texas preacher. That comes from me." The Professor tapped the gate with his finger to draw Levya's attention away from the horse. "What she gave us fits in with Salazar's latest video. He's hinting that he's going to go public with this revolution crap pretty soon. That's why we tend to believe her."

Levya snickered. "Know who shot that video? I did."

That startled the Professor, but he made sure not to show it. "Are you saying you agree with that shit about a . . . what did he call it? A new crusade? Because your girlfriend says you don't."

"Yeah? What does she say?"

"That you told her Salazar was thinking some quote, unquote fucking crazy shit. And that you're not the only one who thinks so. You're not the only one in the organization who doesn't want to be revolutionary. You want to make money. Don't we all?"

"Love does a lot, money everything. Making it is like eating nachos. Once you start, you can't stop until the bowl is empty. And then you order more."

"Is Elvira a truth teller or what?" asked the Professor.

Levya's eyebrows drew together, and he looked down at the thin trench he'd dug with the toe of his boot. He was pondering whether to open up, and how much.

"I told him to his face, 'We're narcos. We're not the fucking Taliban,'" he said, raising his eyes to meet the Professor's. "'You start this revolution shit, we'll have the U.S. Air Force and Navy SEALs down here like that.'" He snapped his fingers. "*La Mariposa*. Would you join a revolution led by a dude who calls himself 'the Butterfly'? The fucking *maricón*."

"Do you think he is, or has he just not found the right girl yet?"

"Ask me if I give two shits. An insurgency, a revolution. *Oye*, man, I'm a patriot and a businessman."

"What about Enrique? Where does he stand on all this?"

"Mora kneels, kissing Salazar's ass. If Salazar tells him to shit, he says, 'In what color, *jefe*? For you I will shit a rainbow.'"

The Professor had heard enough to satisfy his curiosity: the too-good-to-be-true was true after all. "Don Rubén," he said, flattering him with the honorific, "I think it's time for you to do your patriotic duty and work with us to get rid of Salazar, and Mora into the bargain."

"I'm more of a businessman than a patriot. What's in it for me?"

"For starters, you get to avoid going to war with Ernesto. A war you could lose."

Levya puckered his lips and narrowed his eyes into slits. "Elvira told you I'm going to go to war with him?"

"No. But if I owned this horse"—the Professor motioned at the sorrel, nibbling from a hay bale—"I would bet it that you've thought about it."

"'For starters,' you said. What comes after the starters?"

The trainer came in, leading the bay horse to its stall.

"Before you put that one up, saddle this one, the sorrel," Levya said to him. Then, to the Professor in English: "You are shopping for a horse. You want to see what he can do?"

When the gelding was saddled and bridled, they brought him out to the ring, about as big as a baseball infield and surrounded by steel rails. The Professor took off his jacket—the weather had grown warm—and perched on the top rail while Levya mounted up. He sat the horse well as they circled the enclosure at a walk, then an easy lope. Riding to the center, he slacked the reins and put the animal through its paces. Subtle leg cues were all the horse needed to veer sharply left or right, cutting an imaginary calf from its imaginary mother. A curtain of dust sparkled in the harsh sunlight. Far above, turkey vultures soared on the thermals. Levya halted the horse and glanced up at the dark-winged birds.

"They show up every spring, the black hawks with them," he said, with seeming irrelevance. "See 'em, the hawks? Bet you can't, because the hawks look just like the vultures from far away."

The Professor squinted at the sky. "They're called zone-tails. I didn't know you were a naturalist, Don Rubén."

Levya took another spin around the ring, then rode up to the rail, he and the Professor at eye level.

"A good one, this one," he said, patting the sorrel's neck. "He knows what you want him to do before you do. So . . . after the starters . . . ?"

"We know you ordered the hit on two police officers on Christmas Eve. Nothing a cop hates more than a cop killer. After you've done some time in Mexico, the Americans will file an extradition request— you've been indicted there for murder. That guy you put on the floor in Phoenix a couple of years ago. Mexico grants the request to get you off its hands. You get life in a supermax. Solitary twenty-three hours a day. Join us and you get to avoid all that."

Levya, leaning forward on the saddle horn, shrugged off the threat. "You've told me two things I won't get. I need to hear what I will."

This response did not come as a surprise; the Professor regretted hearing it nonetheless. He and Comandante Pérez had discussed what inducements they might offer. They'd agreed that one should be presented only as a last resort. The negotiations had reached that point.

"You cooperate with us, Salazar and Mora go to jail, and the plaza is yours. That doesn't come from me. From high up on the food chain. From the top. You get the plaza."

"That's more like it," Levya said, deadpan. "Except for one thing. Everybody knows that if the Brotherhood is taken down, the plaza is returned to Joaquín Carrasco."

"He's old, he's the past, he'll be taken care of," the Professor stated with crisp finality. Yet it pained him to speak those words. In all his years of double-dealing and double-crossing, he had never double-crossed Joaquín. He might have snitched on a cocaine shipment once or twice to preserve his credentials with his former employers, the DEA, but a betrayal like this—never. "He'll be persuaded that leaving the country is his best option."

Levya had no visible reaction, beyond cocking his head to one side and half-closing an eye in a show of mild interest. "I don't know much about you, Señor Whoever, but I do know one thing: if there was such a thing as a four-sided fence, you could stand on all four sides at once."

Apt, thought the Professor. He laughed sardonically. "Right now I'm on one side, and that's the side I want you on."

At a gesture from Levya, he hopped down from the rail—noticing that the movement wasn't as nimble or sure as it would have been just a few years ago—and unlatched the gate. Levya rode through and dismounted.

"So here I am. Do you want me to kill him for you?"

"We want him alive. We want to parade him in front of the cameras."

"Then what do you want from me?"

"Intelligence we can act on."

Levya looked into the middle distance. He was silent for a long time, seemingly absorbed in thought.

"Maybe I have some. You'll decide if you can act on it."

■ ■ ■

The necessities of his double life had trained the Professor never to betray his emotions; indeed, he'd kept them under restraint for so long that they had atrophied from lack of use. Which was why, as he sped from Levya's ranch, the rapping in his chest and the tingling of his scalp were unfamiliar sensations. He covered the two hundred kilometers to Hermosillo in under ninety minutes. After checking in with Comandante Pérez, he sent an urgent e-mail to the Intelligence Division, requesting aerial photos of certain quadrants in the northeastern Sierra Madre. But the photos Intelligence had on file were years out of date, requiring them to ask their counterparts in the DEA for more recent satellite images. El Paso to Mexico City to Hermosillo—the photos' journey to Pérez's office, where the Professor downloaded them onto his computer, consumed more than forty-eight hours. The delay was not a total waste of time, however; inspired by Levya's casual observation of hawks and turkey vultures, the Professor and Pérez used the time to rough out a plan of attack.

This was what the Professor had learned from *El Tigre Negro* and passed on to Valencia, when he returned to the military base at San Patricio: A fiesta in honor of Salazar's—that is, Julián Menéndez's—forty-fourth birthday was to be held at his Santa Bárbara ranch, which was also his *comandacia*. It was to be an exclusive affair, the guests limited to Levya, Enrique Mora, and the Brotherhood's top lieutenants, together with their guests. Twenty-five to thirty people altogether. The Brotherhood's entire leadership gathered in one place—it could be decapitated in a single operation. Thus had Levya made the too-good-to-be-true even better, without making it any less true. The Professor trusted he'd spoken truth. Experience had taught him to place his trust in a man motivated by greed.

Alberto Valencia's incorruptibility, a virtue almost as extinct in Mexico as the imperial woodpecker, was cemented to his fault: inflexibility. Whether he was incorruptible because he was inflexible or the other way around, the Professor couldn't say; but he was sure that the rigidity in the man's nature produced his single-mindedness and blinkered vision.

That was the only way to explain the captain's reaction to the Professor's report. His first comment was: Why didn't you interrogate Levya about the ambush and the video of the faked executions? The orders must have originated with him, the Brotherhood's *sicario* in chief. Because, the Professor remarked, that incident no longer mattered. Valencia jerked his head, as if slipping a punch. No longer mattered? He stomped around his headquarters, the smoke from his cigarette drawing curlicues in the air as he waved a hand. *No longer mattered?* Well, what could he expect? The deaths of four soldiers would not matter to a cop who had recruited the man responsible for the deaths of his brother officers. Let him off in trade for nothing more than a promise to cooperate. A promise Levya probably would not keep!

Nada mejor que un ladrón para atrapar a otro ladrón, said the Professor. It takes a thief to catch a thief. *Quien con perros se echa, con pulgas se levanta,* countered the captain. If you lie down with dogs, you will get up with fleas. The Professor had lain down with so many dogs he'd become one, which brought another proverb to mind: *No todas las verdades son para dichas.* There are truths best kept to oneself. He'd omitted mention of the promise made to Levya; the arrangement was too far outside the flea-free chamber of Valencia's incorruptibility. Much too far.

"You do see the chance we've got here?" he asked, genuinely curious. If the captain did not, then he suffered from more than poor vision; he was an idiot.

"Of course I do. I don't like what it may cost—that bastard of a butcher walking around free."

He'll be doing more than that, the Professor thought. "A bargain, I'd say."

"We'll find out how great a bargain you struck." Valencia dropped into a chair, facing a TV screen wired to the Professor's computer. "Let's see what you've got," he said.

To preserve security, the clerks and the company sergeant had been dismissed. The Professor pulled down a window shade, shutting out the hard March sunlight, and began his slide show, projecting from the computer to the TV a topographic map showing the Santa Bárbara location, on a high mesa in the Sierra Madre, near the Chihuahuan border. Ten satellite photos of the ranch followed: wide shots, tight shots of the ranch house, a couple of guesthouses, stables, and an airstrip, roughly half a kilometer from the buildings. It was a thousand meters long, the main delivery point for the cartel's shipments of Colombian cocaine. Except for burro paths that even burros would find objectionable, the only way onto the ranch was by plane. Everything for the fiesta—the food, the beer, the musicians—was going to be flown in; likewise, the guests. Levya had already chartered a Cessna for himself and a few bodyguards.

"And, of course, Salazar has more than a few around this rancho," said Valencia, looking fixedly at the screen.

"But not many more," the Professor said, pleased to have focused the captain's attention on the objective. "He relies on the geography. And on the locals to warn him if anyone's coming." A click brought up a photo of a cell-phone tower on a hilltop overlooking the landing field. "So they can stay in touch with him. Levya told me he had the thing flown in in pieces and reassembled. He piggybacks off a network."

"So our problem is, how do we crash his birthday party."

The Professor nodded. Because the military was in charge of Joint Operation Falcon, he said nothing about the plan he and Pérez had devised to solve this problem. He would nudge Valencia into thinking it was his own idea.

"Let me see that topographic map again," the captain said. When it reappeared, he studied it for half a minute. "So, absolutely no way in there by land."

"Except for the burro trails."

"It would take at least a day to move our people in on foot. Salazar's lookouts would know we were coming," Valencia said. "And helicopters . . . too noisy . . ."

"Right," the Professor said. "He'd be warned before they got there. There's an escape tunnel, starts under the main house. Levya's seen the entrance, but he doesn't know where it ends up."

Valencia rose, went to the computer, and clicked back to the image of the airstrip.

"We are left with that," he said. "Fixed-wing aircraft . . ." His glance turned from the screen and fell on the painting that enlivened the dull, functional wall: a depiction of the Battle of Camarón, when the Mexican army defeated the French Foreign Legion. "But that has its problems, too. Our people would have to cover five hundred meters from the landing field to the ranch house. Salazar would have time to crawl into the tunnel."

"But it's not an insurmountable problem."

"Are you suggesting we parachute in?" the captain said, smirking at the absurdity of such a notion.

"No. But I've been thinking: the guests, the cooks, the musicians, everybody is flying in—"

Interrupting himself, the Professor went to the window, raised the shade, and, craning his neck, directed his gaze toward a cloud of turkey vultures soaring above the hill just beyond the base's walls.

"Come over here a minute," he said. Valencia joined him. "Do you see those birds?

"*Buitres,*" the captain said, with a baffled look.

"Not all of them. Zone-tailed hawks are mixed in with the vultures."

"I see no difference."

"Neither would a field mouse or a lizard. Those hawks fly with turkey vultures because they look like them—the same two-toned wings. Deceptive camouflage. So if you were a little lizard or a field mouse, you would think, 'Those are vultures up there, they only eat dead things, I'm safe.' You come out into the open, but you've been tricked. A hawk swoops down and kills you."

Watching the birds—rising, dipping, but always circling, as if caught in a vortex—Valencia reflected on this natural history lesson. His lips stretched into a thin smile. He was stubborn and inflexible, but he wasn't stupid. He got the idea. With a little more nudging, he would be made to believe it was his.

"That *pendejo* of a priest should be here," he said. "He would enjoy hearing you speak in parables."

"We owe the *pendejo* a vote of thanks."

"That's a ballot you cast alone. How much time do we have?"

"Ten days," the Professor said.

CHAPTER TWENTY-SIX

"Y ou never finish a painting, you abandon it," Pamela said to Lisette and Father Tim. "And I'm abandoning this one."

She looked at them, silently appealing for favorable opinions, which she got. His were the more learned—sounded it, anyway. Lisette could manage only a pathetic "It's really interesting."

The painting was one of Pamela's larger works, three feet square. It stood on an easel in the courtyard, allowing the natural light to show it to best effect, and it *was* interesting but in the wrong way: "disturbing" described it better. Not a word Lisette would use, wary of upsetting Pamela. The lithium had restored her equilibrium since the episode in Álamos, but the drug wasn't always up to the task. And she sometimes skipped a dose to give herself a lift. Working furiously to complete the painting, she had become both fragile and explosive, like a hand grenade made of fine bone china. One afternoon, Lisette criticized the placement of a triptych mirror Pamela had hung in their bedroom, above a tall chest of drawers. "I'd have to be six feet six to look into it," she had said, perhaps too sharply. "Why not here"—she crossed the room—"right here next to the door." Pamela shattered in an instant. "If that's where you want it, hang the damn thing there yourself!" she yelled, and she flung the hammer like a tomahawk—not directly at Lisette but close enough to scare her and hard enough to gouge the adobe wall. Remorse followed the outburst almost immediately. "Oh my God!" Pamela cried, flying to Lisette and embracing her. "I didn't mean to. . . . I've been working too hard. . . . I am so sorry. . . . Forgive me. . . . Please say you'll forgive me." Lisette said, "Patch that hole and I will," but with forgiveness already in her voice. Pamela gave her a devouring kiss. "I will, promise. You're a darling." Within ten minutes they were naked and in bed. *Like the hillbillies back home,* Lisette thought when the lovemaking was over. *Fight and fuck.*

Now, addressing Father Tim, Pamela said, "Don't tell me you like it if you don't. I am open to constructive criticism. You may fire when ready."

Her hands as she wiped them with turpentine trembled slightly—a lithium side effect.

"I'm saying I like it because I do," he responded, pitch-perfect. He seemed to sense that she was on edge and not open to any sort of criticism. On the other hand, maybe he had nothing critical to say. "It's striking, original. The blend of styles—Vincent van Gogh meets Jackson Pollock."

"Thank you," she said, giving his arm a light, flirtatious brush, empty of promise. "But I don't see the van Gogh influence."

Father Tim riveted her with a gaze as admiring as the one he'd cast on the painting. Even in her work clothes—a faded flannel shirt worn tails out, paint-spattered jeans, a kerchief wound around her head—she looked beautiful. Any blind fool could see he had a crush on her. A platonic crush, Lisette assumed.

"That . . . that effect in the clouds, that roiled effect," he said, tracing wavy lines in the air with a finger.

Lisette examined the canvas again, and wondered if he was telling Pamela, diplomatically, that he also found it disturbing. The clouds had the chaotic look of ocean waves crashing into a rocky shore; the random smears and points of color bore no resemblance to what they were supposed to be—desert flowers in bloom; and the greenish thing in the middle, representing a saguaro, looked like a tree in a Gothic fairy tale, its arms bent and twisted. There was a derangement in the scene, a distortion of reality, as if it had been painted through a thick pane of leaded glass.

Pamela lit one of her carefully rationed cigarettes and, with her right arm crooked, its elbow cupped by the palm of her left hand, studied her creation for a moment. "I can't see what else I can do for it," she said, then put the cigarette in a coffee saucer and picked up one end of the canvas. Father Tim took the other end, and they carried it into the guest room to dry.

Lisette went to her office, doubting her own perceptions, asking herself, Am I getting a little wacky? Seeing signs of lunacy where there are none? Life with a bipolar person, she'd learned, could upset your own mental balance. After they'd returned from Álamos, she had told herself, "We've made a mistake," and considered ending their affair. But she couldn't bring herself to do it, dreading the loneliness that would follow. Besides, she was responsible for bringing Pamela to San Patricio. It had been her idea that they try living together. She couldn't tell her to pack her bags because of one spell of ugly behavior that hadn't been entirely Pamela's fault. To an extent, Lisette retained the lessons of her hard-shell Baptist upbringing. What her family's minister had preached about faith—it was refined in adversity, as gold is in the fire—was also true of love. If her love for this talented, troubled woman was genuine, it would survive the trial of Pamela's inner demons.

Father Tim appeared in the office doorway and tapped on the door frame. Looking up from her cluttered desk, Lisette waved him in.

"Thanks for stopping by to play art critic," she said, shuffling through a sheaf of documents.

"Glad to. The work she's doing in the church is top-notch. I can't thank her enough. Catching you at a bad time, am I? You look busy."

"Sort of." Lisette scanned the papers, then stuffed them into a manila envelope. "We're off to the States this coming weekend."

He raised his eyebrows. "The States? Holiday?"

"Hardly. There's a Mayo girl, Evangelina Morales, going blind in both eyes. We're flying her to a hospital in Philadelphia for a procedure—a vitrectomy, it's called. Pam got her father to set it up. He's on the board of trustees for the Wills Eye Hospital. It's one of the best on the planet."

A kind smile broke across Father Tim's face. "Well, good for both of you. This procedure, it's for what?"

"Diabetic retinopathy. Hemorrhaging in the eye caused by diabetes, in plain English. Pam and I have to go with her. The kid is only twelve, never been outside her village, much less to Philadelphia, never been in a car, much less an airplane." She held up the manila envelope. "Admission papers, travel documents, airline tickets, papers for her family to sign authorizing us to take her out of the country. All set up and paid for by Daddy Childress and his fellow board members."

"Generous of them."

"Rich people making themselves feel good about themselves. But I'll take it."

The statement caused him to flinch. "Y'know, Lisette, you might try to be a little less abrasive."

"Well, pardon me. This operation isn't going to do Evangelina Morales any good in the long run if she keeps eating crap. But crap is all her mother can afford." She rifled through the clutter and picked up a report from the Mexico's National Foundation for Public Health. "Diabetes: number one cause of death," she said, rattling the pages. "Every state except next door in Chihuahua."

He gave her a quizzical look. "They have better diets in Chihuahua?"

"Nope. Over there, murder has replaced diabetes as the number one cause of death. Anyway, Pam and I are going tomorrow to get Evangelina's family to sign off on the permission papers."

"So it's all right with them?" Father Tim asked, a somewhat dubious undertone in his voice. "I'd be surprised if they have any idea where Philadelphia is."

"Well . . ." Lisette hesitated, the soft ring of doubt in Father Tim's voice giving her pause. "I've got her mother's okay. She wants me to do whatever I can. Evangelina's father is dead, and her mom is illiterate, so her grandfather will have to read and sign the consent forms. I've never met him."

"You said you're heading there tomorrow. Where is there?"

"San Tomás," she answered.

"That's a coincidence," Father Tim said. "We're headed to San Tomás day after tomorrow." He adopted a diffident posture, shoving his hands into his pockets and hunching his shoulders. "But I think we could move it up a day. Would you mind if we caravanned with you?"

"We who?"

"Me, Moises Ortega, César Díaz."

"César? Risky for him to be going up there. That's narco country. What for?"

"A civic-improvement project," Father Tim replied. "Rebuilding a decrepit rope-and-plank bridge that spans the Santa Teresa."

The municipality had promised to fix it but, as usual, had done nothing; so he had taken up two special collections at Mass to buy materials and tools. César had volunteered to do the repairs.

"Turns out he knows something about bridges. He was in the engineers when he was in the army. I never knew that about him."

She looked at him skeptically. "What do you know about bridge building?"

"Zero minus nothing. He wants me to come along."

"Because, with the beloved padre there, there'll be less likelihood of trouble from the bad guys? From what I know, the bad guys aren't crazy about you, either."

"I suppose that's true."

"And you asked if it'll be okay to follow me, because the beloved Dr. Moreno would provide a little extra insurance against trouble. Shame, shame," she scolded in a joking way. "Hiding behind a woman's skirts."

"I'm confident there won't be any trouble."

"Better not be. Pam will be with me. To meet Evangelina and her mother. If anything happens . . . Well, I won't say it."

■ ■ ■

That afternoon, Lisette and Pamela shopped at the *supermercado* on the Calle Juárez, which was super only in comparison with the shabby *tiendas* on the edge of town. Lisette was assembling a food parcel for Evangelina and her mother. She filled the cart, which Pamela pushed, with dried beans, bananas, oranges, *nixtamal*, and whatever else she could find that wasn't loaded with sugar and trans fats.

"Mother Moreno, Mother Moreno," Pamela said in a singsong. "Mother Moreno will make her kiddies eat right if it kills her." She laughed her light and trilling Pamela A laugh, the one Lisette loved to hear; the brittle Pamela B laugh made her grind her teeth.

"I'm looking forward to tomorrow," Pamela went on as they carried the groceries to Lisette's Dodge. "We'll be doing something together, a team. Instead of you doing your thing and me, mine. And I'm eager to see what the Sierra Madre looks like from the inside. There's a kind of mystery to it."

Lisette fished the keys out of her purse and climbed into the pickup. Pulled herself in, actually; with her short legs, she needed the handgrip above the door.

"Don't expect anything picturesque," she said. "It's pretty backward."

"I think I can handle backward," Pamela said, then leaned over and placed a hand on Lisette's wrist just as she was about to switch on the ignition. "Thanks for putting up with me the last few weeks."

"Honey, I'm not *putting up* with you." Lisette threw an arm around her. She felt strong and protective. "It's not like you're a run of bad luck."

"Patient, then. Thanks for being patient. I know I've been difficult. All I can say for myself is that when one of those spells starts, it's like I've been injected with a drug and I can't stop it. Matter of fact, I *don't want* to stop it, because then it's a real rush. I feel like there's nothing I can't do and that everything I think or say is incredibly brilliant. It's only later that it gets bad and the fan belt in my brain breaks."

"Stay on the meds and you'll be okay. Dr. Lisette's orders."

Pamela gave her an affectionate peck on the cheek. At the same moment, as if by design, Paulina Herrera—the woman Father Tim referred to as "the Very Pious Señora Herrera"—emerged from the market, stopped, and stared at them. Lisette pulled away from Pamela's lips, switched on the ignition, and drove off toward the house.

"What the hell was that all about?" Pamela said, with an injured look.

"Someone saw us. Happens to be a patient of mine, and a gossip."

"So? We weren't doing anything."

"It might not have looked that way to her. I probably overreacted."

Pamela let out a breath, flapping her lips. "It does get wearing, all this . . . what's the word I'm looking for? Restraint. All this pretending. We can't show any physical affection for each other in our own house when Anna is there. Or the cleaning lady. Conchita or whatever—"

"Consolata."

"Right. Right. Consolata. No kissing, no touching on the days Consolata comes to mop up. Mess up the bed in the guest room so she doesn't suspect we sleep together. And God forbid if we're walking somewhere and I put my arm around you. It wears me out sometimes."

They circled the plaza, where vans dispensing iced *raspados* vied for space with police SUVs and army trucks; then they headed up the steep Calle Insurgentes.

"I did tell you, didn't I, that we'd have to watch ourselves?" Lisette said. "That this town is more Catholic than the Vatican?"

"It's one thing to hear about it, another thing to live it. Sometimes I feel like I'm back in the day when coming out was what debutantes did."

Lisette threw her sidelong look. "Did you? Come out as a deb, I mean."

"Oh, yeah. The Philadelphia Charity Ball. I was seventeen. My escort looked like he'd stepped out of a Ralph Lauren catalog. And I had to make off that I was entranced, waltzing in his arms, and never ever let on that I'd already experimented with alternatives."

Lisette felt it like a flash fever—that old class antagonism mixed with class envy—as she pictured the tall, pretty girl and the Ralph Lauren catalog boy, whirling under a chandelier in some grand ballroom. She pulled into the alley behind the house and parked.

"My senior prom in the high school gym is what I remember," she said. "Kissing my date in the car after the dance. I grabbed him because I knew what I was and I was fighting it and I thought if I kissed him real hard something would happen."

Pamela looked at her, wide-eyed. "Like what? That the guy would . . . ?"

"Not that. No. That it would change me. It was the reverse of what usually happens. The desire leads to the kiss. I hoped the kiss would lead to the desire. It was the same thing when I got married, when it was more than kissing."

"Yeah, oh yeah," said Pamela, bobbing her head. "Do I know that feeling. I've been there." She looked up and down the alley and said mischievously, "No gossips in sight."

With desire in its rightful place, their kiss was long and avid. It made Lisette feel that she was going to jump out of her skin. "Okay, let's not push our luck," she said, her voice slow and thick.

They got out of the car and carried the shopping bags into the kitchen and dropped them on the table. Recovered from the effects of the kiss, Lisette fetched a cardboard box from under the sink and set it down next to the bags.

"How do you feel about going back to Philly?" she asked.

"Oh, it's different now than it was then," replied Pamela. "All in all, Philadelphia is looking pretty good—"

"I was referring to your mother. How should we . . . uh . . . *comport* ourselves when we see her?"

Pamela pondered the question while they transferred the groceries to the box.

"'Comport'—that's a word I haven't heard in a while. We shall comport ourselves like the adult women we are, and keep contact with Mamá to the minimum possible. She's seventy-seven, but she can still bite."

"I'll bear that in mind," Lisette said, then motioned at the box. "I don't want to forget this tomorrow." She folded the flaps and lugged it outside to the pickup.

Following her, Pamela asked, "Has going back to the States ever crossed your mind? You did tell me you could practice there."

"Sure. And you know what I'd be? Just one more doctor in some medical group or other."

"What's so terrible about that?"

"I'd be easily replaced. 'Fungible' is the word. A fungible cog in the medical machine." She slammed the tailgate shut, a little harder than necessary. "I love these people, Pam. They need me."

"Have you ever thought that you love them *because* they need you?"

"Have you been talking to Nick? That sounds like him."

"I need you, too," Pamela said, turning on her heel to go back into the house. "You're so solid. You're my rock."

■ ■ ■

The drive to San Tomás, two and a half spine-cracking hours in César's farm truck, left Riordan feeling as if he'd been inside a clothes dryer, though he ignored the discomfort. Going into the mountains always invigorated him; it made him feel closer in spirit to Father Kino and the early missionaries, striking out into the wilderness, though at the present stage in history the Sierra Madre was more a moral than a physical wilderness.

They rattled through the village, which was nothing more than a few dozen mud-brick shacks, scattered like puzzle pieces across a flat expanse a thousand feet below the crest of the Sierra Madre, the slopes shaggy with pine forests scarred by the clear-cuts made by pirate loggers. Stringy-looking chickens ambled about, pecking at the ground, and goats nibbled on the abundant rubbish. Plastic tarps enclosing a latrine flapped lazily in the wind.

Riordan spotted Lisette's Dodge parked on a low hill between a house and the rural public health dispensary. Driving at her usual death-wish speed, she'd easily outrun the rattletrap truck. César went down a side road—a burro path, really—turned around, and backed up to within ten yards of the foot of the bridge, flung across a gorge in the Río Santa Teresa, sixty feet wide and as many deep.

"*Mierda*, look at this thing," he said after they got out to inspect it. Standing well back from the edge—as close as he dared—Riordan could see that it sagged in the middle, forming a curve like the rocker of a rocking chair. Planks were askew, separated by gaps a foot wide. Two tall pine trees, spaced several feet apart, anchored the bridge on the near side. The suspension cables—thick ropes—had been wound around them and tied off with half hitches. He could not imagine crossing the rickety, jury-rigged structure. That people did testified as much to their fatalism as to their nerve and agility.

He put on his lined denim jacket. Spring weather, if not spring itself, had arrived in San Patricio, but at this altitude, better than seventy-five hundred feet, winter hung on. From the truck, the three men unloaded two-by-six boards sawn to three-foot lengths, coils of synthetic and manila rope, eyebolts and other hardware, plus power tools and a diesel generator to run them.

César studied the bridge again, hands on his hips, chest thrust out, as if he were confronting an adversary. "First thing we gotta do is tension those suspension cables," he said.

He cranked up the generator, plugged in the power drill, bored pilot holes into each of the pine trees, and screwed eyebolts into the holes.

"Okay, Padre, you and Moises grab the right cable from in front of the tree and you pull on it. Pull hard."

This brought Riordan much closer to the edge of the gorge than he cared to be—within three feet. The rope bit into his soft, priestly hands as, shutting his eyes, leaning backward against the cable's resistance, he stood behind Moises and hauled like a tall-ship sailor raising the main.

From behind, César called, "Leggo now."

Riordan released his grip and stepped back, relieved. César had untied the cable, passed it through the eyebolt, and lashed it to the truck's tow hitch. He then got behind the wheel and eased the truck forward. The bowed cable began to straighten and tighten, and as it was lifted higher than the one on the left, the old, loose planks tipped into the river below. There wasn't much water in it; Riordan heard a sickening clatter as the boards struck bare rock.

Now the cable had to be refastened to the pine. César untied it from the tow hitch. With all three men holding it taut, they circled the tree in what looked like a primitive dance and wrapped it around the trunk in neat coils. César secured it to the eyebolt with an elaborate knot. The left side was tensioned in the same manner, as were the thinner hand-rails above each, and it was satisfying to look at the four lines, now strung ruler-straight over the chasm.

His pitted face flushed from effort, César winced and slapped his breastbone. "Too much salsa on my eggs this morning."

"I don't know why you took this on, but these people will be glad you did," Riordan said.

"I don't know why either." He bowed his head thoughtfully. "Maybe I want to do one last thing for them before I go to El Norte."

"Leave a legacy?" asked Riordan.

César laughed. "Yeah, maybe they'll name this bridge after me. The César Díaz Stupid Bridge. The municipality should be doing this job. We are looking at what's wrong with this country—nobody wants to do anything, but everybody wants to be somebody."

"That's why you're leaving. Mexico is screwed up, you said."

"'Fucked' is what I said. Mexico is fucked, and she has fucked herself. If she was only screwed up, I would stay."

"I would like to talk you out of it," Riordan said earnestly.

"Save your breath. I don't like sleeping with a loaded pistol next to my bed. I don't like walking around with a personal bodyguard. Do you know I was scared to come out here? I came anyway, maybe *because* I was scared. But I'm tired of looking over my shoulder all the time."

"You organized the *autodefensa*. You're fixing this bridge. Mexico needs people like you."

"*Oye*, Padre Tim. Save your sermons for Sundays. The decking comes next."

He took one of the two-by-sixes and, kneeling down, centered it over the suspension cables and drilled a hole into each end, about three inches in. After threading short strands of synthetic rope through the holes, he tied the board to the cables, then pushed it forward and attached a second plank.

"So, that's how we do this," he said, and handed a tape measure and carpenter's pencil to Riordan. "You mark the boards in the exact same place, both ends. Moises, you drill the holes. I do the rest."

And so they began. Very soon they were operating as efficiently as a production line. Riordan traded off with Moises on the drill, the first manual labor he'd done in years. He gloried in it—the drill's whine, the smell of new wood, the thudding generator—and thought of his mentor, Father Batista, never reluctant to pick up a hammer, a saw, a shovel.

Within an hour, the deck reached out some ten or twelve feet. Its weight and the friction of rope on rope made it impossible for César to shove it forward and add new planks from behind. He had to do it from the front end, with a sixty-foot drop in front of him, the bridge swaying each time he walked out onto it. Riordan couldn't watch. He took off his jacket—now, past noon, it felt more like spring up here. Two more planks, another two. The decking reached more than halfway across when César signaled to shut off the generator and called for a break.

He flopped down against one of the pines, the flush gone from his cheeks, his complexion faded from cinnamon to pale sand.

"*Jefe*, you feelin' okay? You don't look so good," Moises said.

"The generator," César said. "Those fumes, makin' me a little sick. Gimme couple minutes."

"Lunchtime, *jefe*. You need somethin' to eat."

Moises went to the truck and brought back a cooler stuffed with

María's chicken fajitas and cold cans of Coke. His normally ravenous appetite sharpened by the labor and the mountain air, Riordan tucked in. César merely nibbled.

While they ate, a trio of young women wearing long Mayo skirts approached. One held a dirty toddler by the hand; the other two carried infants in shawls slung over their backs. Evidently, news of Riordan's arrival in San Tomás had spread; the women asked if he would bless them and their children, which he did, crossing each forehead with his thumb.

"Padre, will you say a Mass for us?" begged the woman with the toddler.

"Maybe, when this is finished."

They thanked him and shambled off in the dust.

"*Muy bien. De vuelta del trabajo.* Back to work," César said, and got to his feet, leaving his lunch half-eaten.

■ ■ ■

Lisette and Pamela waited to see Javier Morales, the blind girl's grandfather, in the kitchen of Cornelia Valdez, his eldest daughter. Evangelina and her widowed mother, Alma, lived with Cornelia, a *curandera* who had attempted to treat her niece's eyesight with herbal remedies. Alma and Evangelina were not there when Lisette and Pamela arrived. They were with Javier, Cornelia said. She sent one of her children to find him; he was the head of the family, so he made all the decisions.

They sat down at a picnic table that must have been salvaged from a trash dump—initials, names, and dates had been carved into its surface. The kitchen, attached to Cornelia's house by two rough-hewn beams, was open on three sides, a kind of ramada roofed with sheet metal laid over woven tree branches, its dirt floor partially covered with tattered straw mats. Ashes smoldered in the oven, made of sun-baked mud; bundles of herbs hung from the crooked rafters. They gave off a mixture of pleasant, if unidentifiable, smells that relieved less savory odors, like the stench from a nearby latrine.

Doing her best to ignore the squalor, Pamela sat with her legs crossed, hands clasped over a knee, a bland expression drawn over her face to hide her discomfort. Lisette had warned her that San Tomás was backward, but she hadn't expected anything quite this backward. The dirt, the stink, the flies, the scrawny dogs foraging in trash piles. She'd gasped when, going to a rain barrel to wash her hands, she'd seen nests of pale brown, long-legged water spiders covering the surface rim to rim. Less than thirty miles away, San Patricio seemed in another world.

Waiting for Javier, Lisette whiled away the time by talking to Cornelia about her powders and potions. Curing Evangelina's blindness was beyond her powers, Cornelia admitted, but she had restored health to other people, a lot of them, and offered to reveal her secret remedies the next time Lisette visited San Tomás.

Finally, Javier, a retired municipal policeman, arrived. He pulled up in a new, chrome-trimmed pickup far beyond the means of a man living on a pension. The rumors Lisette had heard were probably in the bull's-eye: he oversaw the Brotherhood's agricultural enterprises in the region around San Tomás. Entering the ramada, he dismissed Cornelia with a twitch of his head but was courtly toward Lisette and Pamela, doffing his hat in greeting. He was about sixty years old, and built like a mailbox. With his steel-gray hair, bushy gray eyebrows, and clipped gray beard, he looked more like an Old Testament patriarch than a kindly grandfather, and he projected such an air of stern, confident authority that he seemed half a foot taller than his five feet six. Regarding Lisette with the steady but indifferent gaze of a cat, he sat down and said in a voice accustomed to command, "*Muy bien. Usted hablar, vaya a escuchar. Entonces vaya hablar tú, escuchar.*"

"*Dónde están Evangelina y Alma? Se vienen?*" she asked, unsettled by their absence.

"*Ellos están en mi casa. No se preocupe por ellos.*"

"What's he saying? What happened to the girl and her mother?" Pamela whispered.

"He said that I should talk and he'll listen, then he'll talk and I'll listen. They're at his house, we're not to worry about them."

"But they—"

"*Quien es esta mujer?*"

"*Mi amiga. Una americana,*" Lisette replied.

"*Qué está haciendo aquí?*"

He might have been retired, but he retained a cop's suspiciousness. She explained that Pamela was there to meet his daughter and granddaughter because her father had arranged for Evangelina's treatment in the United States. She added a kicker to show that she was not easily intimidated: *"Disculpe, abuelo. No puedo hablar si sigues haciendo preguntas."*

Pamela leaned toward her. "Now what?"

"He wanted to know who you are and why you're here, and I told him. I also told him that I can't talk if he keeps asking questions. You, too, Pam. I'll fill you in when we're done."

Despite her facility in Spanish, she struggled to describe Evangelina's condition and its treatment to Javier in layman's language. Vitrectomy and retinopathy wouldn't do. There was bleeding behind her eyes, she said. A delicate procedure was necessary to stop it. This procedure would take a couple of hours, her recovery about a week. She assured him that she and Pamela would accompany his granddaughter throughout the journey; they would visit her in the hospital as she recovered. Evangelina would be home in less than two weeks. She pulled the airline tickets from the manila envelope and showed him the departure and return dates. He did not give them a second glance; he continued to look at her with his unwavering, neutral stare.

But before his granddaughter could leave Mexico, Lisette went on, these forms had to be read and signed by her parent or a guardian. She explained their purpose and pushed them across the table. Javier did not look at them.

"Abuelo, por favor, lea y firme ellos," she said.

"No es necesario para leerlos. Ella no va a los Estados Unidos. Ella se quedará aquí," he responded in a tone that left no opening for argument.

"No entiendo. Por qué? Por qué razón?"

An implacable look washed the indifference from his eyes as he raised his chin and said, *"Debido a que la matarán y cosechar sus órganos."*

Utterly unprepared for such an answer, she was stymied for a retort. He could not have shocked her more if he'd struck her.

Javier rose and put on his hat and said he was through listening and talking and had nothing else to say. Lisette grabbed his sleeve, pleading with him to wait, to please wait. He could not possibly believe such a crazy thing, could not possibly believe that she would allow any harm to come to Evangelina.

She was doubtless an honorable woman, he said. But she was being deceived. He had been a policeman for thirty years, and he knew what happened to Mexican children in the United States. Sometimes their bodies were found, missing their hearts, their livers, their kidneys.

She demanded to know where he had heard such nonsense.

"*No es una locura, señora, y no tiene sentido,*" he said, with a thrust of his stubborn jaw.

"*Lo siento, perdón, abuelo,*" Lisette apologized, and begged him to reconsider. Evangelina would suffer no harm, except that she would go totally blind without the operation. Shaking with frustration, she tried to punch through his armor of ignorant obstinacy. You are the one harming her by keeping her here, she said, passionately. You, Abuelo Javier—

"*Terminando,*" he replied through compressed lips. "*Buen dia, señora.*"

Helpless, Lisette watched him climb into his chrome-gilt truck and drive off. Then, swamped by a sadness that was first cousin to grief, she gathered the papers and stuffed them back into the envelope.

Pamela frowned in confusion. "What the hell? You said you'd fill me in, so fill me in."

"He won't give his consent. The girl stays right here."

"*What?* Why?"

"You won't believe it."

"Try me."

"He thinks—no, he's certain—that she'll be killed so her organs can be harvested."

Blinking rapidly, Pamela looked at her without speaking.

"I told you you wouldn't believe it."

"My father . . . he thinks that my father would . . . *harvest her organs?* Dad doesn't like to step on ants, and this Javier thinks he would . . . ?"

"It's not personal, Pam. He doesn't know your father from a hill of beans. He's just got this idea that Mexican kids who cross the border end up with their hearts and livers on the black market."

"That poor kid . . . his own granddaughter . . . You couldn't talk any sense into him?"

"I tried. He wasn't listening."

Pamela brushed a wisp of hair from her forehead, then swatted at a fly. "All that trouble my father went through, that you've gone through."

A goat so thin its bones could be counted hobbled up to the ramada and stuck its nose in the ground, as if eating dirt. The sadness welled up in Lisette, her eyes filling as an image of Evangelina formed in her mind, the girl aged and infantilized at the same time, shuffling with the uncertain steps of a woman of ninety, or clinging to her mother's hand like a toddler.

"I should have checked with him before . . ." Her voice quavered. "I should have seen this coming."

Reaching across the table, Pamela clasped her hands. "None of that, okay? It's not your fault that the guy is an ignorant jerk."

Lisette wasn't feeling very rocklike at the moment, only wrung out, defeated. She grabbed the envelope and stood. "Let's go home."

"How do I explain this to my father?" asked Pamela as they went to the pickup. "I can't tell him that the girl isn't coming because her grandpa thinks he's going to kill her for her organs."

"No. But some version of the truth will have to do. I'll e-mail him."

Taking the envelope gently but firmly from Lisette's hands, Pamela pulled out the airline reservations. "It would be better if we told him in person, the both of us," she said, pausing at the car to gaze out over San Tomás's shabby sprawl, the scarred mountains beyond. "I could use a break from Mexico, and I think you could, too."

Lisette swung back into the truck and coaxed the engine to life. "You go ahead. I've got work to do here."

"It can't wait?" asked Pamela, climbing in beside her. "You wouldn't have been doing whatever it is if this had worked out the way we thought it would. I don't see the difference."

"I think you do."

They bumped down the village's single street. Black water flecked with garbage trickled in the culverts alongside it. Pamela tilted her head against the window and let out a long sigh. "Maybe I do. I admire you, Lisette. You know that. But what I really don't see, when I think about that old bastard, is why you love these people so much. I'm sorry to have to say that."

You didn't have to, Lisette said to herself.

They drove on in the bright afternoon without talking, each enclosed in a bubble of her own thoughts, Lisette now more conscious than ever of the distance between them. It had been there from the beginning, albeit concealed, not by love but the longing for it.

■ ■ ■

As fast as Riordan could drill the boards, Moises carried them to César, down on his knees as he extended the deck plank by plank until he reached the far side of the gorge. Riordan, who came from a family where "good with his hands" described a man who could throw a decent punch rather than one adept at fixing or building things, admired César's skill. After the final plank was laid, he uncoiled two long ropes to make support lines between the handrails and the suspension cables on each side. Bending low to loop them around the cables, straightening up to do the same around the handrails, he formed two series of triangles the span of the bridge.

From the far end, he called across the chasm, *"Eso lo hace! Hemos terminado con esta maldita puente!"*

Moises shut off the generator. It was done—a tough job completed in the depths of the wild Sierra Madre. Riordan took a gulp of air, savoring its piney tang, and gazed with satisfaction at the clean, smooth, yellowish decking, the cables and ropes as taut as telephone wires. Sweating from his labors, César tested their work, crossing toward Riordan and Moises at a normal walking pace. When he reached them, he grinned through his sweat, turned, and began to stomp back toward the opposite side. Under his pounding, the bridge undulated and swayed.

Riordan, standing with Moises in front of the two support trees, shut his eyes. Two seconds later, Moises yelled, "César!" His eyes snapping open, Riordan saw his friend flat on his back about two-thirds of the way across, clutching his chest while rolling from shoulder to shoulder. The bridge canted to one side, and he began to slide off, saving himself from a fatal plunge by hooking an arm around a support rope. Now he lay at a sideways angle, his legs from the knee down dangling over the gorge. He let out a loud groan. Moises threw a shoulder into Riordan, intending to shove him out of the way so he could go to the aid of his stricken boss, but inadvertently pushed Riordan onto the bridge.

Without hesitation or a conscious thought, amazing himself, Riordan grasped the handrails and moved forward as quickly as he dared. The bridge swung from side to side, bounced up and down; he felt as if he were walking on a waterbed suspended in midair. He reached César in ten seconds and stood behind him, taking a moment to make sure he had his balance. Then, letting the handrails go, he knelt down and, with cautious, deliberate movements, reached across César's body, grabbed his legs, and swung them back onto the deck.

"What happened?" he asked, out of breath even though the physical effort had not been strenuous.

César looked up. His face had a grayish pallor. "Got dizzy . . . fell. . . . Pain here . . ." He poked his left shoulder. "Damn diesel fumes . . ."

Oh, God, not a heart attack, Riordan thought. He placed his arms under César's, intending to drag him. But it would be impossible to walk backward on the unstable platform while dragging a man as heavy as himself. César would have to make it back on his own two legs. Riordan raised him into a sitting position, then—he didn't know how he accomplished it—got him to his feet and turned him so that they stood facing each other.

Doing an about-face, Riordan said: "Hold on to me, hold tight."

César clasped him around the waist and shuffled behind as Riordan half-walked, half-hauled himself forward by the handrails. They looked like a curious circus act. Riordan gave no thought to the bridge's lurching, to the grinning chasm, to the rocks shining through the thin, clear water below. He was aware only of the necessity to deliver his friend to safety.

When they reached the other side, César released him. He staggered forward, bent over, and dry-heaved. Riordan had him lie down under the trees, telling him to take deep breaths. He did, complaining that it felt like he was inhaling ground glass.

Aspirin. You were supposed to give aspirin to someone having a heart attack. But he didn't have any aspirin.

"Moises, go find Dr. Moreno," Riordan said. "Bring her here quick."

He sat down in the warm loam and rubbed César's chest. "How is it now?"

"A little better. *Oye, Padre. Muchas gracias.* I thought I was going to—"

"Don't think about it," Riordan said, panting. "Take it easy. Rest."

"I fainted," César said, as if embarrassed.

"We'll find out what's wrong and get you fixed up." He smiled reassuringly.

While they waited for Moises to return with Lisette, Riordan alternated looks at the bridge, swung out over the deep rift in the land, and at César's face, now regaining some color.

"Not so much pain now," César said. "I'm okay now."

"No, you're not. Dr. Moreno will have a look at you."

But that wasn't going to happen, not here. Dr. Moreno had left the village some time ago, Moises reported when he returned.

"All right, let's get him in the truck," Riordan told Moises. "You drive."

He extended his hand to César, who grasped it and pulled himself upright.

"No kidding, I'm okay."

"The hell you are," Riordan said. "We're going to bring you to Hermosillo. To a hospital."

He and Moises got César situated in the passenger seat, quickly loaded the generator and the tools, and started off. The road spun down out of the pines into the oaks and junipers, matching the Santa Teresa bend for bend, some turns so sharp Moises had to take them almost at walking speed. On that long, jarring drive, Riordan had a chance to reflect on his actions. In retrospect, they seemed as automatic as reflex; yet there had been nothing automatic about them. They had not lacked intention. He'd seen what needed to be done and he'd done it. He wondered how he'd managed to conquer his abject terror not once but twice, the second time towing a man who weighed at least 180.

These musings did not produce pride in himself. Quite the opposite. He felt humbled, touched by grace; his rescue of César had been an act of love, for one human life and so for God, and grace is bestowed in proportion to the love in the soul that receives it. That, not reflex, not his own will, was what had overcome his dread and impelled him forward. He wasn't worthy of it, but his faith taught that it was the unworthy to whom grace was granted.

At last, from a straight stretch girdling a hillside, he saw the river a few hundred feet below—a ribbon of water that vanished into the sand and reappeared downstream. The roofs of San Patricio peered through the mesquite and palm trees, the twin domes of his church towering over all, crucifixes against a barren blue sky. Westward, the highway to Hermosillo drew a winding black stripe across the Sierra foothills. The familiar landscape brought him to the recognition that in having been touched by grace, he'd been restored to himself and his rightful place in the world. He was skeptical about emotional religion, the ecstatic moment of conversion evangelicals spoke of; yet he felt that he was undergoing something like that now—a reconversion, as it were. After the shock on Christmas morning, he'd played a mental trick on himself to dodge the conundrum theologians and philosophers had wrestled with for two thousand years: how to reconcile an all-loving God with the existence of evil. If they hadn't resolved it yet, he certainly could not. He would have to live with the doubts it awakened. No faith without doubt, he reminded himself. The trick had been the idea that he'd been thrust into an alternate universe, some spiritual black hole in whose depths the laws of moral physics no longer applied. But he was in Mexico, bleeding, suffering Mexico, a Franciscan priest empowered to preach the Gospels, to perform baptisms, to witness marriages, to anoint the sick, to celebrate the Eucharist, and to hear confessions, whose secrecy he was sworn to preserve. To violate that oath was to betray a sacred trust. He'd betrayed it three times; he would no longer. He resolved to end his unholy pact with Inspector Bonham and Captain Valencia, regardless of the cost to himself. Grace is given to the undeserving, he thought. But once it is, your actions have to show that you've received it.

peration Zone Hawk—the unofficial code name was the Professor's creation—got under way with the detention of the mariachi and *norteño* bands hired to perform at Ernesto Salazar's birthday fiesta. The two groups, numbering twelve in all, were quietly rounded up the night before, brought to the air force base outside Hermosillo, herded into a hangar, and assured that they would not be held for long, a day or two at most. Each entertainer owned several costume changes, so there was enough clothing in their collective wardrobe to outfit the Professor, Captain Valencia, and the two dozen *federales* and paratroopers they had handpicked to crash the party. The men would be wearing bulletproof vests under their disguises, however, and this, along with the size differences between them and the musicians, created fitting problems. These were sorted out, though a few men had to make do with mismatched outfits, like the lanky Sublieutenant Almazán, whose pants reached only halfway to his ankles. The Professor attired himself in a black *charro* jacket, a black sombrero, and blue trousers, while Valencia, who considered mariachi suits ridiculous, got himself up as a *norteño* guitarist: flashy shirt, white cowboy hat, lizardskin boots.

They were crammed together in the hangar, the real entertainers and the masqueraders, the former sitting in glum silence until the Professor handed each bandleader an envelope containing $500 in U.S. currency, less than what they would have earned performing for Salazar but sufficient to cheer them up. They got into the spirit of things, helping the masqueraders rehearse "Las Mañanitas," the tune sung at birthday parties from Mexico to Argentina. Some of the troops and policemen could play instruments, and the musicians gave them tips on improving their technique. The lighthearted atmosphere irritated Captain Valencia, wrapped as tight as the coils around an armature. Singing, yodeling, plucking guitars, his troops were behaving like boys on holiday rather than disciplined soldiers about to embark on a critical mission. It would be different if they were in their combat uniforms. These silly outfits—that was what accounted for their goofing off, Valencia decided. It galled him no end to think that he and they were going to meet his big moment decked out like cheap nightclub acts.

Loosen up, take it easy, the Professor urged. The prelude to a dangerous action was always harder on the nerves than the action itself. Think of the costumes as camouflage, like the markings on a zone-tailed hawk's wings.

"There is nothing the matter with my nerves," the captain grunted.

At a little past two in the afternoon, Rubén Levya signaled by cell phone that the guests had begun to arrive.

The frivolities stopped; the men assumed appropriately serious attitudes and boarded the planes, thirteen in each of two air force Cessna Caravans, with the logo of a private air charter service—AEROMUNDIAL—pasted over the military markings. A couple of the instrument cases stacked in the luggage compartment actually contained instruments; the rest concealed FX-05 assault carbines with folding stocks. Sitting in the copilot's seat—not because he knew how to fly but to get a better view—the Professor watched plains rise to foothills, foothills to the crooked spine of Mexico, the Sierra Madre Occidental. The plane bounced in the turbulent air over the mountains, and he recalled the invasion of Panama in 1989, Operation Just Cause. (Though deposing Manuel Noriega wasn't a cause, and its justice had been doubtful; Noriega had simply outlived his usefulness to the world's only remaining superpower.) The Professor was then a young soldier in the 1st Battalion, 504th Parachute Infantry, 82nd Airborne, which seized Fort Amador in a nighttime air assault. Noriega, who'd profited from the Colombian cocaine trade, was holed up elsewhere; but he soon surrendered. With a great deal of poetic license, the Professor could say it was the first time he'd taken part in the capture of a drug lord. And he'd been capturing, killing, and investigating drug lords ever since, when he wasn't working for them.

Actually, he had been employed by only one for all these years since he'd deserted the DEA, and that was Joaquín Carrasco. If the Professor was nothing else, he was loyal to those who were loyal to him. The DEA had not been, abandoning him before he'd abandoned it. The investigation into his partner's torture and murder had been called off to protect the Mexican general who had ordered the assassination. He was a friend to the Juárez Cartel and was related to the defense minister, a friend of Washington's. It was the minister who made a few phone calls and got the investigation quashed. The Professor set off for Mexico on a mission of vengeance—or, as he preferred to think of it, of justice, tracking down and killing his partner's three killers. One turned out to be a top informant for the CIA, which pressured the DEA to rope and tie its renegade agent and bring him back to the reservation. If it failed, the spooks were going to go after him themselves—with extreme prejudice. The Professor fled deep into Sonora and found sanctuary in Carrasco's organization, then at war with Juárez. He offered his considerable skills to Joaquín, if Joaquín would aid him in his hunt for the main target, the general. Carrasco pulled strings and arranged for the Professor to join the Federal Police. In that guise, he developed informants in the general's retinue and then set up the sabotage of a private plane flying the officer to a vacation spa. He died in its crash, an accident to all appearances. Grateful to the drug boss who had made this possible, the Professor honored his end of their deal, taking on every assignment Carrasco gave him. They had stuck together for almost twenty years. Until now. The plaza had been promised to Rubén Levya. Sometimes necessity trumped loyalty.

The pilot, not much older than the Professor had been in his paratrooper days, tapped him on the shoulder and pointed out the window. The mesa lay ahead, a swath of greens and browns ringed by peaks and lumpy hills; in the near distance the cell tower resembled a giant exclamation point. A few second later, the Santa Bárbara ranch became visible: the flat-roofed main house umbrellaed by trees; the long bunk-house behind; the reddish-brown scar that was the airstrip, private planes parked in a row beside the pole barn where coke shipments were stored. The plan was to achieve complete surprise and capture Salazar, Mora, and the others without firing a shot. Actually, that was as much a hope as it was a plan. Mike Tyson had spoken eternal truth when he'd said, "Everyone has a plan until he gets hit in the mouth." The remainder of Valencia's company was assembled at the Hermosillo air base: one hundred troops waiting to be summoned in case things went seriously south.

The altimeter spun: three thousand meters, twenty-five hundred. Below, a single-engine plane, probably with late arrivals on board, was taxiing to a stop. The Caravans swooped low over the ranch headquarters on their downwind leg. The Professor caught glimpses of gunmen loitering by the parked aircraft, a crowd clustered around a smoking barbecue pit in the front yard, a wooden platform—the stage. The Brotherhood's entire leadership gathered in one place: he practically salivated. The plane's radio crackled. He picked up the mike and put the headset on.

"I see you," Levya said, speaking through a handheld Motorola. "You see me? The two delivery vans at the end of the runway. I'm in the blue one; one of my boys is in the white one."

Cargo planes had flown the vans into Salazar's roadless ranch months ago. They served as taxis for his visitors, mostly Colombians.

"Where are Uno and Dos?" the Professor asked, using the code names for Salazar and Mora.

"The main house. They've been in there all day."

As the plane banked to turn into the wind, the Professor toggled the sound-system switch and announced to his passengers, "We'll be on the ground in about two minutes. There are thugs guarding the landing field. When you get off, don't look at them, just get into the vans. Thank you for flying with us today," he added to lighten things up.

The Professor's Caravan touched down, turboprop churning up cyclones of dust, and rolled to a stop. Valencia's plane landed minutes later. Joking and clowning as instructed, the men disembarked, grabbed their instrument cases, and wedged themselves into the vans, the *fede-*

rales into Levya's blue van, the paratroopers into the white one. The vehicles must have transported *mojados* at one time: their exteriors looked to have been beaten with hammers; inside, the seats had been ripped out to make room for twenty migrants in a space meant to hold nine people. Levya drove the half kilometer to the bunkhouse in what seemed like five seconds, the other van close behind.

"You remember what to do?" asked the Professor, sitting in front with his knees in his chest.

"Yeah, yeah. *Sí.* Yeah, I know," Levya said. The ice-veined *sicario* was jumpy, not from fear, the Professor assumed, but from unfamiliarity with his role as a traitor. "He's still in the house. Him and Mora. Drinking. Tea! Fucking tea. Or maybe Mora's blowing him."

"Get him to come out."

They wanted Salazar outside to prevent a getaway through the escape tunnel.

There hadn't been time, during the rehearsals for the raid, to prepare for the unexpected, like the fornicating couple who almost fell out of bed as more than two dozen federal policemen and paratroopers in musicians' garb burst into the bunkhouse. The woman squealed, covering herself with a bedsheet, the man leapt to his feet, mouth ajar, erection wilting. It shrunk to nothing when the Professor, taking no chances on a breach of security, drew a pistol from under his *charro* jacket.

"Back in bed, facedown! Both of you!" he said in a low voice. "Hands behind your back!"

The lovers obeyed, and a *federale* gagged and cuffed them.

In the front yard, blocked from view by the ranch house, Levya was at the stage microphone, playing master of ceremonies. The raiding party in the bunkhouse could hear him clearly. "Hey, everybody, sit down. The music is here. . . . We're going to sing 'Las Mañanitas.' . . . You over there . . . Come on, *muchachos*! Sit down. . . . That's it. . . . Okay! *Muy bien!* . . . I'm going to go inside and get our guest of honor. When he comes out, everybody sing 'Las Mañanitas.'" He shouted: "*Oye! Músicos!* We're ready for you!"

Six paratroopers stayed behind to guard the rear of the house and the couple who had suffered coitus interruptus; the remaining twenty men grabbed their cases and filed outside, led by Valencia's bugler playing brassy *norteño* riffs and another musically inclined soldier strumming a guitar. Precise as a marching band, which in a sense they were, the soldiers formed an L around the yard, a maneuver they'd practiced at the base. They opened the cases, the tops facing outward to hide the weapons from the guests. There were about thirty, seated at two long tables, under piñatas hung from poles. Favorable odds, the Professor thought, fighting to keep his excitement under control. He estimated that slightly better than half were men, swilling cans of Tecate and Dos Equis. A bit drunk already, their attention on their girlfriends. And lightly armed, pistols in waistbands or back pockets, but no assault rifles in sight. They felt secure up here in Salazar's aerie. Very favorable odds.

The Professor and his men took the stage and pretended to be hooking up speakers. The trumpeter and the guitarist continued to play, rather badly; but no one seemed to notice. Levya was taking a long time to produce the birthday boy. The Professor sensed a tension rippling through his team and Valencia's. The guests, too, were growing restless. A narco in a sequined shirt yelled toward the house, "Ernesto! *Jefe!* Come on out so we can sing to you," and then, facing the stage: "C'mon, you guys, start playing! Start singing!"

The trumpeter blew the opening bars of "Las Mañanitas." The man in the sequined shirt jumped up and, raising his beer can, began to sing:

> *Estas son las mañanitas*
> *que cantable a el rey David.*
> *Hoy por ser cumpleaños*
> *te las cantamos aquí.*

> These are the dawns
> that King David sang about.
> We sing here today
> Because today is your birthday.

The Professor's synesthesia switched on. He saw brass cylinders pumping up and down, like organ pipes in motion, as another man joined in, and another.

El día en que tú naciste
nacieron todas las flores.
Ya viene amaneciendo
ya la luz del dia nos dío.

All flowers were born on the day
you were born.
Dawn is arriving and
the light of day is upon us.

Someone else yelled to the musicians, "Play! Play! Where are the guitars and violins?" Another, looking toward the front door, shouted, *"Oye! Don Ernesto! Feliz cumpleaños! Ven afuera!"*

But Salazar remained inside with Levya and Mora. The Professor could feel, as a tangible sensation, control of the situation slipping away. He removed his sombrero, prepared to give it a Frisbee toss—the prearranged signal to make the arrests. A single gunshot cracked inside the house. "Now!" the Professor shouted as he sailed the sombrero across the tables. The well-drilled men quickly pulled their assault carbines from the cases as he drew his pistol and called out: "Federal police! You are all under arrest! Nobody move!"

At that instant, there was a burst of automatic fire from inside, bullets shattering a front window, ripping chunks out of the veranda posts, and smashing a piñata, which spilled candy bars and airline bottles of tequila. The partygoers dived under the tables or ran toward cover, narcos pulling their pistols. The Professor shot one; someone else dropped two others as Valencia and a squad of soldiers charged the house and flattened themselves against the wall, three on each side of the door. The Professor sprinted to them. A paratrooper—it was Sublieutenant Almazán—kicked the door open and stepped inside, the Professor and Valencia behind him. They had a half second's glimpse of a man vanishing down a long hallway.

"Alto!" Valencia commanded.

Enrique Mora spun and fired four or five rapid shots, two rounds striking Almazán's armored vest, flinging him backward into Valencia, who tumbled into the Professor, all three falling into a heap. To an out-side observer, they would have looked like the Keystone Kops.

"*Hijo de puta!*" the captain cursed, untangling himself. The Profes-sor pulled Almazán away from the door. His fancy frilled shirt was per-forated: there would be bruises under the vest's Kevlar plates, but he was otherwise unhurt.

Levya lay facedown near the shattered window, in what looked like a gallon of spilled maroon paint. His pistol was still in his hand. What had happened was a question to be addressed later. The Professor noticed blood drops leading across the clay-tile floor into the hallway. Mora had been healthy enough to squeeze off a few rounds; the blood must have come from Salazar.

With Valencia and the others, he followed the trail down the hall to a closed door at its end. A paratrooper kicked it down and tossed a stun grenade into the room. They rushed inside. It was a storeroom with metal shelving units, one of which had nothing in it and had been pulled away from the wall. In the floor behind the empty case, an open trapdoor revealed a shaft about three meters deep. Red droplets on the ladder shone in the light of the bare bulb overhead. The Pro-fessor climbed down, into the stale air, and stood in front of a steel door that could have come off a bank vault. He grabbed the handle and gave it a shake and it didn't so much as rattle. He squinted. The imperfect fit showed him that the door was dogged tight to a mine tim-ber by three dead bolts, top, center, bottom. The latches would be on the other side, and so was the tunnel through which Salazar and Mora had fled.

"*Capitán*, do you see this?" he said, looking upward.

Valencia's face showed in the shaft opening above. "*Hijo de puta!*"

The Professor climbed out of the shaft and went back down the hall to the front room. Squatting, he picked up Levya's pistol, an H&K like his own. Ejecting the magazine, he found one round missing; on the other side of the room, there were seventeen .40-caliber shell casings.

"What the . . ." Valencia stammered.

"Looks like Levya took a shot at Salazar or Mora."

"What the fuck for?"

"Might as well ask him." He gestured at the corpse. "Maybe they were on to him . . . and on to us. One of them, maybe both, let him have it. He's got more holes in him than a colander."

And we, he thought, have been hit in the mouth.

■ ■ ■

But not that hard.

The operation was a partial success: twenty-four people were arrested and flown to Hermosillo, where three were discovered to be high-value targets. One was Salazar's liaison to Colombian and Peruvian cocaine suppliers; another ran a network of wholesale heroin buyers in the United States; and a third served as the Brotherhood's bribery chief, distributing *mordida* on both sides of the border. Three more bosses had been killed in the brief firefight at the ranch.

Twenty kilos of black tar heroin bricks, more than a hundred kilos of high-grade coke—Peruvian pink—and an arsenal of pistols, assault rifles, and grenade launchers were found in the warehouse. Not the biggest haul in history, but sufficient to further blunt the sting of the Butterfly's underground flight. All the booty was flown back to the San Patricio base with the prisoners, and Valencia's PR man summoned the media.

It took a full day after the raid to assemble a team of engineers and trackers and fly them to the ranch. The engineers blew the steel door open, and the trackers, with their dogs, followed the tunnel almost a kilometer to its exit in a corral, where any scent left by Salazar and Mora was lost in the piles of manure.

An extensive manhunt got under way—roadblocks, helicopters over-flying the mountains, military and police patrols combing them on foot. The media loved it, especially the angle of paratroopers and federal cops disguised as mariachis. Mexico City correspondents for the *Los Angeles Times* and the *New York Times* showed up at the base. So did CNN, filming Valencia and his men, back in uniform, faces masked, posing with the captured narcos, the confiscated weapons and drugs forming a back-drop.

The Professor had always been mediaphobic. This was a matter not of humility but of survival. Keeping his face off television and his name out of the newspapers had kept his body out of prison or a shallow grave, the two places where most citizens of narcoland ended their careers. But for this occasion, he allowed reporters to interview him, on the condition that he not be filmed, photographed, or identified by name. He thought it prudent to tell the press that Rubén Levya had been killed while attempting to escape with Salazar and Mora. "One down, two to go," he said.

■ ■ ■

A day after the news broke, Carrasco phoned on his encrypted cell phone.

"You guys fucked up," he said. "How could you let that skinny *maricón* get away?"

"Good to hear your voice, Joaquín," the Professor said, pleased that betraying him would no longer be necessary. "He's wounded, he's in the Sierra—on foot, most likely. Only a matter of time."

"How is the weather where you are?"

"Warm. It's spring."

"It's still winter up here. Cold as the tip of an Eskimo's dick. What am I doing, freezing my ass off when there's money to be made?"

"Joaquín! You're worth billions."

"I don't mean the money. I mean the action. I miss the action, *Profesor.*"

■ ■ ■

Brigadier General Carrillo, the overall commander of Joint Operation Falcon, arrived at the base with Comandante Pérez to personally commend the Professor and Valencia for their courage and professionalism. In addition to the drug and weapons haul, Salazar's laptop had been seized, its hard drive scoured. Rough drafts of his revolutionary manifesto turned up: a muddle of political rants and religious nonsense that made Ted Kaczynski's ravings sound reasonable. Copies were distributed to the newspapers and the TV networks. A phone directory listing the numbers of state and federal legislators, police chiefs, and mayors, as well as a spread sheet showing the amounts paid to each, were not brought to the media's attention. They conveniently vanished, which incensed Valencia the Incorruptible. This was what bred cynicism and made real change impossible! he fumed. This was why the narcos would never be defeated! Corruption at all levels tolerated, kept secret! Did these compromised officials know that they had taken bribes from a man plotting to overthrow them? He had a good mind to call a press conference and expose every one of them. The Professor advised him to calm down, but Valencia unloaded on General Carrillo, who listened with a solemn expression on his jowly face and said he shared the *capitán*'s outrage; but was this an issue for the army to take on? Of course not. The army was here to protect the nation from external and internal threats, not to concern itself with crooked politicians. Meanwhile, it would be best if the *capitán* kept his thoughts and feelings private. This counsel was given for the *capitán*'s benefit—he had been recommended for promotion to major. This news delighted the *capitán*, and procured his silence.

■ ■ ■

It might have been residual anger that needed venting, it might have been his frustration over Salazar's escape, or his fierce anticlericism, or his bad temper, or all of the above that prodded Valencia into picking a fight with Padre Riordan the next evening. Valencia and the Professor were in the plaza, supervising a changing of the guard: regional troops and state police had been dispatched to garrison the town while the *federales* and paratroopers hunted the two fugitives. After issuing final instructions to the new men, and spotting the priest standing on the church steps, Valencia made an abrupt turn and went up to him.

"Shouldn't you be at Vespers or wherever it is you people go at this hour?" he asked brusquely. "What are you doing here?"

"I believe this is my church," Riordan replied in a tranquil voice. "I wanted to see what was going on." He made a lazy movement at the military and police vehicles ringing the plaza. An electric sunset reddened the desert-beige Humvees and SandCats. "You would think we were under martial law."

"You may consider that you are until we have Salazar."

"I'm quite sure he isn't in town. The news says that he's—"

"I know what the news says."

"Well, congratulations, anyway." He tilted his head at the Professor. "And you, too."

"You are being sarcastic?" Valencia said—an accusation rather than a question.

"No, not at all. The news says that you—"

"I told you, I know what the news says." The captain, who had been standing one step below Riordan, hopped up to put himself on equal footing. "I will be interested to hear what you say in the future. As long as that *hijo de la puta* is on the loose, the war is not over. Who knows? Maybe someone in your parish this very minute is harboring that criminal. And there is some other unfinished business besides. You know what it is." He jabbed the priest in the solar plexus. "I remind you: we are to hear what you hear."

For a brief interval, Riordan shrank back, baffled by the unprovoked aggression. Then, recovering, he leaned forward and traded glares with Valencia. They looked like two fighters trying to intimidate each other before the opening bell.

"I think I know what is aggravating you, Captain," Riordan said, maintaining his pacific tone. There was a change in him, the Professor noticed. He seemed more confident, more at ease in his own skin. "The fact that you had to rely on a priest to get what you need," Riordan continued. "You've just got to prove that you're the big dog. I wasn't going to—"

Valencia interrupted with angry laughter. "Inspector Bonham! Do you hear this? I am being psychoanalyzed by this parasite! This witch doctor!"

"*Alberto. Eso es suficiente,*" the Professor said, embarrassed by the outburst. "*Vamonos.*"

Valencia didn't budge; neither did Riordan. "I was about to say that I wasn't going to mention this until the right moment," the priest went on, but with harsher intonations than before. "But here we are—at the right moment. If I hear anything on the street—and I doubt I will, but if I do—you'll hear it. You're not going to hear anything said to me in confidence. In what you call my 'dark little closet.' You can consider this my resignation."

A plasticity came to Valencia's normally stiff, martial face, his features molding themselves into an expression of contempt and astonishment.

"I warned you about the consequences," he said.

"My bishop is out of the country right now," Riordan answered. "I have an appointment to see him after he returns. He'll hear everything

I've done—from me. And then we'll see what happens. I'm sure you can capture your man without my help."

"Correct," the Professor agreed, attempting to steer the conversation in another direction. "The padre has served his purpose."

But for the captain, Riordan's usefulness was not the issue. "If you were wearing a uniform, I would charge you with desertion. I would have you court-martialed for cowardice," he said, casting a cold gray eye on Riordan. "But since you are not in uniform . . ." He heaved his chest and spat in the priest's face.

Riordan wiped the spit off with his sleeve. "I'll pray for you, Captain Valencia."

"Better that you pray for yourself."

CHAPTER TWENTY-EIGHT

There was no horizon when Riordan gazed eastward to the Sierra Madre. The mountains' blackness matched the blackness of the sky. He could tell the difference only by the absence of stars below a certain altitude. Vega was visible, Deneb barely showed itself, and Altair was hidden entirely. He continued his circle, imagining himself as a tracking telescope as he turned to the south, where Antares glimmered and Spica rode beside the yellowish disk of Saturn. Then he revolved all the way around, through the Milky Way's colorless dust, past the setting moon to Polaris, a glowing white rivet fixed to its place in the heavens. Holding his eyes on it, he felt a buoyancy, as if he might rise out of the earth's sordid atmosphere, out of the shackles of its gravity, and at last out of his own body, his mind liberated to float freely among the cosmos. That was his idea of paradise: his disembodied consciousness touring creation eternally, its beauty ever before him, its deepest secrets revealed.

Altair appeared, seeming to draw the dawn up over the mountains, then vanished in the brightening sky. Before returning to the rectory, he purposely looked at the iron-barred courtyard gate to test himself. The sight evoked a memory of what he had found there three months ago, but without a fresh awakening of horror and disbelief—all the pain of what had been a profound spiritual trauma. He took this to be a sign of recovery.

He walked down the arcade that formed a gallery along the rectory's rear wall, his steps so quick and light that his boot heels made barely a sound on the paving stones, worn to the smoothness and polish of marble. Spanish friars had trod these same stones. He liked to feel them under his feet; they provided him with a physical connection to the missionaries who had preceded him—his ancestors, as it were.

He glided into the bathroom, washed up, shaved, brushed his hair, and changed into his riding clothes. No longer an informant, he felt as if he'd shed a heavy backpack after an uphill hike. The burden would not be fully lifted until he'd confessed to Bishop Perralta. The bishop—the same one who had called for the exorcisms—was a conservative and unlikely to be lenient, though Riordan's motives might be a mitigating factor. How odd that a private citizen would be commended for doing what he had done; yet it branded him an ecclesiastical criminal. Still, he was resolved to make a clean breast of things; and this resolution gripped him so powerfully that he felt as though he'd already carried it out. *Better be careful,* he cautioned himself. *Merely having a good intention isn't the same as doing the thing intended.*

Father Hugo gave him a scandalized look when he appeared at morning prayers wearing a biker's jacket and black leather chaps over blue jeans. The vicar did not say anything until their Lenten breakfast of tea and tortillas.

"Where are you going dressed like that so early?" he asked. It wasn't clear if he disapproved of his pastor's attire or merely found it inappropriate at this time of day.

"Hermosillo. To visit César Díaz. He phoned me last night from the hospital. He wants to see me."

"But it is Holy Week next week, and we have a lot to do," Father Hugo protested. "He is not near death, is he? He cannot wait until he's home to have you call on him?"

"I think he's nervous. They're going to put stents in two of his coronary arteries this afternoon. A routine procedure these days, but the idea of it—"

Father Hugo tore a tortilla in half and dunked it in his tea. "I thought he did not have a heart attack, that he has . . . what is it called?"

"Pericarditis. An inflammation of his heart lining."

"But don't they put in these stents when people have heart attacks?"

Riordan raised his mug and watched the ring of condensation it left on the table evaporate. "They also install them to prevent heart attacks. When they examined César, they found two blocked arteries. So now they're going to fix the plumbing."

"I want to go over the Holy Week preparations with you," the vicar said.

"When I get back. Late this afternoon, probably."

"But the Mayos will be here on—"

"The Mayos will know what to do," interjected the Old Priest, seated by himself at one end of the table. He, too, was fasting, though he was at an age when it was no longer required. His hand as he popped a tortilla shred into his mouth looked mummified. "They have been celebrating Easter here for two hundred and fifty years. Padre Tim is to visit the sick—a corporal work of mercy."

Father Hugo acknowledged the catechism lesson with a little bow. "I have known the corporal works of mercy, and the spiritual ones, too, since I was eight years old."

The Old Priest swallowed and licked his shriveled lips. "Ah, lard," he said.

"Lard? What has lard to do with anything?" said Father Hugo.

"María made these tortillas with lard. Between those made with lard and those with oil, there is no comparison. You and I, Father Hugo, will offer a prayer for César Díaz."

■ ■ ■

Riding a motorcycle, particularly an ebony, chrome-trimmed Harley-Davidson, lent itself to fantasies. Cruising the state road as fast as its condition would permit, which wasn't very fast, weaving around the potholes, Riordan pictured himself as Marlon Brando in *The Wild One*. He rumbled through dusty hamlets and cattle ranges, the roadside gilt by desert poppies opening their petals to the sun, crossed the Río Yaqui, and in three hours reached Mexico 15, the federal superhighway. Military and police checkpoints had slowed his progress; otherwise he would have covered the hundred miles in half that time. He turned north for Hermosillo.

The CIMA hospital was on San Miguel Street. As he double-locked Negra Modelo to a tree in the parking lot, he heard American voices— an older couple crossing the lot, the man pushing a wheeled walker. The hospital was a destination for medical tourists from the States. A fifty-thousand-dollar operation there cost twelve grand here.

César had a private room in the cardiovascular ward. How small and vulnerable that substantial man looked, in bed in a hospital gown tied around his neck, an IV drip stuck in one arm, the other arm hooked to a machine broadcasting his vital signs on a monitor screen. He was watching TV when Riordan entered—some silly daytime game show. He switched it off.

"Padre Tim, good to see you," he said in a slightly hoarse voice. "Did you bring it?"

Riordan drew a chair to the bed and, reaching into his jacket pocket, produced a half-pint bottle of *bacanora.* Mexican moonshine.

"You first," César said.

"No, you. I insist." Riordan unscrewed the cap and passed the bottle to him.

César took a sip, let out a sigh of satisfaction, and handed the bottle back to Riordan, who merely wet his lips with the clear, potent liquor.

"No more than that," he said. "It's not even noon." He nestled the *bacanora* under César's pillow. "How are you feeling?"

"I can't wait to get out of here." César made a sweeping gesture with the arm connected to the IV bag. Everything in the room was white or a shade of off-white, except for the black chair. The sunlight angling through the window looked more like moonlight.

"They've been sticking a thing in me, here," César said, pressing a hand to his ribs. "To drain the fluid, they said. And now they're going to cut me open—"

"That's not what they're going to do," Riordan said confidently. "It's an angioplasty. I talked to Dr. Lisette about this. She told me to tell you not to worry. It's routine."

"To me, it's cutting me open. The doctor . . . *oye*, you should see him, Padre Tim. He looks like a high school kid. First time I saw him, I wanted to ask, 'Where is your father?' He told me that I will have to delay the trip to El Norte for a week. I have to come back for a checkup."

"Where is Marta?" Riordan asked.

"At the hotel. She'll be here before they wheel me in." He motioned at the TV, mounted high on the wall. "Been watching the news. I don't feel so bad now."

Riordan intuited his meaning. "About leaving," he said.

"Yeah. Like I was running out on everybody. It's almost over. The Brotherhood is finished, I think. All those people they caught, Salazar on the run, a bullet in him. He might be dead already."

César grew silent, and the quiet in that white, sterile room lasted long enough to become disconcerting. Staring off into the middle distance, César seemed to be mentally somewhere else.

"You wanted to see me about something?" Riordan asked to draw him back.

"When something happens like what did to me . . ." César paused. "They're going to put me under. You ask yourself, Am I going to wake up?"

With a half turn of his head, he looked directly at Riordan, an appeal in his eyes.

"You want to make a confession?"

"Yes."

He jerked his head at the door. Riordan closed it, then resumed his seat. He felt awkward, knowing about himself what his friend did not know; and his decidedly unclerical outfit heightened his discomfort.

After crossing himself, declaring that he had sinned and that his last confession had been a few months ago, César squirmed and dropped his eyes to his hands, resting flat on his lap.

"Okay . . . Lupita . . . me and her . . ." he began. "You remember at the Christmas pageant? At *Las Posadas*? You saw me with her, and I was a little, you know, *borracho* . . . You remember that?"

"Sure. Go ahead."

"She was . . . you know. . . . She needed someone to . . ."

"Would it be easier if I asked what you did and you answered yes or no?"

"Yeah. I mean, yes, Padre Tim."

"Are you saying you committed adultery? You had sex with your sister-in-law?"

"That makes it worse, doesn't it? My dead brother's wife?"

"Adultery is adultery," Riordan said. "How many times?"

"Three, four, I think," replied César. "She started it. That night. She was feeling terrible, Christmas Eve, her kid dead. *Abrazame*, she was saying, so I hugged her, and, you know . . ."

"One thing led to another. Her starting it doesn't make you innocent, César."

"I know that!" he shot back, affronted. "Why do you think I'm confessing?"

"It's over now? You're resolved not to do it any longer?"

"Sure, yes. It ended more than a month ago. Marta got suspicious, she asked me, Something going on? And I lied to her. So I confess to that, too. Lying. And then Lupita and me stopped and I'm sorry for what I did."

"I'm sure you are. Is there anything else you want to get off your conscience?"

César's gaze shifted, to some point on the opposite wall. His lips parted, then closed.

"Anything else, César?" Riordan repeated.

He made two slow movements of his head, side to side. "But I got a question. The soldiers who killed my nephew and the Reyes boy was that murder?"

"That's not for me to say. I wasn't there. They fired into the air to push the crowd back, didn't they? It was either a terrible accident or fate."

César grew agitated, shifting his weight from hip to hip in the bed, rattling the IV drip on its metal stand. "They didn't need to shoot at all. We weren't attacking them in the plaza. We were holding signs, marching around—"

"What does this have to do with your confession?" Riordan asked.

"Nothing. Or maybe something. . . . Lupita . . ."

Again César paused. It wasn't like him to be so indirect and hesitant. An uneasiness crept into Riordan.

"Before we started," César resumed, "she was saying to me, to everybody, 'The soldiers are assassins, and if my brother was still living, he would avenge the murder of his son.' She got a little crazy. One night, she went outside and screamed it: 'Who will avenge the murder of my son?' Even though I was drunk, I remember what she said to you the night of *Las Posadas*. About the soldiers the Brotherhood killed. Do you remember?"

Riordan thought back. "That she thought it was justice for them to die. Except it wasn't. The four soldiers who were killed were not even the ones who fired the shots in the plaza."

"I know that, and I told her. But she said she was happy they died, and you know, I was, too."

"I still don't see what this has to do—"

"So is that a sin—to be happy for someone's death?"

"Is that all that's on your mind?"

"Yes."

"It is not a thing a Christian should feel," Riordan counseled, breathing a sigh of relief that some new, shocking revelation was not at hand. "If you want to confess it, you have."

"I didn't start with her because I felt sorry for her. It was to calm her down."

This statement dismayed Riordan. Latin machismo. The cure for a hysterical woman was a good screwing. "César, God doesn't care why you committed adultery," he said, with severity in his voice. "Do you think Marta would care about your motives? God doesn't, either. He cares that you committed it. He cares that you repent of it, and that's the end of it."

"After what you did for me on that bridge . . ." César faltered. "I respect you, and I wanted to explain myself. So you respect me."

Riordan took his hand, a hand rough as sandpaper. "I do, my friend. No explanations required. I'm a bigger sinner than you are. Every one of us will be three days in our graves before the devil is done with us. Now say a firm act of contrition."

Pamela left for Philadelphia on a hot, cloudless Saturday morning. Lisette watched the plane take off from Hermosillo International into sunlight so bright it seemed to be sticking pins into her eyes. Driving back to San Patricio, she hummed to herself, happy for the respite from monitoring medications, from keeping her ears tuned for the changes in intonation in Pamela's speech that sometimes heralded a manic flight and sometimes did not but in any case frayed Lisette's nerves.

Yet within a day or two, she found herself missing Pamela as she crawled into bed alone, woke up alone, and, in the twilight after she'd seen the last patient of the day and Anna Montoya had gone home, dined alone in a silence that was palpable. She missed hearing Pamela say things like "Holy moly."

The news had broken only hours after she'd boarded her flight. It was just as well that she was gone. The atmosphere in San Patricio was unsettling, a mixture of excitement and fear. Wild rumors placed Ernesto Salazar in a dozen different places at once. No one strolled in the plaza or on the streets at night, and people locked their doors, despite—or maybe because of—the presence of more police and soldiers than anyone had ever seen in town. They'd resumed their random searches, ransacking houses on the flimsiest of pretexts; and when they did not find the fugitives hiding in closets, they would make off with jewelry or cash to reward themselves for their trouble.

Lisette could not get Evangelina off her mind. Three days after Pamela's departure, she returned to San Tomás with Anna to check up on the girl. Rumors were filtering out of the Sierra Madre that with its leaders in jail or on the run, the Brotherhood had already fractured into freelance bandit gangs. If the stories were true, the risks were greater than usual; but she and Anna made the trip without incident.

She saw Evangelina in the house of her aunt, Cornelia Valdez, the *curandera*. There was nothing she could do for the girl except to note the progress of her growing blindness. Lisette presented another food parcel to her mother, once again explaining that a change in diet might alleviate her daughter's diabetes, which, in turn, might slow the advance of the darkness shuttering her sight. Alma accepted the gift with a tremulous gratitude. Her face had the shape and color of a brown egg, and it wore a timid expression. Maybe her father-in-law had forced more nonsense on her: *Do not give any food offered by the American doctor to Evangelina. It's been poisoned to kill her so her organs can be harvested.* Ignorance! Backwardness! Whenever Lisette thought of Javier, fury surged through her. A fury she had to suppress. Here in these Indian villages, male power prevailed, a power founded on simple physical superiority and a capacity for violence.

Don't take this so personally, she counseled herself as she watched Alma trudge down a dirt street, the parcel under one arm, guiding Evangelina with her free hand.

Villagers began to crowd into the ramada, and Lisette conducted an impromptu clinic, examining kids with bronchitis, a woman who complained of chronic headaches, an old man suffering from COPD. People begged for aspirin, not because they were sick but because they found a doctor's visit a novelty—and the aspirin was free.

When everyone except the old man had left, Cornelia made good on her promise to teach Lisette the secrets of her herbal cures. She plucked sprigs from the plants hanging from the rafters, plants she had gathered herself, scouring the nearby hillsides.

A pail of water steamed on the mud-brick oven, and jojoba nuts roasted in the coals, throwing off a pleasing aroma. Anna sat at one end of the dining table—the picnic table Cornelia's husband had salvaged from San Patricio's town dump—and tended to the old man with COPD. Lisette's pickup was parked alongside the ramada, the nebulizer running off its battery by means of an extension cord.

"Breathe in, deep," Anna said, and the old man went goggle-eyed as he inhaled, struggling to fill his wasted lungs.

Lisette checked the indicator. His blood oxygen level was ninety-two. "Don't let it fall below ninety," she said.

Anna murmured, "I know what to do."

"Señora," said Cornelia in the sharp tone of a teacher calling a distracted student to attention. She was ready to begin her lecture, and was dressed for the occasion in a traditional ankle-length dress speckled with black rosettes. She pulled tuberous roots, like sweet potatoes, from the rafters. *Jaramatraca*, she said. Impossible to find in the mountains. Her husband, the local cattle inspector, had brought her these from "down below." She meant the desert.

Lisette, sitting on a straw floor mat, the pupil at the master's feet, flipped through the booklet in her lap, *Medicinal Plants of the Sonoran Desert. Jaramatraca* was the common name for *Peniocereus striatus*, a cactus.

"I call it 'the Jesus root,' because it performs miracles," Cornelia said, smiling. "First you do this . . ." She peeled the brown skin and dropped the white meat into the pail of hot water. Squatting low, she plucked the jojoba nuts out of the oven and, while they cooled, shoved oak sticks into the coals and blew on them, raising a flame. "Next, you boil the root. When it is boiled, it makes a medicine for the bad stomach. It cures bites from snakes and from these things." From out of a coffee can filled with water, she pulled a drowned centipede as long as a finger.

Lisette scribbled in her notebook, feeling a quiet excitement. She was acquiring hidden knowledge, back in med school, sort of, her professor a Mayo Indian woman who could neither read nor write but was a living encyclopedia of natural remedies. Her teachers at the Autonomous University of Guadalajara would probably regard Cornelia as a witch doctor at best, a charlatan at worst. But these Indians had survived for millennia, so their *curanderos* and *curanderas* must have something going for them.

Cornelia continued: "This is the *matadura*. Grind it into a powder and it heals wounds, cuts, chafes, saddle sores on horses and donkeys. And this, the *yerba del pasmo*, it cures fevers. This one"—she yanked from her pharmacopoeia what looked like a bristly, shrunken apple—"is the *toloache*. It heals swelling, and its juice can make you drunk."

Anna announced that the old man's level had reached ninety-five and would go no higher. She shut off the nebulizer and sent him on his way. Lisette looked up *toloache* in her booklet. *Datura inoxia*, otherwise known as the sacred datura for its powers to induce shamanistic visions, also as *yerba del diablo*, for its intoxicant effect, and locoweed, for the madness it produced in cattle that grazed on it.

"I will show you what I do with the jojoba," Cornelia said, and she scooped up the roasted fruits—they resembled hazelnuts—and poured them into the funnel of an oil press. As she cranked the handle, oil dripped into a small bottle under the spigot. This oil cured diarrhea and swellings from injuries, though not as miraculously as the *jaramatraca*—

A disturbance outside interrupted the lesson. Someone shouted, and people were running toward a dirty, dented pickup that must have rattled into the village only moments ago—the dust it had raised still hung thick over the road below. A vaquero, wearing the inevitable straw cowboy hat, and a skinny teenage boy climbed out of the truck and jogged up to Cornelia's house. Lisette recognized them as Tarahumara by their ankle-strap sandals and the boy's headband (otherwise, he looked like any Mexican street kid: low-rider jeans, a black T-shirt emblazoned with an image of Eminem). The vaquero politely doffed his hat and greeted Cornelia in Tarahumara, saying, "*Cuira*." (Hello.) That and a few other words—*Cumí?* (Where?), *juri* (yes), and *tásirapé* (no)—were all Lisette understood of the ensuing conversation, an agitated one accompanied by much pointing and gesturing. Cornelia said something—jumbled sounds to Lisette's ear—while motioning at her and Anna. The vaquero gave them a puzzled look, as if he hadn't noticed them at first, and asked Lisette in Spanish, "You also are a doctor?"

She picked up on the "also" and nodded, explaining that she was a different kind of doctor.

He turned and, with the boy, hurried back to the pickup.

"Cornelia, what is it? What's going on?" Lisette asked.

There were two other men in the truck, one wounded in the shoul-

der, the *curandera* answered. He had been shot with a gun. The Tarahumara didn't say who they were, but thought they must be narcos. He
and the boy had found them on the road, one man walking, the injured
one riding a donkey.

"They have brought him to me." Cornelia's face furrowed with
worry—no, Lisette realized, with fright. "Señora Lisette, I think it's him.
It must be him."

The news about the raid and Salazar's escape had reached San Tomás
within hours after it happened, by bush telegraph if by no other means.
Lisette's heart rate spiked instantly; she heard a low drumming in her
inner ears.

"I have never treated for a bullet wound," Cornelia declared.

Lisette swallowed and said, "Let's see what we can do . . . together,"
deciding not to reveal that she, too, had never treated a gunshot injury.
Dear God. A few minutes ago, she'd been learning folk medicine; now
she was to be an emergency-room physician, her patient a desperado, the
most wanted man in Mexico. Another tutorial in the University of the
Sierra Madre: everything can change in a moment.

The vaquero, his son, and a tall man with a beer-keg torso walked
the wounded man to the house. They almost had to drag him, his legs
flip-flopping like those of someone afflicted with a neurological disease.
One arm hung limp at his side, the shirtsleeve rust-colored and crusty
with dried blood; the other was draped over the back of his companion's neck, which looked as thick as a thigh. The injured man winced,
then groaned with pain and relief as he was eased down onto the picnic
table's bench, as gently as if he were made of crystal. Yes, it was Salazar.
Lisette recognized him from photos in the newspapers and on TV.

Her insides quivered as the big man, two stainless-steel pistols
jammed in his belt, turned to her and Cornelia, his face teak-colored,
his eyes shiny, black, reptilian. A bristly mustache shaped like an upside-
down U completed the picture of a central-casting outlaw. He had to be
the henchman mentioned in the news reports, but she could not recall
his name.

"Which of you is the doctor?" he asked, in a mild voice that didn't
match his fearsome appearance.

"We are both doctors," Lisette replied.

"The medical doctor," he said.

"I am."

"You must fix him."

"We'll try," she said. Cornelia looked petrified. "What happened?"

"You can see what—he's been shot. There was a disagreement."

"When?" she asked, observing that he and Salazar were dressed in expensive, western-cut silk shirts with mother-of-pearl buttons, fancy cowboy boots. Their clothes were filthy, the boots scuffed from their travels. "You're dressed like you were at a fiesta."

"Sure. A fiesta. We're mariachis, and someone didn't like our music."

"You are a humorist," Lisette said.

"Do you understand me, Señora Médico?" His tone wasn't mild now. "Stop asking questions and fix him."

She directed Cornelia to boil more water; then she and Anna went to her truck, her messy, mobile clinic. Bandages and gauze in this bag, scissors and digital thermometer in that bag, antibiotics and antiseptics in another. Anna spread the stuff on the table, on a clean cloth she'd managed to find.

"How are you feeling?" Lisette asked her patient. "How bad is the pain?"

"I have felt better," he croaked. This was the terrifying boss of La Fraternidad? A slight, almost delicate build, sandy hair cut short, a three-day stubble dusting a light-complexioned, boyish face that still looked a little older than the one shown on the news. The deep lines bracketing his mouth and the cat's whiskers flaring out from the corners of his eyes testified to a man in his forties.

While Anna checked his blood pressure and temperature—the first was low, the other high, 39.7 Celsius—Lisette took the scissors to his shirtsleeve, cutting around the shoulder. He flinched and hissed when she peeled off the cloth. She sucked in a breath, recoiling from the smell. From the shoulder to within an inch of the elbow, his arm was swollen and had turned the color of burgundy; pus oozed from the red-rimmed entrance wound, a thumbnail-sized hole angling in just below the clavicle. There was no exit wound; the bullet was lodged somewhere in bone or muscle.

"If I am permitted to ask a question," she said, with a glance at Scary One, packing the pistols, "how long has his arm been like this?"

"Shot three days ago. Like this since yesterday." It was Salazar who replied.

"Yesterday when?"

"Afternoon."

Speaking slowly and haltingly in a flutelike voice, he said that he'd been wearing his armored vest but had been shot with a *mata policías*, a cop killer. His friend helpfully explained that a *mata policías* was a bullet that penetrated body armor.

"You have been traveling for days on a donkey, with this bullet in you?" Lisette asked, incredulous.

"Yes," the wounded man answered. Light-headed, he swayed as he sat on the bench. "*Es usted una americana?* Your accent," he added, now in English. "You must be . . . American doctor from San . . . from San Patricio."

Lisette nodded. That he knew who she was came as no surprise.

"Me, too. . . . My mother . . . American. I was born in Arizona . . . in Douglas."

Feeling bolder, determined not to be intimidated, she made no pretense to a bedside manner. "Well, you're going to die in Mexico if I don't get you to my clinic and then to a hospital."

He showed no reaction.

"Did you hear what I said? That bullet has to come out right away. My surgical instruments are at my clinic in San Patricio, and then we'll have to get you to a hospital. That's gangrene in your arm. Gas gangrene. It will kill you within forty-eight hours."

He grimaced as a wave of pain rolled through him.

"It will take two hours to get there," she added. "Two at least. We need to leave now."

Salazar made a slight movement of his head, then addressed the other man by name—Enrique—and explained in Spanish what Lisette wanted to do and why and that he thought it was a bad idea. Enrique concurred. Too many cops in San Patricio, too many soldiers. Too many *bloqueos* and *retenos* between here and there.

"We can hide him in the back of my truck," she pleaded. "The police and soldiers always let me through the roadblocks and checkpoints. They know me. And I can sneak him into the clinic through the back door."

She had spoken without thinking. Her proposal drew a low gasp from Anna, one that needed no elaboration. What if they were caught, transporting the *jefe* of La Fraternidad?

"Too much risk. You will fix him here," Enrique said, in a way that foreclosed on further argument.

She made one regardless, pointing out the obvious: without her instruments and anesthetic, she could not fix him. Here or anywhere.

"This woman," said Salazar, inclining his head toward Anna. "Who is she?"

"My nurse."

"Send her for what you need."

Lisette informed him that Anna could not navigate the mountain roads, and even if she could, five hours would pass before she returned. Maybe six, because it would be dark by then. With gas gangrene, every hour counted—

"We can drive her. We know the roads."

This from the Tarahumara, who had been hanging back in a corner with the boy.

The two men approved. "May God repay you," said Salazar. "I pray . . . *Santa Muerte* to grant you . . . safe trip."

"And a quiet one," Enrique added. "You will not say nothing to nobody," he ordered, staring coldly at Anna.

"I am not going to allow my nurse to be on that road at night," Lisette argued. "I'll go."

"You are staying right here with him," said Enrique. *"Claro?"*

A look passed over Anna's small, nutmeg-colored face, a pleading look that begged Lisette to stop objecting.

"Claro," she said, and handed her keys to the Tarahumara. Her truck, beat up as it was, looked to be in better shape than his; and with the clinic's name on the door panels, there was less likelihood of his being stopped and questioned at a checkpoint. She drew up a list in her

notebook—scalpel, probe, forceps, more gauze and bandages—then tore off the page and handed it to her nurse.

"And don't forget syringes and antibiotic, flucloxacillin," she said, walking to the truck with Anna. "Lidocaine for a local. Don't forget that."

Anna nodded, licking her lips.

"It will be all right," Lisette said.

"I pray it will. It is him, isn't it?"

"Yes." Lisette looked back toward the house. "And, Anna, please do as he says. Don't say anything. I'm kind of a hostage here."

■ ■ ■

What a shame that she was no longer in touch with her family. This story would perk up a boring Sunday in Watauga County. *Dear Folks, I had a full day the other day,* she thought, composing an imaginary e-mail. *I took a bullet out of the shoulder of a drug lord, Mexico's most wanted man, and saved his arm from amputation, maybe his life.*

A bit ahead of herself; she'd done nothing of the kind, as yet. Two hours, give or take, had passed since Anna had gone. Assuming no break-downs or other problems, she would be arriving in San Patricio right about now. Cornelia had administered a dose of *jaramatraca* water to Salazar and rubbed his arm with the jojoba salve. Her folk-medicine wonder drugs. Lisette, after putting on latex surgical gloves, had squeezed pus from his wound, causing him to yelp like an injured dog, then cleansed and dressed it with hydrogen peroxide and a gauze compress. She'd cut his shirt into strips and fashioned a temporary sling, bending his arm across his chest (another yelp) and knotting the sling behind his skinny neck. Aspirin to reduce his fever, an oral antibiotic to fight the infection, and she'd done all she could for the time being. Now, covered by a serape against the chill of the mountain twilight, he lay on the pic-nic table, which would have to serve as an operating table.

If he was an American, how and why had he become *el jefe* of one of Mexico's most dreaded drug cartels? Lisette knew better than to ask. Enrique had ordered the curious villagers to go to their homes, which they had done. The smoke of cooking fires twirled into the air. Cornelia began to prepare dinner, and Lisette helped out, to stay occupied and stop herself from thinking too much. She was patting tortillas on a board when Salazar asked if she had a smartphone, one with a camera. She replied that she did.

"Give it to my friend, please."

Despite the civil "please," it was a command. With the aspirin and the antibiotic and, possibly, Cornelia's remedies, he'd recovered a measure of his strength.

Salazar sat up slowly, grimaced, and teetered, on the verge of falling sideways before Enrique grasped him under his good arm to keep him upright. "We are going to make a little video before it becomes dark," he explained, as if this were the most normal thing in the world.

She wiped dough from her hands and handed her phone to Enrique. Tapping the phone's screen, he grumbled that it was stuck in photo mode.

"Don't tap it—swipe it to the left," she said, and performed the action for him.

"Okay, *listos*." He pointed the phone at Salazar, who brushed his light brown hair with his right hand. This was beyond weird. Lisette imagined describing the scene to Nick, and her son pronouncing it "awesome."

"Good evening, brothers and sisters," Salazar began, struggling to inject power into his voice. "This will be a brief message from the Butterfly. The enemies of La Fraternidad . . ." He halted to draw in a breath. "The Federal Police, the army, the *autodefensas*, those who remain loyal to the criminal Joaquín Carrasco . . . they will tell you that the Butterfly has been killed. Yes! That once again I am dead! More . . . lies. As you can see, I live . . . I live. . . . Thank you for watching. . . . Until next time."

The brief effort had cost him. He lay down again, with his head propped on a rolled-up blanket, his eyes shut. *You'll be lucky if you live through tomorrow*, Lisette thought, and asked Enrique what they intended to do with the video. Post it, he answered. As soon as they were in a place with service.

"Now I think you know who we are," he said in that incongruously gentle voice.

"No," she answered, having acquired the habit that was second nature to Mexicans: pretend not to know what you know.

"Yes, you do."

She gulped and nodded, remembering his full name now: Enrique

Mora. He turned the phone off and pocketed it, meeting her request for its return with a look malevolent in its indifference.

A truck pulled into the village. Lisette's heart jumped, then fell when she saw that it wasn't Anna but Cornelia's husband—the cattle inspector—and their two sons. Lisette could not remember the husband's name. He was a sturdily built, handsome man with the complexion of someone who spent little time indoors. Taking off his cowboy hat, he threw a surprised look at her and had begun to ask what had brought her to San Tomás when he noticed the two strangers, one leaning against a ramada post in the shadows, the other stretched out on his family's dinner table.

"Who are—" he started to say, then stopped himself, catching sight of Enrique's pistols.

"We are travelers who thank you for your hospitality," Salazar said, his lilting voice faint, a febrile sheen on his face.

Cornelia exchanged glances with her husband, and he understood that he was not to make further inquiries. He and the boys sat down on a floor mat. Cornelia hung two kerosene lanterns from a rafter, then served dinner: beans, shredded beef, tortillas. Salazar forced himself back into a sitting position. Enrique spoon-fed him with a kind of devoted tenderness, but Salazar could manage only a few bites. Seated on the floor with the family, Lisette didn't do much better. Anxiety had coalesced into a hard little ball in her gut. Enrique devoured his meal like a starving animal. The boys threw looks of awed fascination at him and Salazar, until he said, "Eat your dinner, kids, and stop staring at us." Trying to ignore the presence of his menacing guests, Cornelia's husband said that he and his sons had found a dead calf in a barranca, the tracks of a big cat all around it. A puma, probably, but maybe *el tigre*. No one asked to hear more about this adventure. They ate in a tense quiet, as if in a nest of rattlesnakes that a noise or movement might provoke into striking.

Lisette looked at her watch. A few minutes past seven. Anna should be on her way back. Cornelia offered to rub more jojoba oil into Salazar's arm.

"Put these on first," Lisette directed, handing gloves to her. While Cornelia applied the oil, Lisette checked his temperature—it had risen to 40 degrees—and blood pressure, which had fallen to 100 over 65. Pressing the swollen, blackening flesh produced a crinkling sound, as if she were poking a potato chip bag. The gangrene was progressing, his bloodstream carrying the poison to other parts of his body. She fed him more aspirin.

"You, you, you. Go into the house and stay there," Mora commanded, waving a finger at Cornelia and her family. "You, Señora Médico, remain here."

Cornelia's husband tightened his jaw; being ordered around under his own roof affronted his dignity. Masculine power, Lisette thought. Brute force, and right now the brute and the force were not with him. He meekly shepherded his wife and sons inside. Something furtive in their movements, in the shutting of the door, made her feel abandoned.

Half an hour later, his temperature spiking, Salazar began to hallucinate, babbling about butterflies. Swallowtails. Monarchs. Painted ladies . . .

"Don't talk," Lisette said. "Try to rest."

"Painted lady . . . very beautiful . . . orange and black," he rasped. "God spoke to me through her. . . . Leave Texas. . . . Avenge your mother. . . . Ha! She did not like my butterflies. . . . If you collect them, you become one, a *mariposa*, a *maricón*, a faggot. . . . Leave Texas, save Mexico from the godless tyrants. . . . This came from God, in the voice of the Painted Lady—"

He was using up what strength he had left with his raving. "Stop it!" Lisette cried out, thinking that once the gangrene reached his vital organs, God would not be speaking to him, nor he to God, through intermediaries. "You have got to rest!"

Finally, exhausted, drugged on the painkillers, he let his chin drop to his chest, and he fell asleep. Enrique turned to her, one side of his face illuminated by the kerosene lamp, the other side in darkness, like a half-moon.

"He knows and I know you are the doctor who was with that priest who ratted to the police."

"What? What do you mean?"

"Search your memory, Señora Médico."

She did, and found there the poppy field, the heroin refinery. But hadn't Tim assured her that the raid on them had been a coincidence? That is what she said to Enrique—how the raid, coming so soon after she and the priest had stumbled on the poppy field, had been a coincidence.

"We do not think so."

No matter his temperate, mannerly tone, she sensed that he was keeping the lid on a vast reservoir of violence, and that the lid could blow at any second.

"We also know you were not the finger, and in any case, it is in our code never to harm women," he went on.

It sickened her that she felt relieved and grateful.

"It was the priest, but it is also in our code to warn someone who has fucked up not to fuck up again." He paused and carefully composed a severe expression. "We sent him a warning. To be more careful who he speaks to, and what he says in his church. We are not sure he has taken heed . . ."

Several seconds passed before she grasped what he was talking about. Her ideal self would have come back at him in anger, in revulsion, crying out that whoever Salazar thought communicated to him through the medium of butterflies, it wasn't God. That is what the ideal Lisette would have done. The real one was wordless.

"So, we know who you are, and you know who we are," Enrique continued. "Our code is written in my friend's book. I wish I had a copy with me for you to read. *My Reflections*, it is called. In it he writes, 'It is for every man to fight a battle, to live an adventure, and to rescue a beauty.' So, you see, we do not harm beauty, we rescue it."

"I'm no beauty, and I don't need to be rescued," she said, as certain of the first statement as she was uncertain of the second.

"Oh, but you are beautiful." Enrique's grin, like his stare, belonged in a herpetarium. She prayed it wasn't preamble to a rape. "My friend is a great man. He has been chosen to save Mexico from criminals and tyrants, and fate has chosen you for the honor of fixing him. That is what makes you beautiful. But where is your nurse with your things?"

"It's a bad road in daylight and worse at night," she said. "She should be here soon."

"She had better be. We will be leaving after you have fixed him."

"He has to go to a hospital. His arm may have to come off. He may have to sacrifice his arm to save his life."

"No hospital. We told you that. We will require your truck . . . and you. You will be his hospital. You will be leaving with us to take care of him until he is better."

Her breath caught as the terror that had been lurking in the back of her mind for the past couple of hours barged into her frontal lobe. Now she regretted her last instruction to Anna. She was to be kidnapped, hostage to Salazar's recovery. She felt slightly nauseous. The villagers could not, would not help her. A few men owned old shotguns and hunting rifles, but they would be no match for a professional like Enrique. Besides, too many, like Javier, worked for the Brotherhood. Field hands in the marijuana and poppy plantations, meth cookers, lookouts.

"What if he doesn't recover?" she asked timidly. "What then?"

"Oh, he will. *La Santa Muerte* looks out for him."

Long minutes passed in silence, Enrique fighting sleep. At last, worn to the bone after spending three days in flight from police and army patrols, he succumbed, nodding off in the confidence that she wouldn't try to escape—where could she escape to?—or do something desperate, like steal one of his pistols. Tingling from nervous and physical exhaustion, she stretched out on the floor mat and closed her eyes, but she couldn't sleep, her mind flitting from thought to thought. She mentally rehearsed how she would remove the bullet and debride Salazar's gangrenous arm. She wished she could speak to her son. What was Pamela doing at this moment? In bed, probably—it was early morning in Philadelphia. Nearly ten p.m. here. What the hell was holding up Anna? She'd been gone nearly twice as long as Lisette had anticipated. Dreadful visions teased her: Anna waylaid by a gang, the vaquero taking a turn too fast, the truck plummeting into some black canyon. Ten or fifteen minutes later, she heard the sound of an approaching vehicle, saw headlights piercing the darkness.

His chin on his chest, Enrique stirred but did not awaken. The pickup—hers! hers!—stopped on the road directly below. Lisette's relief turned to joy as she rose and hurried toward it. But before she got there, the Tarahumara and the boy jumped out, ran to their pickup, and sped off.

Anna opened the rear door, the interior light winking on.

"Thank God you're all right," Lisette said to her. "I was so very worried. Did you have trouble?"

"I have brought everything," the nurse replied evasively. "And these, too." She produced an LED lantern and a fleece-lined jacket from a tote bag. Lisette was grateful for both, especially the jacket; she was shivering. She ducked her head inside and did a quick survey. Scalpel. Forceps. Probe. Surgical needle and thread. Bandages and tape. Disposable syringes. Antiseptic. Lidocaine. A proper sling. And a battery-operated surgical saw, in case she had to amputate. It looked as new as when she'd bought it. She'd never had to use it, and hoped she would not have to now. A wild thought flew into her mind—deliberately botch the procedure, for its success would ensure her captivity—but she dismissed this notion immediately: the consequences of failure would be worse.

"You certainly did think of everything," she said to Anna, who made no reply. "Are you ready?"

"*Estoy aterrrado,*" Anna answered.

"So am I. We must try not to be. Or try not to show it. We are both going to need to be steady."

"They have followed me, I think," Anna said in an undertone. "Soldiers. *Federales.*"

"What!" Lisette rasped. "But I told you not to—"

"It was not me," the nurse pleaded. "The Indian man. On our way back, we were stopped at a police *reteno*—"

"*Oye! Señora Médico!* What's going on down there? Get to work! He's awake."

It was Enrique, also risen from his slumbers. She looked up at the house and saw him standing outside, silhouetted against the wavering lamplight.

"How far behind you are they?" she asked Anna.

"*No lo se.* Oh, Lisette, I don't know what will happen now."

Of course, neither did Lisette. Nor did she know what to think, her brain whirling as she tried to sort through the possibilities in a matter of seconds. If she and Anna were going to try to escape, now was the moment: jump in the truck and speed away as the Tarahumara had. Would Enrique fire at them? Could he hit anything in the dark? What if, cornered by the police, he took Cornelia and her family hostage?

"Be brave," she told Anna. "You must not let on that anything is wrong."

The nurse gave a jerky nod, and they trudged uphill to the house.

Enrique cast a serpent's eye on Anna. "What took you so long?"

Visibly trembling, the nurse answered that it was the darkness, the condition of the road.

"Where is that Indian and his kid?"

Lisette stepped in before he could grill Anna any further. "If you want me to fix your friend, Don Enrique, we must start right away," she said, summoning up her best authoritative tone. She reached into the tote bag and shoved an IV drip bag into his hand. "Hold this, please, and do what I tell you."

CHAPTER THIRTY

The Professor was experiencing one of the spectacles synesthesia produced in times of stress or excitement. This being a time for both, the show was a fantastic display of sound and light. The landscape, bathed in the spectral glow of his night-vision goggles, sang a tremulous note in his mind, like a bow scraping a single-string instrument; Valencia's voice as he gave a final briefing to his troops lowered shimmering white curtains into the goggles' greenish, luminescent pools. *I want the son of a bitch alive. We do not move in until she's finished. No firing except on express command. Do you understand? No firing unless I order it. We don't want another fuckup.* Someone murmured, *Sí, mi capitán.* Others followed, each hushed response creating a kaleidoscopic sparkle before the Professor's eyes.

They were twelve, as many as could be mustered on short notice: Valencia with seven paratroopers, the Professor with three federal policemen. They shouldn't need any more to arrest two men, only one of whom was capable of offering resistance. Assuming, that is, that the information they'd pried out of the nurse and those two Indians at the roadblock was accurate. No reason to think it wasn't.

They would approach San Tomás on foot; it was about half a kilometer distant. To draw any closer in the SandCats would give them away. Both vehicles had been backed into an oak grove a few meters off the road and hastily camouflaged with netting and branches. The Professor thought that was unnecessary—it was a moonless night, so the chances of anyone spotting the SandCats under the trees were nil—but the army had its own way of doing things. Leaving the drivers behind to guard the troop carriers, the remaining ten men set off, every loose piece of equipment secured with tape or Velcro straps to dampen the noise. The Professor's sensory spectacle had ended. He was glad; it was becoming a distraction. He heard only the soft crunch of boots, and saw only what was there: the tree-bordered road ahead, looking in his goggles like a tunnel illuminated by faint green lamps.

Valencia halted the column to check his GPS. Two hundred fifty meters, he whispered. There was tension in his hushed voice, a mixture of anxiety, impatience, and a restrained eagerness. This operation was more to his liking, everyone properly equipped and attired—the paratroopers in cammies, the *federales* in black—for his moment of final triumph. If they captured Salazar, Valencia wanted full credit to go to the army, with the Federal Police cast as supporting actors. The Professor agreed. He had no interest in glory, which was nothing more than a word. Maybe the *capitán* would invite him to the ceremony when they pinned a major's star on his shoulders.

A coyote sent up a long call, and the pack answered with what sounded like cackling in a madhouse, raising howls from the village dogs. All to the good. The racket would muffle the raiders' movements. They went on at a brisk walk, until Valencia halted them again. San Tomás appeared ahead. It was as if the lime-colored light of the night-vision goggles had conjured it out of the blackness, a ramshackle Brigadoon, mud-brick huts and shanties scattered across two shallow hills divided by the road. The whole village was dark, except for lanterns glimmering from atop the hill on the right. The house where the gringa doctor was repairing Julián Menéndez, a.k.a. Ernesto Salazar. Valencia deployed his troops, sending two men down the road to block its use as an escape route, two more to circle around to the rear of the house, keeping enough distance between them and it to avoid detection. The Professor overcame, temporarily, his dislike of all things military; he admired the way the men moved— quickly, each one silent as smoke. In a while, three crisp clicks came over Valencia's radio, followed by three more. The blocking teams were in position. Then Valencia, the Professor, and the remaining men, a paratrooper sergeant and the trio of *federales*, sprinted in a crouch to hunker down behind the doctor's truck and wait. The coyotes had ceased their demented warbling, the dogs their howling.

■ ■ ■

She had shot Salazar's arm full of lidocaine and fed him an oral meperidine. He lay flat on the table, semiconscious, his feet dangling over the edge. The bullet had come out more easily than she'd expected, the tip flattened and peeled back so that it looked like a small flower with wilted petals. *Mata policías*. Cop killer. What a lovely term. The round had chewed through his shoulder muscle but had not smashed the bone, the armored vest having slowed its terrible velocity. After cleansing and suturing the puncture, she began to debride his upper arm, which had gone from dark red to purple; it resembled an elongated eggplant. Her scalpel sliced off thin layers of necrotic flesh bit by bit, Anna lifting the strips with the forceps, dropping them into a pail. The two women wore surgical masks to cloak the stench of pus and rot. Enrique muffled his nose and mouth with a bandanna, giving him even more of an outlaw look. Lisette had turned him into an operating-room assistant; he held the drip bag containing flucloxacillin over the prostrate Salazar. For a narco tough guy, he'd proved to be squeamish and whiny, shutting his eyes as Lisette cut, complaining that his arm was getting tired from holding the bag. "Switch hands, then," Lisette snapped. She assumed he wanted to keep the right one free to draw a pistol if he had to.

Her fervent hope was, of course, that he wouldn't have the time, that the cops and soldiers who had followed Anna would swoop in and arrest him and the "great man" without a shot being fired. If, that is, they had followed her nurse. Focused on her task, she'd evicted all thoughts of what might happen to her if she were shanghaied into the role of Salazar's personal physician. Yet an exhilaration ran beneath her fear, the two emotions parts of the same stream, current and undercurrent in seamless friction.

Salazar's eyes were glazed; if not for their occasional blinking, they could have been mistaken for a dead man's. In the light cast by the LED lamp and the kerosene lanterns hung overhead, she sliced and snipped, sliced and snipped. His bicep had a shallow but distinct concavity before she found healthy tissue. There was no discoloration below the elbow; she might have arrested the gangrene's spread. Looking at the bullet wound, stitched up neat as a button, and at the smooth, red scoop in his upper arm brought a sense of accomplishment, of pride in skills she hadn't known she had. Her first surgery, and under conditions a Civil War surgeon would have found familiar. Some baptism. Pulling her mask down, she swiped the back of her hand across her damp forehead, peered into Salazar's face, and said, "It's done."

He rolled his head, mumbling something.

"He will keep his arm?" asked Enrique as he untied the bandanna. Spittle glistened on his mustache. "He must not lose his arm."

"We will see," Lisette said, shocked by the thought that sprang into her mind: *Well, he's got another one.* She told Anna to swab and pack the wound bed with dry gauze.

The nurse delved into the tote bag and said, "We do not have enough. There is more in the truck," in the stilted manner of a kid auditioning for a high school play. She flicked her eyebrows at Lisette, then glanced sidelong, toward the pickup parked at the roadside below.

Lisette understood, or thought she did. A deep fatigue overtook her suddenly; resisting an urge to lie down, she grabbed the LED lantern, telling Enrique not to lower the drip bag. That, she thought, will keep one hand occupied—his right, it was to be hoped.

Outside, as they scurried to the truck, Anna said, under her breath, that she'd been told to vacate the ramada when the operation was over. The police and soldiers did not want to risk getting her or Lisette hurt when they made the arrest.

"The gauze—that's all I could think of to get us out of there."

"I figured," Lisette said.

Prepared for a surprise, she made no sound when, as she stepped around to the driver's side, someone crouching behind the pickup seized her wrist and pulled her down beside him. "Be quiet, stay right here," he whispered in perfect American English. A DEA agent maybe? There were a few more men with him—black, almost shapeless forms pressed against the doors. One of them spoke briefly into a radio, but in a voice so subdued she could not make out what he said.

"Only the two? No one else?" the English speaker asked, his mouth to her ear.

"There's a family inside the house." Her arms and scalp prickled, her heart thudding against her rib cage. Not fear—a weird elation, rather. "Please, no shooting if you can help it."

"We want them alive, don't worry," he assured her; then he and the others rose and started up the hill, jog-trotting in single file. Anna, right next to her, crossed herself, kissing the tips of her fingers.

■ ■ ■

The ramada jutted out from the back of the house. They moved up to the front to conceal their approach. Valencia with his sergeant crept toward one side of the ramada, while the Professor with his men went around to the other. Julián Menéndez had escaped him twice, the first time ten years ago, when he'd rescued the hostages seized by Julián's mother. There would be no strike three. In deposing Carrasco, the skinny *maricón* had wrecked a good thing, a more or less orderly, highly profitable enterprise. And now Julián's head was filled with dizzy ideas of revolution, of waging some sort of holy war on behalf of his mongrelized Christian-voodoo-narco creed. Braced against a wall of the house, the Professor felt an electric current pulsing up and down his backbone— the sensation of unfinished business about to be finished.

Then, voiding himself of all thought and emotion, he stepped around the corner, his H&K in a two-handed grip. In a nanosecond, his brain photographed Enrique Mora, *El Serpiente*, standing with a plastic bag in his hand, the bag attached to Julián Menéndez's arm by a flexible tube, Julián supine on a picnic table.

"Policía Federal! No se mueva. Estás bajo arresto!"

Mora's reaction to the shouted command was as swift and automatic as an eye blink. He whirled and flung the bag at the Professor with the accuracy of a pitcher unleashing a fastball. The long IV tube, torn from Julián's arm, whipped the Professor's face as the bag struck his hands, knocking his pistol from his grip. But in that instant, as Mora went for one of the guns in his waistband, Valencia leapt in from behind and delivered a crisp blow to the back of Mora's skull with a rifle butt. Mora dropped to both knees, tottered, and then fell facedown. One of the *federales* jammed a knee into his spine, wrenched his arms behind his back, and cuffed him with plastic straps. Rivulets of blood webbed the nape of his neck, staining his shirt collar. The cop rolled him over and disarmed him. A matched pair of stainless steel, pearl-handled semi-autos; one of the pistols must have been Julián's. Collecting his own weapon, and himself, the Professor, along with two *federales*, lifted Mora to his feet—it took the three of them to do it, since Mora weighed a good one hundred kilos—then sat him on the table's bench, clamped one end of a pair of plastic handcuffs to his, and bound the other end to the wrist of Julián's good arm, streaked with blood leaking from the vein where the IV tube had been inserted. They maneuvered Julián off the table, onto the bench, and there the fugitive pair sat side by side. Julián, drugged and in pain, his lips compressed, stared in glassy bewilderment. And no wonder, with a stitched bullet hole in his shoulder and, below it, what looked like a salami sliced lengthwise.

"As I was saying, you're under arrest," the Professor noted with a mocking air that concealed a savage urge to pistol-whip Julián. But it wasn't only the desire for revenge, or to punish, that bred the impulse. The Professor felt a bit cheated. The bust had been too easy, too quick; he would have liked a fiery climax.

Valencia removed a handheld from a cargo pocket and radioed the drivers, ordering them to bring up the SandCats. He glowed, he sparkled: Julián and Mora would be taken to the base, the media alerted, and he would perp-walk them past the cameras like a Caesar parading captive kings.

The Professor dug a thumb under Julián's chin, jerked his head up and held it there, forcing Julián to look straight into his face.

"You're not Ernesto Salazar, you're Julián Menéndez—let's be on the up-and-up with each other, all right? It's been a long time, but I haven't changed that much. Do you recognize me?"

Julián blinked and croaked, "No."

"You will when you're feeling better. Care to tell us what happened at your birthday fiesta?"

Julián did not say anything.

"How about you, Enrique? Rubén Levya shot Julián for some reason, then you or both of you killed him."

"There was a disagreement," Mora said, gritting his teeth against the ache in his skull.

"More detail would be helpful. You put at least a dozen bullets into him."

"Only a dozen? We must have missed with a few."

The Professor laughed but without mirth. "All right. These questions can wait. We'll have all kinds of time to get them answered."

"I answer you now," Mora said. "Your trick didn't fool Don Ernesto. He saw you coming out and he knew you weren't *músicos* but fucking *chotas*. We put on our vests and got ready. But that traitor Levya, he drew his pistol and takes a shot at the boss, and then we fucked him up. Okay? Now you know. Now you tell me how you did it. How did you turn him?"

"You don't ask questions," the Professor said. "We do."

"And I have one I want answered," Valencia said. "Three months ago, an army patrol was ambushed, a video made of the soldiers' executions. Who did this? What were the *sicarios'* names?"

Neither prisoner answered. Julián probably wasn't capable of answering. Taking the good-cop role, the Professor told him, in an avuncular tone, that if they had wanted to kill him and his number two, they would have. Personally, he didn't give a damn who had been in on the ambush, who had made the video, who had staged the fake executions; but this information was important to the *capitán* . . .

Julián turned to him. He, too, hadn't changed all that much in the past decade: his face was fuller and more lined, but he had the same sand-colored hair, with its slightly reddish tint, the same faint spray of freckles across his cheeks—inheritances from his half-Irish mother. A startled recognition flared in Julián's eyes.

"You! You!" he cried out, in English.

"Ah, you're feeling better. *Sí, soy yo.* I've waited ten years to put you away." The Professor flashed a jovial, careless smile. "Which do you prefer? English or Spanish?"

Mora made a rumbling sound in his throat, like someone hawking up a lungful of phlegm. "Stop fucking with him. That's a great man you're fucking with. A man chosen to rid Mexico of tyrants, like the ones you work for."

"You seem to be feeling *muy valiente*, Enrique," said the Professor.

"I don't give a shit, that's why."

"Then maybe we should fuck with you," Valencia said, standing close enough to poke Mora's forehead with his rifle muzzle. "If you wish us to fuck with you instead of with the savior of Mexico, we will be happy to do it. We can show you how we fuck with narcos."

Mora's heavy lids fell slowly, then rose again, just as slowly.

"Fuck with somebody else."

"Who?" Valencia made a parody of looking around the ramada. "I don't see anyone."

"Then go fuck yourselves."

"Stop trying to provoke us, Enrique. Your face alone is a provocation. You are extremely ugly. They call you *El Serpiente*, but that is an insult to snakes."

"It wasn't us. . . . Don't need to . . . Not us . . ."

Julián's words were so soft and halting that neither Valencia nor the Professor reacted immediately. Julián's head drooped. Almost in a faint, he leaned against Mora. With the two of them chained together, they looked like some two-headed freak in a carnival show.

"He means we did not spring the ambush," Mora chimed in. "I wish we did. I wish it had been us and that you shits were in the truck when we did."

"Enrique, *escúchame*," Valencia said. "Do you see this?" He twirled the rifle like a baton so the butt end was aimed at Mora's face. "This is what hit you in the head. If you say another word except to answer a question, it will hit you in the mouth. It will hit you so hard that you will be shitting your own teeth for a week. *Está claro?* Inform us. Who was it if it wasn't you?"

The story had hardly begun before it was interrupted by the Sand-Cat drivers, announcing their arrival, and, right behind them, by the American doctor, Moreno, and her nurse. Entering the ramada, both women took in the scene. The Professor noticed that they hung back for a moment, as if they weren't quite sure that they were now safe.

"I thank you for what you've done," Moreno said, stepping forward. "I'm not finished with him yet."

"Then finish and be quick about it," Valencia said.

Which she was. In under five minutes, she had the arm packed with gauze, bandaged, and immobilized in a sling taped snugly across Julián's chest. Then Valencia, in his abrupt, captain-of-paratroopers way, ordered her and the nurse to leave; they were finished with the patient, but he wasn't.

The doctor objected: her patient had to be evacuated immediately and brought to a hospital, because he was in danger of losing his arm.

"I do not give a shit if it falls off this minute," Valencia snarled. "Go."

It was the nurse who convinced her. She was plainly terrified by Mora, who had been glaring at her with pure, implacable hatred. He didn't need superior powers of deduction to have figured out that she was ultimately responsible for the situation in which he and Julián now found themselves.

Mora's account resumed.

Brotherhood lookouts had spotted the army truck on the road. They went to investigate and found two soldiers lying dead outside, two more inside, all four with pictures of *La Santa Muerte* pinned to their shirts.

"And then what?" Valencia said, shaking Mora.

But it was Julián who replied: "Someone . . . tried to make it . . . make it . . . look like us . . ."

"And then what? You expect me to believe you have no idea who those *sicarios* were?"

Unable to go on, Julián slumped into Mora's shoulder like a tired child. All the Professor could feel toward him now was utter contempt. The boss of the dreaded Brotherhood, the would-be revolutionary, had chirped like any small-time snitch, eager to prove his innocence. Innocence. You would have an easier time finding a penguin in Mexico than one innocent man.

"You!" Valencia said to Mora. "Then what?"

"It was Levya's idea."

"What was?"

"The video."

"What about the video?"

"Levya . . . he says, 'Okay, someone wants to pin this ambush on us, let us take credit, but not for an ambush. For an execution. We will make it look like we captured these *paracaidistas* and executed them. To show that La Fraternidad avenges the killing of the kids in San Patricio, so the people of the town will come back to our side. Also to show that we are not afraid even of the great paratroopers—'"

"You think I am going to believe that?" Valencia said.

The Professor had had enough of the captain's obsession. Nudging him to go outside, he followed, then said, quietly, that Mora and Julián could not have fabricated this tale on the spur of the moment.

"They could have made it up before," Valencia murmured.

"There would have been no need to! They wanted to take credit!" the Professor said, now beyond fed up. He pointed out that the story fit in neatly with their own theory that some unknown gang had staged the ambush. There was no sense in wasting another minute on this sideshow. Time to go, time to load the prisoners in the SandCats and start for the base. It would be close to daybreak by the time they got there.

To his amazement—and gratification—Valencia agreed. They went back inside. But the captain was not quite finished.

"So you collected the bodies and you took them somewhere," the captain said to Mora. "You tied them to chairs and you shot them, to make your video more entertaining." His jaw muscles rippled and twitched. "You murdered the murdered men. My men."

"If that is how you want to put it—"

"Are you still fearless, Enrique? Or are you now afraid of us, the great paratroopers?"

"What do you think?"

Mora's mouth and nose exploded, a burst of blood and teeth and saliva, of red and white, like a tomato smashed by a hammer. His head snapped backward from the blow of Valencia's rifle butt, then flipped forward as he tumbled off the bench and onto the floor, gagging and spitting, pulling Julián down on top of him.

"I think if you are not," Valencia said, "you should be."

CHAPTER THIRTY-ONE

A fter Ernesto Salazar's capture, it was as if a thunderstorm had passed through San Patricio; the air felt lighter. The town was no longer under siege, liberated from the Brotherhood's terror and from military occupation as well. The checkpoints on the roads were removed, the *federales* and soldiers withdrawn from the streets and returned to their barracks.

The *Fiesta de la Santa Semana*, when the Mayo reenacted Christ's passion, death, and resurrection, promised to be more festive than it had been in years. Lisette always showed up for the opening ceremonies on the day before Holy Thursday, but she missed them on this particular Wednesday; she was driving Pamela to San Patricio from the Hermosillo airport.

The sojourn in the States had done her good. The woman who returned to Mexico was fully Pamela A, self-possessed and happy to see Lisette, embracing her when they met in baggage claim, giving her a warm kiss in the car before they pulled out of the lot. Despite a long flight and a delay while changing planes in Phoenix, she looked relaxed: the squint lines that came from studying canvases for too long were ironed out, and she was stylishly dressed in a pearl choker and flowing black slacks, her hair pinned up, the way Lisette liked it.

"All right, now you can tell me all about your adventure," she said as they swung off Mex 15, onto the state highway.

Ordeal is more like it, Lisette thought.

Salazar's arrest and the dismantling of his cartel had made the national news in the States. Pamela had phoned right after she'd seen the report on CNN and heard mention of an American doctor, otherwise not identified, who had been treating him for a bullet wound when he was seized.

"I knew it had to be you," she had said, and followed with a rush of questions: "Are you all right? Are you safe? What happened?"

Lisette had confirmed that it had been she, and yes, she was safe. As for what happened, she would give Pamela all the dramatic details when she got home.

"I've got some news, too," Pamela had said, after a pause. San Patricio was not her idea of home.

Now, driving through the scrub desert east of Hermosillo, Lisette narrated the events of those eight or ten hours in San Tomás. The odd thing was that in talking about the experience, she felt as frightened as when she'd lived it.

Out of the corner of her eye, she noticed Pamela staring at her, her lips parted.

"Holy moly! It sounds like a movie."

"It felt like a movie," said Lisette. "Like I was watching myself."

"I don't know how you did it. I would have been a pile of gush if I'd been there. What happened to him? Did he lose the arm?"

"He still had it the last time I saw him. On TV. They were hauling him off to prison. There were a couple of American reporters on the story. They wanted to interview me—what else? I stopped answering the phone and the door. The last thing I need is that kind of publicity."

"Because you had a hand, kind of, in getting that guy arrested?"

"Yeah. Salazar still has loyal followers out there in the boondocks, and they might not take kindly to me if they knew." Lisette slowed down as a cow and her calf ambled across the road ahead. "I asked one of the cops, this strange guy—looks and talks like a gringo; I think he might be DEA or something—I asked him not to say anything to the press about Anna's and my involvement. Just tell them that they found us taking care of Salazar. Which he did."

"More and more like a movie," Pamela said. She looked out the side window at the pools of Mexican poppies collected beneath the saguaro and organ pipe cacti. "Kind of weird being back here."

Lisette ignored the remark. "So how did it all go in Philadelphia? In your last e-mail, you said your father took the news about Evangelina pretty well and that you got along okay with Lady Iago."

Pamela huffed. "I can't say I got along with her. I told her all about you, about us, and I guess she finally accepts what I am. Didn't stop her from getting in a dig, though."

"Which was?"

"That she's resigned herself to not getting any grandchildren from her one and only daughter. That even if her lesbo daughter took out a sperm-bank loan, she's now too old to have kids."

"How sweet."

"Forty-four isn't too old."

"It is cutting it kind of close," Lisette said.

"I have a cousin who had a perfectly healthy boy at forty-six," said Pamela, with a feeble ring of hopefulness. "And there's always the adoption option."

Did she want to have kids? Lisette decided not to pursue that subject.

Pamela fell silent—perhaps brooding over her mother's charming commentary—and gazed out the window again, at underfed cows plodding along a barbed-wire fence, from which white plastic bags flapped like tattered flags of surrender. She reached into her purse, checked her phone, and muttered, "No service."

"And there won't be any for the next twenty miles," Lisette said. "All right. What's your news?"

Placing the phone in her lap, Pamela replied, "It's good. Two pieces of good news."

"C'mon. Shoot."

The first piece was that a cutting-edge Philadelphia gallery, the Wexler, had seen photos of her latest work and liked what they saw and agreed to exhibit the paintings in June. She'd signed the contract—a sixty-forty split on any sales.

"They're going to pair me with Roberto Lugo," Pamela added with a catch in her breath.

"Enlighten the philistine, please."

"He's a ceramicist mostly, but does some work on canvas. Very hip. He grew up in Philadelphia, too. In North Philly. The Puerto Rican barrio. The idea is two artists from the same town, way different backgrounds—"

"The Latino street kid and the Main Line Wasp?" Lisette said, her eyes fixed on the winding road as it climbed into the Sierra foothills.

"That's it, yeah." Pamela did not say anything for a few minutes, looking at her phone or out the window, seemingly preoccupied.

"I'm going to be a whirling dervish the next couple of months!" she exclaimed, breaking her pensive silence. "Going through the stuff I've done, turning out a few new things. I feel like I'm on the launch pad. . . . No . . . the relaunch pad. . . . And counting down to"—she shot a fist at the roof—"blastoff!"

"I'm happy for you," Lisette said, as if reading from a greeting card. She wasn't sure what this development would mean for their relationship, and Pamela's exuberant outburst put her on edge. "What's the second piece?"

"I don't want to say just yet. I'm waiting to hear."

"Give me a hint."

"Really. I'm superstitious about some things. I'll tell you as soon as I know."

■ ■ ■

The next day was Holy Thursday. Following the script for the Mayo Easter-week fiesta, the Pharisees, led by men swaddled in blankets, their faces hidden by fierce-looking, wooden masks, took possession of the church and captured a statue of Jesus, which they would hold until defeated by the armies of Christ on Holy Saturday.

Unable to resume her restoration work, Pamela occupied herself with selecting canvases for the exhibition and with a new painting: a mad swirl of clashing pigments and shapes suggesting blossoms with vulvas at their center. When she took a break, it was to check her phone for a message confirming the second piece of good news—whatever that was. Absorbed, she paid no attention to the patients who passed through the courtyard to Lisette's clinic, and not much more to Lisette herself. She'd entered her own world. *Wherever it is, it isn't here,* Lisette thought, feeling the peculiar loneliness that descended when you were living with someone who wasn't living with you.

Late on Good Friday afternoon, Lisette had a walk-in: Cristina Herrera. Still in her dark blue and white uniform, shouldering a backpack full of books, she must have come straight from high school.

"You have some time, Dr. Lisette?" she asked modestly.

"It happens that I do." Lisette pushed the microscope and the slides she was preparing to one side of her desk, then indicated a cast-off kitchen chair that now served as a seat for her patients. "Please, sit down. What brings you here?"

Dropping the backpack, Cristina sat with her shoulders squared and her hands clasped firmly in her lap. She had her mother's long, narrow face and downturned mouth, but where Señora Herrera's features reflected her dour personality, the effect on Cristina was one of melancholy.

"What are those?" she said, motioning at the slides.

"You've studied biology in school?"

"Yes."

"Well, these are slides of bacteria from the water in one of the villages in the Sierra. There has been an outbreak of dysentery and diarrhea there, because the people don't boil the water before they drink it. I'm going to show them these bacteria through the microscope so I can convince them to boil their water. Would you like to see what the germs look like?"

She inserted a slide under the scope. Cristina came around to her side of the desk and squinted through the eyepiece.

"Like very little worms," she said. "But short and fat and furry little worms."

"*Shigella sonnei.* That's their scientific name," Lisette said in what Nick called her "lectury" voice.

Cristina sat down again.

"But you didn't come here for a biology lesson. What seems to be the trouble?"

The girl threw a quick, shy glance at Anna, who was rearranging a supply cabinet.

"Anna, would you mind leaving us alone for a while?" Lisette said.

The nurse closed the cabinet and went out into the courtyard.

"I have been bleeding when I should not be," said Cristina, after Anna had left the room.

"When?"

"In between, in the middle of my month. When it's not supposed to."

"Is the bleeding heavy?"

"No, not too much. It's like small spots. But I'm worried it might get bad, like before."

"Before? Before when?"

"In January. Things like little red peas came out."

"Clots," Lisette said, and frowned.

"They said it would stop, and it did." Cristina gave a determined smile. "But now, more blood, and I am worried."

Lisette returned the smile. "Who is 'they'?"

The girl hunched her shoulders and cast a nervous glance at the ceiling. Lisette took a moment to give her time to answer, but none came.

"Cristina, I have to ask you this—did you have an abortion?"

With a rapid twitch of her head, she affirmed that she had. She was near the end of her first trimester when her boyfriend, Eduardo, brought her to the public health clinic in Hermosillo. It would not admit her because she lacked proof that she'd been raped. A nice lady at the clinic, however, referred her to a man who would do the procedure. A woman worked with him, maybe his wife, maybe not, and she was not so nice. It was done in a room in their apartment, which was dirty and in a rough neighborhood. Afterward, they gave her pills for pain and to prevent infection, and that was the end of it. Except now there was this bleeding.

"It's not unusual to have spotting between your periods. You said you're in the middle of your cycle?"

Cristina nodded.

"I think it's nothing to worry about."

The girl's face brightened. "Honestly? I have been hiding the napkins in the rubbish, like I did after the, you know. I am worried my mother will find them and start to ask questions. I told her I had a miscarriage because she says that women who have abortions burn in hell when they die."

Sounds like something my mother would say, Lisette thought. "I need you to take your clothes off so I can have a look and be sure," she said.

"All of my clothes?" Cristina asked.

"No. From the waist down."

She shyly reached under her dress, wiggled out of her underwear and, with the dress rolled up to her waist, lay on the examination table at the back of the room. Lisette moved a folding privacy screen between it and the door, and slipped on latex gloves.

No fever, no abdominal swelling, spotty blood with no clots and no bad odor, pulse and blood pressure normal, cervix closed . . . Cristina Herrera, so unfortunate in what had happened to her, was lucky in this instance. The exam over, Cristina dressed, and Lisette gave her pain medication and an antibiotic, assuring her that she would be fine.

"I am happy it is gone," she whispered, returning to the chair beside Lisette's desk. "It was the child of the devil, you know."

"It was the child of a rapist, *mi querida*, not the devil," Lisette responded gently.

"That is what Padre Tim tells me."

"You've seen him?"

"I went to confession before I came here."

"I can't imagine that he said you will burn in hell."

"No!" Her eyes widened, the brows lifting into arcs. "He told me about the sinful woman in the Bible who was going to be stoned. And the Lord says to the men with the stones to throw them if they have no sin. They go away, and then the Lord asks the woman, Where are the men who accused you? Haven't they condemned you? And she says that no one is there to condemn her. Then He says—"

"'Neither do I condemn you, go and sin no more,'" Lisette cut in, somewhat startled that she remembered anything from her childhood Bible study.

"That is what he said, Padre Tim."

"Sounds like him."

Cristina looked down at her hands, folded in her lap. "I cannot pay you, Doctor Lisette."

"Can you make enchiladas?"

"No. But my mother does." She smiled slowly. "It is said they are the best enchiladas in San Patricio."

"Then ask her to bring me some when she has the time. Enough for two people. With green chili sauce."

"I will, but I will not tell her the reason."

"That goes without saying."

After the girl left, Lisette massaged the back of her neck, musing on something she'd heard from a politician she knew in Álamos—"We have laws for everything in Mexico, but we don't enforce them until we need to." Evidently, there had been no need to enforce the law against Cristina's rapist but great need to enforce the one requiring her to prove that she had been raped.

She went out to the courtyard, where Pamela was swiping a house-painter's brush across her canvas; and she was swiping it like a house-painter, in long, careless strokes.

"Shit, shit, shit," she muttered to herself.

Looking over her shoulder, Lisette saw that she was covering the work she'd done—in black.

"Does it ever stop?" Pamela said, swinging the brush back and forth. "It's hard to concentrate with that racket."

She meant the fiesta, whose sounds—drumbeats, flutes, guitars, and chants—drifted up, faintly, from the plaza.

Swat. Slap. Swat.

"Why are you covering the whole thing up?"

"Because it's derivative. Bargain-basement, secondhand Georgia O'Keeffe. The Wexler people would see that in a heartbeat. The Wexler's a big deal. I can't turn in crap."

"The other day you were on the launch pad, now you're where?"

She was swabbing black over the black, the strokes vertical, horizontal, diagonal.

"Maybe you could use a drink," Lisette said.

"Tequila on the rocks. How do you say it? *En el rocas.*"

"*Las*, honey. *En las rocas.*"

"That's what I need."

■ ■ ■

By Saturday morning, people had come out of the Sierra in the hundreds, some walking, some on horseback, some in pickup trucks with dust-curtained windshields. They pitched tents in the hills embracing San Patricio and in the afternoon streamed into the pueblo, the women wearing everything from shorts and halter tops to long Indian skirts, the men in jeans and straw cowboy hats, all surging toward the plaza to watch the final confrontation between the *fariseos*—the Pharisees—and the allies of Christ: the *Matachines*, the deer dancers, and the old men of the fiesta, the *pascolas*.

The noisy celebration made it impossible for Pamela to work. She and Lisette went out into the street. A human tide swept them down Calle Insurgentes, into the town center. Crowds five and six deep surrounded the plaza on three sides, kids riding their fathers' shoulders so they could see. The fourth side, facing the church, was kept open as an arena for the climactic struggle. There, in the palm trees' half-shade, musicians scraped battered fiddles, strummed guitars, and plucked homemade harps while the white-clad *Matachines* danced. They danced in lines and in circles, twirling and shaking gourd rattles. Some men came forward as others fell back, the choreography like a high school band's at halftime: the same pattern over and over again, lines bending into circles, the circles breaking back into lines, advancing and retreating as the fiddles and guitars played a repetitious melody on a strange scale. This went on for nearly half an hour in the hot sun, the air dense with the scrambled odors of mesquite fires, sizzling meat, bodies innocent of soap.

Now the *pascolas* and the deer dancers, wearing the antlered heads of real deer, joined the *Matachines*. Lisette climbed onto a bench to get a clearer view; even Pamela had to stand on tiptoe. Stripped to the waist, the deer dancers had the torsos of lightweight boxers; the *pascolas* wore masks dripping horsehair braids and carried banners emblazoned with red and green crosses. All of them shuffled toward the church and formed a human barrier at the bottom of its steps. At the top, Father Tim, Father

Hugo, and the Old Priest stood in their brown habits, a choir behind them. Several women poured ashes from plastic pails onto the street facing the church to mark the boundary of holy ground.

The *fariseos* arrived, parading in two long columns up the Avenida Obregón, led by men who carried a straw effigy of Judas. The *fariseos* were also masked, their masks imitating witches and sorcerers and beasts. Some banged on handheld drums and beat wooden knives against wooden swords with a quick rhythm. The cocoon rattles wrapped around their legs hissed like rattlesnakes. They marched into the plaza, then turned to face the *Matachines* and *pascolas*, lined up at the foot of the church steps. The *fariseos* charged, but as they neared the boundary of ashes, Christ's allies bombarded them with flowers—paper flowers and real flowers, gold, lavender, orange, and red. The *fariseos* fell back, reformed their ranks, and charged again, urged on by frenzied drumbeats, only to be repulsed a second time under another barrage of flowers.

At last, after a third attempt, the *fariseos* retreated in confusion, tossing their swords and knives aside, tearing off their masks. The church bells rang out, and the choir began to sing the "Gloria" while the *fariseos*, admitting defeat, set fire to the straw Judas and threw their masks into the flames.

"This is supposed to be *Catholic*?" asked Pamela, looking up at Lisette, perched on the bench.

"Not quite."

"It's very exciting, but what's it all about?"

"The Pharisees have been defeated by flowers. Christ's blood was supposed to have turned into flowers. Flower power, you might say, has overcome the power of swords and knives. The triumph of good over evil."

Her eyes watering from the smoke, Lisette looked over the flags, the blossoms scattered across the plaza, the mass of burnt-umber Indian faces, timeless faces that could have been lifted off a daguerreotype from a century and a half ago. A wave of love rolled over her. *I belong to them,* she thought. *I belong here.*

■ ■ ■

On Easter Sunday afternoon, Lisette was in the kitchen baking a ham while Pamela sliced potatoes for *gratin dauphinois*.

"What do I do now?" she asked when she'd finished.

"Put them in the baking dish, pour in the milk and cream," Lisette said, reading from the recipe. "It says three cups, but it's just the two of us, so make it a cup."

Pamela brushed the slices off the cutting board, into the dish.

"Okay, now salt, pepper, a clove of garlic, nutmeg."

"How much?"

"Teaspoon of salt, quarter teaspoon pepper, pinch of nutmeg."

Her brows pursed with concentration, Pamela measured the seasonings precisely as directed, except for the nutmeg. What constituted a pinch? Cooking wasn't her strong point.

"This isn't a chemistry experiment," Lisette said cheerfully. "Put a little between your fingers and sprinkle it over the potatoes."

She did that, then placed the dish in the oven with the ham. Lisette set a timer for forty-five minutes and they went into the courtyard and sipped the margaritas she had made earlier. The mellow-yellow hour had arrived. The fountain bubbled, the stream from the griffin's mouth flicking droplets into the oblique sunlight.

"I'm glad that fiesta's done with," said Pamela. "Peace and quiet—I can work."

Lisette always had difficulty thinking of what her lover did as work. Cutting and baling Christmas trees, as she had in her girlhood, was work. A soft chiming came from the bedroom, and Pamela's head turned quickly.

"My phone!"

She went into the room, practically at a run. Not half a minute later, Lisette heard her whoop, and she came twirling out, pumping her arms like a twenty-year-old cheerleader.

"Whoo-hoo! I got it!"

Lisette set her glass on the table. "Got what?"

Pamela spun toward her, waving her iPhone. "An e-mail! The job! Got the job! And we've got something to celebrate!"

She fell into a chair, slouching, her whole face alight, and wrapped her fingers around the margarita glass. Raising it, she said, "Let's toast me! Whoo!"

They clinked glasses. "What job, sweetie?" Lisette asked. "You never said anything about a job."

"That's what I didn't want to tell you in the car the other day. I was afraid of jinxing it."

While she was in Philadelphia, the Wexler Gallery's director mentioned that he'd had lunch with the dean of the Yale School of Art the previous month. The Department of Painting and Printmaking was losing two faculty members and looking to fill the vacancies. The gallery director said he would find out if the positions were still open and recommend her—if that was agreeable to her.

"Agreeable? Of course it was agreeable. Agreeable squared. I mean, Yale! I got the call the next day, the dean told me to shoot him a résumé and some photos of what I'd been doing, and I was on that so fast I should have gotten a speeding ticket. So the dean e-mails me back and says the résumé was being reviewed but if it was up to him all by himself, he'd be thrilled to have me on board. His word, Lissie. *Thrilled.*"

Lisette rose and, leaning over the table, kissed Pamela's forehead. "And I'm thrilled for you. Congratulations." Actually, "thrilled" might have been an overstatement, though it did please her to see Pamela happy, as opposed to being in a state of over-the-top excitement. "It's great when all those connections pay off," she said, realizing as she sat down again that the statement had come out wrong. A little resentment had sneaked into it, as if Pamela's connections had come through an inheritance rather than her own merits.

But Pamela hadn't noticed. "I start as a lecturer. In July. The summer term. But it's a tenure track. I won't have to worry about money again."

Lisette squeezed lime into her drink.

"I didn't think you'd ever in your life had to worry about money," she said.

"Everybody worries about money. People with money worry about money. If they stopped worrying about it, they'd lose it."

"That would be one way for their worries to be over."

Pamela fixed her gaze on Lisette. "Something on your mind? You don't sound as thrilled as you said you are."

"Well, I am. It's only that this news is unexpected, and I'm wondering where it leaves us."

"You're my rock, my anchor, Lisette. I think if I hadn't had you in my life the last couple of months, I would have floated away, like one of those party balloons."

"You will do just fine," Lisette said, bothered by the description of herself as a rock and anchor. It seemed to confer a responsibility she might not be able to live up to, and didn't want.

Right then the timer dinged, and they walked briskly into the kitchen, took out the ham and the potatoes, and carried them to the table. For the next fifteen or twenty minutes Lisette hardly uttered a word while Pamela went on about Yale and the exhibition, stopping only to take a bite of her food, which wasn't often. She looked burnished, as lovely as Lisette had ever seen her. Yet she felt that peculiar loneliness again— of being in the company of someone who wasn't present.

As if aware that she'd been yammering too much about herself, Pamela stood and wrapped her hands around Lisette's neck.

"I was in a bad way after U. of A. let me go and you helped me through it."

"Gratitude will get you everywhere."

"Really? Where would that be?" Her voice was teasing.

"You pick the destination."

"Have you ever read Catullus?" she asked.

"I'm afraid I've never heard of him."

"A Roman poet. 'Let us live, my Lesbia, and let us love, and let us judge all the rumors of the old men to be worth just one penny!'" She bent down and kissed Lisette on the mouth, tongued her ear, nipped her earlobe, and kissed her lips again. "'Give me a thousand kisses, then another hundred, then another thousand . . .'"

■ ■ ■

"Now, was that a great idea or what?" Pamela said afterward, a long leg thrown over Lisette's waist.

Lisette agreed it was, though it seemed that in the act she had traded places with Pamela. It was she who had been present and not present at the same time, her heart somewhere other than her body; that is, while Pamela had made love, she had been fucking.

Pamela sat up, her back against the headboard, and pulled the bedsheet over her breasts in a sudden onset of modesty. Lying on her side, Lisette looked at Pamela's shoulders, smooth as a girl's, and was glad of the twilight; it concealed the wrinkles in her skin, dried out from too many years in arid climates.

"You said you wondered about where all this leaves us. I was wondering, too, on the flight back," Pamela said. "I had a lot of time to think about what to do if Yale came through."

Lisette, a bit drugged from the postprandial lovemaking, or fucking, whichever was appropriate, mumbled an "uh-huh."

"Are you interested in what I was thinking?"

"Sure."

"I'm going to have to start pretty soon, looking for an apartment in New Haven. I'd like to be looking for a place for *us*."

Now Lisette sat up straight.

"I don't want to be apart from you," Pamela went on, fully in the persona of Pamela A. "You are my rock and my anchor, and you did say, *twice*, that you could practice medicine in the States. And it's been legalized in Connecticut. Gay marriage."

Oh, my God.

Pamela leaned over and cupped Lisette's chin to gently turn her head so they faced each other. "I'm asking you to marry me."

Lisette was silent.

"This was supposed to be an experiment, to see if we got along?" said Pamela plaintively. "I think we did pretty well, all things considered."

All things considered.

"You didn't think I could stay down here forever, did you? You couldn't have possibly expected I would."

"No."

I don't want to be a rock or an anchor.

"I know I caught you by surprise. I don't expect an answer right away. You need time to think it over."

There is nothing to think over but everything, too. A split screen switched on in Lisette's mind, neither showing attractive images. Screen 1: a medical office in some dull Connecticut town, filling out Medicare forms, commuting home to Pamela, gallery showings, lots of Brie and white wine. Screen 2: here, this courtyard, eating by herself a dinner cooked by herself in the long shadows of endless evenings.

"I need a couple of weeks to finish a mural in the church. I'm not leaving right away," Pamela said, crinkling her eyes. "It's a big step, asking somebody to spend the rest of her life with you."

Lisette could promise to think it over, but she knew with a mathematical certainty that it would be an empty exercise. A cold resolve welled up in her. She made sure to keep the coldness out of her voice but not the resolve. "Baby, I've got to turn you down. I've got to say no."

Pamela's upper lip quivered, but she caught herself.

"I'm giving you time to think it over."

"I'm afraid I don't need to," Lisette said, laying her hand on Pamela's. "I don't want to spend the rest of my life with anyone. It's not you."

"Who if not me?"

"For one thing, I don't believe in marriage, gay or straight. That poem, about not giving a damn what old men say? All these gays demanding the right to marry, they're giving a damn. They want to be accepted, respectable, middle-class people. That's not how I see us."

"Okay," said Pamela, with a forced evenness in her voice. "Please tell me what you see."

"We could spend time together when I'm in the States. You could come here on summer breaks—"

"A shuttle romance? Oh, please. My . . . my condition, is that it? You can't deal with that? Or don't want to?"

Lisette shook her head with more vigor than was necessary, because, in truth, Pamela's condition was on her mind, and it violated her best image of herself to think that she could not cope with it.

"You know, when you love someone, you want to spend your life with her. So how should I take the fact that you don't want to spend yours with me?"

"I never expected you to throw your whole life over for me," said Lisette irritably. "Why do you expect me to throw mine over? I don't see myself in Connecticut or Massachusetts or California or anywhere but here. I can make a difference here. That's all I've ever wanted—to make a difference."

"I was feeling pretty damn good half an hour ago," Pamela said, her sadness and hurt curdling into anger. She got out of bed and into jeans and threw on a shirt, buttoning the top button in the wrong hole, so that it hung askew. "How about the difference you made to that blind girl? These people haven't changed in a hundred years, but if you think you can change them, hey, you're welcome to keep kicking a rock with your bare foot." Her face reddening, she pantomimed a kick, then turned and made for the bedroom door. "I need another drink."

CHAPTER THIRTY-TWO

Riordan sat in his room, making notes on what he was going to say to His Excellency, Bishop Arturo Perralta. He felt like a jailhouse lawyer preparing his own case. The meeting, postponed until after the bishop's trip abroad, was scheduled for Thursday, the day after tomorrow. He would first confess to what he'd done. But absolution from the sin would not remove the excommunication that arose from it. That would have to be appealed. Convincing the bishop that his case had merit would be the hard part. He was determined not to hedge or shade the truth, but also to avoid excessive self-recrimination. He had to present his crime in the proper light, hoping Bishop Perralta would give him a favorable recommendation when he sent the appeal to the Vatican.

He was interrupted by his cell phone. It was Marta Díaz, and she didn't bother with a hello.

"You must come over right now," she said, in a taut, nervous voice.

"Marta, it's six-thirty in the morning and I . . . It's not César, is it?"

"Es una emergencia. Por favor, ven ahora."

She hung up.

His heart, Riordan thought. He dressed, climbed on the Harley, and in ten minutes was there, finding César not only healthy but lugging a heavy, rope-bound suitcase out of the house. Moises and the other two bodyguards were loading furniture into the bed of a farm truck, the same one they had taken to San Tomás. César shoved the suitcase into his pickup, parked in front of the truck. Tension showed on everyone's face, and there was a panic-stricken quality to their quick, jerky movements. To Riordan, they looked like figures in a film running at the wrong speed.

"What is this?" he asked. "Marta phoned me . . ."

The look in César's black eyes was not one he'd seen before. Dread.

"We're leaving for El Norte now," he said. Reaching into his pocket, he produced a business card and gave it to Riordan. It read:

EXCELSIOR PRODUCE DISTRIBUTORS LLC

3019 N. GRAND AVE., NOGALES, AZ 85621

IGNACIO DIAZ, WAREHOUSE MGR. 520-761-1313

ig.diaz@epd.com.

"My brother. I wrote his home number on the back. I will phone you when we've arrived at his house, but if you are not hearing from me, call him. Tell him to contact the U.S. consulate. The one on the Mexican side of Nogales."

This was all more than Riordan could absorb.

"What's going on?" he said. "Leaving now? There's your heart—"

"I'll have it checked in the States. Right now, it's the last thing I have to worry about," César said, his voice strained. "You didn't hear what happened last night?"

"No."

"Come inside and see for yourself."

What Riordan saw were a desk drawer thrown on the floor, the contents strewn about, a bedroom dresser tipped over, clothes torn from an armoire and tossed everywhere, kitchen cupboards flung open, shards of glass and broken dishware scattered across the tiles.

Soldiers—paratroopers—had battered down the door at three in the morning, César related, rousted him and Marta out of bed, and, after forcing them to lie on the floor at gunpoint, ransacked the house. A sergeant informed César that they were looking for drugs and weapons because they had information that the *autodefensa* was trafficking in narcotics.

"What?" Riordan exclaimed. "That's—"

"*Loco, sí!*" said Marta, hastily picking up the scattered clothes and stuffing them into plastic trash bags. "*Loco y más loco!* They are as bad as the narcos! Worse!"

"They did not find any drugs, of course, but they took my rifle and pistol, and all my records," César went on. "From the *autodefensa*, from my orchard, even my insurance papers. Every document they could get their stinking hands on."

"But not these," Marta said, pulling the couple's Mexican and U.S. passports from her handbag. She raised them and her eyes toward the ceiling, as if in offering. "*Gracias a Dios*, they did not find them!"

"They raided other houses at the same time," César said. "All belonging to my men." As he spoke, he grabbed a corner of the toppled dresser. "Help me with this, Padre Tim."

Riordan took the opposite corner and they stood it up, then slid the drawers back into place. Moises and the others came in and carried the dresser out to the truck.

"We have Lupita to thank for this!" Marta said, furiously balling up shirts and blouses and cramming them into the trash bags. "Tell him, César, tell Padre how we have to thank her."

He's confessed to her! Riordan thought, and pressed his palms to his temples.

"Where is she?" he asked, hoping to divert the conversation.

"I've sent her away, with her girls. To Magdalena," César replied. "She has people there. Maybe we'll try to get her into the States legally. If not, then we'll hire a coyote. She's in as much danger as we are."

Something else, then.

"She deserves to be!" cried Marta. Moises stepped back into the bedroom, and she tossed a bag at him like a stevedore. "This goes in the pickup!" she snapped. Out of all of them, she was, or seemed to be, the least frightened; her anger had either overcome her fear or was masking it. "Maybe I would be as crazy like her if I lost a child, I don't know.

Screaming in the middle of the night for revenge, talking to everybody that the killing of the soldiers was justice. A madwoman!"

With an abrupt wave, César motioned for Riordan to go into the front room, now empty. A sadness jabbed the priest's chest when he saw, on the wall where the photo of the Christ of Atil had hung, a square of blue paint lighter than the rest.

"Let me tell you, quick, what happened," César said.

Not two hours ago, he'd received a warning: Next week would be too late to leave Mexico; tomorrow would be too late. He had to leave now. The reason given for the raid had been a pretext; Capitán Valencia was collecting "evidence" that César, with a few militiamen, had ambushed the paratroopers in December and tried to make it look like the work of the Brotherhood. Proof was to be offered that the bullets had been fired from their guns, including César's rifle. He was going to be arrested soon, possibly as early as today. And he well knew what would be waiting for him.

"It was that federal cop who called," he said. "The one who looks like a gringo."

"Bonham?"

"Him. Who else would know what that fucking Valencia is up to?"

Riordan couldn't fathom what Bonham's motives might have been. Valencia: that brutal officer was an example of what happens to a man obsessed. Expelling these thoughts, he asked, "What about the others? The ones whose houses were searched?"

"They can do what they want. They're on their own. I have to think about myself and Marta. And Moises and those other two. They protected me, now I got to protect them. They're coming with us."

"But they're all deportees. They'll be arrested as soon as they cross the border."

"An American jail is better than what will happen to them here."

"Have you told your brother about this?"

"No. Only that I'm coming today instead of next week. I don't want him to worry."

There was nothing further to be said. Riordan offered to help load their belongings. César shook his head. Not necessary.

"Please give us a blessing," he added. "We'll need it, I think."

They returned to the bedroom, where Marta was still packing frantically.

"Padre Tim is going to bless us," César said to her.

She paused, dropping a blouse or two, and the couple assumed a reverential pose, hands crossed over their waists, heads bowed. Riordan drew the sign of the cross in the air and prayed for God to grant them a safe journey. They crossed themselves and raised their eyes to him.

"*Abrazos, Padre Tim,*" said Marta.

"*Sí. Abrazos, mi amigo,*" her husband echoed.

And as they all three huddled in an embrace, a sense of loss swallowed Riordan up. He was embarrassed to discover himself crying.

■ ■ ■

He rode slowly to the rectory to avoid making too much noise. After he locked up his bike, he sat in the courtyard, on the stone bench by the weather-stained bust of Padre Kino, and tried to find a clear signal in the static crackling through his head. The Old Priest, watering his herb garden, bid Riordan good morning and said that they'd missed him at Lauds and at breakfast.

Riordan murmured, "There was an . . . an emergency."

Wanting solitude, he resented the presence of the back-bent figure holding a watering can; but the Old Priest wandered to a far corner of the garden without waiting for further explanation.

A nation of sheep and wolves, Riordan thought. *And this wolf wears a paratrooper's uniform, and what is in his predaceous mind?* He forced himself to engage in a mental soliloquy: *So start with Valencia, a monomaniac fixated on finding who was responsible for ambushing his troops. . . .* He put the interior monologue on pause, thinking back to the conversation when he'd had lunch at Valencia's headquarters. *Even though it looked like the Brotherhood perpetrated the massacre, the captain had been disposed to consider alternate possibilities. . . . Now enter Lupita, calling out loud for justice, broadcasting her satisfaction with the soldiers' deaths to anyone who will listen. . . . Eventually Valencia hears about her ravings. He thinks, "If not narco assassins, who else had the motive and the means to pull off this heinous act? Who else but Lupita's brother-in-law and the uncle of Hector Díaz?"* Riordan probed his memory, and in a few minutes he recalled that the patrol had been sent to investigate an anonymous tip about a . . . what was it? A poppy field. *So Valencia's next Sherlock Holmes deduction would be that César Díaz assembled a handful of his most trusted men, called in the tip, and lured the soldiers into a trap. . . . Easy enough to print pictures of* La Santa Muerte *and plant them on the bodies. . . . The major missing piece is, what's convinced Valencia that the Brotherhood did not commit the crime?*

Riordan slumped on the bench, his eyes on the ground. He had hoped that Salazar's capture would bring, if not an end to his parish's afflictions, then a long respite from them. César would be safe once he crossed the border, but what about the other militiamen on the captain's list? What was to happen to them?

Suddenly he sat up straight, startled by the realization that in reconstructing Valencia's logic, he had unintentionally built a case against César. Not an airtight case, but a plausible one. His thoughts leapt back to the day in the hospital. *Surely, facing a heart operation, César would have confessed if he'd anything to do with it. . . . Surely he would not have regarded the act as justified. . . . But this is Mexico. Six years—no, it's seven now—of unremitting bloodshed might stretch the firmest conscience to accommodate committing murder without remorse or guilt. . . . But no! Stop it!* he argued with himself. *He's not capable of that kind of treachery, that kind of violence . . .*

He looked at the Old Priest, hoeing at the far end of the garden, and recalled the myth of Azazel and the sacrificial goat that bore the sins of the people. *Chivo expiatorio*—expiatory goat. Riordan thought the Spanish sounded better.

He went quickly into his room, unlocked the cupboard in his desk, and took out the encrypted burner phone; but he hesitated. What did he hope to accomplish? Then, determined to get some questions answered, he punched in Bonham's number. Following the instructions given months ago, he ended the call after three rings, then waited for a response. When several minutes passed in silence, he redialed and waited again, once more without a callback. This was unbearable. He needed to finish his note-taking and to psych himself up for what was bound to be the most critical hour of his life. His vocation, his reputation, his standing as a communicant Catholic—everything, in short, hung in the balance. But his brain felt frozen. A couple of hours, give or take, since he'd watched César leave with Marta, Moises, and the other bodyguards. It had looked like a scene out of *The Grapes of Wrath*, the farm truck piled high with furniture, bedding lashed to the side slats with old ropes. They would be in Hermosillo by now, turning north on Mex 15 for Nogales. Three to four more hours would bring him to the border and, Riordan hoped, safety.

Knowing that he would be in no fit mental condition for anything till he heard from César, he pocketed the phone, got up, and entered the church to quiet his mind. Ladies of the parish were removing Easter decorations, and Pamela Childress stood high on a platform, rubbing some sort of compound onto the mural of Saint Mark. One of the women stopped work and approached him—the Very Pious Señora Herrera. She wished him a good morning, her face pinched and somber in the dim flickering of the Paschal candle. His own face felt as if he'd been walking into a cold wind, so much so that when he manufactured a smile he thought his skin would crackle.

He asked what he could do for her, silently praying that the subject would not be her daughter. Prayer answered: Two boys were giving her trouble in catechism class; she'd scolded them but to no avail. It would help if Padre Tim gave them a good talking-to. Of course he would, but not today, nor tomorrow or Thursday—he would be in Hermosillo on Thursday. Friday, then? she wanted to know. Yes, yes, fine, Friday, he replied, trying to keep the irritation out of his voice. Now, if she would pardon him. . . . He broke off the conversation and shambled down the side aisle to where Pamela was at work on the mural. He stood beneath her for a half minute before she became aware of his presence.

"You're just the man I wanted to see," she said, and began climbing down the scaffolding.

"I'm much in demand today," he said.

Reaching the floor, she rubbed her hands with a cloth and faced him. In two seconds, her expression passed from serious to cheerful and back to serious, as if she couldn't make up her mind which was appropriate for what she had to say. She was, with regrets, giving him notice; she would be leaving in about two weeks—

"You, too? Everybody seems to be leaving here," he said, with no attempt to conceal his disappointment. "Where to and why?"

"To Connecticut, to look for an apartment. I landed a teaching job at Yale. Then it's on to Philadelphia for an exhibition of my work."

"Good for you," he said. "If that doesn't sound sincere, it's because it's not. I'll be very sorry to see you go. And Lisette? I hope she's not leaving, too."

"She'll be here forever."

He caught the mixed disappointment and resignation in her tone. "Did you two have a fight?"

"Uh-huh. But we more or less patched things up. We're very good friends. That sounds like such a cliché, but . . ." She pursed her lips and glanced up at the mural. "I meet my commitments. I'll have San Marco done before—"

The phone vibrated in his pocket. "Excuse me," he said, and sprinted through a side door into the courtyard.

"*Hola*. Inspector Bonham? Can you hear me all right?"

"A little faint, but good enough. What did you want?" Bonham said. He sounded annoyed.

"I need to know a couple of things, like why you warned César Díaz."

"Why would a priest need that kind of information?"

"Inspector, please. I'm only trying to get at the truth."

A short, sarcastic laugh. Even over the phone he could see Bonham's penetrating eyes boring into him.

"Padre Tim, you should know by now that the second most dangerous thing in Mexico is knowing the truth. Because if you know it, you'll do the most dangerous thing, and that's to speak it."

"Would you please tell me."

After a brief pause, Bonham said, "I take care of my assets."

"César? That's how you knew he was planning to leave the country? You mean César was—"

"What do you think? For all practical purposes, he was San Patricio's chief of police. Valencia doesn't know I recruited him. He's got a bigger hard-on for Díaz than he does for you."

"If we could talk in person for a few minutes," Riordan pleaded. "Could you stop by the rectory this afternoon?"

"I'm in Hermosillo, tying up loose ends. The joint operation is over. The Federal Police are being reassigned."

"Valencia's troops, too?" he asked, with a timorous hope in his voice.

"They'll be pulling out in a few days," Bonham responded.

Another reason for the captain's haste, Riordan said to himself. He needs to tie up some loose ends of his own. Then to Bonham, in a tone of stiff formality: "I would appreciate it if you could tell me . . . did César have anything to do with that ambush?"

Bonham let out a long, loud breath. "Put it like this: We're in Mexico. We'll never know who did it."

"But Valencia seems to think . . . He's going to frame César, isn't he?"

"Listen to me," Bonham broke in. "If I were you, I would stay out of it and away from Captain Valencia. Like I said, I take care of my assets, right up to when they have to take care of themselves."

And the line went dead.

■ ■ ■

Riordan attempted to do just that—to stay out of it, whatever "it" was—by evicting all thoughts of César and the others and attending, with a kind of furious concentration, to mundane tasks: going over the parish books with Father Hugo (they hadn't found a replacement for Domingo Quiroga); working out the Mass schedule and who would visit which sick parishioners; reading his breviary. Focusing on these daily affairs required such mental effort that he was exhausted by midday; and yet he could not sleep at the siesta hour. He lay on his bed wide-eyed; then, giving up on rest, he hopped on his bike to run a couple of errands and gas up at the Pemex station. By that time, news of the events of the previous night had reached almost every ear in San Patricio. People at the gas station and in the market were murmuring that the army was preparing some sort of move, arrests were going to be made . . . César Díaz had fled the country! On his way to El Norte! The rumors must be true—he was a narco. Otherwise, why would he have left so suddenly?

That was the sole topic of discussion at dinner. Father Hugo, to Riordan's distress, repeated the slanderous whispers. The guilty man flees when none pursues. Except in this case, someone was in pursuit, and the pursued wasn't guilty. Couldn't be guilty. Affecting a sober air, Riordan pointed out that Díaz had been planning to move to the States for some time; he'd merely left early.

At eight-thirty, after Compline, he retired to his room. Under normal circumstances, this was the hour for an examination of conscience and serene meditation, but on this night, he gazed at his smartphone screen, willing it to ring or to flash a text message. Thirty minutes of this was twenty-nine minutes too long. He removed Ignacio's business card from his wallet and called the home number. The voice-mail reply infuriated him. "Damnit!" he muttered. "Answer!" He rang off and tried again in a little while, receiving the same recorded message: "No one is available to answer your call. Please leave a message after the tone. For other options . . ." This time he left his name and number.

It might be Moises and those others, he reflected as he stripped down to his underwear and went into the bathroom. Maybe the Americans detained them, and César and Marta with them. He banged his knee on the commode—the bathroom had barely enough space to turn around without bumping into something. He brushed his teeth and pissed and got into his pajamas. Certain that sleep would elude him, he shuffled back into the bathroom and swallowed a sleeping pill, wishing he had some of César's *bacanora* to wash it down. He dropped into his narrow bed, and with Marcus Aurelius's *Meditations* in his lap, sought a haven within himself: *Nowhere can man find a quieter or more untroubled retreat than in his own soul . . . the ease that is but another word for a well-ordered spirit . . .* His spirit was a long way from well-ordered. It would have kept him wide-eyed half the night if not for ten milligrams of Ambien.

CHAPTER THIRTY-THREE

Riordan woke up at his usual time—four-thirty—but not with his usual vigor and alertness. The sleeping pill had left him too groggy for his habitual stargazing. Otherwise, he clung to the consoling rituals of his morning routine: wash up, shave, don his scratchy Franciscan robe; sing Lauds in the church with Father Hugo and the Old Priest. At seven-thirty, he said daily Mass for a sparse congregation, then ate breakfast. By nine o'clock, he was in the parish office, occupied with administrative work. Trying to be occupied, that is; his mind was elsewhere, dwelling on Bonham's inelegant words: *He's got a bigger hard-on for Díaz than he does for you.* Riordan grasped the reasons for Valencia's hostility toward his own person, but the still deeper hatred for César had other sources. The captain had been infected with the same malignancy as the criminals he pursued: a moral rabies, as it were, but of a peculiar kind, in that he didn't blindly snap and bite at anyone or anything that crossed his path. He singled out his victims. That his suspicions had fallen on César and César's fellow militiamen was not without logic; yet, the suspicion had grown equal to conviction in the court of Valencia's mind. It was a logic birthed by an irrational impulse: to make someone pay for the deaths of his troops. Retribution, the curse of Mexico: Blood must compensate blood.

The cell phone's ringtone almost made him jump out of his skin. The caller ID read, IGNACIO DIAZ.

It was Ignacio's wife, Consuela. She apologized for not returning Riordan's call last night. She and her husband had been at the border crossing in Nogales, asking the customs agents if they had any record of César's having entered the U.S., or if he'd been detained. There was no record of any kind, she said. Nor had they heard from him since yesterday afternoon, when he called from Magdalena to say that he was about an hour from the border. They were, naturally, very worried that he'd met with an accident.

Riordan felt a slight chill.

"Mrs. Díaz, have you contacted the American consulate?" he asked, feigning calm.

Her husband was in fact at the consulate, and the people there were asking the Sonoran state police if there had been any traffic incidents.

"He's not in any trouble, is he?" she asked.

What to say? He settled on "I don't know for sure"—which was true as far as it went—"but I think the consulate should look into that, too."

"Oh, my God—"

"Please, Mrs. Díaz." It took some effort to keep any note of alarm out of his voice. "I don't want to cause you any unnecessary worry. I'll find out what I can down here."

This is impossible, he thought, setting the phone on the desk. For conscience's sake, for the sake of César and Marta and the militiamen yet to be arrested—if they hadn't been already—he would have to ignore Inspector Bonham's warning.

■ ■ ■

He rode his Harley up the Mesa Verde road, taking the turns slowly, uncertain what he would say to Captain Valencia; uncertain, for that matter, that he would be allowed to see him and not sure what could possibly come of it if he was. But he had to try. César, Marta, and the others had been apprehended, somewhere in the sixty miles between Magdalena and the border—of that he was reasonably sure. Reasonably,

ha! As if reason had anything to do with what happened in this beautiful, sorrowful, blood-spotted country.

He rounded the final bend before reaching the crest, where the rock
pinnacle soared on the left side of the road and the cliff plummeted on
the right, into the waterless Santa Teresa. He was surprised to find that
the *bloqueo* was back up, its orange cones sheering him toward the left.
Instead of the usual squad, only two soldiers were manning it today, and
when they got out of their SandCat, he recognized the same pair who
had accosted him months ago: the squat, powerfully built private and
the sergeant with the lupine face. The temperature had shot up twenty
degrees since daybreak; in his leather jacket, he felt the heat when he
stopped.

"I'm going to Mesa Verde," he lied as he stood, left boot on the foot
peg, the right on the pavement, the idling bike leaning into him.

"Shut the engine, get off!" the sergeant ordered.

"You must recognize me. I have to get to Mesa Verde."

"Sure, I recognize you. Shut the damned engine, get off the motorcycle!"

To underscore the command, he swept his submachine gun back and
forth.

What now? No reasoning with a man with a gun. He did as he'd been
told.

"You are under arrest," the sergeant barked, pulling from his rear
pocket a plastic zip strap.

Before Riordan could protest, the private seized him by the
biceps, in a grip so strong his arm went numb, spun him around, and
yanked both arms behind his back. The sergeant cinched his wrists,
gave the strap a hard jerk, and shoved him to the roadside, facing the
pinnacle.

"You're not going to make me lie in the dirt this time?" Riordan said,
figuring the least sign of weakness would only excite these two predators. A mistake. The sergeant ripped off his helmet and struck him with
it, where his neckbone joined his spine. His head snapped forward, into
the cold, fissured rock. As he reeled from the twin blows, the sergeant
patted him down, shoulders to ankles, and confiscated his cell phone and
wallet.

"Keep your mouth shut and don't move one centimeter."

His skull pounding front and back, afraid he would topple over, Riordan pressed his sore forehead against the rock. Like a natural air conditioner, it was releasing the chill it had absorbed during the night. The cold, he figured, might keep any swelling down. He was sweating nevertheless, rivulets dripping down his ribs. Behind him, he could hear the sergeant speaking into the SandCat's radio. Under arrest—they must have been waiting for him! But how . . . ?

Sometime later—it might have been half an hour—a car approached, but he resisted turning to look at it. He heard a door slam, then voices in undertones: the sergeant's and Captain Valencia's. Footfalls on the road, then—

"Turn around and look at me, priest."

He obeyed, galled by his own docility, though it was the only intelligent way to behave. Valencia, in his beige camouflage, maroon beret cocked dashingly to one side, regarded him with a look of benign curiosity, as if he were some odd, harmless animal in a cage.

"I should thank you; you saved me the trouble of going to look for you," the captain said.

He had Riordan's cell phone in his hand. Without further word, he held it up to Riordan's face, the screen showing the call log, then produced Ignacio Díaz's business card. His expression didn't change.

"The reason you have been arrested," he said in neutral tones, "is that yesterday morning you assisted in the attempted escape of a man suspected of murdering four members of the military. You know who that is."

Riordan noted the emphasis on "attempted." He said nothing. His forehead throbbed. His tongue was sticking to the roof of his mouth for lack of saliva.

"This is Mexico and I am an army officer, in case you have forgotten," Valencia said. "You do not have a right to remain silent, you do not have a right to a lawyer, you do not have any rights at all. I asked if you know who that is."

Riordan cleared his throat and answered, "I didn't realize it was a question. César Díaz."

"Who is also under investigation for narcotics trafficking."

"He's done nothing wrong, and I didn't assist him in escaping. He wasn't escaping. He'd planned to move back to the United States. He's a U.S. citizen, you know."

"But first a citizen of Mexico," Valencia said. "How is it that you know he's done nothing wrong? How do you come by this information?"

"It's ridiculous to think that he's a narco, or that he's capable of murdering your soldiers. Or murdering anyone."

The captain's eyebrows arched. "So I am ridiculous?"

"You know that was not my meaning."

"I said he is suspected of murder and narcotics trafficking, then you said it is ridiculous to think that. Which makes me ridiculous."

"*Lo siento, Capitán,*" he said with a slight, obsequious bow. Submit! The average Mexican, the Mexican not born into privilege or power, ingested that lesson with his mother's milk. But it made Riordan feel painfully small. "My meaning was, if you knew him as well as I do, you would know he's not a killer or a trafficker."

"I am certain that Díaz and I will become better acquainted soon. Then maybe I will form the same judgment as you. But maybe not."

"Would you tell me where he is?"

"Why should his whereabouts concern you? To find out if your assistance was successful?"

"I did not assist him. He asked my blessing for his journey—"

Valencia threw his head back in laughter, then cast glances at the two paratroopers. "His blessing. Did you hear that, *muchachos*? Bless me, Padre, so I can escape!" The soldiers laughed as well, stiffly and artificially, as if in obedience to an order. "You fucking priests and your blessings. Tell me, do you bless the altar boys when you stick your dicks up their asses?"

Good God! Was all this, at its root, about his violated brother? Or another demonstration of his power? Both?

"Where he is . . ." Riordan began. "Not my concern . . ."

He couldn't put a coherent sentence together.

"Good!" Valencia said. "You got something right! It's not your concern. I am amazed that you and he would think I would allow him to take off without alerting our people to be on the lookout for him. What stupidity! No, it's arrogance!"

"It's his brother. He's worried . . ." Riordan stammered. "His brother is at the American consulate. . . . The consulate is making inquiries . . ."

The captain clenched his teeth, and his gray eyes appeared to push back into his skull, darkening to lead as they did.

"Making inquiries? That's what they're doing?" he shouted, poking a forefinger into Riordan's chest. "You are telling me that it is I who should be concerned because the Americans are making inquiries? Do you think I give a fuck about that? Do you?"

The suddenness of this violent response caught Riordan completely flat-footed. He lurched back from the jabbing finger. As swiftly as he'd lost it, Valencia recaptured his self-control; but it wasn't like the composure of mere seconds ago—more like a leashed rage.

"Never mind the gringos' inquiries," he said in a low voice. "You haven't answered *mine*. How did you come by this information that Díaz did nothing wrong? What brings you to this conclusion?"

Riordan was silent, aware now that he was dealing not only with a man mastered by a morbid obsession but with a psychopath. *Say as little as possible,* he told himself. *Say nothing if you can.*

"I thought so," said Valencia. "You have no idea how you came to that conclusion. Because it is a false conclusion. A fucking lie."

"He would have told me. I would have known."

"Maybe we're getting somewhere. You mean, he would confess to you his crimes. Which I am sure is what he did." The captain brushed his upper lip with his fingertips. "You visited Díaz in the hospital not long ago, is that correct?"

Pointless to inquire how he knew.

"Yes."

"Why?"

"He asked to see me."

"For what purpose?"

"He had a heart condition, he was going in for an operation—"

"Yes. Exactly! Such medical procedures can be dangerous, so he wanted to make a confession and clear his conscience. But he didn't confess that he had missed Mass or had beat his wife or had fucked some whore."

Riordan met the captain's harsh gaze as steadily as he could manage. Heat waves shimmered off the asphalt road. "I can't tell you what he said. I can't even tell you *if* he confessed. I thought this was settled between us."

"I don't recall that we settled anything. You . . . how to put it? . . . tendered your resignation. I don't accept it. You heard his confession in that hospital room. And what did he confess?"

"I can only tell you what I already have. Díaz never killed anyone."

Suddenly, the captain's expression softened, and his tone grew milder.

"Look, you can spare your friend a great deal of unpleasantness. I have evidence that will implicate him, and when I show it to him, it is I who will be hearing confessions."

"Then what do you need me for?" Riordan cried out.

"To spare Díaz unpleasantness."

"I doubt that anything I might say would spare him."

"Consider sparing yourself, then."

He had to get out of this, but he couldn't think how. He could barely think at all. A recollection popped into his mind. Something the inspector had said weeks ago. The name of the game in the Sierra Madre was dominance. And that was the name of this game. Valencia didn't want information; he wanted to break Riordan to his will, to force him to grovel and beg and say whatever he wanted to hear. Riordan was resolved not to break. In twenty-four hours, he would go before the bishop in another kind of interrogation, and he could not face that man if he surrendered now.

"Canon law, article 1388," he said, managing—just barely—to sound firm. "It is a crime for a confessor to betray a penitent by words or in any other manner for any reason."

"And it's not a crime to aid the escape of a suspected criminal? Not a crime to conceal what this criminal has said to you about his crimes? You had been cooperative, and then, after seeing this criminal in his sickbed, you help him try to get away and stop being cooperative. What am I to make of that?"

"That I damned myself by cooperating, and now I wish to make up for it and save my soul."

That sounded pretentious even to Riordan himself; yet he was glad he'd said it. Valencia trembled slightly. He could all but see the molecules in the captain's brain swirling in Brownian motion, then rearranging themselves.

"If I were you, I'd be thinking about saving my fucking life, not my soul."

With a flick of his hand, Valencia signaled his soldiers. They seized Riordan's arms, the private clamping a hand over the back of his neck, and pushed and pulled him across the road. Riordan kicked and twisted. The private released one arm, swung around, and drove a fist into his solar plexus, the punch taking all his wind, buckling his knees. Then the two men shoved him to the edge of the precipice and stood behind him, the sergeant holding him by the belt, the other soldier gripping his neck, digging a thumb into a pressure point behind his ear. Head bent, gasping to regain his breath, he could not help but look down. The bare rock wall bulged outward near the top, creating the impression of a bottomless abyss. Only by looking straight out, toward the rolling foothills beyond the riverbed, could he achieve any sort of perspective. Which was no comfort. The drop had to be three hundred feet. Riordan, whose acrophobia had undergone a mere temporary remission on the rope bridge, was paralyzed and nauseous. Fearing he would fall from sheer dizziness, he inhaled deeply and raised his eyes toward the sky, the spring desert sky, itself a desert of purest blue.

"No, look at me," Valencia said.

Riordan was only too glad to. Anything but down. The captain held his motorcycle helmet out over the edge, gave it a flip, and counted, "One one thousand, two one thousand, three one thousand, four . . . Ah! There! Did you hear it hit the rocks?"

Riordan hadn't heard a thing.

"About four seconds, and you would be conscious all the way down, conscious when your body crashed into those same rocks at, oh, I would say more than two hundred kilometers an hour. We paratroopers have to make such calculations when we free-fall. *Velocidad terminal*, it is called. Terminal velocity. You should think about the terminal part."

He's enjoying himself again, Riordan thought.

"*Por lo que, una vez más.* What did Díaz tell you in the hospital?"

All you have to do is hold out. Show him that you're not going to be forced or frightened into anything.

"It is a crime for a confessor to betray a penitent by word or in any other manner for any reason," he repeated. He sounded like a POW—which, in a sense, he was—refusing to give anything but name, rank, and serial number.

"You must think I'm bluffing," Valencia said.

He walked quickly onto the road and rolled the Harley across it to the cliff's edge. With two hard shoves, he sent Negra Modelo over. Riordan shut his eyes, but he heard the crash below, and the sound of it, the bang and clatter of shattering metal, was more sickening than the sight would have been.

"A tragic accident!" the captain shouted, gleeful. Drawing closer, he spoke into Riordan's ear with loathsome intimacy: "Do you know what, priest? I'm begging you to answer me. Really, I am."

At this point, Riordan didn't know what terrified him more: being hurled to his death or that, in his terror, he would do and say whatever Valencia wished. Was he committing suicide with this fidelity to a principle? Had he fallen suddenly in love with martyrdom? As these thoughts flew through his mind, he could not believe that his life might be but minutes, perhaps seconds, away from ending. Then, as unexpected as a hurricane gust on a placid sea, an icy blast of despair struck him. He did not feel assured of heaven; he did not, for that matter, feel convinced that any existence succeeded this one—that his consciousness, loosed from flesh, would sail the cosmos forever. He could not help himself—he began to sob.

"Stop it! You're disgusting!" said Valencia. Then, in a tone of odious compassion: "Listen. I'll give you an out. I will ask you questions, you only have to nod or shake your head. You won't have to say anything."

"Not by word or in any other manner," Riordan said, choking. "There is no reason for you to do this."

"No reason is necessary," Valencia said, then backed away a couple of steps, his hands on his hips, his head cocked a little, quizzically.

"You are not a priest to me. You are not a priest to anyone. You are nothing more than a snitch. But a snitch who has stopped snitching, a finger that no longer points. What can be more useless?"

Someone with an active nature compelled into submission can bear it only so long. Riordan willed himself to look into the emptiness beneath the jutting cliff. He could see the front wheel and fender of his bike, yards away from where it had struck, the bent chrome tailpipe, bits of shiny metal. How would they explain the strap around his wrists? he wondered. Maybe they would find a path down into the riverbed and cut it off. Maybe not, for this was the Sierra Madre, where accountability and questions of guilt, like the mountain rivers, died in the desert. No explanations would be necessary; whoever found his body would know what lies to tell, and beyond the telling, to believe them.

"And you're no soldier to me," he said to Valencia. "You're a thug in a uniform. I have nothing to say to you."

The captain made a movement like a head feint. The sergeant jerked Riordan's wrists, pulling him back a few inches. He felt a sawing motion, the flat of a knife blade against his skin. The sergeant was cutting the zip strap. So they were worried about that after all; they had to make sure it looked like an accident. *Whose sins you shall forgive, they shall be forgiven; whose sins you shall retain, they shall be retained.* It was he, Timothy Riordan OFM, who would be the goat of expiation now. It was he who bore the sins— his own sins and César Díaz's and every sin he'd heard confessed in his lifetime as a priest. He would atone for them all. A rapturous tide roared through him, sweeping away his fear, his despair, his regrets as Christ's words tumbled into his mind: *I lay down my life that I may take it up again; no man takes it from me, I lay it down on my own.*

■ ■ ■

With a desperate swing of his shoulders, he wrenched free and stepped out into space.

ACKNOWLEDGMENTS

My sincerest thanks to my editor, Michael Signorelli; my agents, Aaron Priest and Lucy Childs; and my lady, Leslie Ware, for her patience and help in the revisions to this book. Also to Molly Malloy, for the tale she told me and taking risks she did not have to take; Dan Cantu, for sharing his knowledge and experience; Father Bill Cosgrove, for his advice and insights; and above all, to Elizabeth Pettit, a selfless servant of the dispossessed who opened my eyes to a Mexico seldom seen by tourists.

ABOUT THE AUTHOR

PHILIP CAPUTO is an award-winning journalist—the co-winner of a Pulitzer Prize—and the author of many works of fiction and nonfiction, including *A Rumor of War*, one of the most highly praised books of the twentieth century. His novels include *Acts of Faith, The Voyage, Horn of Africa*, and *Crossers*. His previous book, *The Longest Road*, was a *New York Times* bestseller. He and his wife, Leslie Ware, divide their time between Norwalk, Connecticut, and Patagonia, Arizona.